EROSION

RUTH ESTEVEZ

Beaten Track
www.beatentrackpublishing.com

Erosion

Second Edition
Published 2020 by Beaten Track Publishing
First edition published 2012 by Parkinson and Archer
Copyright © 2012, 2020 Ruth Estevez

All rights reserved.

Paperback ISBN: 978 1 78645 441 6
eBook ISBN: 978 1 78645 442 3

Cover Design: Miranda Estevez-Baker

Beaten Track Publishing,
Burscough, Lancashire.
www.beatentrackpublishing.com

With thanks to God's Own Country
Yorkshire

Praise for *Erosion*

Erosion is a beautifully written, surprising novel. Ruth Estevez smartly combines lush, descriptive prose with believable, down to earth dialogue. The characters are all extremely well drawn and live and breathe on the page. The plot is pacey and plausible with some very unexpected twists and a very satisfying conclusion. This is an excellent book, which deserves to receive greater exposure and will reward repeat readings.

—Bob Stone (Owner of Write Blend bookshop; author of *Missing Beat*)

The quality of the writing sucked me in, and the carefully constructed plot kept me reading. It's always great to see a writer who has control of their material, and who understands the need to layer meaning into their work - the 'erosion' in many senses of the word. Recommended.

—Dan Malakin (Author of *The Regret*)

You can hear the sea and feel the cliff beginning to slide. The tension between the characters is tangible. The players are rounded and convincing. I thoroughly enjoyed reading this novel.

—Gill James (Lecturer at Salford University International)

'Erosion' is a beautifully written novel in which Ruth Estevez consistently captures atmosphere, mood and a sense of place with a perfectly chosen word or sentence. The plot is intriguing because

we sense all is not well in 'this world' but we are not quite sure why. This leaves us fascinated to discover what is really going on and, consequently, keeps us turning the pages. The characterisation of the main protagonists is distinct and very strong and the pace of the novel builds towards a compelling conclusion. 'Erosion' is also a very thought-provoking book with themes which question society's attitude towards those on the periphery (quite literally in this case!) of our communities. I enjoyed this novel very much and would definitely recommend it to others.

—Amazon Customer

I loved the setting for the book, reminiscent of seaside holidays on the east coast of Yorkshire with the constant awareness that coastlines were changing year by year due to the ravages of the sea. I felt a connection with the characters, perhaps also from my own past. Gripping end to the book with gently unfolding love story. Well written and memorable!

—Elizabeth Wheildon (Headteacher)

EROSION

EROSION

Chapter One

THE SEA ROARED, battering the land. On the cliff edge, a row of chalets trembled. In her scramble to get out of bed, Lizzie tripped over her unpacked suitcase, limped to the bedroom window and yanked back the curtain.

Rain teemed down, making it difficult to see. She rubbed away condensation with her palm. Outside, grey mist obscured the other chalets. A rumbling drummed across the ground. The floor began to shake, and she pressed her hands against the window frame. Tremors like this didn't happen in town. She'd been mad to take up the offer of shelter in this remote chalet park even if the accommodation did come free.

The movement subsided, and she pressed her nose against the smooth, damp surface, her breath clouding the glass. She wiped it clear with her sleeve. The first signs of daylight cast a dull perspective over the surrounding buildings, but driving rain still distorted her view. Even so, she could tell something was very wrong with one of the chalets.

She wiped the glass again. With a booming crack, the chalet jolted backwards, roof severing, and its reverberations stampeded over the grass. Holding tightly on to the sill, Lizzie braced herself. The walls shook. As soon as the movement stopped, she hurried from the bedroom, across the living area and, unlocking the front door, swung it open. A strong gust howled around her, bringing with it the cold breath of a northeast wind. Slamming the door closed, she returned to the bedroom, dodging the suitcase, and pulled on jeans, boots and a jacket over her pyjamas and sweatshirt. The curtains at the single-paned window fluttered, and she pulled up her jacket zip.

Outside, the sound of rupturing stone, rock and wood blasted across the ground and hit her full in the chest. She gasped, feeling the weight of the elements pressing her backwards. Only by bending her head against prevailing gusts and driving rain could she force her way towards the cliff edge and the precariously positioned chalet.

It was harder than she'd thought. Immediately drenched, her hair stuck to her face, and her trousers clung cold and wet against her thighs. Keeping her shoulders hunched, she fixed her eyes on the building, annoyed that she had left the comfort and warmth of her bed without thinking what she'd do to help.

A dog barked. The chalet's front door slammed open against cracked frontage, banged closed again, then once more blasted wide as a gale ploughed through gaping fissures and broken windowpanes. Lizzie glanced to her right along the line of dark buildings then over her shoulder at the ones behind. No lights shone out. Not one door opened. No sight or sound of curious neighbours. She told herself that others were dragging on their boots and coats and at any minute would appear and rush towards the collapsing chalet.

Then she saw the couple. Several feet inside the broken doorway, an elderly man and woman clutched each other. They were dressed in outdoor clothes, though seemed in no hurry to leave.

"Hey!" The wind snatched away her voice. "Here, come on!" Frantically, she waved her arms. Water, heavy as granite, smacked white foam against the rocks before heaving to explode again. At the sound, she stepped back and glanced once more towards the other chalets. They remained silent and dark, still nobody in sight. She looked back at the couple. They'd disappeared. She edged nearer but still couldn't make out where they had gone. The dog kept barking.

"Here, boy." Lizzie stared deep into the gloom of the building. Two figures knelt on the floor, heads resting on each other's shoulders as they clung together as though praying. They seemed oblivious to the barking dog, her frantic shouts and their chalet collapsing around them.

"It's this way." She edged closer. "Come on, get out."

Barking wildly, the dog ran towards her, but the couple didn't even turn their heads. The dog ran back, looked at Lizzie, then again at the couple.

"Get up!" The force of the wind and rain fought her voice. Waves thundered against the cliff. She clenched her wet fists. "It's going to go!"

Still they didn't acknowledge her. She glanced around once more, wondering what to do. Hesitating for barely a second, she crept forward, carefully extending one foot through the doorway. Creaking, the chalet shifted. Lizzie screamed, jumping onto solid ground and staggering backwards. She looked again at the surrounding buildings. Still no-one appeared, and she began to sweat in spite of the cold. All doors in the outcrop of buildings remained resolutely shut, not one sliver of light leaking through tightly drawn curtains. A pale grey clung to the grass, and only the sound of rain, wind and crashing surf permeated the misty air.

Lizzie trudged to the nearest chalet. Grabbing the handrail, she leapt up the steps and hammered a fist against the wooden door. It didn't open. She wiped away the rain streaming down her face.

"Hello?" she shouted. "Is anybody in?"

No answer. She banged again, but the building remained in darkness. Grasping the door handle, she shook hard. It didn't budge.

Sliding on the mossy timber beneath her feet, she hurried to the next building and grasped the rail as she climbed the treacherously drenched steps. She struck the door with a numbed fist, but once again, it remained closed and locked. Tears pricked her eyes. The pressure in her chest was almost unbearable.

She stumbled to the third chalet, but on seeing wide-open curtains and darkness behind, she immediately headed to the next. This time, the moment her hand hit the door, it opened.

The outline of a tall, youngish man leaned forward. "Hello?" Lizzie pointed into the drizzle. "One of the chalets."

He peered at her more closely. "Who are you?"

"There are people in there." She wiped a trembling hand over her wet face. "The cliff is giving way."

Her voice sounded weak, but that was as loud as she could make it. Stepping back, she willed him to hurry. He stared past her for a moment before flicking on a light, which illuminated his towering, wild-haired figure. Rain gusted across the veranda, and Lizzie hunched her shoulders as a squall sliced through her thin coat. She caught an unexpected whiff of the ripeness of apples. All at once, stars speckled her vision, and she reached again for the rail in an effort to stop from swaying. She focused on a pile of driftwood propped against a cheerful blue kitchen unit. And then he reappeared.

"Which one?" he asked, brushing past so close she almost fell over. "Close the door." He didn't even look back to check she'd heard.

She skidded on the grass, trying to catch up. He had a long, sure stride. With his collar up and hat pulled low over dark hair, she couldn't fathom what he would do. The twisted shape of the chalet loomed in front of them. Within seconds, they reached the edge.

He cupped his hands and shouted, "Shelley? Gordon?"

Hearing squelching footsteps, Lizzie turned to look behind. An older man, probably in his early seventies, hurried awkwardly towards them until, finally, he slid in the mud and only held himself up by grasping at the taller man's arm. He squinted directly into Lizzie's face.

"Who the hell are you?"

"I tried to help," she stuttered. "I was telling…" She paused, but the taller man didn't offer his name. "There's two people trapped in there with their dog. We've got to get them out."

The older, stockier man pushed her roughly aside and pulled at the other's sleeve, turning him away. Sensing movement, Lizzie glanced at the chalet. With a whisper of crumbling soil, it shifted again. Then a huge slice of land fell away. The chalet tilted towards the sea.

"Oh my God," Lizzie whispered.

The chalet teetered precariously on towers of turf and stone. The back and one of the side walls had broken away, and between them, the wind and gravity slid furniture across the floor. Curtains flapped, bedding tore off a bed, ornaments smashed against walls, and interior doors ripped free of their hinges.

"Where are they?" Again, the wind snatched her voice, and the others didn't appear to hear. She saw the elderly man inside the chalet, balanced on the edge of broken floor, and instinctively reached out. Without warning, the cantankerous older man blocked her way and jabbed a finger in her face.

"Get back to your chalet."

The wood groaned and splintered. Lizzie slipped past, but he grabbed her coat sleeve and yanked her back. They faced each other, ready to spar as the wind tugged at their coats and trousers. The ground shuddered again, and chunks of soil tumbled into thundering waves.

"Can you see him?" Lizzie called to the younger man.

"Gordon?" he shouted.

The chalet lay almost completely on its side. Several figures hurried out of the mist towards them. Another old man appeared. He shook his head and gesticulated towards the building. About twenty metres away, the woman from the sole caravan on the site desperately held a man back from approaching further.

"They're still inside!" Lizzie cried. "We've got to get them out!"

The old man glanced at the half dozen people who had gathered nearby.

"Someone's got to go in!" Lizzie pleaded.

"Anyone got some rope?" the taller man shouted.

Someone hurried forward and handed over a massive coil of hemp.

"Jez!" the old man interjected.

Lizzie grasped at the name as Jez tied the rope around his waist. The man who had handed it to him wrapped the other end around a concrete post.

Jez caught Lizzie's gaze. "See what you started?"

"What?" Lizzie saw a gleam of amusement in his eye before he turned and inched his way to the cliff edge. "Take care!"

She grabbed his arm, holding his gaze as rain streamed down his face, dripping from his nose and lashes. Even in this terrible situation, there was warmth in Jez's eyes. The dog yelped and leapt through the air, head-butting Lizzie's leg and then scampering in circles, ears down, tail flailing. She looked back at Jez and saw doubt flicker across his face. Together, they turned as a steady cascade of crumbling earth grew into a thunderous rumble, and the section of cliff collapsed metres from their feet, taking the chalet crashing with it into the sea.

Chapter Two

G RADUALLY, THE SKY turned a pale yellow over the quietening sea. Waves scraped back from the rocks, and gulls wheeling overhead cried for scraps. The rain petered out. The wind dropped, leaving the air damp and chilly. Along the clifftop, emergency services abandoned their vehicles and approached on foot. Figures clustered around one of the weather-beaten chalets that stood about fifty metres from the cliff edge. The foul-mouthed seventy-odd-year-old from the night before lit a cigarette.

Inside, sheltered from the grey morning, a woman in her sixties poured tea into mugs for the small crowd gathered in her chalet. She pushed one towards the police officer who was interviewing her. He nodded his thanks and glanced at the bag of sugar on the worktop.

"Mrs. Cummings? D'you think I might have a couple?"

She smiled for him to help himself and addressed a pleasant-looking man standing close by. "Trevor? Would you mind?"

He kissed her cheek and picked up two of the mugs. "John?" He handed one to a tall, emotionless man in a neat jacket before placing the other in front of a nervous-looking woman sitting on an ancient sofa. "Drink it, Joyce," he said. "It'll warm you up."

Joyce Carmichael, looking pinched and pale, cradled the cup in her hands. Mavis Cummings, rounder faced, hurried from the kitchen area and sat beside her, almost spilling her drink. Their husbands stood apart, gauging the second, squat officer by his questions as Jez explained that Peter Hawksworth was visiting his family near Leeds and the other missing resident, Marilyn Hopper, always stayed in Rook Bay on Friday nights.

The Bowles had remained in their caravan, as they didn't want to leave the children. Meanwhile, a third officer talked to Lizzie Juniper in the chalet next door.

Gordon and Shelley Weston's retirement home had stood furthest from the track that led to the main road. It had also been nearest the cliff edge. Adjacent, but further inland, stood the Carmichaels' chalet, then the Cummings', then a brightly painted celebration of a wooden house that had remained unoccupied the previous night. Beside that stood Jez Maiden's and finally Peter Hawksworth's neat building next to the rough track leading steeply up the hill and onto the coast road.

Those who owned chalets nearest the sea were immediately forbidden from returning until representatives from both the Environment Agency and council had ascertained that the land and buildings were safe—and only then to organise evacuation. The chief officer recommended they be out by the end of the week at the latest, preferably in the next day or two. Luckily, there were no more storms forecast and bright, warm weather was predicted. Even so, they would need to move out as quickly as possible because the land remained unpredictable. The council official wanted them to leave that morning, but backed by the Environment Agency's assessment and carefully judged agreement, everyone promised to be out by the coming Friday—5th November.

The old man threw down his cigarette and glanced at the neighbouring chalet then down the line to the Bowles' rusting caravan. He didn't once turn his head to look at the deep gash breaking into the field where the Westons' chalet had stood.

***

Lizzie struggled to keep her eyes open as she stared at the mug of sweet, milky tea in her hands. She felt sick. It must have been obvious because Police Officer Greg Taylor glanced up and said, "This won't take long—unless you want to get out of those wet things first? I can wait. Or do you want me to fetch one of the medics?"

Lizzie shook her bedraggled head. She couldn't summon the energy to strip off her dirty wet clothes or even rise from the chair where she slumped. She didn't know how to begin. Already it felt like a nightmare that she struggled to remember. Only the terrified look on the old man's face, the sound of the dog barking, the thunder of crashing waves and the cold of Jez's oilskin against her cheek remained in her head.

They sat in silence, ignoring distant shouts and throbbing engines. In the unbearable stillness of the room, she began to tremble. The liquid in the mug she held rippled, and she stared at the widening circles as if it were the most important movement she had ever seen.

"I'll come back," Greg said gently, rising from his chair. Lizzie looked up at him and frowned. "You're going to catch your death—get changed. There are others I can see. I'll go talk to some of them and come back to you."

She let out a long breath. The police weren't usually thoughtful. If her eyes hadn't felt so dry and painful, she would have cried.

"No," she said. "Ask what you want. Get it over with."

Greg looked unsure but cleared his throat and read out her name, address and phone number, much to Lizzie's confusion.

"When did I tell you those?" she asked.

"Just now. Do you want me to put that down for you?" Before she could answer, he took the mug out of her hands and placed it on the table. "Those details are correct, aren't they?"

Lizzie pressed her lips together. Tears began to rise at being shown unaccustomed kindness. "I only moved in yesterday."

"Oh. Right." Greg frowned. "I don't think you'll be allowed to stop here if that's—"

"I'll be out by tonight," she interrupted.

"Good." He relaxed slightly. "Glad to hear it."

"I've got friends. They wouldn't let me stay here even if I wanted to."

"Right," he repeated. "I'll, er..." He waved his pen. "Can you tell me what you saw?"

"I saw it fall."

"Do you know what time it was?"

She shook her head.

"Can you tell me the order it went?"

She stared at her hands, trying to remember, and glanced up at the officer. He was slightly flushed and inappropriately neat and clean in contrast to her dirty fingers and cropped nails. Briefly, she wondered if her mascara had run. What had woken her? She couldn't recall. The driving rain and gusting wind had practically dropped now, and the quiet made her uneasy.

"I don't know," she admitted and covered her mouth to stop her jaw shaking, but her hand trembled unhelpfully. Tears brimmed in her eyes, blurring the officer's features. His face seemed too close. Tears trickled under the curve of her chin, and she wiped them quickly away.

"I heard a noise," she said, breathing deeply. "I looked out of the window. There was something odd about the chalet over there, and then the floor started shaking. I got dressed and went outside, but it was cold, really cold and windy, and the rain was horrible." Her voice cracked, and she stopped.

"D'you want a tissue?"

"There's some toilet paper," She pointed towards a door at the far side of the room.

He stood and moved away. The fluorescent light came on, and Lizzie flinched and averted her eyes. Almost immediately, he came back, holding the roll out to her. She unravelled several sheets, then balled them up in her fists.

"What did you do?" he asked.

"I couldn't see anyone, and...I think I heard the dog barking, so I ran to the chalet, but I was scared. I tried. I did try, but they wouldn't come out, and if I started to go in, I made the chalet rock more, so I shouted for them to come out, but they couldn't hear me. It was terrifying. I live in Rigby. I'm not used to mud and the ground and…" She unwound a fresh length of toilet paper and hid her face. "I tried," she reiterated, "but there was only me."

"So what did you do?" He made it sound as if it were her fault, and she wondered if this was where it would end. He must've thought she was mad or a coward or a terrible person, but she was none of those, and she had never taken the blame without a fight.

"I got hold of that tall guy with the hat—Jez, someone called him—and he came out, and then there were other people, but it was difficult. Someone had some rope, and they tied it up, and he put it round him, but then the cliff started to go, and it just fell away, and the chalet…oh my God, the chalet." She paused for breath before whispering, "You could hear it. Every sound. And they didn't scream. I'd have screamed—why didn't they?" She started crying in earnest, shaking her head as she tried to stop herself.

"What did you do then?" he asked.

"I watched."

He didn't say anything.

She wiped away the tears and stared at him, at his pen moving over the paper. She no longer cared what he thought; he hadn't been there. She remembered the waxy feel of Jez's coat and the firmness of his large hand on the back of her head as he'd pressed her face against his shoulder so she could no longer see.

"Did you know the couple?" The officer's voice jarred. Angrily, she shook her head. "Can you name the other people that were there?"

"I don't know anyone."

"Right, well, is there anything else?"

Lizzie had never seen a rock fall or even a landslide before. She'd seen it on the local television news, but now that she'd witnessed firsthand the reality of the devastation, of how waves could lacerate a cliff so that it collapsed, she was petrified. For the first time, she felt the terror of hearing land and everything on its edge crash into the sea.

"That's all I remember," she said, picking up the mug of tea and taking a gulp of the now-cold liquid.

Chapter Three

G REG CLOSED THE door quietly behind him and looked up at a turquoise sky. The sea fret had cleared.

Alone in the chalet, Lizzie wandered into the dingy bathroom and turned on the shower before peeling off wet clothes. The water alternated between freezing and scalding but eventually settled on a comforting heat. She watched her pale skin turn a deeper pink. Reaching for the soap, she realised she'd left it, along with the shampoo and towel, unpacked in her case on the bedroom floor. Dripping, she pattered across the flowery carpet, dug out the plastic bag and returned, shivering, to the bathroom.

Soapsuds coursed over the slight curve of her stomach, and she let the heat cleanse and penetrate until she found she had been standing so long her legs gave way.

Light-headed, she turned off the shower, stepped out of the cubicle and, picking up the towel, wrapped it around her tingling body. She slumped onto the end of the bed. Her wet hair clung to her over-sensitive skin. For several minutes, she stared at the tumble of clothes overflowing from the suitcase, too tired to move. She eventually flopped backwards and gazed up at the mould-stained ceiling. Noises outside continued. The air smelt damp. She shivered and crawled under the duvet, determined to close her eyes for five minutes or until the knot in her stomach went away.

***

An ambulance pulled up the hill as a fire engine had done half an hour previously. Several police cars remained parked at the bottom of the track, and uniforms made their way across the grass as other figures in overalls approached the cliff path. A length of police tape already fluttered between two posts denying access to the beach.

The caravan door remained closed. Inside, Simon Bradbury, the officer talking to the Bradford-born Gary and Sandra Bowles, began to succumb to fatigue. He found the early shift as exhausting as interviewing people. In full flow, Gary gave an in-depth account of events before moving on to share his opinion of the government and lack of compensation residents would receive. Sandra repeatedly added to his monologue while she rammed children's sweatshirts and trousers into sports holdalls. She sounded angry but looked upset.

Gary was matter of fact. He told Simon that the weathered caravan was worthless, but they were getting off lightly compared to others whose chalets were now worth no more than a pound and would cost a great deal more to demolish and remove from the site as they were bound to do. He wouldn't be them if someone paid him. He planned to abandon the caravan where it stood; no-one could prosecute him for that. They would definitely save and go abroad from now on, and hopefully, over in a sunny resort, they'd meet people more like themselves. This crowd was a strange bunch of his parents' and grandparents' generation; old codgers who had nothing to do with them.

Sandra nodded in agreement. "Holidays are supposed to be fun. We have enough doom and gloom at home, don't we, Gary?"

Finally, Simon prised himself to his feet and closed the caravan door behind him with relief. He yawned deeply as he wandered across the field to the cliff path. Greg beckoned him over, and without speaking, they studied the retreating sea. Below, on the rubble-strewn beach, they recognised their senior officer Harry Sayles' distinctive figure by the way he moved. Others circulated around him, stretching metres of tape across the shingle, wrapping it around posts that others hammered into the sand. They watched him slipping around on seaweed, picking his way around rock pools and eyeing the smashed drawers of wet, unrecognisable clothes. They made out sodden food packets and submerged tins of baked beans and peaches.

Oblivious to them, Sayles paused to examine piles of sodden knitwear, buckled pans and broken dishes, bending idly to study any writing that, ultimately, turned out to be indecipherable. He looked around. A chair remained inappropriately upright, its feet deep in sand, and he stood beside it as if to sit down.

"What d'you reckon?" Simon asked.

Greg crushed a lazy wasp with his boot. "He'll be searching for an address book, some form of identification, maybe a safe or a strong box with that kind of stuff in. From what the neighbours say, doesn't sound like there's any family to contact."

"What happens to the bodies if no-one claims them?"

"I think the church deals with them or maybe the council. They might not be religious." Greg shrugged. "I don't know anyone who's not had someone to do for them. Sad that, isn't it?"

"That you've not known anyone?"

"That they've no-one, you pillock."

They looked out at the calm sea. Sayles bent to pick up a dark wooden cross, large enough for them to recognise.

"Catholic." They both nodded.

Simon scratched his cheek. "Complicates things."

The wind ruffled the grass again. Greg brushed his boot over the blades.

"I don't get these people," said Simon.

Greg glanced over his shoulder. "You should have heard what the medics were saying."

"Yeah, well, they see all sorts."

"Think if it were your mum and dad." Greg watched the gulls gather noisily over the debris.

"I keep telling you, they've moved to Spain."

"Can you imagine the chaos if the Costa del Sol collapsed like this?" Greg's parents still lived in Beamstown. "They'd be some pretty pissed off ex-pats over there."

"Don't even joke about it. I'm thinking of joining them myself."

"You won't go."

"Don't be too sure." They watched Sayles kick a small Belling oven. "He thinks it's a safe." Simon laughed.

"Glad we're not cleaning this mess up," Greg said, turning away. "C'mon. Is there anyone else we need to talk to?"

"Geoff's finishing off." Simon shifted his boots to catch the sun's beams shining on them. "Suppose we could cordon off that part of the cliff. It's not been done yet."

"Let that lot do it. They know what they're doing."

"Why don't these people just move?"

"I asked that, but it's like I'm from another planet. Let the council sort them out, I say."

Simon took off his hat and ruffled his red hair. "Not the nicest way to go."

"Bloody nightmare, this place." Greg stared at the chalets. "You've got to feel for the beggars."

Within three hours, the police officers and land experts had meandered back across the shingle carrying small bags of personal effects and obscure hints about the moment the Westons had died. Their faces didn't give anything away as they reached the steep path that zigzagged its way up the cliff.

Soon, they were all back on the tops, pulling off wellington boots and overalls and loading up cars and vans. Sayles held up the crucifix with its splayed figure of Christ as if it were a trophy and, reassured that the residents were starting to move out, ordered his officers to leave. Immediately, they clambered into vehicles, slamming doors before speeding away up the track, just as, unnoticed, a wiry sixty-year-old man strode up the cliff path and ducked under the fluttering tape.

***

"We've got to rethink this," Trevor blurted out. Left alone once more, they had all crowded back into Randolph's chalet.

"I want—" began Joyce, but John interrupted.

"Rethink?" He raised his voice. "It's not a question of rethink. It's bloody scrap it completely."

"John," his wife tried to placate.

"I didn't think it would be so awful." Mavis's hands shook. "Please, Trevor, I want to go now. You were right—we should have gone years ago."

"'Course, love." Trevor nodded. "Whatever you want."

"You what?" Randolph turned on him.

"Everyone, let's sit down." Jez gestured to the sofa and chairs. "Peter? You sure they didn't see you?" The wiry man shook his head and Jez nodded. He scanned the group. "Right, well, even if we started packing up this second, it's going to take a few days."

"I don't care, I'm—" John began.

"The weather is good. What happened last night was because of the heavy storm. Gordon and Shelley could have got out. We were there, and the newcomer was desperate to help them, but they chose not to. They stayed inside their chalet."

"Exactly, the newcomer," John grumbled. "What are we going to do about her?"

"What's her name?"

"Lizzie something," said Mavis.

"Bloody hell. What's she said to the police?"

"Shelley was always adamant about this," said Jez.

"We all are."

"No, buts, this is ludicrous. We can make sure this doesn't happen again. I certainly don't want to be clinging on to the kitchen table for dear life." John slapped his hands together.

"The forecast says sun for the rest of the week." Trevor's soft voice rang out.

"It's unstable. It's an absolute farce," persisted John.

"It's all right, Mavis," said Jez. "We will leave."

"And how do we do that, MasterMind?"

Jez glanced up at Randolph's sharp words.

"We can all be out by the end of the week," he said. "But, Mavis?" He bent down and took her hands, holding them in her lap and looking into her pretty, gentle face. "We don't want to leave the chalets behind when we go because they'll just be flattened by a bulldozer, and people won't give a toss about the place. They won't know we even existed. I'm sorry." He glanced at Trevor and back to Mavis. "If we don't make a stand, it'll happen again and again to people like you and Trevor and me and Joyce here."

"I know," she said. "Don't worry, I do know."

She remained quiet. Sunlight warmed the wood of the coffee table. Trevor breathed too loudly. A curtain scraped the sill as a breeze wafted in.

"If we can pull this off, it'll make politicians and leaders around here have to do something other than throw a few boulders down at Rook Bay." Randolph's face reddened. "Putting these people's heads on the line is the only way to get them to do anything. Why d'you think I've been trailing down with those sodding letters every week?"

Jez still held Mavis's hand.

"It's not about us, is it?" she said.

"Christ." John crossed his legs away from the others.

Mavis looked unsure.

Trevor glanced up, his face more youthful than usual. "We'll think of something," he said quietly to Mavis.

"It's a coward's way out whichever way you look at it," said John.

"Weren't you listening?" Randolph grumbled. "This is about more than you protecting your sodding reputation."

"If you look at it as helping people in the future then it's not cowardly, it's brave," said Jez.

"No-one else lives in a god-forsaken hole like this."

"You'd be surprised. You don't venture beyond Rigby high street do you, John?" John flushed, stony-faced. "No disrespect, John, but it's not going to get any better."

They all waited for his response, but when John cleared his throat, folded his arms and crossed his other leg, they turned back to Jez.

"This gives us control of where we're going," said Randolph.

"And when," Peter chipped in.

"And when," Jez paused, but no-one added anything else. "So that's established. We want control?"

"Of course we do," muttered John.

"We don't forget this." Jez held up a sheet of paper covered in handwriting.

"I told you, I've changed my mind." John slapped his hands on his knees, poised to stand.

"John." Small, wiry Peter Hawksworth spoke with unaccustomed force. "Our backs are to the wall. We have two options as I see it. One, we surrender and live the rest of our lives like battery hens like on that estate at Rigby. Or two, we fight and do it our way. There is no other way of looking at it."

He noticed their bewildered faces.

"In the army, you always consider the group," he said. "It's not about individuals. I've been held captive and fought in conditions you wouldn't believe..."

"Tough guy." John leaned back.

"I know what I prefer." Peter sat back down.

No-one spoke. Jez glanced at Randolph then at Peter, then at John, who remained impassive.

"It's different for you." John folded his arms again.

"I was in bomb disposal," retaliated Peter. "Most of the time, we prevented anyone from being maimed or killed, but sometimes there was nothing we could do. No-one's asking anyone to purposely kill anyone."

"Why do we have to give up our homes?" Mavis grasped Trevor's hand. Tears dripped onto her skirt, forming dark smatters. In the ensuing silence, the breeze wafted a curtain again, and in the distance, waves brushed over wet shingle. The tide had turned.

Chapter Four

A N HOUR LATER, Lizzie awoke to the sound of shouting. Disorientated, she rolled out from under the duvet, leaving behind the damp towel. She pulled on the first clothes to hand, and zipping up a fleece, she rammed her feet into boots. At the door, she hesitated, wondering how long she had been asleep. There was no sound of the engines that had been so noisy earlier.

A voice bellowed outside. "You fucking traitor!"

"Stop it, Randolph!"

Hand on the door handle, she waited. Should she grab her suitcase and drive off, or brave the strangers and see for herself what the rumpus was about? Glancing across the living room, she spied the duvet piled untidily where she'd pushed it back, the wrinkled, damp towel and clothes crumpled and discarded on the bedroom floor. The irate voice sparred again, and this time, she recognised it. She hated bullies. She'd give that cantankerous old git what for.

She rounded the front of the chalet to a bombardment of vicious expletives. Stunned at the sight of Randolph careering towards a man ramming a cardboard box into the boot of his car, she realised this was no ordinary argument. The younger man turned, his face empty with surprise as Randolph seized the open car boot and slammed it down hard. The edge scraped the man's knuckles as he swiftly pulled his hands free. A dark-haired woman stood in the caravan doorway.

"Gary?" Her voice was tinged with anxiety.

From the woods that stretched north of the park, two young boys appeared and sped past Lizzie. She watched in disbelief as a neatly dressed man grabbed and held them both even though they struggled desperately to break free. Looking back to the car, she flinched as Randolph smashed his fist across Gary's jaw.

"Shit," she muttered, striding towards them.

Gary garbled obscenities as he swung back at Randolph. She broke into a jog. She really hated bullies. If need be, she'd punch Randolph's lights out. She'd almost reached them, fists clenched, when someone took hold of her arm. Furious, she spun around. Tall, wild-haired Jez held her gaze. He didn't say anything, merely pressed her gently backwards. Anger flushed across her face, and she threw off his hold. He glanced quizzically at her, then focused his attention on the brawling men, leaving her standing, fingers tingling.

"Randolph." Jez strode swiftly towards them. "Randolph!"

Gary, flailing under the onslaught of Randolph's blows, struggled to hit back. Crying, the dark-haired woman who'd hovered in the caravan doorway hurried to separate them.

"Stay back, Sandra." Jez yanked Randolph's shoulder, and with the old man caught off balance, Gary managed to land a punch on his jaw. Sandra continued to pull at her husband's shirt sleeve.

"Get off me!" Gary yelled, whipping himself clear and sending her sprawling across the grass.

"Mum!" The younger boy wriggled free.

"Get off!" the elder boy shouted.

"Watch out." The neatly dressed man, someone called John, raised both arms as he relinquished his hold.

Another man, in a green cardigan, shambled across the grass.

"Steady on," he said. "Let's talk about this. Mavis, see to Sandra."

Grey-haired, pleasant-faced Mavis bent down stiffly next to Sandra.

"I was trying to help you," Sandra yelled over the woman's shoulder at her husband.

Lizzie glanced from one to another, amazed that people who'd seemed so insipid last night could now be so antagonistic. She started to say something, but Jez already pressed Gary away and holding out his other arm spoke in a low voice.

"Randolph. Back off," he ordered. "Come on, calm down."

Almost immediately, Randolph's entire body drooped as he let his fists fall by his sides. Gary cradled his damaged hand, straining half-heartedly against Jez's hold, his face erupting in bloodied bruises.

"What are you on about, you sick bastard?" Gary's voice shook.

"Who said you could call the fucking police?" Randolph stabbed the air.

"There's dead people out there, you mad tosser!"

"What else was he supposed to do?" Sandra said. "Of course he called the police."

She paused, disbelief and horror flashing across her face. Randolph launched again at Gary, who wrestled desperately out of Jez's hold. Unleashed, the two men locked arms and pressed the other for submission as if they were pit bulls.

"Someone stop them," begged Sandra.

"Jez, stop them."

"Randolph."

"Gary."

"Dad?"

"Stop it!" Lizzie screamed, heart pounding and hands clenched so tight her fingers cut into her palms. "There are kids."

For a moment, her words seemed to hold everyone enthralled whilst she stared incredulously at the mix of astonished, dazed and still angry faces. And then the scene erupted again into noise and mayhem. Sandra called out as she reached for the two boys running towards Gary. Gary, with renewed strength, came to his senses just as Randolph heaved back his fist and smacked him hard across the cheekbone. Gary collapsed onto his knees. The two boys flung themselves on Randolph, who shoved them flailing to the ground.

"Now get out of here," Randolph threatened.

"Mavis?" Jez touched her shoulder. "You ex-nurses always have good first-aid boxes, don't you?"

Mavis hurried towards her chalet, and everyone focused their attention on the Bowles', pushing the boys forward now to their parents, attempting to calm Gary's anger and Sandra's indignation, encouraging them in their decision to leave, almost providing reasons for haste with offers of assistance.

Standing on the edge of the circle feeling unqualified to help or offer advice and completely ignored, Lizzie watched Randolph march away alone along the clifftop, shoulders rounded, oozing animosity. She turned back to say something, but Jez's attention was focused on Mavis, who returned and knelt awkwardly on the ground. Gary held out his hand, and the older woman took it, settled herself then pulled a wad of cotton wool from an old square biscuit tin, neat with bandages and plasters. Jez proffered a bowl of water, and Mavis carefully dipped in the cotton wool.

Transfixed by the gentleness of their faces after the ugly violence of the previous minutes, Lizzie watched. Very carefully, Mavis dabbed smarting cuts on Gary's face whilst around them others wiped away tears and calmed an extremely vocal Sandra. Lizzie continued to watch silently, increasingly reluctant to break the atmosphere that settled over the now quiet group. She couldn't believe they'd allowed Randolph to walk away without any attempt at a reprisal, but most of all, she was shocked and disappointed in Jez after the lead he had taken the previous night.

Gary appeared to enjoy the attention, but Sandra looked more fed up than ever, and their sons, silenced, glanced now and then with resentment that their dad had come off worst. All of them ignored Lizzie. Half hoping they'd notice, she turned to go. But no-one spoke, and left unchallenged, she determined she would have nothing more to do with any of them and strode back to her chalet, working out that she could be driving up the track and out of the place within fifteen minutes.

Half an hour later, she was almost ready to leave. She couldn't hear any noise outside. Assuming they were all busy packing up as well, she rammed trainers into a plastic bag amongst wedges and heels. She didn't want to bump into Jez or Randolph or any of them. She never wanted to see the chalet park ever again. Her suitcase already in the car, she felt relief that there wasn't much more to load. Bundling up the duvet, she marched outside and, seeing everyone had disappeared, threw it angrily onto the rear seat. Back inside, she stripped the bed of its sheets and pillows, scooped up the bag of shoes and hurried down the steps, shoving them all into the open boot. Turning around, she jumped. The grey-haired, cheerful-looking woman called Mavis held out a bacon sandwich on a small blue plate as if nothing untoward had happened.

Chapter Five

LIZZIE BIT THROUGH the white bread into crispy bacon, watching the man in the green cardigan approach. He tripped and almost dropped the tray of mugs in his hands.

"He makes the best tea," the woman said.

"Mavis is right," He held out the tray. "I hope you don't take sugar. I haven't put any in."

Lizzie looked at the two steaming mugs and shook her head, wondering if this was a last-minute effort to ditch all their food.

"What about you?" she asked, crunching on her sandwich.

"Oh, Trevor's had his." Mavis took one of the mugs and pressed it into Lizzie's free hand.

She glanced behind them at an abandoned lawn mower. Trevor smiled and shambled back over the grass, discarding the tray and empty blue plate on the coal bunker by the chalet door. Mavis turned expectantly. Slightly uneasy, Lizzie forced a smile and walked quickly back inside, banging the mug over-zealously on the table so that tea slopped onto the Formica. Ignoring the spillage, she grasped a toilet roll discarded from earlier on the sofa, dropped it on top of a food box and, picking it up, turned to the door.

Mavis blocked her way. "D'you need a hand?"

"I'm sure you've got plenty to be getting on with yourselves." Lizzie manoeuvred past, and as she pushed the box into the boot, Mavis followed, clutching the mug left on the table.

"I wiped up for you." Her eyes looked nervous even though her lips smiled.

"I bet you're really organised with your packing up, unlike me," Lizzie said, closing the boot.

Mavis glanced over her shoulder, then back at Lizzie. She nodded and raised the mug again for her to take. Lizzie wondered if she dared say something, anything, about the couple who had died only a few hours previous. It was as though it had never happened, but the broken cliff edge gaped otherwise. Reminding herself that the expressions on the old couple's faces had been real, she shivered again at the sound of waves and the memory of the vicious fight between the two men. She glanced around at the chalets. Randolph's rough voice and sheer force of inexplicable violence made her uneasy; fortunately, he hadn't reappeared. She'd seen men and women brawling in Rigby. She knew the damage bare knuckles could inflict, but this had been different. A stranger didn't usually make her feel unsafe, but this old man sent prickles across her scalp, and the chalets made her think of the children's home.

"We've been coming here for years." The sound of Mavis's voice startled her. "When they were little, my girls used to love playing on the beach. It's a shame they don't make it up here anymore. People lead such busy lives nowadays, don't they?"

Lizzie gulped down the tea. She wanted to get out of the place as quickly as possible, place her feet on safe ground, talk to someone who didn't sound as if they belonged in an institution.

"One lives in London and the other in Brussels," Mavis said.

Lizzie nodded. Maybe these people weren't so strange. Maybe they were in shock and this was what old people did when they were in shock. She wondered if she could have coped with a mother like this woman who cooked bacon in the mornings, remembering her children playing years ago and ignoring the fact that her neighbours had died horrifically in front of her eyes.

"Trevor used to drive back to his work in Leeds from here on Sunday nights," continued Mavis. "I used to feel quite lonely all week, just me keeping an eye on the girls. Other people always seemed to have such big families to help out."

Lizzie didn't know what to say, so she lifted the mug to her mouth even though it was empty.

"It's a shame you're leaving before the picnic," Mavis said.

"Picnic?"

"Tomorrow."

Lizzie frowned. "Aren't you all moving out?"

"The weather's going to be kind to us."

The woman had definitely lost the plot, Lizzie decided. Maybe they were all 'care in the community' and Prince Charming of the Big Hall had forgotten to tell her. It would explain a great deal.

"Well, I hope it goes well." She handed back her cup and walked around to the driver's door.

Mavis followed, swinging the empty mugs, looking more like a young girl than an elderly woman. "Are you sure we can't tempt you to stay? Marilyn makes the best chilli in the world."

Lizzie glanced up, her hand on the door handle, trying not to like the woman—whose flower-covered apron was thread-worn around the pocket and whose hair had obviously not seen a hairdresser in years—or to ask who Marilyn was, when she noticed a man in a suit, trousers tucked into wellington boots, assuredly pushing a measuring wheel from the end wall of the chalet nearest the sagging police tape to the cliff edge.

"They do it every so often," Mavis said, absent-mindedly still swinging the two mugs as she headed nonchalantly back towards Trevor.

Before Lizzie could ask what she meant, Mavis had gone inside her chalet. Noting the ostentatious silver car, Lizzie turned her attention to the man as he dropped the wheel at his feet and, raising a clipboard in his other hand, wrote something down. Unable to stem her curiosity, she strolled over to where he stood. The man, dressed in a grey anorak, the bottom of his suit jacket protruding beneath and a shirt and tie visible at the neck, walked from the corner of Mavis's chalet, trundling the apparatus to the edge. Trevor seemed to take no notice, pushing the lawn mower as if tending a lawn in the suburbs.

"It's dangerous," Lizzie automatically called out, striding more quickly towards the man, but he merely raised his head, paused in thought and scribbled on the clipboard again.

She frowned, wondering why none of the residents seemed interested enough to come and talk to the man, but then Mavis had said he did this every so often. The next chalet stood a lot closer to the edge than she had thought, and a wave of anger hit. How on earth had the authorities let any of these people live here? It wasn't safe. From where she stood, it was impossible to ignore the long drop to the beach and waves that rhythmically beat against the cliff base at high tide. Nervously, she looked around. A woman in cords and long sweater, arms folded with hostility across her chest, stared back. Lizzie glanced again at the man with the clipboard. He tapped his pen against the board as if he noticed nothing untoward.

"This you?" he asked.

Lizzie shook her head and pointed over her shoulder. The man followed the direction of her eyes.

"Not immediately at risk, then." He stamped his boots on the turf.

Stop, you idiot! Lizzie was horrified. *Do you want the entire cliff to collapse with us standing on it?*

The woman with bright-red hair, who had stared so aggressively, shuffled in a pair of old clogs down the steps of the chalet emblazoned with the name Sunset Boulevard.

"I didn't realise until I actually stood here how near these are to the edge," Lizzie said, turning her back on the woman.

"It shakes people up when they see it written in black and white." He headed towards the gaudily painted chalet. The woman kept her arms folded across large breasts, turning her head to look out to sea at a passing freight ship. Lizzie followed, noting that the woman was still attractive in spite of her long, unbrushed hair and previous day's mascara clogging her eyelashes. It seemed odd suddenly, that Lizzie had never seen any of the people who lived here, either in Rigby or anywhere else.

The scruffily dressed woman wandered down the side of her chalet, ripping dead leaves from bushes as she did so. The man began rolling his measuring wheel.

"Are we going to get a copy of this in writing?" the woman croaked without giving him the benefit of her attention. "We're all on tenterhooks to know when we're going to end up down there."

"Hopefully, you'll have moved out before that happens, Ms. Hopper," he replied, buzzing the *Ms.* like a wasp.

Lizzie stared aghast. How could anyone be so blasé when the ground they stood on might collapse at any moment and any one of them could be clinging on, as terrified as the old couple that had died so horrifically last night? She was about to speak when she saw Jez striding over the grass, and the sight of him filled her with relief. Immediately, the redheaded woman trudged up the wooden steps and disappeared back inside, discarding the last of the leaves she had gathered. Without knowing why, Lizzie felt glad she had gone.

"What's the distance?" Jez asked as if he hadn't seen her. In spite of herself, she flushed.

"Thirteen metres five." The man balanced the wheel.

That does it, Lizzie thought. *They're not both going to ignore me.*

"Now, this is the one that matters to you, isn't it?" The man raised his voice again to Jez. "Nine metres exactly. Luckily for you, it's not changed since last time."

He marked the measurement down.

"Is everyone aware how fast this cliff is disappearing?" Lizzie asked as she stepped between the men.

Jez leaned against the chalet wall. "Can be up to a metre, metre and a half a year." He glanced past her at the man for confirmation.

"Doesn't that frighten you?"

"It's Peter's next." Jez nodded his head, looking at her for the first time. "Appropriately named, Sea Rest. Mine's Driftwood. Yours is The Holiday Inn."

"Did you name them?" Lizzie pursued.

"Twenty metres." The man studied the wheel before strolling diagonally inland, missing out the derelict bungalow opposite Sea Rest and the old caravan where the Bowles' car stood packed and ready to leave.

"Aren't you curious to know how far your landlord's chalet is from its demise?" Jez gazed across the park.

The man had already rolled the wheel casually back toward the sea. Lizzie glanced towards Randolph's chalet, which stood only slightly further back than the one she'd attempted to sleep in.

Randolph was her only real concern. She didn't care if he stayed in the chalet park or not, but she worried he would erupt with unexpected violence, as he had done earlier, once he knew there was an official on site. The seemingly irrational ferocity of the little old man made her instinctively shy away.

"He's not my landlord, I'm not staying," she said, watching the official make his final journey to the cliff edge.

"Ah. I hope we haven't frightened you off."

"No-one frightened me," she retorted. "I just don't stay in places that are falling into the sea."

"Neither do they, apparently." Jez nodded towards the caravan.

"What about that woman with the apron? Mavis somebody— she was talking about some picnic tomorrow."

"Thank you for your time," Jez shouted, and the man raised a hand in acknowledgement as he walked back towards his silver Vauxhall.

"How far am I from the edge?" Lizzie called after him, but the man appeared not to hear. "Idiot," she muttered under her breath, glancing at Jez to see if he had heard. Something else had caught his attention.

Marilyn, dressed in seemingly nothing but a long red kimono and holding what looked like a hot water bottle, hair now in a carefully brushed coiffure and face heavily made up, sauntered down the steps of her chalet. She meandered clumsily in the tatty-looking clogs she had worn earlier across the narrow stretch of grass towards Jez's chalet. His face remained unreadable. Slowly, swaying her hips, Marilyn mounted the steps. Then she opened the door with a grand sweep and disappeared inside. Lizzie glanced questioningly at Jez, who, face expressionless, continued to stare after the curvaceous woman. Lizzie flushed for a second time, angry at herself for the pang of jealousy that hit her stomach.

"Think what you're missing," he said before heading across the expanse between the two lines of chalets. He was gone before she had time to retaliate.

Chapter Six

LIZZIE CAST HER eyes over the worn furniture, determined there would be no reason to return to the chalet. It seemed ludicrous to hang around, but knowing that once she drove away, she'd never see the place again, she loitered, annoyed yet unable to help herself. On top of all that, she felt anger sizzling in her head again that Andrew had let her spend a night with lunatics in a chalet park that was crashing into the sea. She shouldn't have listened to him. She should never listen to him. She must find somewhere to stay that had nothing to do with him.

"You agreed to it, Lizzie Juniper." She tapped her leg with the car key in frustration. "You kissed him and said, 'Thank you, you've saved my life.' Again."

She looked for one last time across the grass, surprised at the tranquillity of the old buildings standing against the now aquamarine sky and equally bright sparkling sea. It was beautiful. It really was beautiful. And quiet. She wasn't used to quiet. She couldn't help but look. There was no apparent movement from Jez's chalet. She turned. Mavis stood by the ancient Renault watching Gary Bowles carrying a suitcase down the steps of his caravan. Lizzie walked to her car.

"Are you and your husband leaving straight after that picnic?" she asked, opening the driver's door.

Mavis looked questioningly for a moment as if she'd forgotten who Lizzie was.

"Yes, yes." She perked up. "But I think we've got a bit more packing up to do than you have."

Lizzie smiled. Of course, it would take these people days to put their lifetime of belongings into boxes and bags and load

33

them into a van; she'd been stupid to think otherwise. Who would organise this, and would they all travel together to a home in Beamstown with windows looking across the bay? Ideally, they would be able to take their time, but this wasn't any old move. This was evacuation.

"I'm sorry about your friends," she said.

"They hadn't been here as long as the rest of us."

Lizzie didn't know what she'd expected to hear, but that wasn't it. She thought of their terrified faces and the little dog barking. She wondered where it was lurking when Gary Bowles slammed a car door, making them both jump.

"Pity they chose this weekend to come over." Mavis wiped both hands down her apron.

Realising Mavis meant Mr. and Mrs. Bowles, Lizzie nodded as if she knew what the woman was talking about. "Don't they live here all the time?"

"You couldn't live permanently in a touring caravan," Mavis said. "It's holidays and weekends only for something like that. But I have to say, they've never been this late in the year before."

"I suppose if the weather's good?" Lizzie looked up at the expanse of blue.

"It wasn't yesterday." Mavis frowned. "Yesterday, we had that storm that…"

"You did a good job looking after Mr. Bowles," Lizzie said. She couldn't stand the thought of waiting for Mavis to fill in the gap about what the storm had done.

"The wound is superficial." Mavis sounded distracted again. "And he's not a wimp." She smiled suddenly, taking Lizzie by surprise at how pretty and young she appeared under the freckles and wrinkles.

"How come you live here?" Lizzie turned to look at the Bowles' car, packed and ready to go.

"You didn't go abroad when we were young," said Mavis as if she hadn't noticed. "No-one had money for that. And we liked it. It's hard to explain to people nowadays. They think nothing of jumping on a plane and flying all over the world, but back then, you didn't go far, and you certainly didn't get the holidays there are now. People worked long hours and lived in the same place for most of their lives. When we first came here, when Trevor retired, we didn't see any reason not to move here properly. That's how we came to buy this place. It was lovely. Same kind of people as us, wanting a quiet life, getting the garden straight, more time to grow our own fruit and vegetables, joining local clubs, sea air. After living in the centre of Bradford, it was good to see proper open spaces."

"It's very...well, cut off from everywhere," Lizzie said.

"There were more chalets and caravans then, and we did have a shop with a little café. We liked it, didn't we?"

She glanced across at her husband as he walked towards them, and Lizzie felt a pang in her gut for the years the couple had shared.

"But you stayed," she said.

"Why wouldn't we?"

"You've seen how close you are to the cliff."

"Oh, yes." Mavis nodded.

"Then why haven't you moved?"

"I know it seems daft, but it's caught us off guard. There was word from the council, but it just seemed like scare tactics. The cliffs weren't bad at first. Someone came down to talk to us recently, though, didn't they, Trevor?"

"A year ago," he said as he joined them.

They didn't sound mad, Lizzie thought; just old and forgetful.

"Randolph talked to them in the main," Mavis went on. "I didn't want to go. It's my fault. You thought we should, didn't you, love?" Her eyes began to fill.

"We like it here," Trevor said.

They stood, each momentarily caught in their own thoughts, Trevor in his muddied wellington boots, a bunch of freshly picked parsley in his hand, Mavis still wearing an apron around her waist.

All three of them watched as Gary Bowles rammed a freezer bag into the well of the passenger seat. His wife, Sandra, closed the caravan door. She smiled sheepishly at them.

"No use locking it." She shrugged. "It'll never sell, and what would we do with it anyway?"

Trevor raised his hand.

"Good luck, dear," called Mavis.

Gary strode around the car, checking the rear doors were locked. Barely visible inside, amongst pillows and duvets and assorted bags, sat their two young sons.

"Aren't you getting in?" he asked Sandra as she hesitated, staring at the closed curtains of the caravan.

"Yes." She snapped back to consciousness. "Bye." She waved.

"Look after yourselves," called Mavis. "And the boys."

Trevor waved his parsley.

Sandra smiled and clambered awkwardly into the passenger seat, pushing against the freezer bag with her shin to make more room. She closed the door and wound down the window, leaning out as if she wanted to say something important.

"You take care as well." Her words were barely audible.

Lizzie glanced to see if anyone else had come to wave goodbye, but no-one had, so she watched alongside Trevor and Mavis as the car struggled up the bank under its heavy load.

"Oh dear," said Trevor when the vehicle stopped and looked as if it were about to slide back down the hill.

"I'd better get off as well." Lizzie ducked her head to climb inside the Renault.

Mavis smiled as if she hardly saw her, nodding and blinking slowly to clear tears that welled in her eyes.

Lizzie sat behind the wheel for a moment as she took a last lingering look at the chalets before turning the ignition key, releasing the handbrake and moving forwards. In the rear-view mirror, she glimpsed Trevor putting his arm around Mavis's shoulders and leading her away. Relieved, Lizzie drove down the centre of the two lines of wooden shacks, noting for the first time how well kept some of them were, with benches and gardens of late flowering roses, Michaelmas daisies and faded hydrangeas. Stones had been brightly painted around one, and wind chimes jangled in the breeze. Someone had some ladders out, and a line of shirts flapped between two posts, but there was not a soul in sight now Trevor and Mavis had disappeared. Lizzie wriggled her shoulders, reminding herself not to get involved.

Nearing the track that led up to the main coast road, she noticed police tape fluttering across the top of the cliff path. Intrigued by its movement against the vast reach of sky, she stopped the car. Watching it dance and flicker in the expanse of blue, she leant her arms on the steering wheel, realising that soon this place would no longer exist. She checked in the mirror again. Still no-one in sight.

After a moment's thought, she turned off the engine and stepped onto thick grass, automatically glancing over her shoulder at the chalets. The park seemed deserted, and she carefully stepped towards the edge and looked down at the beach. Far below, the wooden roof, floor, walls and doors of the collapsed chalet lay broken and battered across the distant shingle. Around broken planks, still recognisable as the structure of a building, the sodden, ruined contents spewed over the sand and rock pools. Amongst seaweed and tins of baked beans and tomatoes, a painting of two indistinct people staring up at the sky caught her attention. In a rush, the panic and fear she had felt from the previous night came flooding back. She bent down, hands clasped to knees, hair dangling over her face and, closing her eyes, took deep breaths. After several minutes, she straightened up and with another intake of sea air walked shakily back to the car and leant against the door frame. She didn't care if anyone shouted out now or asked what she was doing. Reaching across the seat and fumbling in her bag, she pulled out her mobile phone and pressed in a well-used number.

Chapter Seven

FORTY-THREE-YEAR-OLD ANDREW BOOTH slipped his hand inside his jacket pocket. Instinctively, he muted his mobile phone because he knew that if it rang at that moment, it could jeopardise the uneasy balance between himself and his thirty-five-year-old wife. Judith was uncannily astute as to when another woman phoned, and this was not a time to unsettle the delicate truce they had reached. He glanced sideways at her, chastising himself for having mistaken confidence for lasting attractiveness.

As they rounded the side of the house, the unlit bonfire rose in front of them, a mass of dry branches, broken-off pieces of fence and gate, cracked fruit and seed boxes and irreparable furniture. This autumn, it towered higher than Moorland Castle had seen for years. Andrew surveyed it with pride as Judith strolled around its perimeter, eyeing it for any stray piece of wood that might become dislodged.

"It's looking great, isn't it?" he said as she joined him.

She looked back towards the drive. "Jim Wright's not done a bad job for once."

"Why do you always call him by his full name?" Andrew tapped some sticks into place with his foot. "Why can't you just call him Jim?"

"What's the bill for burning Guy Fawkes this year?"

"It's worth it." He kicked a fir cone across the grass. "And we make quite a bit on the food and beer."

"That's because I'm in charge of the catering."

"Everyone's happy, then."

"I'd be happier if we sold tickets. Ten pounds a head. People would pay that."

"Families around here can't afford that," said Andrew. "I'm not charging people."

"You love being the benevolent Lord of the Manor, don't you?" she mocked.

"Any boss will tell you that goodwill is essential. Besides, it's tradition."

"This isn't some big conglomerate, and these people aren't your loyal workforce." She fingered the cashmere scarf around her neck. "They don't give two hoots about you, Andrew."

"Don't start, Judith. You knew this was part of our life when you married me. You can't start complaining now."

"When are you going to learn you have to change in order to survive?"

"Tradition is more important." He steered her around to face the mullion windows of the library. "Estates hold a delicate balance between owner and worker, and whatever happens in the outside world, in here—" he gestured across the gardens "—we're all a part of the same community."

"Ah, yes, *Downton Abbey*. What they really want is a flash car and a big television and holidays in Florida. I know you like to pretend that nothing ever changes and that if you give someone a bale of hay, they'll give you a barrel of beer in return, but it's not like that anymore."

She stood in front of him now, hands confrontationally on hips, unable to conceal her frustration.

"I think things will go back to it," he said. "But I'll expect at least a case of Château Margaux this time around." He forced a smile. She still looked good.

Judith had clearly picked up on his thoughts, but she wasn't going to give in yet.

"A family on the Rigby estate probably has more ready cash than we do," she said. "It's ludicrous us paying for their entertainment when they're erecting satellite dishes as fast as they're having kids."

Andrew stared at the pyramid of wood looming behind her head and the chair balanced like a hair adornment waiting for the final touch of the guy.

"As I said, I think things are coming full circle." He turned away, keen to change the conversation. "The bonfire and fireworks are free to locals. The tourists can subsidise them."

"Everyone's envious of us—even so-called friends," Judith changed tack. "You know when they're commiserating with you as you tell them you've got to find another seventy thousand to fix the roof, they're secretly wishing it were them."

"Bloody stupid if they are." Andrew bent to straighten a branch that didn't need straightening.

"Nobody sees the reality behind the coat of arms and well-polished silverware."

"That shows we're managing, eh?" Andrew kicked a two-legged stool, and the surrounding branches shifted.

"My God!" Judith watched him fiddling around. "The things we end up talking about. Makes you wonder how we keep the magic alive."

He smiled—the smile that had captured her in the first place. "You know what keeps the magic alive."

"Says the man who takes weeks building up a pile of wood and then strikes a match and burns it down in a few hours."

"That's exactly why foreigners descend in hordes," he said, noticing the scarf slide from her neck. "They love our strange traditions."

She dangled the strip of tomato red cashmere. "I sometimes feel as if I'm locked up with a family of eccentric aunts and uncles."

Andrew strolled away from the bonfire. Judith followed him, unbuttoning her jacket.

"Fancy a gander round the gardens while we're at it?" He quickened his pace without turning for a response.

The castle grounds were no longer what they had been. There were no regiments of colour in the knot garden or sweeping profusions of flowers in the borders. Jim Wright and his assistants tried hard to maintain control over the beds, planting self-propagating clumps of hardy perennials and lace-capped hydrangeas. Jim had a special love for the rose garden, to which he allotted more time than he should, but having been there longer than either Andrew or Judith, they left him to tend the gardens, deal with pests and manage the annual shoots.

Walking around the far side of the building, Andrew pressed the window surrounds, pulling back a straggling piece of ivy and mentally noting the ragged edges of grass.

***

Judith watched a rook fly off one of the chimneys. "I could do with a holiday right now."

"We'll be closing up the house in less than a week," Andrew said. "You could go to your sister's, though your brother might be a safer bet. More to do in London, so you wouldn't get so bored."

Judith thought of her brother in his stark apartment overlooking the Thames. It was tempting. She could never see the point of staying with her sister in the mid-terraced house in York that had nowhere to park her four-by-four.

"I want to go somewhere warm," she said.

"We'll have to do something about that." Andrew nodded at the protruding stem of a buddleia growing out of the pointing on one of the many chimney stacks.

"We could leave Carol in charge of the winter clean-up. She's highly capable and we could disappear off to Spain early."

He glanced at her. "A spot of surfing would be good."

"You could sit at the bar and chat to Javi." She smiled. "Business and pleasure."

"I'm not convinced we should leave Carol in charge of the clean-up. She's only been the manager for a year."

"Two," Judith corrected.

They had meandered down to the greenhouses and wandered past dusty glass panes marked with driven rain and cracked by forgotten accidents. Stacks of terracotta flowerpots leaned precariously next to plucked vines and ravished tomato plants. This was Jim's terrain, and Judith half-expected to see him emerge at any moment, pint mug of tea in one soiled hand and a cutting of some description in the other. But he must have been working elsewhere, as the kitchen garden straggled empty except for the persistent rook that had flown down from the roof and now stabbed at the turned earth.

Andrew pointed at this and that—a plant that needed staking or a wall that had lost one of its coping stones. Judith pushed her hands in her jacket pockets and merely nodded, staring blankly when he indicated objects in need of repair.

Her mind wandered as she imagined living in a pristine London flat like her brother's. His life seemed so simple and clean like his freshly painted white walls and angular furniture. She could see herself there, dressed in blocks of colour, looking ten years younger. She would have all the most up-to-date gadgets—a plasma screen on the wall and a remote-control music centre. Not a book or ancient DVD in sight. There would be no dust lurking in dark corners because there would be no dark corners, only light from floor-to-ceiling windows cleaned by a contracted firm of specialists; the perfect place for a lover.

Andrew was slightly ahead of her now, her thoughts having slowed her feet. At the gate, he turned and waited, holding it open until she walked through, and she knew he'd noticed her taut jumper, revealed through the open jacket, and her long, bare neck unencumbered by the scarf.

She strolled past. "You're behaving yourself at the moment, aren't you?"

"That's a sudden change of subject." He caught hold of her hand and rubbed his thumb into the softness of her palm.

"Well, you know how you are when you're not behaving."

"Is this how I am?" He smiled.

"Have you sold that old chalet off as I asked?"

"No buyers yet."

That wasn't the answer she'd expected; she'd assumed it had gone long ago, and the fact that it hadn't made her suddenly angry.

"You're not going to be able to sell it now."

He ran a hand over her twice-weekly-exercised buttocks. "It's a case of do I keep up repairs or let it go to ruin?"

She wriggled, but he held her close. "Let it go completely."

"Other people still live down there. It looks bad next to the ones that are still being kept up." Distracted, he admired her body with his hands.

"It's a waste of money maintaining any of them when they'll soon be in the sea. Just forget about it."

"You're right," he said, kissing her exposed neck.

She let her head fall back, knowing what she was doing, knowing he'd soon do whatever she wanted. "Aren't you tired of this dilapidated old house?"

He ran a thumb over her lips. "You always say that at the end of the season."

She pressed against him. "This year, I'm particularly fed up with it all."

"I know. The house needs more doing than usual."

"Don't you hate the cold and never-ending rain? I just want to feel the sun on my skin." She wound her hand around his shoulder.

"You deserve a holiday." He kissed her cheek. "Your skin feels gorgeous to me."

"Every way we turn at the moment, someone is screwing us."

"We'll soon be in Spain."

"And your thoughts will only be for me?" She pulled him closer, keen to feel that there was no going back for him.

"I do. I will. You're always first."

"Kiss me."

"Yes," he sighed. "Spain. A fresh start. Not come back here until March."

She grabbed his shoulders and dug her fingers tightly into the tweed. They stumbled backwards until, pressed against the ivy, she felt the stone wall of the house, solid behind her back.

Chapter Eight

LIZZIE SHOVED HER phone into her pocket. She hated this coast. You could never get a signal. She turned on the ignition and looked at the clear sky through the windscreen. She didn't know where to go. Not Moorland Castle. Andrew must be with his cow of a wife. She couldn't face going back to Rigby. The thought of the old flat was too depressing. She took hold of the handbrake. The passenger door opened, and someone, Jez, dropped into the seat beside her. He'd appeared from nowhere.

"What are you doing?" she demanded.

"Can I have a lift?"

"I doubt I'm going where you're going."

"How do you know where I'm going?"

"I'm sorry, I'm late for work," she said. "I'm not joking. You'll have to get a lift with someone else."

"John's in a mood. He won't let me borrow his car." He patted the console as if to say 'Let's go!'

"Top of the bank and that's it." She was more annoyed with herself that she felt pleased to see him again than because he'd had the cheek to jump in and catch a ride.

"Belt?" He pulled the strap across his chest and nodded at her.

Pressing down the accelerator, the car skidded over loose earth. She drove more steadily up the track.

"Did you even know this place existed before yesterday?" he asked.

"I know now."

"And now you're leaving."

"That's just it! Why doesn't anyone seem to care what's happened? You lot go around beating each other up and shouting and then handing out bacon butties. I can't believe no-one's reported that old man. He should be banged up."

Neither spoke again until the car reached the top of the track and she pulled on the handbrake, keeping the engine running.

"It's a shame you couldn't have come here before all this started," he said.

She glanced at his door then away again, tapping her fingers on the wheel. There was no way she could look at him.

"Those people were killed," she said. "I should never have come here in the first place."

"Would have been nice to get to know you better."

She couldn't bear it; men always said something too late to draw you in when they wanted something. She should have known; should have guessed he'd be like all the rest.

"How come you're so calm?" she asked.

He strained his neck, trying to see himself in the driver's mirror. "Do I look calm?"

She stared at the wheel, all the questions in her head seeming superfluous, all except one.

"Why haven't you moved out already?"

He settled back in his seat. "Lack of an alternative, I think is the phrase."

"Of course there's an alternative. You must have been told that. I can't believe you've been allowed to stay here."

More questions brewed in her head.

"We're going now."

"Yes, sorry, of course you are. It's none of my business." She looked up at the blue sky. "You should give that other old couple a hand. They're not sure where to start."

"Sounds like you're developing a soft spot for them."

She shuffled in her seat, readjusting her grip on the wheel. "I've got to go."

"If it wasn't for last night, would you stay the week out?"

It wasn't worth arguing, and she was too tired to make the effort. All she wanted was to get away, away from him, the chalet park, the entire Yorkshire coast. Yorkshire. England. The planet.

"I wouldn't stay the week," she said.

"Where you off?"

"I'm late."

He didn't move.

"Are you going past Moorland Castle?"

She waited. Still, he didn't move, so she lowered the handbrake hoping he'd get out without saying anything else. Talking drew her in, it always drew her in, and he unsettled her, and she didn't want unsettling. He must have known she worked at the castle. She hated the fact everyone knew everything about you around here. She looked at him. He didn't move, but a muscle in his cheek twitched, and she wondered if he were smiling.

They sped along the cliff road, the sea on their right, farm fields to their left.

"Thanks for the lift," he said.

She pressed her foot down harder on the accelerator. "I can't believe you're carrying on as normal. Don't you care what happened to...what were their names?"

"What do you want me to say? They were like a mother and father to me? Every time I smell cherries, I'll think of Shelley? When I hear someone whistle a Tom Jones tune, I'll think of Gordon packing up his fishing stuff? We don't show it to outsiders, but just because we're not taking photos and writing about it, doesn't mean we don't feel anything."

"I'm only asking." Lizzie glanced at the sea, wishing she hadn't asked.

They drove in silence again, she, annoyed she'd said anything and annoyed he sounded annoyed. They were almost there; she could ignore him by keeping her eyes on the road. She concentrated on how she'd ask Andrew to sort her out somewhere decent to stay. For all she knew, this bonfire business could take up all day, and then she'd be asking him at the last minute and he might be going out by then or distracted or—worse—Judith may be hooked around his neck.

She wondered if she could change her mind, say she wasn't going past the castle and drop him off before then, but they were already skirting the estate walls and the entrance gaped just ahead.

"What do you do?" he asked.

He knew she worked at the castle. She hated questions when the answer was obvious. She definitely couldn't arrive with him gawping into her affairs.

"I'm Mr. Booth's personal assistant," she said.

"So you know the place quite well."

"Of course."

She tried to think of a question to ask him, to shut up the sound of his brain working. The entrance gates loomed. She looked ahead at the long, bleak road to Rigby.

"Just one thing for you to think about before I get out," he said. "You spent one night in the park, and you seem, to me—I may be wrong, but—you seem to care about some of the people you met last night. I remember you crying and screaming at me to save Shelley and Gordon, and now you're concerned about Trevor and Mavis getting packed up in time. Why don't you pop back and help them get sorted?"

She slowed the car. "Think that would be a bit patronising, don't you?"

"What you did last night takes a lot of courage."

She kept her eyes fixed on her knuckles. "*You* were going to go in and save them."

"I knew them. You didn't."

"What's your point?"

"Stop here, would you?"

Relieved, she pulled over and looked at him expectantly.

"Mavis and Trevor want to leave, but they're scared where they'll end up," he said. He undid his seat belt. "So are John and Joyce. In some ways, Gordon and Shelley are better off."

"Don't say things like that."

"Nobody knows who they are. Nobody cares."

"'Course they do."

He raised his eyebrows. "I think you know that's not true. Their lives and their homes are worthless. They've no money and no-one to turn to."

"The council will help them." He was right. No-one did care. The council would do the absolute minimum they had to. Too busy. Not enough resources. Always someone else in more need.

"You know what it's like when you haven't a clue what's best, so you just stay still and hope for divine intervention?"

She knew how that felt. She'd curled up under a duvet often enough. Days coming out only for a drink of water and the bathroom; days of numbness; days wishing she were dead.

He turned to face her. Her cheeks flushed. The air in the car seemed too hot, but she hesitated in lowering the window. She didn't know what to say. There were no suggestions to be made. She knew what it was like to lose touch with people, to have no contact with a family whose faces you barely remembered. Families and friends didn't want to know about people who were of no use to them and who would only infringe on their time. Mavis's daughters wouldn't want to have their worlds disrupted, and Lizzie knew what it was like to have to depend on the state. The only thing she didn't know was what it was like to be old.

"Don't worry," he said, opening the car door. "We'll sort it. Don't give Mavis and Trevor or any of us another thought."

She wanted to tell him that wasn't what she meant; tell him he was being unfair and how dare he put that on her when he didn't know anything about the way she thought. She mustn't shout, she told herself, or she would lose the argument before she could formulate a response. He was closing the door and patting

the roof. Through the rear-view mirror, she watched him walk
back the way they had come. He strode away without turning
to look back or to either side, and she couldn't take her eyes off
him. Instead of turning into the drive, she pulled out her phone
again and, scrolling down, pressed Andrew Booth's number.
This time, she got a signal, but he didn't answer. She threw it on
the passenger seat and glanced in the mirror again. Jez still
didn't turn around, and she looked at her hands, clenched tightly
together to stop them from trembling.

Chapter Nine

CAROL BAILEY, THE house manager, raised her blonde head on hearing the door of the gift shop open.

She smiled brightly at the small group of men and women dressed in anoraks and flat shoes. "Your guide has arrived!"

Lizzie ignored the handful of visitors browsing with little interest amongst the shelves of books and knickknacks. "Where's Andrew?"

"Thank you for your patience." Carol's French-polished nails flashed. "Lizzie will be ready to take you round the house in five minutes." She leaned forward and lowered her voice. "You have two seconds to get changed."

"I need to speak to him. Where is he?"

"You can pay now for any purchases," Carol announced. She lowered her voice again. "See him in your own time."

"Can't you take them round? This is urgent."

"No, I can't. Helen's phoned in sick, so I'm on my own, and I've a ton of other stuff I'm supposed to be doing for the big night. Just put your green jumper and badge on and get back here fast." She hissed at Lizzie then announced breezily to the room, "Two minutes!"

Lizzie glanced at the men and women trying to look as though they weren't listening.

"You don't need to get changed for us." A large man, unable to contain himself, raised his voice.

"Lizzie will be with you in one minute," said Carol. "If you'd like to take that time to look around the shop?"

"We've looked." The man rested a large hand on the counter. "The sign says the tour starts at eleven."

A tall, bony woman pressed a Moorland Castle brochure next to his squat digits, and Carol took the ten-pound note from her freckled hand. Lizzie pushed her way out of the shop again, heading straight across the entrance hall for the door marked 'Private' just as Andrew sauntered through the main entrance.

"Why aren't you answering your phone?" Lizzie stopped when she saw Judith emerge from the porch with a bunch of Michaelmas daisies in her hand. "Hello, Mrs. Booth." She nodded quickly as Judith glanced at Andrew.

"Shouldn't you be taking our visitors round?" Judith's face remained unreadable as Andrew headed for the library.

"D'you know about the chalet park?" Lizzie kept her voice steady.

"Our chalet is no longer in use," Judith said, gazing coolly at Lizzie. "We have absolutely no interest in the place."

"Lucky for you, then." Lizzie glared back. "Because the cliff collapsed last night, and one of the chalets went with it."

"Which one?" Andrew's attention caught, he stopped by the library door.

"Please say it's ours?" Judith said.

"Was anyone hurt?"

Lizzie shook her head, trying to keep the tears at bay. She didn't want to talk about it. She didn't want to remember, but it was too late to backtrack.

"You should go down and see for yourself," she said. Andrew glanced at Judith and felt in his pockets. "I thought you'd have heard."

Andrew pulled his mobile out of his pocket and studied the screen. "Fifteen missed calls. You wouldn't mind finding the Range Rover keys for me, would you?" he asked, turning to Judith. "They should be in the top drawer of my desk."

Judith dropped the flowers onto the hall table and strode towards the library, leaving the door open wide.

"I'm not lying to you," Lizzie said. "It was horrible."

"Shush." He briefly touched her shoulders.

"I've got all my stuff. I can move straight into the gatehouse today."

"We'll talk about that later." He glanced again towards the open door. "I'll have to go straight down to the chalet park and see what's going on."

"The whole cliff fell away, and this couple—"

"It'll have to wait." He frowned, seeing Judith in the doorway swinging the car keys and Carol appearing from the shop at the same time.

"Oh," Carol looked both annoyed and relieved. "Good morning, Mrs. Booth. Did you get the phone call, Mr. Booth?"

"If it's about the park, Lizzie's just told me, Carol. Thanks, Judith." He took the keys.

Lizzie wanted to grab his arm but didn't dare in front of his wife. He looked tired. Judith must have given him a hard time. She swallowed, silently begging him to ask her to accompany him but dreading that he would because that would mean returning to the park and seeing Jez and all those people again. Andrew was already turning away.

"I'm not sure how long this is going to take." He nodded to Judith.

Swiftly, he strode back through the front door, and they all watched him go, momentarily silent. Lizzie crossed her arms over her stomach; if she pressed hard enough, she could hold everything in.

With a loud cough, Carol interrupted her thoughts.

"The visitors are waiting," she said.

Judith gathered up the daisies. "Doesn't she need to get changed?"

Lizzie thrust her way into the staff changing room. She could hear Judith's and Carol's voices even though she couldn't make out what they were saying. It didn't matter; she was safely away from the chalet park, safely away from Jez—from all of them. Andrew was already distancing himself. The duvet beckoned. All she needed to find was a bed to hide in.

Looking in the mirror, she scraped back her hair. She looked as tired as Andrew. As always, when dressed in the dark-green uniform worn by the guides at Moorland Castle, she was surprised how different it made her feel. Today, drained and miserable. Tomorrow, she would be over all this. She dabbed Vaseline onto her lips. Ready.

"Welcome to Moorland Castle," she announced to the eight visitors, "which has been home to the Booth family since 1593."

There was a pause as though they and Lizzie spoke different languages.

She pointed hastily to a coat of arms hanging high on the entrance hall wall. "But the castle is older than that and was first owned by the Carter family. Unfortunately, they were Catholics, and during Elizabeth the First's reign, they lost it to the Protestant Booth family, who were keen supporters of the queen."

"You'd put up a fight if anyone tried to take your home away from you, wouldn't you, Ted?" The freckle-handed woman tapped the arm of a large man at her side.

"What happened to these Carters?" Ted demanded.

"Lord Carter was hanged until he was almost dead, then castrated, quartered and finally disembowelled."

Silence. She didn't know why she'd blurted it out so brusquely. Maybe she wanted them to feel what she felt every time she drove away from the house, every time someone told her to get out, every grey morning when she felt cold winter air strike her face. Even if she told them how harsh Yorkshire was, they wouldn't see past its beauty. Visitors didn't. You had to live there to know how unforgiving it could be. She racked her brains for how to bring the topic back to the script she had learnt, but Ted's wife spoke first.

"What's disembowelled?" she asked.

There was no going back. There was never any going back. She had to make them understand.

"It's not pleasant." Lizzie stared at their faces, all lit up with eagerness to hear about the suggested pain. "You're cut all the way down the middle lengthways, from here to here." She ran her fingers down her torso. "Then across your stomach horizontally, then the executioner hacks out your innards. You'd die in excruciating pain sometime during all that." There was silence again, but Lizzie didn't hold back. She felt the anguish of her inwards spewing out on a regular basis—well, they could learn something about how that felt.

"Lady Carter wasn't put through that, though," she said. "She wasn't stupid. She wanted to survive, so she married a Protestant from Hampshire and changed her faith." She paused. They studied the room. "If you'd like to follow me upstairs, we'll start at the top of the house and work our way down." She grasped the Newel post to steady herself.

"What happened to their children?" A woman in a lilac anorak followed. "Were they disembowelled as well?"

"Now come on, love," a bald man said, turning to her. "Be realistic."

"Their children were grown up when all this happened," said Lizzie. "They were given the chance to leave the country, so they went off to France. Lots of young Catholics did. Over in Europe, they could talk about getting their own back. It was an ideal breeding ground for terrorists."

"They don't sound like terrorists to me," said Ted, directly behind Lizzie. "Sounds like they were just planning on claiming back what was theirs. I'd do more than that if someone took my house away from me and butchered my old man."

"And your wife got on with her life," added the woman.

"Too right, I would, Vera."

"Some of these Catholics planned on blowing up the Houses of Parliament and any innocent people who happened to be there," said Lizzie. "I wouldn't give them too much sympathy."

"You're talking about the Gunpowder Plot," said a man dressed in navy.

"I read somewhere that Guy Fawkes was from around here," the lilac-clad woman said, glancing at the nearest paintings.

"York," Lizzie said. "And you're very welcome to come to the bonfire and join in the celebrations if you want." She faced them all. "You can get details in the shop from Carol—the woman with the blonde hair. She'll be pleased to help. The fireworks are supposed to be better than those in London."

The tall, thin woman looked at her husband. "Won't we be in Edinburgh?"

"I'm guessing there's a big charge?" he asked.

"No, it's free," said Lizzie. She could feel her heart inexplicably pounding. She dabbed the slight sweat that had appeared on her forehead with her fingertips.

"Does the Booth family still live here?" the man in the navy jumper asked as they followed Lizzie up the staircase.

"Of course. They open up the house to visitors from Easter until Bonfire Night, but they keep certain parts private for their own use." She breathed in deeply. "I'm going to show you the smallest room in the house first, then we'll make our way to the grandest." She set off along the heavily panelled corridor, willing them not to ask more questions.

They passed several closed doors and pale faces staring out of dark oil paintings. A recess held a glinting armoured figure that made Vera flinch and Ted shake his head. Lizzie had seen every reaction before. Halfway down the long corridor, she brought them to a halt, and they crowded nearer as she silently pressed an area of panelling. With a slight creak of old wood, it opened outwards, revealing a short flight of stone steps ascending into darkness.

"The space is very tight," said Lizzie, flicking an incongruous light switch. "So if half of you want to look at the portraits here, I'll take the first four in, then the rest afterwards. The pictures are of Booth family members from Queen Elizabeth the First's time to the present day. Is that all right?" she asked in a way that made it clear she didn't want a response. There were disappointed agreements from those in the group farthest from the opening. Disgruntled, they hung around until, realising they really would have to take their turn, they wandered off to reluctantly study Andrew Booth's ancestors.

Eagerly, Ted, Vera and two others, Joan and Keith, obviously close friends, ascended the narrow stairs, steadying themselves by sliding one hand up the plastered wall as they watched that their feet firmly trod on the narrow, spiralling steps. The room at the top opened out, and they stood at a loss, gazing into the confined space exposed in the light of a bare bulb wired precariously from one of the walls.

Lizzie gestured with both hands. "The priest hole."

Keith ran a hand over the rough wall. "I've always wanted to see one of these."

"Priests lived here?" Vera asked sharply.

"For a while," said Lizzie. "And only one at a time. This room was built into the chimney space specifically for a priest to hide in. Could be for days, often months. Sometimes, it might not be a priest but a well-known Catholic who needed to hide from the government's men."

They looked around again at the comfortless stone walls and floor.

"If that door in the panelling was discovered, they'd soon be up here," said Ted.

"Yes, and that's why this isn't a normal priest hole. It's special."

Lizzie lifted her leg over a huge stone beam, gestured for them to follow, and so, with each other's help, they clambered over the obstruction to find themselves in a second even smaller area and, like the first space they had entered, devoid of any furniture or ornament.

It's what's called a Double Priest Hide, and it is one of only three left in the entire country." Lizzie explained. "Now, if you bend down, you can make out a narrow gap. That's it. I know, you have to get right down. Just mind your heads. That opens out into another hole, and that is where the priest would hide, not in this first one. So if soldiers did want to search the house and the family was very unlucky, they might find this hole, but not the second one underneath. Originally, there'd be wooden panelling running all the way along here, but that's gone now. A very famous Catholic, Edmund Campion, hid here for a while."

"I can't see how anyone could fit through." Keith, squatting, tilted his head to one side in an attempt to make out the gap.

"People tended to be thinner and shorter in those days," said Lizzie.

"Think if we'd come after lunch," laughed Joan.

"Ow!" Ted's knee joints cracked.

Lizzie let the visitors gaze around the cramped space and wonder at the possibility of spending months in such a tight, inhospitable hole with death highly possible. It seemed obvious that traitors should have chosen to escape across the sea to France.

"I won't ask you to climb in." She smiled, crouching to check out the space. It yawned pitch-black and smelt stale and cold. Standing, she suddenly felt a rush of blood to her head and swayed, putting out a hand to find something concrete. Stars rushed in. Her skin turned cold and sweaty. Darkness beckoned. She couldn't help it. She fell.

***

Carol heard the commotion before she saw anyone. Annoyed at being interrupted, she marched out into the hall to see what the rumpus was about. Looking extremely pale, clasping the balustrade, Lizzie crept downstairs, supported by the big man of the party, followed by the women and behind them, three other men.

Carol rushed to the bottom of the stairs. "What is it?"

Vera waved her brochure in the air. "She fainted."

Carol opened the door to the library, and Ted supported Lizzie through, with the others eagerly following and making no pretence about looking around.

"What happened?" Carol asked Ted and Vera.

"Nothing," said Lizzie.

"She passed out." Vera nodded.

"We were in that weird little room up some stairs."

"The priest hide."

"Hole."

"One minute, she was bending down, the next, standing up..."

"The next, passed out in Ted here's arms."

"Quite the charmer."

Lizzie slumped onto a chair and dropped her head between her knees so that all any of them could see was a tangled mop of red hair.

"I'm sorry your tour has been cut short," Carol said. "I'll reimburse you, of course. If you'd care to follow me?"

She ran the receipts through the till, and they took the money happily enough even though they had enjoyed the drama. Soon, they were back in the main hall with Carol announcing they were welcome to attend the Grand Firework Display as special guests. Somewhat disappointed, Vera said they had an intense itinerary which they could not deviate from but would have loved to come. They were heading for Rigby Abbey and the shops that afternoon, then York with the Minster and Shambles—whatever they were—the following morning, and then on up to Scotland and Loch Ness.

"That's a shame." Carol swept them along, trying but failing to hide her relief. "It's a massive community event, and the Booths are known for their hospitality."

The lilac-dressed woman came back into the entrance. "The minibus is ready to go," she said.

"The driver can wait until we're good and ready," blustered Ted. "Now, you look after that little lady."

"Don't get yourself upset," said Vera. "Thank you." She nodded to Carol. "I hope that young woman looks after herself. There are far too many young women who don't eat properly nowadays, and it doesn't do to get too peaky and go climbing about in places like that priest hotel thing."

"Thank you for visiting Moorland Castle," Carol reiterated. "I hope you enjoy the rest of your stay in Yorkshire."

Outside, Carol impatiently watched Vera follow Ted onto the minibus. The engine throbbed noisily, and the driver stared straight ahead, ignoring the vibrations. Everyone else waited in their seat. Eventually, the bus pulled away.

Hurrying back inside, Carol found Lizzie already in her coat and pulling her phone out of her bag.

"I don't think you should drive yet," Carol said.

"I'm okay." Lizzie studied the screen. "It was just a head rush."

"You look terrible," Carol said coolly. "One of those women thinks you're pregnant. Are you?"

Chapter Ten

A NDREW DIDN'T ANSWER. Lizzie let her phone drop onto the sofa, curled on her side and stared down at a can of Lilt Carol had placed on the floor. She closed her eyes. It felt better not seeing anything. If she couldn't see the room, she could imagine she were somewhere else.

The click of Carol's heels and the beep of the till reminded her of reality. Finally lifting her head, she sat up and listened to the noises of the house. In some ways, it would be easier to remain in the library, pretending to be asleep until darkness fell, rather than open the door and return to a world that stretched inhospitably from the main house, down the drive and across the bleak stretch of road to scrub and grey sea. She leant against the back of the sofa, wondering what was the matter with her that made even the decision of whether to get up so difficult. No way was she pregnant. She knew better than that. Eventually, last night's events began to take hold and practicality kicked in. She picked up her bag. She didn't want to think about the chalet park and the dead couple's faces. She didn't want to think about Judith and Carol either. She knew which was worse.

She tiptoed across the hall and put her ear against the study door, but the wood was so thick no sound could be heard from the other side. She listened again—still no noise—and pressed down the handle at the same time as Judith appeared through the front entrance.

"Can I help you?" Her voice travelled over the open space as Gloucester the Labrador padded across the flags.

"I was going to let you know I've finished for the day." Lizzie let go of the cold metal. "But, well, you're not in here." She smiled. Felt stupid. The dog rubbed against her legs as if it knew.

"Have you seen Carol?" Judith turned away, not willing to wait for an answer.

Both Lizzie and Gloucester followed.

"That woman, Marilyn Hopper, just ran into me with her bloody bicycle." Judith swept through the open door.

Carol looked up from carefully separated piles of coins on the counter. "Are you all right?"

"I'll live," Judith said, glancing at the meagre amount. "Is that it?"

"I think I've met her," Lizzie said. "I mean, I've heard the name." Judith turned to face her. "Don't tell me she's a friend of yours?" She remembered Marilyn's bright hair. "She lives at that old chalet park. You know, where you have a chalet?"

It was as if the air froze. Lizzie's chest tightened. Her breathing stuttered. She looked down, not wanting them to notice she trembled.

Judith walked past her towards the door. "We all knew that was on the cards."

"An old couple were killed." Lizzie's voice shook. "I was staying there. I saw them. I...I think that...Marilyn Hopper, was it? I heard her name mentioned. She lives there too, so I think she must have known them pretty well."

Judith spun around in seemingly slow motion and looked at her with heavy, scornful eyes.

"I think Lizzie's trying to say that this woman was probably so upset she wasn't concentrating on where she was going," Carol said.

Judith studied Lizzie. "She wasn't upset, Carol, she was drunk." "Oh."

"What's up with you?" Judith demanded, looking at Lizzie.

"You still look pale," said Carol. "Why don't you sit down?"

Lizzie shook her head. It all seemed like a dream. She could feel herself pulling away as they faded into the walls. She put her hand on the counter.

"I was wondering," she began. "As a big, big favour, Judith—I would be really grateful. Would it be possible for me to move into the gatehouse?"

"How close are you to the edge?"

"The edge?" Lizzie had already begun to fall.

"Lizzie looks pretty shaken up, Judith," Carol cut in. "I don't think that chalet park is a good place for her to be staying. Come on, you. Sit down."

"It's not my chalet," said Lizzie. "I don't own it. It was one night. I don't want to stay longer—"

"Whose is it?" Judith asked, jangling keys loudly in her hand.

Lizzie watched the dog scratch itself. She winced at the overloud noise.

"I think it's yours," she said. "It's the estate's—the Booths own it."

There was a long pause. No-one spoke.

"The gatehouse is a holiday cottage, so it isn't viable to have a tenant." Judith's voice grated. "Besides, it's always rented out over Christmas and New Year."

"It's November. No-one is in it in November." Lizzie struggled to keep her voice calm.

"You could stay with me," Carol said, "but my boyfriend's just moved in, and the place is tiny."

"It wouldn't be for long." Lizzie dared Judith to look at her. "A few days until I find somewhere permanent."

"I'm sorry." Judith fingered the open cash register drawer. "This is the time of year repairs from the summer get sorted before the busy winter lets. There are plenty of properties to rent in Rigby now that the main season is over, I suggest you look into that."

"The place is full from now until Halloween. You know that." Lizzie wouldn't be able to control her voice for much longer.

"Carol, have you given Lizzie her wages? That will help with a down payment." Judith reached into the till and took out a twenty-pound note. "As it's the end of the season, a little bonus."

Lizzie eyed the twenty-pound note. "I'm only asking for a day or two. I didn't sleep at all last night, and I don't think I'll be safe driving on that road to Beamstown. You've no idea what it was like at that chalet park."

"And you have no idea what it's like running an old pile like this," Judith snapped. "Do you think I enjoy having people traipsing through my home, peering at my personal belongings? Imagine clearing up after a group of twenty-year-olds who've rented the cottage for a weekend and trying to turn around any profit! Don't whinge to me about living where you don't want to and dealing with people whom I wouldn't normally give the time of day." She paused and looked briefly aghast at what she'd said, then straightened her jacket. "I'm sure you'll find somewhere in Rigby if you get off now. Otherwise, I suggest you go back to the chalet park."

Slowly and in silence, Lizzie took the twenty-pound note from the counter.

"You know this is the time we lay all the casual staff off," Judith said.

"Helen will be finishing as well." Carol nodded reassuringly.

"I think you should visit the chalet park." Lizzie's voice was barely audible. "See for yourself what it's like. It's battered by the weather. The chalets are awful. They're damp and rotten and ready to fall down."

Carol took Lizzie's arm as if supporting her. "D'you want me to come out to the car with you?"

"I'm not asking for anything outrageous." Lizzie flushed, angry now. "It's only until I get myself fixed up."

"I'm sure someone like you has friends." Judith was already leaving the room.

Lizzie hesitated. She'd packed the car. She couldn't go back to the chalet park even if it was safe. Carol held her arm as they walked outside. She didn't say anything but looked concerned. Lizzie couldn't bear her pity.

"Don't worry." Lizzie forced a smile. "It really was just head rush."

Reluctantly, Carol left her, and she leant against the car, taking deep breaths. She couldn't say what really made her want to black out the world.

A couple of youngsters waving branches jumped over a low wall bordering the gardens to the right. The older boy turned around and grinned. An overwhelming desire not to be alone surged over her.

She tried not to sound desperate. "Suppose you want a lift?"

"Got our own wheels, ta." Whooping, he broke into a run.

She should have known, but at least an old battered Renault like hers was safe from carjackers like them.

Chapter Eleven

Normally, she loved the time between day and night when people turned on the lights but refrained from pulling curtains so that you could peep inside. Even the sparsest room looked inviting. Shops remained open for another hour or so, which meant she didn't feel excluded by hurrying along almost-empty pavements.

She turned into a narrow opening where lights from tiny fishermen's cottages shed their glow onto flagstones. Exhausted from lack of sleep, she wished she'd come earlier.

"Sorry, any other time." Bill shook his head. "You should know this is one of the busiest weekends in Rigby."

"But you *can't* be full." She wouldn't believe it. No stranger to Rigby would think that the narrow, dark entrance could open into a pretty nook flanked by inviting little houses. Bill's little B&B was so well hidden in the back courtyard, it never ceased to amaze her how he made a living

"Now that's where you're wrong," he said. "I'm on all sorts of websites. These people love my place. Can't hurt me telling them smugglers lived here and we're chock-a-block with ghosts." He laughed, pleased with himself. He didn't open the door further than halfway.

She tried to keep the tremor from her voice. "Can you think of anywhere else that'll have a room going?"

"What about that place you work?" He glanced over his shoulder towards the voices within.

She shook her head.

"You must have a mate with a settee," he said, retreating into the warm glow of the narrow hallway.

Footsteps coming into the yard made Lizzie turn around.

It was no-one she knew. Just a young woman shoving a key into a neighbouring blue door, which she pushed open with her knee. Lizzie forced a smile, and the woman, weighed down with shopping bags, shrugged before kicking the door shut. Light from the small window cast squares on the yard.

Doors closed to her, Lizzie remained in the dusk, alone. She had banked on Bill having a spare bed, and now she didn't know where else to try. Anyone she called a friend was probably sitting on someone else's sofa.

Heading back across the bridge, she dodged figures in long, black dresses, tight, black jeans, black hair, purple eyes, silver crucifixes and dark nails. They streamed past in droves, taking over pavements and bars, narrow streets and fish and chip shops.

And every bed in town.

Head down, weaving past them all, Lizzie racked her brains where she could try next. Everywhere screamed full. She trudged past charity shops, the tattoo artist and old jeweller's, encountering fewer and fewer goths as she headed up the hill towards the supermarket car park where she'd left the car.

Driving around the top of the recreational ground, she pulled up, flicked the lock on the door and clambered into the back seat, hugging the duvet around her. It was too early to sleep, but she was tired and no longer cared. In the morning, she'd go to the café and scrounge a breakfast for clearing a few tables. That would set her up for the day, and then she'd see about finding proper work. And somewhere to crash.

She slept and dreamed she was five years old with a bright-yellow hat, running happily to the headmistress's office. A man laughed and waved at her, and she waved back. She knocked at the closed door. Again and again. Louder and louder. *Come on, answer!* A dog barked, and she half-awakened but was determined to lull herself back into that dream world again. The noise thumped inside her head. The persistent knocking became a rhythm. She opened her eyes. A face pressed against the window. She screamed. A hand tried to open the door, and she tugged the duvet up to her cheekbones.

"Open the door."

She recognised that voice and the uniform.

"You're going to ache in the morning," Phil Chorley shouted before gesturing for her to flick open the locks.

As he let in the cold air, she shuffled back, pulling the cover tighter.

"What you doing?"

"Trying to sleep."

"Here?"

"Are you offering me a bed?" *Leave me alone. Why can't people leave me alone?*

He slumped into the passenger seat. "You can't stay here."

"Why don't you go arrest a wife batterer?"

"I saw you," he said.

"Well, hi, now bugger off."

"I've got to move you on."

Her thoughts had already moved on, her mind focusing on alternatives. "What about your flat? I know you're staying with Carol now, so it's free."

"One of the lads at work is getting divorced. He couldn't wait to move in as soon as he heard I'd moved in with Carol. Sorry. If I'd known..."

A scream already rose up, threatened to pour out, envelop them both.

She kept her voice steady. "It's one night, Phil. Tell him to go home. He's got somewhere—I haven't." Already, she knew it was hopeless, but she had to go through the motions. Last year, two months ago, even last week, she'd have wheedled her way around him, but she couldn't be bothered now. Maybe the chalet park had affected her. Maybe she didn't care if it was her body falling off the cliff and into the sea.

"I know you can't go back to that chalet park." Phil tapped his fingers on the dashboard as if he'd read her mind.

"How do you know that?"

"It's not safe, is it?"

"How d'you know I was at the chalet park?"

"Carol. What about that ex of yours?" He turned to look at her. "Colin. Why don't you go there?"

She shook her head. "No, it's all right, I know where I can go."

"Where?"

"Are you going to let me over?"

He climbed out of the car, holding the door until she was in the driver's seat. The bunch of keys still dangled from the ignition; turning it, she glanced up at Phil.

"Seat belt," he said.

Sighing, she pulled the strap, and he stepped back to let her close the door. In the rear-view mirror, she saw him watching her pull away.

"I'm going!" she shouted.

At the other side of town, she parked up again.

Thirty-four-year-old, dark-haired and bearded, cigarette in hand, Colin Fisher opened his front door. She watched him, no longer caring what happened. He could refuse, acquiesce— she no longer had an opinion. Sleep was the priority.

"I need a bed." Lizzie barged past him into the dingy ground-floor room.

Later, having drunk more than she had in some time, she slept.

***

Colin finished his beer and put the empty can down with the rest on the crowded coffee table. Strolling out of the room, he soon returned, throwing a sleeping bag over her inert body.

***

The next morning, she padded into the bedroom and looked at the empty, unmade bed. On the pillow lay a sheet of paper.

It read: 'We're out of bread and milk.'

Creeping under the duvet and curling it around her, she lay still, willing herself to disappear. Sleep didn't come. She turned over. The sheet crinkled beneath her. Damp silence. A car drove past the window. She wandered into the kitchen. Memories flooded back of how she'd hated living there because nobody really lived there. They came in and went out. Drank, slept and passed through. Passed out more often than not.

He rarely cooked. There were coffee and teabags, sometimes some milk in the fridge. Sometimes sliced bread and the extras that went with that. Always biscuits.

She knew Colin had been taken with her; this young girl who would strip off without flinching and model in front of a crowd of would-be artists. Somehow knew the tools for knocking together picture frames. He had thought, as a pseudo-bohemian himself, that he had found his soul mate. In time, disappointed to learn that she was actually only playing the part as she played any role, he turned as cold as his flat and treated her as a sub-class test case that would never rise to the heights of a muse. Lizzie had not been hurt. She had already moved on. It was not her policy to rely on one person alone; in her experience, that never worked out.

She glanced up at the kitchen clock. It was a little after nine. After a while, she filled a glass from the tap, drank it and refilled it several times before eventually placing it on the drainer. The sink smelt as it always had, being stacked with mugs filled with brown, congealing liquid. She turned away. Her bag lay on the living room floor; on the wall, a rough painting of her pubescent naked body, a barely recognisable canvas from a distant past. She opened the unlined curtains and looked across the road at the car park with the leaning masts of jostling boats running parallel to parked cars. A camper van pulled in. She watched it drive around until it found a big enough space. A couple sat in the front.

While he awkwardly manoeuvred the vehicle, the woman folded a road map. Lizzie turned away, back to the grey room.

Part of her wanted to stay because she wanted the old times back when she thought she loved him. He had seen her walking home from school and said she had a model's face. He'd been sitting in the marketplace, sketching credible portraits of tourists, and he had drawn her for free.

"You could make a living doing this," he'd said.

And she had slept with him.

Only she soon realised it wasn't love when he expected her to do as he said, do as he wanted; do what she was told to do when she no longer wanted to do it.

"What do you love about me?" she'd asked.

He hadn't answered and she hadn't asked again.

Slumping on the sofa, she pulled on her boots, then sat, head aching and throat dry, but she couldn't stomach any more water. Dragging her coat across the seat, she slowly pushed one arm into the first sleeve. A faint noise made her stop. The flats in the daytime were usually silent. It had been something she'd hated, that feeling of being the only person with nothing to do and nowhere to go. Only after she'd left did she find out that during the day, most people were sleeping and not, as she had thought, busy with proper jobs and friends to share their lunchtime sandwiches.

The noise started up again, and she twisted around. A rhythmic scratching came from just inside the kitchen. Standing slowly, she pulled on her coat and tiptoed towards the noise, unable to work out if it came from under the floor, behind the walls or in the room. She peered into the kitchen, nerve endings twitching. Stretched up against the overflowing rubbish bin, eyes gleaming, a long, dark rat scratched with its claws. A second later, its hunched shape dropped on all fours. When it snaked its long, thick tail, Lizzie stumbled backwards, and the rat, startled, sent a biscuit wrapper scurrying.

Lizzie leapt back. Sweat broke out across her forehead and the palms of her hands as she stared transfixed at the kitchen doorway. For several excruciating minutes, silence pounded. She glanced at the front door. Colin always locked it. The spare key hung as it used to, on a hook to the left. If she grabbed her bag and then the key, and if she rammed it straight into the lock, she'd hopefully get out before the rat moved again.

Through the kitchen doorway, she saw its claws appear first, tapping, scratching, and then its nose. She stepped up onto the sofa. It stopped as if listening. She breathed heavily. It moved forward and turned slowly so that it faced her. Its whiskers quivered. Tentatively, it plodded into the room. Head splitting with possibilities, she reached down to the coffee table, grabbed one of the cans and hurled it. As it clattered against the wall, the rodent shot across the floor and under a chair.

"Shit," she said. "Shit, shit, shit."

Turning around slowly, she almost overbalanced as the soft cushions gave under her weight. No movement from the chair, she glanced at the door again, her bag and then the key. The chair again. Silence.

Tensing, she leapt onto the floor.

"Aggghhh!" she shouted, stretching to grab her bag and stamping her feet, but the bag, wide open, spilled its contents. Trembling in her haste, she desperately scooped purse, brush, keys, tin of lip salve—all the bits that she kept there—back inside. Seeing nothing left to gather, she looked around again before running for the door, bag in one hand, the other extended towards the key.

Chapter Twelve

SHE SPOTTED ANDREW halfway across the castle's front lawns and called out. He turned, still speaking into his mobile phone. Lizzie clenched her fists in frustration.

He took her arm as he finished the call. "Where've you parked?"

"I've just had the worst night of my life," she said. "I hope you're satisfied."

"What's happened?"

"It doesn't matter now." She looked away; there was too much to explain.

He steered her across the grass. Already she regretted coming, knowing everyone thought she was a nuisance and wanted her to disappear. *"But where?"* she wanted to scream. *"Where am I supposed to disappear to?"*

Well, she'd take everyone down with her. She went over it all in her head. If she couldn't have the gatehouse for one week until Rigby was clear of all those goths, she'd tell the papers what a shitty landlord Andrew was, how he was fucking her and how he didn't really care about the locals he always said were the salt of the earth. Why should she always be the one that got the raw deal? *"Give me the gatehouse and I'll stay under the duvet for an entire week and not bother a soul,"* she wanted to say. But she said nothing.

"Are you in the bottom car park?" he asked. He seemed preoccupied.

"Out on the main road. I don't want to upset things for you." She tightened her jaw, hurrying to keep up with his long stride,

73

wishing she were the type that gave men a hard time because that's the only way you seemed to get what you wanted.

"I've done all I can," he said, pocketing the phone. "Beamstown Council keeps an eye on the chalet park now. It's out of my jurisdiction. They've got specialist equipment. I haven't. If anyone needs reporting for negligence, it's them." Andrew steered her away from the house, towards the main drive. "Never underestimate how much I care about the people round here," he said. "I'm merely a custodian. My hands are tied. This shouldn't be happening to the poor buggers."

She realised he was trying his best; he must have been worried about what had happened at the park. Still, he hadn't said he cared about her, only those strangers. She was unlovable.

She folded her arms. "What do you suggest I do?"

"Not to ask each other for anything was the deal." His voice gave nothing away.

Beginning to curl inwards, she pressed her arms tighter across her body. "It's the big Halloween weekend, and everywhere is full. I can't go back to that chalet. It's not safe, and there's a bloke there who's off his trolley." She was jabbering, she knew, but she couldn't stop herself.

"Can't you stay where you were last night?" He glanced at her for an instant like a teacher looks at an aggravating pupil.

"I can't stay there, and I can't go back to the chalet park." She raised her voice, frustrated, angry, that familiar feeling of wanting to lash out.

He carried on walking. "The residents are having a party this afternoon," he said.

"What's that got to do with anything?"

"This is the big event of their year. I'm going, and I think you should. It'll do you good. Few drinks. Help you relax."

"You're having me on. Is this that picnic? The big event of the year?" She laughed, hollow. "Is that what they're calling it?"

"They'll be vacating the place tomorrow—as soon as they've nursed off their hangovers."

"Stop sidetracking me. Can I stay at the gatehouse? You won't even know I'm there."

He stopped, studied her, then set off walking again.

"How can they have a party when someone's just died?" If she took a different tack and kept talking, they'd get to the end of the drive, then she'd try again when they were actually outside the gatehouse. He wouldn't refuse when they were standing right by its front door.

"It's not a party as such. I used the wrong word," he said. "It's All Souls' Day, and it's a mark of respect, not really my thing, being a Catholic tradition, but I like to give my support. This year, it's more important than ever."

"Stop it, Andrew." She heard the edge in her voice. "They can't be having a party. You didn't see how they died."

In truth, she didn't want to be reminded of the old couple's faces and the dog barking, sliding in the mud, the old man swearing at her and the smell of Jez's jacket. She could still hear the wind and feel the stinging rain and hair whipping across her face and how much that hurt. The sound of cracking wood, breaking glass, rumble of ground and sea and realising how terrifying the sound of waves crashing against a cliff could be. She couldn't face going down there again. She wouldn't be able to look at the gash in the land where the chalet had stood. The place made her shiver. It was impossible to go back.

He put his arm around her shoulder. "It's all right," he said. "If they're willing to do this, we've got to respect that."

"I'm not stopping them."

"You're judging them."

"I'm not."

"I have an invitation. I'm showing my respect by attending." He sounded genuine—the Andrew she liked.

"Up to you." She shrugged, but his arm remained tight across her shoulders. "I've never heard of All Souls' Day."

His voice softened. "You've not been part of anything, have you?" She hated the way she was so easily drawn back in and shook her head. He kissed her hair gently. "Traditions help people. This helps them say goodbye."

Helps who? He was testing her, waiting for her to say yes, she'd come, yes, she thought it was the right thing to do, that they weren't freaks and he was right. She vaguely remembered the Leavers' Assembly at school and how most of the girls had cried. She hadn't, but she remembered that feeling of wishing she could.

"All right," she said as they reached the gatehouse. "But if I agree to come, what are you going to do for me?"

She'd asked. Now it was up to him. A car horn blared on the main road. Andrew hesitated for barely a moment before grabbing her hand.

"Did you pull your car up on the verge?" He dragged her behind him, not listening for an answer.

"You're now saying I can stay?" Incredulous, Lizzie tripped over tendrils of bramble hidden in the long grass in her haste to follow him to the back door.

Andrew jiggled the key in the lock and didn't see her stumble, only felt her arms around his waist as she turned her clumsiness into a caress. He fell against the door, turning the key and the handle at the same time. The door opened with a jolt and, grabbing her hand, he pulled her inside. Immediately, she wrapped her arms around him again.

"What's all this?" he asked, returning her kiss.

***

Judith steered her large black four-by-four through the main gates. She'd seen Lizzie's old Renault parked on the roadside. Anger tore up her spine, she tensed her shoulders, readying herself for an onslaught of words with Andrew. A movement by the back door of the gatehouse caught her eye, and she slammed her foot on the brakes. The crack of metal hitting metal rang out as a car carrying four Japanese tourists slammed into the back of her.

"What the hell do you think you're doing?" she yelled, jumping out of the car and storming towards the silver saloon.

The four equally irate tourists leapt out of the Audi, waving their arms and bombarding her in Japanese.

***

Andrew looked up.

"Shit," he muttered, positioning Lizzie behind him. "We've got to get you out of here."

"What's happening?" She put her hand on his arm, but before she could see, he pushed her firmly away. She didn't need telling twice. She'd learnt that lesson a long time ago. "Okay. See you later?" she said.

"At the park."

She slipped through the doorway and around the back of the building, forcing her way through spindly rhododendrons until, reaching the wall, she felt her way to the gatepost. Still hidden by bushes, she glanced back down the drive. A mass of gesturing figures issuing a torrent of indecipherable sounds jostled around Judith, who, undeterred, shouted at them to be quiet. Andrew, meanwhile, strode towards the group from the other side.

Judith glared at him as the tourists' car reversed back through the gates. Lizzie pressed herself flat, nervous they would misjudge the wall in their haste. But they were exacting and, having reversed, sped away again in the direction of Beamstown. Lizzie's attention returned to Andrew and Judith.

"Were you showing someone round the gatehouse?" Judith demanded.

"I was seeing if anything needs doing."

"I do hope you're not planning on moving someone in behind my back." She paced up and down, kneading one hand into the other palm and looking over his shoulder for signs of movement that would reveal someone was, in fact, inside.

"I wish you'd give me more credit. I was checking it's in order for the Christmas lets." Andrew put his hands in his trouser pockets in an attempt to look relaxed, managing instead to look like a guilty schoolboy.

"Listen to me carefully, Andrew." Judith spoke slowly. "No-one is moving into the gatehouse, least of all one of your hareem. Is that clear?"

Andrew pulled out his handkerchief and wiped his nose. "I don't know what you're talking about."

Judith grabbed hold of the open car door. "Don't make a fool of me."

He reached out to touch her with his free hand, but she pulled back, glaring at him. She slipped behind the driver's wheel.

"I promise you. You know I love you. I wouldn't hurt you," he said.

"You can't hurt me," she replied coldly. "I asked you not to make a fool of me. Can you promise not to do that?"

"Absolutely! There's nothing for you to worry about."

She turned on the ignition, revved the engine then slammed the car door closed and drove off, smattering his feet and trouser legs with gravel.

Lizzie waited, but Andrew didn't look in her direction. The dust settled, and she stepped out from the bushes onto the drive, but he still didn't turn around even though he must have heard her footsteps.

Chapter Thirteen

S HE WOUND DOWN the window and let her arm droop in the rush of air. Daydreams often set in when she was driving. Engine humming like a lullaby, blurred countryside like a picture book. She could put things in boxes in separate rooms and not think about them. It did no good thinking too much; she'd always known that. She'd look through her suitcase and dig out something pretty to wear for the afternoon. She'd change in the cold chalet, and if he came down straight away, he might catch her unawares and warm her up. Make up for ignoring her. But the picture in her head wasn't of Andrew; it was of Jez. *Block it out*, she told herself. Block all images out; get through the day; that was all she had to do. She could do that if she dulled herself down. She could stand the chalet park for one more afternoon if it meant snuggling up in a warm bed in a solid stone house that night. Andrew or no Andrew.

The sea sparkled. Grass flickered. White streaks wisped over the blue sky. She tapped her foot on the brake. Silhouetted, a figure sat on the grass verge. Slowing, she recognised Jez, sitting on a little folding stool at the top of the track with an easel in front of him. She sat with her hands on the steering wheel and watched him. He could have been a painting himself, only he made tiny movements—a brush stroke and then unmoving again against the canvas.

It was as though nothing else existed; she, sitting in the car, he, on the stool, and that was all there was. She decided he wasn't going to move and, as always, she would have to be the first to either speak or drive past. She couldn't decide. The effort of reacting at all seemed to open up so many dangers.

As if he read her mind, he turned his head.

Of course, she got out and strolled over to where he sat, glancing from the canvas to the two rows of buildings that stretched along the cliff edge. Jez continued to make small downward strokes on the expanse of cliff he had already painted. The sea filled the space beyond the green field, and above it, blue sky domed, marked only by two black seagulls and flimsy traces of white cloud. She glanced again at the real chalet park. A dog, the one that had escaped from the collapsing chalet, scampered across the grass. A small, lean figure walked towards the second building. The man crouched down near the cordoned-off cliff edge.

"What d'you think he's doing?"

"Thought you'd left us." Jez waggled the brush in the jam jar of grey water, then continued to make small strokes, careful, exact, covering the white.

"I've heard there's a party today as a sort of farewell to this place?" She waited for what he would say, but he said nothing. Unable to bear the silence, she scrabbled around for a topic of interest. "They've got those huge walls along the beach at Rigby and massive rocks at Rook Bay," she said. "You'd think they'd do something like that here."

"You know why they don't."

"I don't."

"Look where we are. Which do you think is worth the millions of pounds it costs for sea defences?" He paused, eyes on the horizon.

She looked down the sloping field at the scattering of old-fashioned chalets and out at the vast, fathomless sea. Even a warm, Indian-summer-type October couldn't make the park attractive. Surveying it from the top of the hill, the chalets, weathered by gales off the North Sea, now appeared more depressing than the council houses she had always dreaded. There were no shops or young people here. The two boys she had briefly seen the other day seemed like ghosts somehow, not really having belonged now they had left. Decay surrounded the buildings as well as the land,

and she realised, studying the small human movements of the tiny, angular-looking man, that neglect was even present there.

She looked down at the painting again. Jez daubed in the chalets, marking their positions with small, grey strokes. Lizzie counted three, plus the caravan in the row nearest them, then five running along the clifftop and then the land gouging a wide bite where the Westons' chalet had been. The dog barked again.

"Which is yours?" Lizzie asked.

"Don't you remember?"

"I was distracted."

"Second from the track."

"Aren't you worried?" Her gaze wandered over the jagged cliff edge towards the one he mentioned, but her eyes fixed on one that was boarded up and stripped of paint. It looked as if it hadn't been lived in for years. She could make out corroded pipes and bleached wood. Wind and rain made a battering onslaught here, the sea air, filled with sand and salt, stippling the slats and peeling the paintwork.

"Why d'you live so far away from everything?" she asked. "It must be a real pain when you run out of stuff."

"No distractions."

"Where do people work?"

"Only I work." He smiled lazily. Beautifully.

"But, well..." She hesitated, caught out by his tone. "Do you have much in common with the others? They seem... well, you're younger than most of them." He didn't answer. "Are they all retired? That family that left didn't live here permanently, did they?"

"It's the most secluded place on the whole of this coast," he said.

"Well, thank God the tourists haven't found it." Half a laugh in her voice.

"They've got Rook Bay and Rigby."

"And Beamstown," she added.

He looked up. "Not a whiff of money here."

"Or boutique gin."

She caught the flash of his smile again, ignored it, looking instead at the chalets dotted in the field and the only vehicle, an old battered BMW parked near a line of washing that flapped in the breeze. Waves hit the shore with a shrouded rumble.

"Do you sell many paintings?" she asked.

"Some."

She thought about telling him about the art club, which met weekly in a village hall, and that people sometimes sold their pictures, but that would have been against her well-learnt principle of not proffering information. Besides, he wouldn't fit in.

She studied the canvas propped on the easel. The roughly drawn chalets were in the right proportion to the landscape. Waves interlocked colours in the background. Sky, high and vacant, gave a sense of scale. His hand hovered uncertainly, and she wondered how he'd capture the bark of a dog, the sound of crinkling foam swooshing at the water's edge and the cry of a lapwing, but somehow, she knew he would. But he wouldn't be able to capture how the place made her feel.

"What have you decided?" he asked.

He caught her off guard. "How d'you mean?"

"Are you staying or driving past?"

Here was her chance. *Get in the car and keep on going.*

"I wouldn't want to miss the All Souls' Day celebrations and a chance to pay respect to that couple."

She'd said it aloud; mentioned them. Now she'd find out if he remembered holding her against him the other night. She clenched her hands together.

"That's up to you." His voice was gentle as foam.

"You don't mind, do you?" She always pushed people too hard, too fast, and she didn't know how to stop.

She watched as he stood, straddling the stool and lifting the canvas off its low stand. He glanced briefly at her as he closed the lid on the paint box, folded the easel and then paused, stool in one hand, canvas in the other, easel under his arm. The box lay on the scrub. A gust of wind swept through the grass, and the car engine ticked away its heat.

"Could you?" He nodded to the box.

She picked it up. "I won't offend anyone, will I? It seems a nice thing to do." *Will it be enough? Will it make me likeable?*

"You can have your moment to remember them if that's what you want," he said. "It is All Souls'. We remember the dead."

"Oh, no. I'm okay. I didn't know them, it's fine." She looked down.

"Well," he said. "We're going to be celebrating their lives, and anyone else's life people want to celebrate."

She frowned at her stupidity. She couldn't tell him there was no-one to remember and no-one to remember her when she died.

"D'you need a lift down? Not that you usually wait to ask for a lift." She walked back to the car, wishing she had met him in another place sometime earlier, years ago, hoping he understood her clumsy attempt to tease.

"You don't have to make it so hard." His voice carried otherworldly through the late autumn haze. She stopped with her hand on the door. There it was again, that lilting sound that drew her to him. She opened the door, determined no-one was going to hurt her again.

"You've nowhere to go, have you?" he persisted.

Several soft thuds sounded from behind, and she bent her head, resting her chin on her chest; a hiatus; jumping as his hand brushed her shoulder.

"It's all right," he said. He stood very close, blocking out the sky. "This stretch of cliff is the only place I feel safe. I don't have to prove myself to anyone here. I don't have to talk or do anything I don't want to. I can just be. All I have to do is breathe, eat, drink and be myself." He studied her face, his eyes trying to read hers. She grinned, embarrassed by his proximity, aware that he probed, that he could see behind her pretence.

"And paint," she said.

"Randolph's sorry about his behaviour. He apologises for frightening you."

"It's that Gary bloke he needs to apologise to."

"Hasn't anyone ever apologised to you before?"

"No-one's ever had to."

"Randolph thinks he's driven you out."

"It's the bloody cliff that's driven me out."

"I told Randolph it was him."

She let out another short burst of laughter, but he only stared at her.

"I've found somewhere else to stay," she said and turned awkwardly, trying not to touch him, even by accident. He stepped back, somehow aware.

"So why is it you're bothering coming to the picnic?"

She knew she'd lost the thread, the battle, whatever it was she wanted to hold on to.

He studied her. "There's something else."

For some reason, she didn't want to tell him about Andrew and that she was a Protestant invited by another Protestant to a Catholic tradition.

"You're dead right," she said, climbing into the driver's seat. "I'll stay well away and wish you a great time." She could kill a few hours, go back to the gatehouse later. She knew how to wait.

"Everyone wants to see you." His voice smiled. "Just drive down. Mavis'll make you welcome, probably find some job for you as well."

"I suppose you're saying that because you want a lift down?"

"No, I'm stopping up here. I've forgotten to put something in the painting, and if I don't do it now, the light'll be different and it won't blend in."

"But you've just packed everything away." For some reason, she didn't want to go down to the park without him. "And what about this box?" She held it out.

"Ah, yes," he said, taking it back. "You go sort yourself out. Look, I can see Mavis and Joyce. Tell them you saw me and I won't be long, then we can talk again."

She hesitated, but he began re-erecting the easel, and Mavis and Joyce waved as if beckoning with open arms.

Chapter Fourteen

S HE PARKED UP the car and watched two men moving between the chalets, collecting chairs and tables. One was the horrible man from the night before; the other was the thin man who had been wandering about. To her relief, they both ignored her in spite of what Jez had said. Marilyn, wearing a pink apron and red dress, bent over a trestle table, chopping a mound of onions, mushrooms and other vegetables. Mavis beckoned, and Lizzie, glad not to be on show, followed her inside one of the chalets. The strong smell of vinegar hit as they entered, and she caught her breath. With a sheet of crumpled newspaper, Joyce wiped the windows then dipped her hand into a yellow bucket before wiping the glass again. With each sweep of her hand, she studied the man outside as he laid out tools on a painting table erected under the open window.

"Is this your way of saying goodbye?" Joyce didn't camouflage the frustration in her voice.

"Is that yours?" he replied, his voice clearly audible through the open window.

As if sensing their presence, Joyce turned her head with a look of embarrassment on seeing Lizzie. She dropped the ball of newspaper into the bucket. "He gave up a very good job to come here," she said.

Lizzie nodded uneasily and wandered into the kitchen.

Mavis smiled and went back to sieving flour into a bowl of creamed butter and eggs. "Joyce has a bigger oven," she explained.

Joyce moved on to the next window. Lizzie followed her gaze to the sparkling sea. It seemed almost blue this morning, as if it were mid-summer. *How dare it! How dare the sun shine and sea sparkle and this well-dressed woman clean windows as if nothing has happened?* She watched Joyce drag the damp newspaper over the glass, pushing with her fingers into the moist corners and around the wooden rim, frowning at the thick, dark gunge. The spectacular view outside rose above ragged ground, and Lizzie wondered how the two women could bear to be baking cakes and cleaning house.

Strolling to the door, she watched the dog scamper across the grass as if nothing had happened to his owners. Someone had obviously taken him in. Joyce didn't look like a dog person, but there was definitely a damp animal smell mingling with the vinegar. She stepped outside, walking across the grass to see what had caught his attention. The aroma of spices wafted through the open door of Marilyn's chalet; holding a hand to shade her eyes, Lizzie looked around. Without warning, the small scruffy dog reappeared, and she ruffled his coat.

"Lizzie, leave Campion be," Joyce called from the top step, crumpled newspaper still in her hand. "We usually have a nice cup of coffee about this time. We might even be able to beg something fresh from the oven."

The warm aroma of freshly baked cake replaced the vinegar smell, and Lizzie felt a strong pang of hunger. Andrew had been right: they really were going to hold some sort of banquet. She would never understand people; Colin said that was in her DNA. That was another reason she'd left him.

"You're very brave doing this today," Lizzie said, glancing all the way across at the flapping police tape and ragged cliff edge. Joyce dropped the paper in the bin. "I suppose you feel you must do something before you go." She stopped, realising too late that Joyce wasn't the sentimental type.

"Mavis," Joyce looked at her hands, "are we ready for a coffee?"

A voice from inside said, "Kettle's on."

"Shoo! Shoo!" Joyce flapped her hand at Campion.

"It's fine, Joyce." Mavis sounded tired. "I like seeing him around." She stood in the doorway, behind Joyce, her eyes looking smaller than Lizzie remembered, and the smile a little forced. "I'm so glad you decided to come back."

"Are you sure you want to stop what you're doing?"

They gathered in the kitchen. Mavis moved the bowl of fresh cake mixture out of the way. "Everything's under control."

"Something smells good."

"Victoria sandwich cake. It'll be another twenty minutes or so, and then I can pop this one in. Are you hungry?"

"I'm hopeless at cakes," Joyce said, spooning granules into the three mugs as if this were a regular occurrence.

"Your flans outdo anybody's," said Mavis. "Fruit or savoury. Go on, sit." She indicated a chair.

Lizzie peered into the mixing bowl standing on the work surface. "How many are you making?"

"Just two. I'm waiting for the first one to come out so I can reuse the tin." Mavis moved the bowl next to the oven. "I've got a pudding and some jacket potatoes in there as well."

Lizzie reached past Mavis towards the bowl. "I love cake mixture."

"It's not good for your tummy like that." Mavis tapped Lizzie's hand. Surprised, Lizzie recoiled. "Best wait until this one's done— you can have a slice at the picnic. Now, come and drink your coffee. It's perfect with one of my oat biscuits. Joyce? Can you bring the biscuits over? They're still warm."

Lizzie sat on a chair facing Mavis and Joyce, who looked expectantly at her from the sofa. Two women couldn't look more different, and Lizzie tried to imagine what it was like in winter, spending the short, dark days with someone with whom you had nothing in common. But now, in sunshine with the distant sound of male voices drifting through open windows along with the odour of paint and vinegar, it seemed almost an option to live here.

"Do you like cooking?" Mavis asked as Joyce held out the plate of biscuits.

"I never learnt." Lizzie picked up a knobbly shape.

"Oh dear, that's a shame," said Mavis. "Not even at school?" Lizzie shook her head.

"I suppose you preferred needlework?" guessed Joyce. "I know I did."

"I hated everything about school."

"That's the trouble with these big comprehensives. I expect they aren't very nice places to be at the best of times. They should never have got rid of grammar schools."

"It was okay." Lizzie was sure they weren't really interested in what she had to say about her school days and were merely talking about anything other than Friday night.

Mavis held out the plate. "Have another biscuit."

She took another and lifted her mug, sipping the hot liquid as she kept her eyes on its murky depths, weighing up whether she should ask if they were all right.

"I was brought up in a back-to-back in Leeds," Mavis said. "At least you grew up in beautiful surroundings."

Lizzie shrugged; they obviously couldn't face talking about it.

"Yes, at least you could see all this when you opened your bedroom curtains," said Joyce. "That must have been lovely as a child."

"If you want to talk about your friends, I don't mind." Lizzie took another sip.

They remained silent. *Please, please let them say something about how scared they were and how terrible they felt that they didn't act quickly enough to help save their friends.* She wanted to apologise for something she wasn't sure she'd done or not done but didn't know how unless they said something first. But they said nothing, and the crunching of biscuits and slurping of coffee grew increasingly awkward.

Lizzie drained the rest of her drink, shivering as she caught a glut of sugar granules on her tongue.

"Thanks for the coffee and biscuits," she said. "I'd best get on. I want to get changed and—"

"I met Trevor at Crompton's," Mavis blurted out. "Over a shepherd's pie. I was a dinner lady. He was on the floor."

"I met John at a dance," said Joyce.

"Have you a young man?"

"No. Er...no," Lizzie said.

"I knew as soon as he put his arms around me and we started to dance."

"Can you smell burning?" Lizzie screwed up her nose, and with a small cry, Mavis hurried into the kitchen.

Lizzie held Joyce's gaze for a moment until the elder woman stood, awkwardly straightening her skirt. Campion let out a high-pitched yelp and crouched in a corner.

"What's happened?" Mavis's voice filled with panic.

The muscles on Joyce's cheeks tensed. "Stupid dog."

Lizzie put her mug in the cluttered sink. The perfectly baked cake stood on a cooling rack, and Mavis was already pressing fresh greasy butter wrappers against the base and sides of the warm tin. The mixture in the cake bowl reminded her of a similar bowl she'd licked clean when she was six years old and then had her hand slapped hard.

"I'd best be off," she said.

Mavis waved the spoon by way of acknowledgement; a large dollop of soft cream splatted on the floor.

"Bother," she muttered, turning around for a cloth, but before she could retrieve the sweet yellow mixture, Campion bounded excitedly past Joyce and swiftly slavered it up.

"Oh, no! Don't do that!" Mavis pushed him away with her leg, but it was too late. The mound had disappeared. Wagging his tail as if pleased with himself, Campion pushed past Lizzie so that she almost fell over. She turned to smile at Mavis, hopefully making a light moment out of the dog's antics, but Joyce remained speechless in the doorway between the kitchen and dining room, and Mavis looked up, tears brimming her eyes.

They both watched Campion scamper across the field.

"It was hardly any," Joyce consoled.

Blinking repeatedly, Mavis turned back to the baking bowl and quietly spooned the rest of the mixture into the tin.

Keen to leave them, Lizzie hurried across the grass, catching Trevor and John in her peripheral vision.

"Hello!" Trevor called out.

John made a sweeping gesture across the table. "Thought I'd give them a last clean."

Trevor picked up a hammer. "Want to come and see what we're up to?"

They were mad. They were all mad, but Lizzie didn't know what else to do. Looking at rusty tools with two old codgers was the last thing she wanted to do, but there seemed no alternative without appearing rude, and after what had happened during the night, she didn't want to hurt them. It seemed ludicrous. She could quite easily repeat what she'd said to the women, but it didn't seem right to lie to this pair, and besides, it would take two seconds to change and then, with time to wait, she'd drive herself mad, willing Andrew to arrive. She glanced up the hill. She couldn't see Andrew or Jez. Sighing, she turned to face the two old men.

Trevor placed the hammer back on the table.

"These things always fascinate me," he said, picking up a spirit level and balancing it between his thumb and index finger until the bubble settled in the centre of the two lines. "Always wonder who invented these things. You know what I mean? Who sat down and drew it out and decided that the way to check a thing's equilibrium is by a bubble suspended between two black lines?"

John held up his fist. "This is the original tool," he said.

Trevor nodded as he picked up an immaculately maintained Phillips screwdriver. "You see my point, though. Which was made first, this?" He waved the screwdriver. "Or the screw to fit it into?"

"Chicken and egg," Lizzie said.

"Exactly." Trevor smiled as if pleased.

"Every problem has a solution," said John.

"Bit like us and this place," said Trevor.

"How's the painting going?"

"It's going. Keeping me out of Mavis's way. She's at her baking, so I'm staying well away until she calls for us to start setting up. Saw you've been helping?" He looked at Lizzie again.

"Oh, Joyce and Mavis seem to have it all organised," she said.

John dropped a minute amount of oil into the hand drill. A drip spotted onto the table, and John's jaw tightened. Trevor watched in silence until John laid the tool back down and wiped up the oil spill.

"I'll leave you to it," Lizzie said, glad of their awkwardness for giving her an excuse. John rubbed the table.

Trevor pushed his hands into his trouser pockets, and she walked slowly away, trying not to look like she was hurrying. She had no idea what time it was. She was hungry, and the smell of baking only made the pangs in her stomach stronger. She should have taken another biscuit.

Looking back over her shoulder, she saw John pick up the bevel-edged chisel and run his thumb over the sloping side, letting it pass smoothly up and down. He then held it as if he were going to put it to use, pushing it with tiny movements in the air as though carving out a niche in a piece of wood. The thoughtful expression on his face dropped suddenly, and he laid the chisel back down between a pin hammer and small hacksaw. She turned quickly away again and caught sight of the wiry man strolling along the clifftop; these really were an odd bunch of people.

As she dragged her suitcase out of the boot of the car, she realised she no longer wanted to talk about Friday night with anyone. They were afraid, but there was something else, and she was beginning to despise the two men fiddling around with their hammers and pliers when they should be packing boxes and organising vans, or maybe it was pity she felt. Either way, she didn't want to give them space in her head. Determinedly, she focused on what she needed to do before Andrew arrived. She'd shower and change, and then she'd eat and drink, and soon, she'd be out of this place forever. These people would fade into the past as everyone did. All she needed to do was not think too deeply and she would be right as rain.

Chapter Fifteen

S HE LIKED THAT feeling of dressing after a shower. Who knew when she'd have a chance for this again? Skin clean and glowing, hair damp and smelling of shampoo, stains washed away—it was as though you could begin again. Like a Catholic after confession.

Dabbing her hair dry with a small towel, she stood by the bedroom window watching Trevor run a brush carefully along one of the window frames of his chalet. He dipped the brush into a tin of black paint, then dragged it along the now gleaming surface again. She glanced at the sky, registering the still clear depth of blue. This year, the Indian summer had lingered longer than anyone could have hoped, as if it wanted to give them a reprieve from the battering of a harsh Yorkshire winter. She watched Trevor pass the brush along the windowsill one more time. Curious at the ordinariness of the sight after what had happened, she undid the catch and pushed open the glass.

The tang of paint singed the air, and then came the smell of frying onions and the distinctive aroma of chilli. The normality of activity puzzled her: they should be packing up instead of pottering about as if nothing had happened. It were as if the cliff hadn't collapsed, the chalet hadn't crashed onto the beach, and no-one had died. She shivered. She would never forget the howling wind and the old man's face.

Right now, solid azure sky glazed over the chalets, and shadows danced across the grass as if there had never been a wind rattling windows and rain churning the ground. The sun-filled room felt cosily warm, the gentle breeze refreshing and danger of land collapsing under them seemed unimaginable. Even laughable.

93

She rubbed her hair again and turned toward the bed to survey the three dresses. At least Andrew's presence would mean she knew someone here.

But Andrew didn't arrive to take her by surprise. Time passed, and Lizzie grew increasingly uneasy as smells floated through the open windows and the sounds of activity grew louder. Glancing outside, she saw the central area had been turned into an arena of rugs, cushions and deckchairs. She couldn't wait any longer.

"You look nice," Mavis called, intercepting her as she came down the steps. "We need your help, don't we, Joyce?"

Joyce nodded.

Lizzie tried to extricate herself. "I'm sorry, but I've got stuff to do."

"Let her get on with whatever it is," John said gruffly as he passed on his way to Trevor's chalet.

"The chairs are leaning against the side wall," Joyce called after him.

"Unless Trevor is painting that section, and then goodness knows where he's moved them to. You'll have to ask him," Mavis added loudly before turning back to Lizzie. John waved his hand dismissively behind him. "That's a pretty dress," she said.

Lizzie set off towards the car. "I have to go."

"Where?"

"Tell her about the luncheon," called Joyce impatiently.

"Usually, we're all snuggled up in Marilyn's," Mavis said. "She's very good about it, but just fancy, this year, we can be out on the grass. Isn't that marvellous?"

"Yes, that's great."

"Stop for a minute, will you?" Mavis laughed, holding a hand to her chest. "I'm not as fit as you."

"Why don't you have it in summer if you want to be outside?" Lizzie waited for Mavis to catch her breath and as she did so noticed the curtains of Jez's chalet pulled closed.

Mavis began talking again, tugging at her attention. "But it wouldn't be anything to do with All Souls', then, would it? We've brought it forward as it is. Now, I know someone who needs your help." Taking Lizzie's hand, she led her across to Jez's chalet and rapped her knuckles on the door.

Lizzie glanced up the bank, hoping the door would remain closed at the same time willing him to appear. "I don't think he's in," she said.

Undeterred, Mavis pushed open the door and marched into the dimly lit room. "I've found you a little helper."

To Lizzie's amazement, Mavis began opening the curtains. As the light flooded in, a shape on the sofa moved. Arms stretched up and the figure yawned. The room beamed with bright sunshine. Out of the shadows, Jez sat up.

"Don't you tell me painting's tired you out," Mavis fussed. "Lizzie's here to give you a hand moving your things outside. Put her to good use, or I might have to take her back to help me." She smiled conspiratorially at Lizzie as she bustled past, pulling the door closed as she left.

Confused, Lizzie shuffled self-consciously, wondering why he'd gone to bed without coming to find her.

She grabbed the door handle. "I'll see you later."

"Don't you want to earn your plate of Marilyn's chilli?"

She had smelt the spices, seen the cake that Mavis had made, and her stomach caved in hollow.

"What needs taking out?" she asked.

"My easel."

She crossed to where it stood.

"I'll need that as well." He pointed to an old wooden stool covered with several jars of brushes and dirty water. Before she could respond, he disappeared through the doorway, dangling another stool from one hand.

Automatically, she moved jars and brushes onto the floor and then, hearing voices, glanced through the window. Jez stood, stool still in hand, chatting idly to Marilyn. They were laughing, and then he said something else. Her head rushed with heat. It was inexplicable. What was she doing? Being ordered about and him flirting his head off. She caught the stool as she stepped back, and a jar smashed onto the rug, water and brushes spilling out. She glanced through the window again at Jez and Marilyn, still laughing. She stood for a moment listening to the jollity, then strode back outside and across the grass towards the track.

Keep walking, she told herself.

"Lizzie?" Mavis's voice rang out.

She kept going, angry at the dull ache in her ankle from where she'd bashed it against the table leg as she'd hurried out of the chalet.

"I'm sorry, Mavis," she said, loud enough to be heard without turning around, "but there really is somewhere else I have to be."

"I'll come with you," Jez's voice cut in. He sounded close; he must have snuck up fast.

"I'm meeting someone." She wanted him to see Andrew now, see Andrew coming to meet her, and she hoped he'd be jealous— jealous as she'd unexpectedly felt seeing him with Marilyn.

"Go away," she muttered. "Go away, go away."

"What about my easel?" He caught her up.

"You seem to be coping," she snapped.

"Male or female?" He grinned.

She stopped. When he didn't say anything, she turned to face him. The breeze caught her hair.

"What d'you mean?"

"Who are you meeting? Male or female?"

"Andrew Booth. Lord of the manor."

"That's all right, then." Jez pulled a roll-up out of his shirt pocket.

"He said he comes down every year for this thing, and I'm his guest."

"Did he say what time he'd be here?" His vo[...] morning's sea.

She wished she'd put on her sunglasses and [...] dark plastic.

"He knows the way. He's been comir[...] Jez gestured for them to return.

"Well, he does own property here! Of course he knows the way!"

"Exactly," he said, looking back at the picnic area. "So you don't need to meet him."

She couldn't *not* look into his green-brown eyes. He knew Andrew. She was so stupid; of course he did. She concentrated on the grass and tyre ruts and drying mud. When they reached his chalet, without a word, he crouched down with his back to her and prised open a can of light-blue emulsion. The pungent smell filled the air. Picking up a large brush, he held it out to her, placing the can with his other hand on the old stool he'd carried out earlier. When she didn't take the brush, he dipped it in the can and swept it horizontally along the slats of the chalet.

Lizzie glanced over her shoulder, but the others seemed preoccupied. "Why are you doing this now?"

"Upkeep."

"Are you taking the mickey?"

"When you were running off, I was telling Marilyn that I thought Trevor was on to a good thing. It won't take long if you help me."

"I wasn't running off! I told you—I'm supposed to meet Andrew."

"D'you want some overalls?" Jez reinforced the presence of the brush.

"I'm fine. Shouldn't you concentrate on getting ready for this meal, celebration—whatever you call this thing?" She glanced again at the arrangement of rugs and chairs.

e need to use up the paint because we can't carry it out of
e." Jez made another sweep with the brush. "And it'll be cool if
the place looks smart."

He didn't look at her, and she couldn't decide if he was teasing
or if his meaning was more pointed. She took the brush and,
dipping it in the tin, made a long smear of blue along the faded
wood. The clean, slightly sharp aroma of fresh paint rose up again.
She dipped the brush deeper into the thick sludge and pressed the
bristles in a slow, long sweep, and then back again. It felt good,
therapeutic, a distraction. She'd have to be careful, though, not to
get any on her dress.

Taking up another brush, Jez worked more quickly, reaching
up to the eaves easily, while Lizzie concentrated on the lines of
bristle. She could do this: she could make vast sweeps of blue with
the warmth of the sun on her back and let her mind drift. Jez didn't
break the pocket of escape with conversation. He remained quiet,
moving from tin to wall to tin to wall in fluid movements and
didn't berate her for taking her time. As far as she was concerned,
this could go on forever.

But finally, they stood with their backs to the sea. The high
tide crashed onto the beach below, churning over shingle so that
the distant voices of other residents sounded remote. They stood
separate from the others. And Andrew still hadn't appeared.

The roar of the waves rushed through her ears. "Food must be
about ready," she said.

Jez barely smiled. He didn't seem to notice that the edge of cliff
fell raggedly away a short distance from where they stood. Lizzie's
heart pounded. She tensed all her muscles against the strong
breeze off the water. Danger shot a bolt of excitement through her
body. The surf thrilled her senses, and the warm sun made her
relax. She really could stay here all day. This was the first moment
in a very long time that she'd felt free to enjoy herself, with no
sense of that anxious knot in her stomach. She glanced at him.

"Not scared, are you?" he asked.

She breathed in. She *was* afraid, but it was a different sort of afraid to normal.

"I think I'll leave you to it." She held out her paintbrush. "It's only fair I help Mavis as well. Earn some of that cake she was baking."

He stopped with his brush mid-air and then balanced it carefully on the rim of the tin. He looked at her, as if for the first time really taking her in, and then, slipping an arm around her waist, swung himself behind, cradling her between his body and the chalet. She froze. If they hadn't been in such a precarious position, she would have shoved him away, but she didn't want either of them to fall.

"We've almost finished," he said. "And then we can eat." He put his head to one side, his mouth almost touching her cheek. She could feel his breath and warmth and his hair brushing her skin.

Carefully, she reached up and took the brush. He immediately wrapped his hand around hers and pushed it in a sweep over the wood. Her arm extended fully with his, taut where his remained slightly bent. As he stretched her arm down to the tin, his hand eased her body to bend, the curve of her bottom scooped into his legs. The intimacy peppered her head with doubt.

He stretched her through the movement again, and she remained tense, her brain unsure of letting someone manipulate her.

"Relax." He shook her arm, his fingers lifting slightly then enclosing hers once more.

She closed her eyes. She didn't care about anything anymore— if they fell; if they finished painting the chalet; if she ate or not. They moved easily together as if in a dance, and the brush flowed smoothly. It was as though she were being lulled by the gentle rhythm of the waves. They reached up to the right, her back flexing, then to the left, curving around, then swaying from side to side, feet touching, then down, down, until they bent together and then began again, cradled within him, and all the while the waves below surged forward against the cliff.

In all too short a time, brush balanced back on the tin, they surveyed the finished wall. She gazed through the window. A man and a woman stared out from a canvas.

"Isn't that…?"

"John and Joyce. Would you like me to paint you?"

"Why would you want to do that?"

"Jez, it's ready!" Mavis called.

She turned to face him and squinted in the dazzling rays of the sun. His eyes, almost jewel-like, were all she could see in the yellow glare.

"Thank you for trusting me," he said.

She *had* trusted him, and she realised that for once, it felt like the right thing.

She dropped her head out of the light. "I still think it's a crazy thing to do."

"Painting the chalet or standing on the cliff edge?"

"Trusting you."

"Jez?" Mavis called again, and he stepped backwards, taking Lizzie's hand and leading her around the side of the building. Immediately, the sound of the sea receded under the noise of plates and glasses and voices. It didn't matter that one or two specks of blue flecked her skirt.

Chapter Sixteen

IT WAS AS though they were on holiday. The women wore dresses and the men light-coloured shirts. Trevor had rolled up his sleeves; John's were neatly fastened at the cuff. He and Peter both wore ties.

The atmosphere crackled with excitement, colour and sunshine. Jez continued to clasp Lizzie's hand, and she looked around self-consciously. No-one seemed to notice. Her eyes automatically strayed to the cliff edge, miraculously cleared now of any remaining debris. Everyone seemed purposefully occupied and no-one seemed upset by the fact they were remembering or celebrating or whatever it was they were supposed to be doing. She was part of this. Part of the little community. She and Jez strolled together until, gently, he let go of her hand and Mavis led her to a seat. She shifted in her chair, took a long drink of Trevor's elderberry wine and squinted up at the sun. *If only this would last,* she thought, already affected by the dark, red liquid in an empty stomach. *If only this pocket of in-between time would stretch into infinity.* Jez was right: this place, on an afternoon like this, with people like these, did make you feel cut off from the rest of the world.

Trevor spread out on a rug, arms behind his head, gazing up at the clear sky. Jez squatted on a stool, easel in front, erected low so that he could see over the top. The sound of his brush striking the side of the jar as he rinsed it punctuated the early afternoon chatter. John busied himself, refilling people's glasses, constantly on the move. He didn't look at his wife once. She didn't look at him either as she painstakingly cut bread.

Marilyn balled her hand. "Chunks, not slices," she said.

Joyce didn't reply, turning the loaf on its side and continuing to cut neat squares. The huge pot of chilli steamed in front of Marilyn, who spooned generous amounts onto plates stacked beside her, reaching across and dropping two or three pieces of bread on the side from a basket Joyce fastidiously replenished. She handed the platter to Peter, who passed it to Mavis and on around the circle. Jez put down his paintbrush, stood and lifted the easel behind before picking up a plate that rested on the grass near his feet.

The combined smells of cigarettes, chilli, fresh paint and sea air coupled with the early afternoon alcohol made Lizzie light-headed. Mavis quietly chewed a hunk of bread. Trevor, his mouth full and cheek stained by sauce, beamed. Joyce and John self-consciously balanced plates on knees. Peter, who had barely exchanged a word, nibbled a crust. Randolph, whom she didn't wish to speak to, ate as if it were his last meal, and Marilyn refilled her glass and left her plate of food to go cold. All of them, so busy ignoring the absence of the dead couple.

Their avoidance of the tragedy suddenly made Lizzie want to stand up and demand to know what they were still doing there. She would have, but she was too mellow, her stomach satiated, dizzy with friendliness, woozy from too much wine and a sun blazing too bright. What she really wanted was to curl up on the grass and fall asleep. She took another long drink of Trevor's homemade liquor. Reaching across for the bottle and refilling her glass, she caught Marilyn's eye. They both sipped. The wine smelt and tasted of dark fruits.

Peter raised his heavily laden fork to Marilyn. "Thank you," he said quietly.

"Hits the spot," said Trevor.

"Spicy," murmured Joyce, dabbing her mouth with a white napkin.

The breeze rippled through the grass. Forks scraped plates. No-one mentioned that two of their number were missing. At the point when Lizzie thought she could speak up, they heard someone approaching, and all turned to watch Andrew swagger noisily across the grass, lugging a crate of beer. Randolph rose from his chair, and between them, they half-dropped the crate on the ground, making the bottles ring out.

"Thought it would help," Andrew announced, sweeping one up and taking an opener from his pocket. "Christ, it's warm." He took a long swig as he surveyed the group. Lizzie didn't look up, resenting his presence now he had finally arrived.

"D'you want some?" Marilyn lifted her plate.

"Why don't you sit down?" Trevor pushed forward a chair before Andrew could answer.

"Thanks." He took the plate from Marilyn. "Your fruit bushes always do a lot better than mine, Trevor, and I've got a full-time gardener looking after them."

"We're sheltered here," Trevor said. "Must be something to do with the hill behind us."

Randolph flicked his bottle top onto the grass. Lizzie concentrated on the sparkling liquid in her glass, trying to calm the anger she felt. Like a cuckoo, Andrew had invaded her nest, and she hated how she lurched from feelings of need to rage to sheer panic. Luckily, talk began again. Jez nudged her shoulder and held out an opened beer. Automatically, she took it, willing him to sit down, but with a half-full glass of wine in her other hand and a plate balanced on her knee, she couldn't make up her mind what to do. Decisively, she downed the wine and, resting the glass on its side, turned to Jez, but he had returned to his seat on the other side of the circle. John uncorked another bottle.

"You're really pushing the boat out," Andrew said. "Not that I'm complaining. This is marvellous. I'm just...well, impressed by the scale of it. Well done, Randolph. All of you. You've surpassed yourselves."

"It's a significant year," Randolph said.

Lizzie looked across at Andrew, who seemed totally at ease amongst the group, and she wondered why he'd never mentioned how well he knew them.

"What about some music, Randolph?" Mavis suggested.

Having already put down his beer bottle, Randolph reached behind and slid a dark-wood guitar across his knee. Eyes averted, he began to play, agile fingers moving over the strings, his other hand sliding deftly along the neck.

Lizzie watched and listened. These people never ceased to amaze. She hadn't expected an old sod like Randolph to play such heart-rending music. The strings quivered under his touch, chords dripping with melancholic thrums. She glanced at Jez, who had repositioned the easel and once again dabbed a brush over the canvas. The others continued to eat as though there was nothing extraordinary about the scene, and Andrew tapped his foot with inappropriate jauntiness as if it were a light-hearted ditty and not an ode to death.

The sky spread wide and blue. Lizzie breathed in deeply. Her head swam and limbs drooped. In the haze, she noticed Trevor, lying on his back, snoring gently, and Joyce sliding in her chair. Peter shook his head to a proffered bottle of beer. Mavis moved stealthily around the circle, gathering plates, swaying slightly as she tried to make the music into a dance. John leant back in his chair, pretending to be interested.

Andrew lowered himself next to her and swigged his beer. "You seem at home."

"So do you." Her voice slurred.

"I'm asked every year," he said as if he hadn't noticed. "It's tradition, whatever you want to call it."

She watched him, seduced by the music, knowing that his breath would smell of hops. He patted her thigh but stood as John strolled towards them. The pair of them splayed their legs territorially, admiring the light flashing on the sea.

"Beats working," said Andrew.

"Just what I was thinking," said John.

They fell silent, and Lizzie listened to the waves and the guitar until the men started talking again.

"I'm glad those cutthroat days are behind me, if I'm honest with you," John said, and when Andrew merely grunted, added, "I was with BMW for years."

The guitar chords faded, and Andrew made a show of applause. "What would you say makes a man happiest, Randolph?"

Randolph raised the beer bottle to his mouth. "God's own country."

"So this is what your average man wants, is it?" laughed Andrew. "A good view of the North Sea from solid Yorkshire soil?"

"Ask any man, and he'll tell you he wants to earn over a hundred K," John cut in.

"Your average man wants his own bit of land," said Randolph. "And to be king of it."

Jez smiled without looking up. Trevor snorted as he woke.

"That's right," said Mavis. "Time to join the party."

John remained silent.

"I'm right, aren't I?" Randolph nodded to Andrew.

"When you've as big a house and as much land as I have, of course you're right." Andrew guffawed, and a ripple of laughter followed.

Joyce stood. "Have some cake." She held out the plate of carefully cut slices. Andrew took a piece, smiling his thanks, but John remained within his own thoughts. Thus ignored, Joyce was forced to pass on. Lizzie shook her head. The colours blurred.

Marilyn cleared her throat. "Let's end with a story," she declared, rubbing stained hands together.

Randolph propped up his guitar. There were noises of agreement. John turned to look at the sea. Andrew strolled back to his chair.

"A story of passion and salvation," said Marilyn, wafting away the cake that Joyce held out. "A lady, attractive and youthful looking." She giggled. "A lady who, on tumbling from her golden chariot, lay in a dimple of ground under a long stretch of copper beech and rustling chestnut trees beside an isolated road. Cocooned from all around as if cradled in her own nest."

"Is this a true story or made up?" Mavis asked, smiling around the group for support.

"That's entirely up to you," Marilyn said. She looked thoughtful. "Our beautiful lady lay on the grassy verge, staring up at a bleached sky, a little disorientated and a little amused at her plight. The wheels of the chariot whirred, clicking gently as they spun, mingling with the hum of a gorging bee, pounding waves and trembling leaves. There was another noise. What was it? What could it possibly be? She lay still. She listened. It sounded as if someone was groaning. And they were close by."

She paused, looked around, hands poised to create tension. "It couldn't be someone hurt, could it? She hadn't hit anyone with her speeding vessel. A passing cyclist continued on their way. Other than that, the road seemed empty. She listened to the groans, trying to decipher what they could mean. Minutes passed. It grew hotter in the little nook in the midday sun—so hot, moisture trickled down her neck and pooled here." She touched the palm of her hand on her chest. "Mesmerised, the lady listened to the repeated sound. It was a voice. A human voice. Our lady slipped her hand under her skirt to wipe away the perspiration that trickled between her legs."

Randolph lit a cigarette.

"Her skin glistened," Marilyn continued, shifting in her seat and tipping back her head. Lizzie glanced over at Randolph; he drew deeply on his cigarette. She looked around the circle; they all waited, some looking down at the rug, others studying their hands. Some held their eyes fixed on Marilyn. Jez continued to paint as if not listening. Holding the cold beer bottle against her hot cheeks and hearing the soporific tone resume, Lizzie closed her eyes.

"Amongst the lushness of green, on the other side of the iron railings, two people stretched as she did, cocooned in the long grass and looping fronds. They moved, slowly, methodically, and she began to move with them, feeling what they felt, echoing the sounds they made."

"I don't quite get it," Mavis interrupted. "Is this some sort of fairy story?"

Looking at Andrew, Marilyn continued. "The undergrowth wafted." She motioned with her hands.

Randolph threw down the butt of his cigarette. "I'm going for a slash."

Lizzie watched him walk away, wishing she'd thought of that. Her bladder had grown uncomfortably full. She could walk in the other direction. She could waddle back to her chalet. Marilyn took another mouthful of beer, swirling it around before she swallowed, letting the bottle dangle in her hand.

"It went on and on, growing in strength, so that everything sounded louder—the waves, trees, insects—until she could take it no longer and suddenly she let herself go with one long animal cry, and then, spent and exhausted, she curled on her side like a baby."

"I know how she feels," said Joyce.

"But what about the person she heard moaning?" asked Mavis. "Were they all right?"

Marilyn lifted the bottle and took another long drink, flapping her hand over her face as if to cool herself.

"Later, much later, when sleep had evaporated, our lovely lady opened her eyes. Crushed into her palm were three ten-pound notes. One blew out of her hand, and a foot stamped down, trapping it. It flapped, trying to escape, but the man, a prince in another lifetime, bent down and retrieved it. She was too exhausted to speak, but when he put the raggedy old note back into her hand, forcing her to hold on tightly, she asked him if he had ever loved her."

She paused again. Lizzie couldn't look anymore; she could barely listen. From under her fringe, she glanced at the others. John feigned sleep. She couldn't see Trevor's face. Mavis looked scared now. Lizzie wanted to know what Jez thought, but he continued to concentrate on the canvas, and no matter how hard she willed it, he would not look up. Andrew stared at the bottle clenched in his hands as if trying to battle with some strong emotion. Marilyn began to speak again, and no-one stopped her.

"He told her that he did still love her, and that's why he gave her money. With Herculean strength, he picked up her chariot and gallantly guided her to her feet, smoothing out her dress and brushing her down so no grass clung to her clothes. He kissed her then, telling her that he would love her forever. But she pushed him away. She had heard those words before. Bereft, he stood back as she climbed slowly onto the chariot but not before she gave him back the money, forcing him to take it. She didn't accept love, in whatever form it came, but especially in the form of money."

Marilyn took another swig of beer and waited for them to respond. After what seemed an age, someone clapped forcefully. Lizzie looked around. It was Andrew, smacking his hands slowly. She looked at Jez, but he continued to paint, dabbing the brush over and over on the same spot.

Lizzie's limbs felt heavy. Joyce began to clap and then Mavis. Peter tapped one hand against his knee. She wanted to tell them to stop but knew that if she did, her words would slur. If she stood, she'd fall over. She glanced at Andrew, but he glared at Marilyn, holding his beer bottle in both hands as if strangling it.

Lizzie couldn't bear it anymore. She needed to pee. She couldn't cross the rug. Couldn't reach her chalet. Looking over her shoulder, she saw Andrew's Range Rover. The shining vehicle with its large wheels stood out. She could rest her head against one of those wheels and wait. But first, she squatted around the far side, pulled up her dress, held her knickers aside and let steaming liquid splash over the pristine tyre.

Euphoric with relief, she crawled over the ground and sighed to sleep with her head on the bumper.

***

The light began to fade, and with it, the sun's warmth. Footsteps swished over the grass.

Hearing the driver's door open, Lizzie scrambled to her knees. The driver's seat creaked as he climbed in. He still hadn't seen her. She felt her way to a standing position. He turned on the ignition. She leaned on the bonnet.

He looked up. "Bloody hell!"

Staggering around the side, she yanked open the driver's door.

"I thought you'd gone," he said.

She looked over her shoulder at the muted figures. "I peed on your wheel."

He studied her for a moment. "You're very drunk."

"Can you get my bag?" She looked again at the distant shapes moving in the dusk.

"I don't think you're in any state to go anywhere."

"You don't want them seeing me talking to you, do you?" She swayed.

"No, it's not that. A good night's sleep is what you need. Will you find your chalet all right?"

She laughed, and he glanced back to the site of the picnic, but only two figures remained, folding up rugs.

"Get a good night's sleep, then." He attempted to close the door again.

"Could two people live in the gatehouse?" She leaned in, trying to maintain her balance. She'd said it, let it out, begun to put into practice her train of thought.

"You get to bed and sleep that wine off."

She wanted a bed, a soft pillow and a warm thick duvet.

"He can paint," she slurred.

"Who?" Andrew's face blurred before her eyes.

The mauve sky, shadowy pink, high, high above, pulled further away. She wanted to lie down right there. Sleep. Stop moving. Andrew fingered his keys. They clinked. Fairy bells. He sighed. A gust of wind. She spiralled away from the car and, bending down, rested her hands on her knees.

"I feel sick." She slumped onto all fours, aware that as she stared down at the sharply focused blades of grass and black soil with all its intricate specks that her knees drew up the cold and her palms sank into the dirt. The side of the vehicle loomed over her head, shiny and reflecting like a skyscraper. The grass swirled and sounds merged overloud. She arched her back like a cat then let it fall, resisting the urge to let herself roll sideways and lie still, cooled by damp-smelling earth and grass and creeping darkness.

Drooping her head, weighted by the heaviness of her brain overfull with schemes and excuses, she let the sea gently lull her into oblivion. Annoyingly, hair dangled, obscuring and tickling, but she couldn't push it away. She closed her eyes. Blackness came as a relief. If she curled up to sleep, like a baby, the sickness would go away. A car door slammed. Footsteps, heavy feet. The grass smelt ripe. Legs outstretched, arms star-like, head cradled in a dip of cushioning soil. She liked the smell, liked the coolness. She turned like a catherine wheel, fizzing, sparking, head bubbling like a can of Coke, and spewed over his shoes.

Chapter Seventeen

Judith Booth glanced with disdain at the dishevelled spectre of her husband as he stood in the library surveying two large suitcases.

"What are these for?"

Judith grabbed her handbag from the sofa. "Where've you been? I told you I needed the Range Rover tonight."

Exhausted, Andrew strolled towards the long windows. They were cold to the touch. Outside, dark pressed. The sound of her rummaging through the contents of her bag filled the silence. He itched to shout his frustration.

"Jim filled it with petrol for me. You'd better not have used it up."

"Judith, be reasonable." He turned around. "We never go until after the bonfire."

All he wanted was to fall into bed; he didn't even have the energy for a shower and here was his wife, packed and demanding to leave for the airport that night. He was too tired to travel anywhere but upstairs. He stared at the matching luggage.

"Can't we decide this in the morning?" His voice came out flat and dull, not really asking a question but pleading for her to understand this was all he was capable of doing.

"I've booked two seats," said Judith. "Come or not, it's up to you."

"But we always wait until after the sixth."

"All the details are sorted with Carol. I've covered everything, she knows exactly what needs doing. We won't be missed." A key fob jangled as she pulled it out of the bag, sending lipstick, a comb and other keys sprawling across the cushions.

"This is ludicrous," he said.

"It's up to you."

He glanced at the cases again. "Is it?"

"I'm not arguing." Judith gathered everything back into the bag.

"No. We'd all know about it if you were."

There was an uneasy silence again as Andrew turned to look back into the darkness and Judith's shoulders grew more rigid.

"I thought I'd have to order a taxi," she said. "Is the Range Rover outside?"

"Wouldn't a taxi make more sense?"

"I had hoped you'd drive me." She picked up her long wool coat from the sofa.

He'd had enough. "So you assumed already that I wouldn't come?"

"Are you going to drive me to the airport?"

"I shouldn't have driven here." He slumped into a chair, and it sagged under his weight.

She gave him that withering look he knew well and waved an elegant hand. "Will you at least put in the bags or has all chivalry gone with your sense of pride?"

He glanced at the cases again, incongruously new in the jarring light that showed up the shabbiness of their surroundings. He wanted to turn off the glare of the wall lights and central chandeliers and switch on lamps that sent out a diffused glow that wrapped the room in a time warp; reminding him of his childhood and a time she hadn't existed.

"Why are you angry?" He didn't say 'this time' or even mean to phrase it as a question. It was another statement thrown in desperation. He didn't want to lift heavy cases and go outside into the cold night and have to make the decision whether he would climb behind the wheel again or not.

"Andrew, I'm tired as well. I don't want to argue, I just want to go. I need to get away from here, and quite frankly, right now,

I don't care particularly if you come or not. I'll leave the car at the airport and you can get Jim to drive you and pick it up later."

She looked at him now, her striking blue eyes as beautiful as ever, but their sparkling veneer had turned diamond hard years ago.

"I thought everything between us was fine." He rested his hands on his thighs, readying himself for the long haul of discussion.

***

Judith clenched the keys into her palm. It had taken all day to pack the cases, soothe Carol's panic at being left to run the bonfire and fireworks, and telephone the caterers and pyrotechnic teams to confirm they were in complete control of their part in the proceedings. Angrily, she had dragged the cases down the front stairs, telling herself good sex wasn't enough anymore. Her back, head and fingers ached. She felt weak with hunger but refused to waste time eating. At that moment, she hated Andrew more than she hated the house. It was impossible to spend one more night there; impossible to work out if this marriage was worth the status it brought.

"I'm trying, Andrew. I'm really trying to stay calm, but you make it very difficult."

He looked down at his hands. "I'm sorry I had too much to drink. It was a party."

"It isn't that. I don't mind driving. In fact, I'd prefer it, but if you want to stay here, then that's the end. I'm not doing this anymore." She picked up her handbag. "Please will you bring out my cases? Is the Range Rover at the front?"

"I can't just up sticks at a moment's notice. I haven't packed, and I'll need to speak to Jim with all the people coming. I can't do that until tomorrow."

"There are such things as telephones and email, even video calls, but as I said..." She pulled gloves over her freshly painted nails.

"Jim doesn't do any of that," he said and looked away. "I can't even get him on the landline. You know what he's like—always out and about, never in the office."

"You should make him carry a mobile like normal people."

"I'm not going to force him. It's always worked well enough."

Scorn blazed in her throat.

"Carol is more than capable of holding the fort. And I've locked up the private rooms." She forced her voice to remain even and low, knowing how much he hated it when she used that tone of disrespect for his home.

"Judith, give me a break. You know I go to the All Souls' Dinner every year and I'm always late back. You know what that lot are like. Once a year, for Christ's sake. Once a year." He stood now, pacing out his anger, as if he was only now realising she'd never been the right one for Moorland Castle. "And this year, we were remembering Gordon and Shelley Weston. How the hell could I rush that? I couldn't turn up for just five minutes. Be reasonable. I know you're not completely heartless, whatever people say."

"Don't you dare get all sanctimonious on me as if you're some devout Catholic when you hardly even qualify for C of E." She raised her voice to match his. "You don't care about these people. You don't care about anyone. The only person you care about, Andrew, is yourself."

"Once a year," he repeated as if she hadn't heard. "And it's not about being a Catholic or whatever. It's about respect and tradition, not something I suppose you'd know anything about, coming from your father's soulless business monster of a gaping vacuum."

"My father's money has made it possible to keep this house from completely going to ruin." Her voice trembled, belying her carefully perfected appearance.

"You think everything's about balance sheets and deadlines." Andrew stopped pacing and faced her head on. "Christ, I should have listened to Jim."

"You know what? I don't want you to help me." She caught hold of the nearest suitcase. "Stay here. I don't want you in Spain with me either, pining away as you always do for this pathetic place. We have nothing in common, nothing. You're just a boring has-been who deserves this cold, depressing hovel. You can do what you like and rot here with your precious gamekeeper and band of deluded groupies."

"Go!" He waved his arm, turning his back on her. "Go and do what you bloody well like yourself."

She stared at him, taking in the well-tailored but old trousers, the saggy country jacket and still fine head of hair.

"And don't worry about the bags. I'll manage on my own the same as I manage everything."

***

Andrew, despite her telling him not to bother, picked up the larger case and marched out of the room, noisily dumping it by the front door before reappearing and snatching the smaller case from her hand.

"I'll put them in the back then I'm going to have a shower and go to bed," he shouted over his shoulder.

"You'll have to retrieve Gloucester," she said, following him. "I've left him with Jim. I should have listened when he said you'd be too inebriated to drive."

"Jim would never say that."

Her heels resounded on the wooden floor. "He talks to me as well, you know."

He hated her then; hated her more than he thought possible, and the overwhelming vividness of that single thought shocked him.

He dropped the second case next to its partner by the front door and, hands shaking, looked back at her—this woman, neat in a pale-grey suit, a darker grey coat tasteful on top, her blonde hair combed into an immaculate bob, earrings and necklace, just visible, perfectly matching, her gleaming patent shoes, deep-pink thin lips, tightly gloved hand tapping the side of her thigh…

"Can you get the door?" he said, bending to pick up the cases again.

"You'll have to move."

Andrew could feel his anger rising. He had toed the line for so many years, he had lost count of his compromises. His parents had said nothing when he announced his engagement to the beautiful blue-eyed daughter of a distribution company owner. His younger sister had shrugged and said at least the children would be good-looking. His friends had been more graphic. It was only Jim, the old gardener, who had commented low under his breath.

"What did you say?" Andrew remembered how unchar-acteristically aggressive his response had sounded.

"Nowt," Jim muttered.

"No, you said something."

Jim had looked him straight in the eye. "All the best to you both."

It hadn't been what he'd initially said. Andrew had known she was the wrong one to marry, but she was beautiful and perfect as if she'd just stepped off her father's assembly line, smelling like the make-up counters at the department store in York. It wasn't anyone's fault they couldn't have children, but that didn't stop them masking how they each cast blame on the other.

She sledgehammered into his thoughts again. "When I get back, I want to put the house on the market."

"What?" Their feet crunched over the gravel.

"I've already contacted Grove, Thatcher and Amos."

"It's not yours to sell." *The last straw*, he thought and swung the cases with renewed vigour. "Open the boot, would you, you hard-cased crab?"

She looked at him scathingly and, pressing the key fob, marched past him towards the flashing vehicle.

Chapter Eighteen

H E LIFTED THE cases into the back of the Ranger Rover as if they were weightless. Judith liked tall, strong men, but Andrew, although both these things, wasn't disciplined enough to be the business highflyer she craved. She thought when she first met him that he would always dress in new, locally designed shirts and suits, looking smart and debonair. She'd admired the fact that he didn't send to London but supported local tailors. It seemed quaint and what real money did, but it came as a jolting disappointment that in reality, his clothes were well made so that they didn't wear out, not because he liked spending money on looking good.

With nothing left to say, she strode back inside the house one last time to check she hadn't forgotten anything.

"It'll take me a few minutes to pack a small bag," he said, avoiding eye contact as he always did when he was angry.

She hesitated, wondering if she should let him. If she should believe him. She glanced at her delicate, gold watch before strolling to the downstairs washroom. She took her time. Tried to pee twice. Washed her hands. Dried in all the cracks. Hand-creamed, then wiped her hands on the towel again. If he was to come, then he'd have to wait for her, not her for him. When she reappeared, pulling on the second tight leather glove, she found the hallway empty.

"Andrew?"

No response. Buttoning up her coat, she waited for any noise that would betray him, but the house remained quiet. Resting one foot on the bottom tread of the wide staircase, she listened again.

Glancing up, she noticed the glow of a light. Unable to believe that he was taking so long, she trotted up the stairs to issue a pithy summons. As she strode along the hallway past her husband's great-great aunts and uncles and fresh-faced grandparents towards the master bedroom, a torch beam flickering through the open door of the priest hide caught her eye. She flicked the light switch on the wall. Nothing happened. Her anger increasing with each step, she ran one hand against the wall to follow its curve as it took her up the short flight, until she reached the small room at the top.

She stared incredulously at Andrew's shadowy figure on the far side of the low wall that divided the room. "What on earth are you doing?"

Torchlight panned around the room. "It sounded as if something had fallen over."

"I can't hear anything."

"Like a bang. I was walking past…"

She let out a gust of frustration.

"The bulb has gone," he said.

"Well, that could have been the noise you heard, but you don't need to change it now." She turned to go.

"I think someone's been up here. Listen."

Faintly, there came a trickle of crumbling plaster.

"I thought you were packing?"

His head disappeared from view.

"This is ludicrous." She could no longer hide her annoyance.

"I can see something."

"If this is meant to stop me going, it won't work."

"Give me a minute. There's definitely something."

"Andrew, I thought you'd be downstairs waiting, and I've had to come all the way up here to find you."

"I was on my way when I saw the open door—I was about to shut it when I heard a noise. And I want to find—"

"It's symbolic, Andrew," Judith interrupted. "You will do anything rather than leave this place, won't you?" She stared into the dark, watching the flicker of his torch. "I'm going."

"There's something definitely wrong here." His voice came out muffled.

She shivered; the cold struck through her coat.

His shape loomed over the wall. "Do me a favour? Just come over here and see if you can see anything."

"You've got to be kidding."

He stretched out his hand. "Please?"

She took it, and he helped her awkwardly straddle the low wall. "Well?" she demanded.

"Bend down and look."

He flashed the torch into the second hide. She bobbed down and glanced quickly at the uneven stone. Shadows merged with the pocked surface.

"What am I looking for?"

"The walls." He shifted the torch. "Can you see any damage?"

Of course he was worried that the house was falling down. It was always the house, the grounds, traditions, the locals, that chalet park—anything rather than her needs.

"I can't see a thing." She put one leg back over the narrow wall, careful not to snag her tights.

"Don't be like that." He grabbed her arm. Exasperated, she flung him off. Caught off balance, he staggered, flashing the torchlight across the ceiling.

Reaching the steps, she trotted down the narrow flight until she stood at the bottom, in the light of the landing, waiting for him to appear. When he didn't, she imagined his tall figure leaning against the wall of the priest hide above, calculating how long it would take for her to run back up the stairs. Well, she wasn't going to. She remained still, determined that he should come down to her. She put her hand against the door. Still no sound. She felt the familiar hatred towards him for ruining what should have been a well-balanced alliance rising in her stomach. She told herself she would never return, that she'd open a sports complex in Spain, find a young Spanish hotshot and start a new life without Andrew and his soul-draining ancestors.

She leaned forward to listen. Still no sound of him climbing over the low wall. Exasperated, she stepped back into the corridor and slammed the secret door. With both hands, she dragged the wooden 'No Entry' sign into position to bar the entrance. She hoped he would jolly well walk straight into it and do himself lasting damage. That would teach him to put a crumbling pile of stone before her. She looked at the sign's gleaming oak supports for a moment, wondering how much pain it would inflict, before turning back to the main staircase.

Standing by the hall table, she looked back up the stairs. The landing light still illuminated the top steps. With a sharp click, she turned it off. Holding the front door open for a moment, she listened again, wondering if he would text her at the airport.

Outside, the glare from the security light illuminated the dark drive, highlighting her every move. She glanced up at the main bedroom windows. The curtains were drawn, and she tried to recall if she had pulled them. She couldn't remember. She walked over to the Range Rover and climbed into the driver's seat, wriggling the key into the ignition. The engine ticked as she sat for several minutes tapping her foot on the accelerator.

The front door remained closed, but still she stared, expecting it to open at any moment and for Andrew to sheepishly appear. It didn't. He didn't. She couldn't wait any longer. The security lights extinguished. The wind swayed the treetops. She hated that sound. It spoke of winter and cold and isolation. She pulled the seat belt across her chest, revved the engine several times, then released the handbrake. Gravel churned under the tyres as she pressed her foot down and the moon broke through billowing clouds, lighting her way.

Easing up after an initial burst of speed, she looked in the rear-view mirror for a last sighting of the castellated house lurking in the moon's white glow. She'd miss the prestige of living there, but that would be all. Other places would be more beneficial for a wealthy soon-to-be divorcee. Driving with gathering relief past dark rhododendrons and towering horse chestnuts that bordered the main gates, she sighed with relief. For the first time in her adult life, she looked appreciatively at the moonlit waves to her left. The full, circular orb surrounded by its brown and lilac aura hung heavy in the midnight sky, and she took it as a sign of approval.

In all the years living there, she had never seen what so many described as the beauty of the coast. She found the long stretches of grey road and expanse of brown scrub and blanched moor barren and depressing. The sea always seemed uninviting, and she shivered even when the beaches were inundated with holiday-makers. The sky always seemed too vast and bleak, speckled with common gulls, the air pungent with salt and sand. She could not remember the last time she had walked along sweeping stretches of shore, stony with rocks, green and slimy with beached seaweed. Not since childhood had she felt shells cracking underfoot or heard the sound of fossil hammers tapping the cliff's downfall. She didn't miss it. Age, tradition and memories were not for her. Maybe she was more sentimental than she thought. The sea, an expanse she normally ignored as a backdrop to the day's list of tasks suddenly appeared promising and beautiful, bathed as it was in magical beams.

An outcrop of trees sent their vertical shadows horizontally across the road. On her left, the black expanse of water splayed its white, shimmering panel of moonlight. There were no other vehicles in sight, and she liked it that way. She was glad Andrew hadn't come. Without him, there were no reminders of decaying buildings or ancient traditions, just airports filled with strangers and the white concrete enclaves of Spain. Those were images and places she preferred. She'd closed the door on musty velvet curtains and the smell of furniture polish. No more pings of the pathetic cash register or tourists emerging from coaches. She tightened her grip on the steering wheel. Onwards. Into the future. She pressed her foot down on the accelerator.

Through dappling shadows, the road veered to the left. She turned the steering wheel but realised too late that by taking her eyes off the deceptively lit tarmac she had misjudged the bend, and the Range Rover bumped over scrub directly towards the cliff edge.

Chapter Nineteen

WRENCHING THE WHEEL hard to the right, Judith slammed her foot on the brake, but the tyres slid on moist grass. Holding her breath, she squeezed her eyes closed, willing the car to stop before the cliff edge. She tensed for the fall. Opened her eyes. She'd stopped in time. She waited. The engine had stalled. Relieved, she rested her head on the steering wheel.

For several minutes, she didn't move, listening to waves hushing against rocks below. Eventually, raising her head, she stared at the moon dappling its reflection on the water. She yanked up the handbrake and let out a long, quivering breath. Her legs ached. Her fingers hurt. The sky shrouded cloudless. Not a soul in sight. Breathing deeply again, she turned the ignition key. The engine refused to start. She tried it again. It wouldn't even turn over. Releasing her seat belt, she pulled her handbag out of the foot well and set it on the passenger seat. Her hands shook, but she didn't need to rush. It would be all right; she'd catch a later flight if she had to. She took out her mobile. Her voice would wobble if she spoke to anyone. She might even cry. She slid it back into the bag and took out a packet of cigarettes.

Swinging open the door, cigarette rigid between fingers, she stepped onto the grass. The cold wind hit, and she gasped. Turning, she pushed hair from her face. The wind had got up. She couldn't see. She pushed back her hair again, but in her annoyance, her foot slipped on the soft ground. She reached back for the car door. On the night-damp grass, her feet slid from under her. She thumped down, hard. Twisting, she felt behind for the Range Rover's bumper. Her fingers scraped the smooth metal. It would be comical, seeing herself splayed on her stomach, but right now, just damn annoying, dirtying her new coat. She tried to scramble to her knees, but the ground wasn't there. Her legs stretched into open air. She gripped the lush grass and held still. Soil under her stomach shifted, then crumbled, then completely gave way. She screamed, grasping for something to hold until her hips pressed into the edge, her legs dangling in space. Crashing waves made her tighten her hold. Blades of grass tore, and she ploughed her fingers through the soil, digging her toes into the cliff below. Wind caught her hair. Caught the cigarette. A swirl of light.

She tried scrambling, heaving herself. A shoe spiralled. She pressed her forehead on the earth. Soil under her stomach sagged, and she lost her grip. The ground dropped. She scrabbled for a hold. She tried to grab the edge, the rock, rough grass, anything. Air howled. Rushed. She plummeted, fingers ripping the air. Her skirt rode up. Her remaining shoe eased off. Falling made her blink and blink and blink. Heart churning. Stomach lifting. She fell. Down, down, down. Barely turning but flailing. Her stocking feet hit the water. Pain shot up her legs. Waves exploded into froth. The swell lifted, holding her body on its crest. She gulped in salty water. The wave wrapped around her. She beat against its power. It threw her against the cliff face. Her shoulder cracked. Tossed, she watched the sweep of water. Her head seethed. Her arms floated. She sensed it coming closer. Water, rock, cold, fear merged. Blurred. Sighed between her teeth. When her body mulched into the rock again, she felt nothing.

***

Hours later, dawn broke. A gunshot echoed out of the woods and across damp fields. John Carmichael strode through the grey light, his boots lacquered in dew, his coat and hat covered in heavy November chill. Raising his rifle, he killed his second rabbit of the day as a third leapt out of the bushes and sprinted across the clearing, zigzagging towards nearby trees. He raised his gun, aiming to catch it in his sight. The rabbit darted from side to side, and he expertly tracked it until, working out which direction it would run next, he bent his finger. The animal leapt low under bushes. John fired, and the sound cracked through the trees. He waited a moment before lowering the barrel to see a rabbit's tall ears disappear into the scrub.

He trudged forward, scooped up the dead rabbit and placed it in the bag hanging taut across his body. Checking his watch, he calculated that he'd stay for another half hour; hopefully, in that time, a pheasant would appear. Joyce had said she wanted Trevor and Mavis to have a nice meal; it wasn't an everyday occurrence, and a bird seemed fitting somehow. Kicking through the grass, he glanced to his left and right, on the lookout for a well-rounded prey.

All the animals in the woods seemed to have disappeared with that final shot, but John doggedly prodded through undergrowth and scoured the middle distance for movement. With dawn retreating, resigned, he turned back in the direction of the chalet park, realising as he walked that he had come further than intended. He wished the bag bumping against his leg were heavier and filled with game that would make a feast to satisfy everyone instead of being what it was. He could imagine it now if he had. Randolph would gruffly nod, giving little ground; Trevor would be embarrassing with praise, Peter full of restrained gratitude. He could never read Jez, but he should certainly admire his aim with a gun. And the women would fuss and dither and organise and plan, and he would be treated like a successful big game hunter.

He lingered, cocking the rifle and walking in a state of readiness. He didn't pray; he didn't believe in God. He left that to Randolph and, to a lesser extent, his wife, whom he felt played at church-going for want of anything better to do.

She had raised her voice on one of those rare occasions. "It's free, isn't it?"

He couldn't really argue with that because the time spent in flower arranging and meetings and worship meant she wasn't wishing she could redecorate or buy something, anything, as had been her wont when they lived in the big house in Roundhay.

He muttered that he should be grateful for small blessings. The barely filled bag scraped against his side again, and he felt a pang at the contrast between his life then and the life he led now. He knew Joyce was bitter at his failure to provide into their old age. She never said anything directly, but she looked at him less, the stance of her body tense with resentment. Her growing silences told him all that he already felt.

Sometimes when out hunting, he'd thought how it would be preferable to turn the gun on himself, but he abhorred the cowardliness of such an act. He wished he was still the driven, single-minded executive he had once been, but here, it held no sway. His chest, like his shoulders, had been stronger then.

Trudging on, putting these thoughts aside, he kept alert until he stood on the edge of the woods, looking down across fields to the sleeping chalets and the sea. He waited, urging a pheasant or even one last meandering rabbit to make an appearance. None came. There was something else, though. The light caught the top of a vehicle, standing proud on the cliff edge facing the eternity offered by the sea.

"Bloody show-offs," he muttered.

He looked around for one last time. Gulls cracked warnings. *Bugger them*, he thought and set off again, squaring his angular shoulders and dropping the barrel of the gun so that it moved in unison with his leg as he strode through the long, wet grass.

Joyce was already dressed. She watched him take the two rabbits out of his bag and lay them on the newspaper she had spread over the kitchen table.

She walked back through the living room and into the bedroom. "Call me when they're ready."

He slipped the bag from his shoulder and hung his jacket in the cupboard. After washing his hands, he skinned the pair of rabbits then scrubbed their thin bodies under the tap, drying them thoroughly as he had done many times before. He glanced at the cleaver lying ready on the table then at the two rabbits rigidly exposed side by side, heads together, back legs outstretched as if taking one final leap. Skinny without their fur. He clenched his jaw again, picked up the first animal and chopped off its back feet and then its head.

Later, Joyce draped small pieces of rabbit in a tray of shallow boiling fat and, turning them, browned the meat. The pieces sizzled. She did the same with the four flaps of skin John had removed with a sharp knife, embarrassed that someone would have to eat them when this meal was supposed to be a cordon bleu feast. She scattered halved carrots and small onions that filled up the tray and finally dropped sprigs of rosemary like flowers in a coffin. It would be enough with potatoes and peas, followed by a blackberry tart for the four of them and some remaining for Randolph and the others to eat if she was frugal with portions. Placing a lid over the casserole, she pushed the dish into the oven, ready to cook later on a low heat. Resigned, as she'd learnt to be, she gathered the peelings, took them outside and tipped them onto the compost heap.

Gulls circled overhead. She would be pleased to see the back of them. Even though they no longer woke her as they had when they'd first holidayed at the coast, she still thought them as common as the starlings that had swooped through Leeds city centre on her way to the bus station after work. Even then, she had felt she was above the cry of common birds.

That had been before she met John Carmichael. She wondered what would have happened to her if he had not come into the department store that day. As soon as he strutted into the leather goods section with the intention of buying a purse for his mother, she knew she was destined to marry. Most of all, she knew she would be safe; safe from the banter of the front steps and the embarrassment of washing lines strung across the street and the indignity of passing an uncle on the stairs. And now she was aware again of how common gulls were and how they reminded her of starlings at dusk.

***

Overlooking the park, Lizzie shivered, head aching and throat dry. It was the only place to get reception for her phone. As she pressed in Andrew's name for the third time, she glanced to her left, seeing a dark four-by-four speed towards her. She recognised it. Andrew was coming for her. She raised her hand. Waved. It sped up. Brakes screeched behind her. Andrew's Range Rover raced past, wafting up dust. She turned to watch it speed away. The Royal Mail van had come to a standstill several feet away to her right.

"Pillock!" the postman shouted out of his open window as the black vehicle curved around the bend towards Beamstown.

"You nearly hit me," Lizzie said.

"Bloody toffs think they own the roads." He held up his hand by way of apology before heading down the track to the chalet park.

Lizzie pressed in Andrew's name again and let it ring. As the phone went into message service for a fourth time, she swore. She looked around. Andrew had kept driving. She shivered. The red van pulled up at the bottom of the track. It was all so normal. She set off back down to the park.

The postman was knocking on the first chalet's door. Peter, unshaven and with dishevelled hair, opened it. The postman glanced down at the large parcel at his feet and held out a keypad. "I need you to sign."

Lizzie watched as she drew closer. Peter took the bulky contraption in one hand, curving out his signature awkwardly with the small attached pen. He handed it back, and the postman returned to his van without checking that Peter could lift the parcel off the floor. Lizzie gave but a cursory glance as she trudged across the grass. The van swung around, and she slammed her chalet door closed, feeling nauseous once again. One hand on her forehead, she downed a mug of cold water before meandering across the room and shuffling under the flowered duvet.

***

Randolph stood on the beach, wellingtons sinking into wet sand. As he ferociously dug, water refilled the hole, the sand growing darker under each thrust of his spade. Jumping into the hole that now reached above his knees, he pulled in the sides, scraping together the fallen sand and tossing it out onto a growing mound. He worked around and around, extending the space until, digging down again, the shovel hit boulders. Clambering out, he stabbed the spade into the sand and bent to roll the rigid corpse of the dog into the hole. It splashed into the shallow water and lay partly submerged. Swiping up the spade, he shovelled in loose sand until the mound was flat and Campion completely covered. He then stamped over the area, pressing down hard. He smoothed down the edges with his boots so that it melted seamlessly into its surroundings. Finally satisfied, he made the sign of the cross over his chest. Using the spade as a walking stick, he crossed the beach towards the cliff path.

***

Lizzie pulled the slightly grubby duvet up to her cheeks. Wriggling, she straightened the cardigan that had bunched under her back and turned carefully onto her side, waiting for the room to spin and sickness rise up as she knew it would after a night's heavy drinking. Pain stabbed her head. She winced. She'd kill Andrew. He should have put her up in the gatehouse. He should have stopped. Why hadn't he bleeding well stopped? Maybe he hadn't recognised her because he was driving so fast.

What a state she must have looked! She closed her eyes again, remembering the cold, damp smell of soil and the sweet sickness of Andrew's shoes. Little wonder he hadn't stopped.

***

Peter studied the parcel on his kitchen table. He cut through the thick tape with a Stanley knife, pulling away the brown wrapping and tugging it gently from beneath the box. He held his breath. Waited. He put down the knife, folded the paper and placed it on a chair. The box stood about two feet by two and a half high. It seemed overpowering on the inadequate table in his small kitchen. Laying his hand gently on the top as if feeling for life inside, he breathed in deeply several times, then, picking up the knife again, ran the blade along the tape, slicing it apart.

***

Randolph panted heavily as he cleared the clifftop just as Peter emerged from his chalet. Even at this distance, Randolph could see there was something amiss. He lumbered across to intercept him. As soon as he was within reach, Peter grabbed Randolph's arm, casting his eyes over the other chalets. Randolph followed him inside. The box stood open on the kitchen table. Peter closed the door. Randolph peered inside the box before turning his head with a smile.

Chapter Twenty

LIZZIE GULPED IN the cool air. Mesmerised, Mavis stood on the bottom step. Trevor looked up at them both from a short distance away.

"Are you sure you're feeling well enough to be out here?" Mavis asked. "You look very pale."

Trevor held out a steaming mug. "I've made you a good strong cup of tea," he said.

"He makes a lovely cup."

Lizzie still felt the sickness of alcohol. She shouldn't drink— she always told herself that the morning after. It always landed her in trouble, made her be in places she didn't want to be. She nodded briefly. Mavis took the mug from Trevor and held it out for Lizzie to take. The scent of the tea only made her more nauseous.

Two vehicles negotiated the bumps and potholes of the track.

"Who can this be?" Mavis untied her apron as she retreated down the steps.

"I recognise the blue," said Trevor. "It's that Miss Harper from Housing. Where's Randolph when you want him?"

"Why d'you need him?" asked Lizzie.

"We wouldn't be anywhere without Randolph," Trevor mumbled.

The large, once-white Audi and blue Focus bumped steadily down the bank and curved onto the flat, where they stopped. Two men and a woman, all wearing dark suits, climbed out and strolled towards Trevor. Mavis anxiously hurried to stand by him.

"We've had all the discussions we're going to have." Randolph's voice rang out of nowhere. Lizzie looked around and spotted the squat, old man outside Peter's cabin. "Vultures don't take long, do they?" he shouted, hobbling down the steps.

"Hello, Mr. Brook." The woman held out her hand. "You know why we're here."

"He'd better not upset Miss Harper," Mavis whispered.

"Mr. and Mrs. Trevor Cummings?" The one with the pen and clipboard glanced at Mavis and Trevor, ignoring Randolph. "And you are?" He looked enquiringly at Lizzie. She didn't answer.

"Elizabeth Juniper," Mavis eventually said. "That's right, isn't it, dear?"

The man raised his voice. "Susan? Did you know new residents had moved in?"

"You're not signing up more recruits, are you?" the woman—Susan…Miss Harper—fired at Randolph, who glowered back.

"I'm Steve Ingalls, from the Housing Department," the man told Lizzie. "We don't seem to have you listed."

"I'm not," she said, wishing she had stayed in bed.

Steve Ingalls wrote on his clipboard.

"We'd like to talk to everyone," said Susan, staring directly at Randolph and Peter, now standing side by side. "Do you want to call the residents together, or should I?"

Nobody needed the meeting to be announced. It was as if the tapping noise emanating from Peter's chalet had caught their attention, and they now appeared as they had out of the dawn mist two nights previous.

Everyone watched in silence as a skinny, black-haired lad in a cheap, trendy suit tacked a piece of laminated card to Peter's door. Randolph jumped back up the steps and, pushing the lad roughly aside, pulled the piece of card free from its tack.

"What's this?" he demanded.

"Notice of eviction," the skinny lad said, palpably annoyed that he had lost dignity for a moment and looking at Susan for permission to retaliate.

Randolph ignored the lad and strode menacingly towards Susan. "I've told you before—this is private property."

"You will be rehoused, Mr. Brook. Carl..." Susan gestured to the young officer to carry on.

"This is my home and it's none of your business." Randolph spat the words.

"Within a year, your home won't be anyone's, Mr. Brook. It will be down there." She pointed to the sea. "This entire row could be down there next week." She appealed to Peter. "Mr. Hawksworth, we've been through all this. You must see, particularly after what happened to the Westons." She turned to Trevor and Mavis. "Mr. Carmichael, Mrs. Carmichael... Come on, Mavis. Enough is enough, isn't it?"

"You can't force us to do anything we don't want to do," said Randolph.

"Now that's where you're wrong. We have an obligation to ensure your safety." She straightened her shoulders. "We can evict you if we provide alternative housing."

"Just you try."

"I'm here to offer all of you some very good accommodation not far from here. If you want to get yourselves sorted, we can take you now to view the properties."

"We don't want to go," said Randolph before anyone else could speak.

"Solid homes in safe locations."

"In Rigby?" For the first time, John made his presence known.

"Beamstown." Susan looked pleased he was taking an interest.

"I bloody hate Beamstown," muttered Randolph.

Lizzie closed her eyes. Beamstown wasn't what the chalet park residents would call 'nearby'.

"It'll cost, won't it?" John shook his head as he dug his hands in his pockets.

"How will we afford it?" Trevor joined in.

"We planned to end our days here," said Mavis.

"It won't cost you a penny," said Steve Ingalls, looking slightly unnerved as the residents closed in.

The ensuing silence lasted barely a moment.

"You'll be changing our way of life," Randolph said. "That always costs."

"Where's Marilyn?" Susan glanced over Steve Ingalls' shoulder at the clipboard, touching his arm to reassure them both. Carl stood at a distance, halfway between the rows of chalets as if caught in no-man's land.

"What about compensation?" John demanded.

"Nothing's changed, I'm afraid," she said, "but you are getting somewhere to stay."

John turned away. Joyce tightened her lips.

Here we go, thought Lizzie, and she sat on the step, cradling the mug of tea between her hands, content merely to listen to events that didn't concern her.

"Our pensions won't cover this." Mavis's voice trembled.

Trevor gently touched her arm. It was them that Lizzie felt most sorry for.

"If it's all right with you, we'll be staying," Trevor directed at Susan Harper.

"You don't need their permission, man," Randolph snapped.

"Sixth of November," said Susan. "Then we send in the bulldozers."

"Now just a—"

She waved her hand, and Carl jolted back to his senses.

"That's less than a week."

Lizzie looked up.

"I suggest you take up the offer, then." Susan turned again briefly. "Who's ready to go? I can take four of you, Steve and Carl another three."

Lizzie studied the eviction notice the lean-faced Carl had shoved into her hand.

"They know this land can't be sustained." Susan shot her a second glance. "Now, Mrs. Carmichael, Mrs. Cummings, would you like to come with me?"

Lizzie put her mug down on the step. "Are you saying this land isn't worth saving?"

"If you'll excuse me, Miss?" Steve Ingalls interjected. "D'you want to come with me?"

Before Lizzie could respond, Susan Harper cut in again.

"You haven't been through the process and consultations that the rest of the residents have been through. It's impossible to sustain every stretch of land on this coast."

Lizzie could tell by the sound of her voice, this woman had had enough.

"You need to fuck off out of here," Randolph warned gruffly, but Susan remained calm.

"I'll call the police if I have to."

"You can't threaten people."

"I'm advising you, Mr. Brook—" she motioned to Carl as she spoke "—you will be evicted in one week because demolition men are coming in, and they will flatten these chalets, burn the remains and whatever you *choose* to leave behind. If you haven't taken up the council's offer, you will officially be homeless, and you will be free to blame nobody but yourself. That's your choice, of course. Now, nail up the rest of those notices, Carl."

"Why is she being so rude?" asked Mavis.

"Because she's worried about us," said Trevor.

"This is a bit heavy-handed, though."

"She's just doing her job."

Carl nailed up another notice; Lizzie wondered how much he got paid and if it was worth it for doing a job like this.

"You can't dictate to us." John Carmichael stepped forward. "If you're not going to pay us anything for the privilege."

"We've been through that, Mr. Carmichael. You were aware ten years ago when you were offered moving costs. What we can offer now is social housing, and I strongly advise you to take it this time."

Lizzie glanced across at Jez, who leant against his chalet wall, lighting a cigarette. She forced herself to her feet and walked slowly over to join him. He held out the roll-up, but she shook her head.

"Aren't you bothered?" she asked, looking back at the others.

He inhaled deeply, then blew out smoke.

"It doesn't mean anything," he said.

"They're serving notice. You have to go."

"No, we don't."

Lizzie frowned and reached for his cigarette. She didn't care if she was sick or not now. As she took it, she touched his hand gently, long fingers, sinewy tendons, prominent knuckles. She peered up at his face, but he was looking down at his hand against hers.

"Are you going to take it?" he asked.

"How come your hands are so soft?"

He caught her gaze, his eyes almost completely amber in the sunlight. *Where did the green go?* As if he had read her thoughts, he smiled, retracting his hand to take back the cigarette.

"They're not," he said, matter of fact. "Too many nicks with the pallet knife." And then the moment broke as he threw down the butt. "This is getting nasty." He pushed himself off the wall, brushing her arm as he took a couple of paces towards the small crowd.

Voices, now raised, could not be ignored.

"Get off my property," John demanded, tearing down the notice. "Get off!"

"John…"

"Let me deal with this, Joyce."

"Come on, John," Trevor appealed, taking his arm.

"Leave him alone, Trevor," Joyce warned as John shook himself free.

John pushed Carl down the steps. "You are trespassing, young man."

Susan Harper beckoned her assistant away, but John had already grabbed the younger man's jacket and shook him hard by the lapels.

"John, stop it."

"How dare you?" His face shone livid. "I paid for this property fair and square. I own my chalet and the plot of land it stands on. It's mine. You think I'll take charity and live in a council flat next to a family of twenty wasters? I was a managing director at BMW, for Christ's sake."

"Mr. Carmichael, you need to stand back. Leave Mr. Grant alone," Susan Harper said, striding forward.

Trevor shook his head. "This isn't right."

"We'll deal with this," Jez said, pressing the obviously shaken Carl away.

"Hypocrites!"

The grating voice silenced everyone. Marilyn stood in the doorway of her chalet, her words projecting like bullets. Everyone had forgotten her. "You left us to rot all this time, and now someone's dead you start bothering?"

"We'll be back at one this afternoon to take you to see some properties," Susan Harper said, gesturing to her associates to retreat. "Hopefully, you'll be ready to go by then." She nodded again to her colleagues, and all three strode back to their vehicles.

As Steve Ingalls passed Lizzie, he caught her eye. "Have you a car?"

She nodded.

"Take this." He handed her a sheet of paper. "There's a map on the back. If no-one else, try and get the old couples to have a look with you. We've marked which ones we think will suit."

"But…?"

"I'll meet you at the first address."

She could tell by the look on his face that he didn't hold any hope that the residents would change their minds. She scanned the list of addresses. She recognised the estate. It was the largest on the North East coast. She glanced around for Jez, but he had disappeared. Susan Harper leant on the car door of her Audi as the two others climbed into the Focus.

"I'm warning you, Randolph, if you're not all out by November sixth, the police will oust you and they will not be gentle. By then, you'll be trespassing, and we can legally force you off this land. I'd recommend you all be ready at one."

"And I recommend you fuck off," Randolph shouted.

"It's not me that's taking your homes away from you," Susan shouted back. "Cast your eyes out there." She pointed towards the sparkling waves. "If you want to put the blame on anything, put it on that."

She climbed into the driver's seat and slammed the door. Within seconds, the tyres churned up the grass as the car spun in a circle and made a run up the hill. The other vehicle followed.

Trevor helped the visibly shaken John sit down on the chalet steps. Without speaking, Mavis, dabbing her eyes, walked away and Joyce briskly followed, leaving Lizzie alone with the cold cup of tea.

Chapter Twenty-One

JOHN CARMICHAEL SAT, shoulders angular and rigid in the passenger seat of Lizzie's car as his wife and Trevor and Mavis shuffled silently into the back. In his usual quiet manner, Trevor had been very persuasive.

"Let's do it for the ladies," he said discreetly to John. "And let Lizzie drive. It'll make her feel useful. I think she needs to feel useful."

John turned the car keys over in his hand before putting them carefully back in his trouser pocket and glaring at Trevor.

Lizzie drove them up the hill to join the A171. They all remained silent. The sun wasn't as bright as it had been during the previous few weeks, but still Lizzie put on a pair of sunglasses. She turned up the music and no-one commented on her choice.

"Are you going to the bonfire?" she asked, unable to stand the tension in the air any longer.

John hesitated before clearing his throat. "It's not my cup of tea."

She glanced in her rear-view mirror. Both women stared out of the side windows while, sandwiched in the middle, Trevor studied his hands.

"I didn't see Campion this morning, Joyce," Lizzie tried to engage her in conversation.

"He's off on the beach," Trevor said.

"Didn't want to think he'd been locked out."

She drove the rest of the way without saying another word, relieved that the nausea had passed and all she needed to deal with now was the lingering headache. She let the music play, grateful that the tunes stemmed the awkwardness of the pulsating quiet. She could think her own thoughts and make her own plans in the small pocket of time it provided between the chalet park and the housing estate.

"Did you ever consider going to live with either of your daughters?" Joyce's voice broke through a pause in the songs. Lizzie glanced in the mirror, surprised to hear the restrained woman's voice.

"I don't think they've room, have they?" Mavis looked at Trevor. He kept his face down. She turned back to Joyce. "Have you?"

"You won't get me kowtowing to my kids," John said.

Lizzie gripped the wheel tighter; she could always tell where resentment brewed and where it may lead. She glanced in the mirror again. Both Joyce and Mavis looked upset. It seemed strange they spoke as if they were strangers when they'd lived as neighbours for so many years.

"Would you like to have done that, Joyce?" Lizzie asked. She felt sorry for the woman, squashed by such a domineering man.

John shifted in his seat as if to shut her up by his presence. No-one would make her shut up.

"Do they live in York?"

"I don't like cities," Joyce said, catching Lizzie's eye in the mirror.

"I bet this place'll suit you, then."

"You think we'll like a pokey squat with pit bulls barking next door and kids kicking a football against the front wall?" John broke in again. "Putting up with that crap before we're shipped off to another council-run home where every chair you're forced to sit in smells of piss and you're lined up like old bangers watching reruns of *Midsomer Murders* and bloody *Downton Abbey*?"

"John."

Lizzie concentrated on the road again. She couldn't bear John's voice. She itched to shout that they were lucky they were still alive and were being given a new start, and that she was driving them, so they didn't have to do a thing, but she didn't. Instead, she stared at the red traffic light, willing it to change. Trevor lowered the window, and the draught swirled into the car.

Veering off the main road, Lizzie entered a large housing estate where every turning and building looked the same. Pulling over, she checked the map the man in the suit had given her. She was glad that he had. Left, right, left. She drove past houses with green fenced-in front gardens and wide verges. She hoped the council officials had the sense to turn up before her passengers changed their minds. Spotting a blue Focus, she drew in at the kerb. Immediately, Steve Ingalls climbed out of his car, and Lizzie eagerly stepped onto the pavement.

"We're here," she called over her shoulder to Trevor.

"One double bedroom. Central heating. Double-glazed throughout," she read cheerfully from the sheet of paper while Steve helped Mavis out of the car.

"Good to see you all," Steve said, shaking Trevor's and Mavis's hands. He bent his head to greet the Carmichaels, but they both remained in their seats. "Ready to have a look at your new homes?"

"You're not putting us in one of these hen hutches," John said.

"Not if you don't want." Steve smiled.

"Then we'll wait here until you show me the one you've in mind for us."

"Well, it's practically the same..." Steve's upbeat tone dropped.

John stared straight ahead.

"Right," Steve said. "You two stay here then, while I show—" He glanced at his sheet of paper. "—Trevor and Mavis." They stood unsmiling, looking like children who'd had their sweets taken away.

After a moment, they followed Steve inside, Lizzie trailing behind, not sure what else to do. She felt suddenly exhausted and wished she'd merely ticked the box and agreed to whatever they gave her. Parched, she craved a drink and wished she'd brought one.

There was no furniture in the ground-floor flat, only carpets and curtains and the chill of emptiness. The fireplace in the living room had a three-bar gas fire protruding over a grey-tiled base, and Lizzie knew instinctively how Mavis and Trevor would hate that. She didn't want to see their expressions as they stood close together just inside the door, and in an attempt to appear nonchalant, she walked over to the window that looked onto a front lawn and the road. She could see the Carmichaels motionless and unspeaking in the car.

"It's a tidy place," Steve encouraged.

Lizzie glanced back at the Cummings. They looked unexpectedly vulnerable and at odds for a couple who had become practically self-sufficient with their vegetable garden and careful, meticulous recycling. They more than any of the others should fit in on the estate. They were the most friendly and sociable of the chalet park residents, ordinary, hard-working people who had happened to retire to a doomed spot, and Lizzie had thought they'd relish the camaraderie of neighbours. Looking at them now, though, standing small and unsure, it struck her that they weren't normal in the sense of people living here. They had been too long removed from daily bustle, and its noise and ways frightened them. They didn't own a television; they had never heard of celebrity culture, and they spoke with the softness of isolated farmers living high up in the northern dales.

She felt ashamed for having brought them to a place as alien to them as Newcastle would have been. Ironically, this building, standing shoulder to shoulder with streets of similar homes, protected from the town by the fast A-road and backed by the old railway tracks, felt bleaker and more barren than that clifftop field ever had.

"Is it a shared garden?" Trevor asked.

"The man upstairs doesn't bother with it. I'm sure he'd let you do what you want," Steve said, trying to stay positive.

Trevor peered over his shoulder through the back window at the tall, brown fence.

"Do you want to look at the kitchen?" Steve gestured, and they all shuffled back into the narrow hall.

The kitchen looked half decent, and Lizzie turned to see their reaction. The sun had come out and shone through the window, making the room with its white units and appliances wincingly bright.

"You could bake some terrific cakes in here," Trevor said quietly.

"D'you want something to drink?" Lizzie touched Mavis's arm gently.

"I'm just tired," said Mavis, near to tears.

Trevor took her hand. "Come on, love."

Lizzie stepped away from the doorway, catching Trevor's eye. She could tell from the way he shook his head that they weren't going to take the place. She glanced at Steve, who, rubbing his hands, followed them back into the hallway.

They walked in and out of the reasonably sized bedroom as a matter of courtesy and stepped one at a time into the tiny, square bathroom. Even Lizzie could see it all seemed soulless compared to their home that brimmed over with knickknacks and pots of seedlings that would eventually transform into luscious plants.

Neither of them said a word when they got back to the car and John twisted around to gauge their response. Joyce sat tight-lipped, pressing her fingers against her handbag and gazing at the bronze clasp.

Lizzie waited for Steve to make a suggestion as to what to do next. A tortoiseshell cat rubbed itself against her leg and mewed loudly. Ignoring it, she studied the row of two-storey buildings with slightly long grass divided by narrow slab pathways leading directly from the pavement to front doors.

"They're scared of change, aren't they?" Steve said.

"They're just scared." Lizzie felt sorry for him but didn't know what to say. She hardly knew the people in the car so couldn't explain how she knew this place wouldn't suit them.

"Here." He held out a key ring with two keys attached. "The other's round the corner. Number 15C. I'll wait here and you can bring the keys back when you've finished. Throw them out of the car window as you're passing if you want." He managed a smile.

"I'm happy to take this one," she said.

His eyes flickered with gratitude.

"Brilliant. I'll have to check at the office, as you aren't a registered resident at the park, but there shouldn't be a problem. Thanks—maybe you doing that will get them thinking. It's better if people aren't forced."

She glanced back at the bleak building then at him.

"Here's my number." She held out her mobile, and he hesitated. "And my name's Lizzie Juniper," she added. He nodded and punched in the digits.

"I'll ring you tomorrow. Definitely."

"Is the next one ground floor as well?"

As soon as she sat behind the wheel, an unexpected wave of anger engulfed her.

"You should have come in," she said, looking at Joyce in the rear-view mirror. "Your one is exactly the same. Do you want to tell them how great the kitchen looked, Trevor?"

"What?"

"We can drive round if you're serious about this," she said.

"Of course I'm serious," snapped John, scrutinising Steve, who strolled up and down talking on his mobile. "What's he doing? Isn't he going to show us around?"

"I've got the keys." She turned on the engine.

As they pulled away, they began to notice people around, women pushing prams, solitary men, the odd one with a companion, someone going shopping, a child on a plastic tractor, and in the background, dogs barking. These people hadn't a clue that a place like the chalet park existed, and she wondered what the point of her discovering its existence could be when it was on the verge of destruction.

She'd been offered a flat; she must remember that. If only she hadn't seen the freedom of the park, even if it was crumbling into the sea, she could be happy here, settled for the first time, not having to do things she didn't want to do. *Keep that in mind,* she told herself, *there's no question about not taking it.*

Pulling up at the house, John bobbed his head to one side and contemplated the building from his seat.

"Ready?" Lizzie asked.

She hadn't expected him to release his seat belt. But he did. And straight away. He opened the car door and eased himself out. Immediately, a child's wail forced him back. Lizzie sprang out of her seat. The three in the back darted their heads around like startled chickens. A toddler sprawled screaming on the road beside an upturned tricycle. What must have been the kid's mother, flapping her arms, came scurrying towards them. She arrived, sweeping up the tricycle with one hand and the boy with the other, swinging him to her breast so that he clasped his hands around her neck and sobbed snot onto her collar.

"Did you knock him off?" she demanded.

"He was right there," John stammered.

"Effing moron!" she yelled. "I could sue you for this!"

"Don't talk nonsense. Where were you? A small child should not be let loose on their own!"

"If he's got brain damage, you'd better be ready," she retaliated, taking in the car and the others in the back of the vehicle. Before John could reply, she marched away, the child peering red-faced over her shoulder.

John slowly lowered himself back into his seat, and Lizzie bent to speak, but he had already pulled the seat belt across his chest, the click of the fastener snapping loudly.

"What are you doing?" she said. "That's probably as tame as it gets around here." They all stared at her. "These houses are dry and clean, and they're safe. They're not going to fall off the cliff. Don't any of you want to get out of that death trap you're living in?" Her last words reverberated around the car. "Those chalets are shit. You have to admit that. They're damp, they're rotten, and they're falling apart. For God's sake, you've got the chance to live somewhere decent. What's wrong with all of you?"

Chapter Twenty-Two

FINDING THAT ANDREW still didn't answer, Lizzie shoved her mobile into her jacket pocket. She looked back at the car, parked on the verge, then down at the chalet park where she'd unceremoniously left the others. Dusk snuck in quickly and she shivered, unsure what to do next. The sea loomed in a solid-looking mass to the horizon. It would be a cold night, but at least Officer Phil wouldn't move her on from a remote spot like this. She couldn't face spending another night in the park however uncomfortable her car became. Low clouds hid the moon and a wind picked up. She opened the rear door and slumped onto the back seat, pulling a rug around her and staring out of the side window. Leaning forward, she pressed down the locks on all four doors.

She slept fitfully, waking to check her phone for messages that never came and staving off the urge to pee. Her mouth felt stale and dry and her stomach empty as she chewed a last piece of gum. Pulling the rug closer around her, she winced with the stiffness of her back and hoped it would soon be light and she'd get a call from Steve telling her she could move into the flat right there and then.

The next time she woke, the moon hung large and the night pressed silvery against the windows. She couldn't make out any lights down below, only a shimmer of water behind. Closing her eyes, she pushed the image of Mavis's tearful face from her mind. Dreams crept in and disappeared. The rush of waves shushed through her head. Sleep again.

Stomach rumbling, she stared at the grubby roof, creamy white above her. A yellow dawn shivered inland. No sound. She could stay there all day, never move, listening to the quiet, catching a gull's cry and the crunching tyres of a passing car, snug and warm and safe from contact with another human being. Her stomach rumbled again, so empty she felt sick. The thought of biting hot chips reeking of vinegar made her salivate. She glanced out of the window. A tall figure stood on the verge with his back to the car. She pushed open the door.

"How long have you been there?" she asked.

"Can I come in?"

Shuffling up, Jez tucked the rug around his knees. "You can tell winter's round the corner." He draped his arm around her shoulders.

"What are you doing?"

"Sorry." He dropped his arm. "I thought you might be cold too."

"I'm fine."

"Yes, I see that now."

They sat in silence, staring at the road through the windscreen. She could have snuggled up and let him put his arm around her, but she wasn't ready to let him in. Remaining as they were, side by side, not talking, not moving and not caring if their breath sounded too loud or faster or slower than the other was a first step.

"So how did it go yesterday?" he asked.

She pulled up her coat collar, wondering what the others had said. Time did move at a different pace in the remote chalet park. One day here seemed like a week; she couldn't imagine how a year must feel. The housing estate seemed a million miles away and months ago. Normality had no place here, no-one leaving for work or returning for tea. No shops pulling down metal shutters. No car horns or tyres racing through puddles on grey Monday mornings on their way to work.

She shrugged. "It went."

"Why did you sleep up here?"

"Why not?"

"Come on, I'll make you breakfast." He pushed back the cover. "You must be starving."

He climbed out, holding the door, bending to watch as she moved to the front seat. She gazed at the now uninterrupted expanse of turquoise breaking through yellow behind his head. She caught his eye.

Maybe it was the teasing lilt in his voice. Maybe it was the challenge of trying to gauge what thoughts hovered behind his eyes. It could have been her body seizing up or maybe it was as simple as her stomach demanding to be fed. The breeze wafted her hair. She scraped it down.

Driving carefully down the track while Jez, hands in his lap, sat quietly beside her, she looked warily at the chalets for signs of activity.

"It's still early," he said as if reading her mind.

She glanced sideways at him. "Too early for seat belts?"

"Ha-ha."

She drew the car to a standstill and turned off the ignition.

"Are we going to get out?" he asked.

There it was again: that tone as if he knew her well. It was more unsettling than the old man's violent temper or the two women probing for information or Andrew ignoring her calls. It made her think that she didn't really exist on the edge of everyone else's lives but in the centre of someone's.

Buffeted by the breeze, she shivered again as she climbed out of the car.

"Come on," he said.

The heat of his chalet hit as soon as he opened the door.

"The wood needs using up," he explained, gesturing to the stove by way of explanation.

She walked around, rubbing her arms, trying to loosen up and appear relaxed. He pulled off his coat, discarding it on a chair, and busied himself in the kitchen, bringing eggs and margarine and milk from the fridge.

"What d'you want me to do?" she asked.

"Nothing."

He switched on the kettle, looking around for clean mugs amongst the pile in the sink. Playfully, she nudged him out of the way and tipped up the bowl of water, letting it drain noisily down the plug hole, relieved at finding something to do.

"You'll need water from the kettle," he said.

She nodded, pushing up her sleeves while he broke eggs into a bowl. She liked the surety of his boots on the bare floor, the ordinariness of domestic noises, the camaraderie of his movements and concentration on his face. And then the kettle boiled. She refilled it as he beat the eggs. There was his familiar easel holding a blank canvas. Jars and paints, brushes and cloths clustered nearby. It wasn't like anybody's place she had been in before.

"Are you going to do that washing up?"

It was easy. It had never been easy with Colin, who hated anyone in his kitchen even though he never cooked. Never easy in the hostel with too many hands and bodies and voices. But here, with him, they were in tune, each somehow knowing where the other would move next.

She devoured the scrambled eggs on toast, drank two mugs of tea, then munched through five biscuits. Jez ate slowly and methodically. They barely spoke, and it didn't matter. Afterwards, he wouldn't let her wash up again and, rolling up his sleeves, plunged his arms into a replenished bowl of hot suds.

"I don't believe it," Lizzie said, pacing up and down. "They were nice flats. The people around were okay. No real oddballs and there were gardens. Trevor could grow carrots or potatoes or whatever. You tell me. Why won't they move? It seems crazy."

"Have you asked them?"

"John and Joyce didn't even get out of the car to look. I think they're all scared of something new."

"Maybe they don't want to move," Jez said, picking up the pan that had held the scrambled eggs.

"Any sane person would move if their house was going to crash into the sea, but they don't seem to want to. Isn't that scarier than moving?"

"Maybe they're more philosophical about it."

"How can anyone be philosophical about it? I'm terrified of this place and I haven't seen half of what you lot have."

When he didn't reply, she looked at him standing at the sink scrubbing hard at the pan with its remains of scrambled egg. Colin never made her breakfast even when they'd first got together; even when the sex was okay. Andrew merely handed her a coffee from the jug already made and told her to help herself to a cellophane-wrapped flapjack or a chocolate bar from the shop. No-one cooked for her, and they certainly hadn't washed up afterwards.

"There's a flat for you if you want it," she said. "Even one for me."

"Tell me why the others didn't like them."

Tell him what? How could she tell him that she'd been so angry she could have kicked them out of the car and left them to find their own way back? She had hated them for turning down a home offered so easily when she'd only ever been offered a room in a hostel. She couldn't tell him she had felt useless and a traitor but also indignant and angry and superior all in one congealed mess of emotion.

"I drove them up to East Moor and we met the housing officer," she said, folding her arms. "Trevor and Mavis looked round one of the flats, but Mavis didn't like it. John wouldn't go in and Joyce didn't even get out of the car. No sorry, no explanation, just no."

"Did you say yes?"

"What I really want is a spaceship out of Yorkshire."

He rinsed the cutlery, forks and knives clattering against each other.

"It doesn't matter what the places are like." She shrugged. "Anywhere is better than here."

He didn't say anything, and she knew she'd insulted him. It wasn't what she meant. His chalet with its paints and driftwood and boxes of apples and wood carvings was better than anywhere she'd been, just as Mavis's china ladies and chipped cups were more endearing than a matching set of mugs. It always went wrong. She always said the wrong thing or didn't say the right thing or didn't say what other people would understand.

"I didn't mean—"

"Maybe they're being cleverer than you think."

"I don't understand."

"If they wait until they're thrown out then Susan Harper's mob will have to pay moving costs."

His shoulder blades kept moving as he scrubbed the pan again. His head slightly bent somehow made him seem taller. She hadn't expected them to be devious.

"I'm impressed." She wondered why she had assumed them to be naïve. "But what if the cliff collapses before Friday?"

"The forecast is good. We should be okay." He rinsed the pan, though scrambled egg remains still coated the inside. She didn't care; she'd seen worse.

"But the others have turned the flats down," she said. "The housing people don't like that. I know. I've dealt with them before. Maybe I should say something in their defence? I could say they're doolally, or you could."

"Why are you so bothered?"

"I'm not." She turned away. What was the point when nothing ever changed? "I mean, I'm going anyway. It makes sense they come as well. Two birds with one stone."

"You sound angry that they're not grateful."

"I'm just frustrated. It doesn't matter two bits to me. Why would it? I just felt we'd trailed down there…but it's fine. Other people will take them up." She hesitated, remembering how Joyce had tried to voice her opinion and had changed her mind.

"John probably has his eye on something better." Again, it was as if he were inside her head, and she knew he was right. They'd probably be offered a mansion with a swimming pool attached. Some people always came out on top.

"You should do the same," he said.

"Hold out for something better?" It was so ludicrous she almost laughed.

"Wait until Friday then they'll have to find somewhere we all agree on." He made it sound simple, as if they'd get a cottage in Rosedale, flowers around the door and a cat curled up by the fire.

"Stay here until Friday? That's not an option."

She walked to the window and looked outside at the other buildings. Randolph was going into Peter's chalet. That was it. No way was she staying in the place.

Chapter Twenty-Three

S HE DROVE ERRATICALLY. Seeing Randolph again after Jez's kindness made her inexplicably panic. This was typical of the way she behaved, but she couldn't help it. She had to get out, get away, do something rather than stand still. At the top, her phone went off. A text from Steve. She couldn't have the flat until the following day. Characteristically, she took that as if she'd never get the flat, that they'd find some reason tomorrow to give it to someone else. Annoyed with herself for believing the tide had turned, she drove too fast until, aware of the speed dial, she took her foot off the pedal and turned through the gates. *You have a choice, you have rights*, she told herself as she pulled up in the main car park. *Use them.*

Inside the entrance hall, low voices emanated from the shop. Lizzie headed straight towards them to find Carol handing three staff members their wage envelopes, the same as the one she'd received barely a day ago.

"Where's Andrew?" she demanded, determined not to be fobbed off any longer.

Carol looked at her with annoyance as the other two turned in surprise.

"He's—" Julie, the raven-haired girl from Maple, began, but Carol interrupted.

"Why?" she asked, slamming the till closed.

"Is he in the library?" Lizzie walked back to the door.

"What d'you want him for?"

"Is Judith with him?"

"You two can start cleaning the Blue Bedroom," Carol said.

"Is the hoover up there?" Julie asked, still looking at Lizzie, where she hovered by the door waiting for Carol to answer her question.

"You'll have to get everything out of the cupboard," Carol said. "Ken? Will you give them a hand?"

Ken followed the two women out of the room as they reluctantly left, obviously desperate to speculate about Lizzie and Andrew. Lizzie didn't care; she didn't care about anything any longer now panic unravelled faster than she could scramble it back together.

"Andrew and Judith are in Spain," Carol said, closing the door and walking back to the till.

"Very funny. Is he out with Jim? Did he say what time he'd be back?"

"I'm not joking. They went last night and left me in charge."

Lizzie looked pityingly at Carol. "You won't mind if I check, will you?" She moved to leave again; she'd find Andrew if she had to tear the door off every room.

"What? Come back here." Surprised, Carol took a moment to follow, but Lizzie was already striding across the hall and pushing open the library door.

Finding the room empty, she turned back to Carol. "Is he upstairs?"

"They're not here." Carol looked embarrassed as she blocked the way. "And you'll be trespassing, Lizzie. We haven't got the run of the house anymore."

Lizzie nudged past without a word and headed directly for the staircase.

"I've told you," Carol said, hurrying in pursuit. "They've gone."

But taking the steps two at a time, Lizzie had already reached the top.

"Come back here!" Carol dashed up the stairs as Lizzie ran along the corridor, opening doors and shaking those that were locked.

***

In the pitch-dark of the priest hide, hearing noises, Andrew tried to move, but his limbs didn't seem to belong to his brain. He didn't feel as if he had any body, merely a sensation of his head being so heavy it felt comforting. Footsteps.

"Help," he rasped. "Help."

***

"What did they say?" Lizzie demanded. "When are they coming back?" Her chest tightened with panic. "What did he say?"

"Come back downstairs," Carol said. She had seen Lizzie like this before.

In the vast master bedroom, with wardrobe doors and drawers showing empty closets, Lizzie swung around to face Carol, who stood in the doorway.

"They never go to Spain this early." Lizzie walked to the bay window and pulled back a curtain. The bonfire looked bigger than ever.

"Cup of tea and we'll slag them off all you want," cajoled Carol.

"He must have left a message for me."

Carol didn't know which was more pitiful—Lizzie's face or her voice. She shook her head slowly. They stood in silence. The empty cupboards, Judith's bare dressing table and the pristine bed said everything.

***

Andrew listened to the throbbing silence. Someone spoke. Who was it? He didn't recognise the voice that called out from his throat. His own voice was robust and confident. The voice that slunk out into the room sounded afraid.

***

Lizzie moved as if in a trance. She tried to think what to do next, where to go. It wasn't only Moorland Castle closing down.

Carol hurried down the main stairwell in pursuit. "I wasn't here when they left."

"Why didn't you phone them?" Lizzie asked, reaching the bottom.

"They're not answering. Believe me, I'm as cheesed off as you are."

"When did they say they'd be in touch?"

"You know Mrs. Booth."

"Then you can make all the decisions?"

They stood by the central table, Carol willing Lizzie to leave; Lizzie felt as incapable of making a decision as Andrew's dog. She could see Ken and Julie loitering at the top of the stairs with the Hoover.

Resting one hand on the table, she tried to clear her head. "Okay," she said. "I'll tell you what this is about." She paused, waiting for Carol to ask, but Carol merely put her head on one side. "Andrew said I could stay in the gatehouse as it's empty, and he said to pick up the key this morning."

Carol still didn't say anything, and then she sucked in her breath and shook her head.

"No-one said anything to me," she said.

"Obviously, but I'm telling you now."

"Is it his?"

"What?"

"Does Judith know?" Carol stared at the floor.

"Oh, for God's sake." The penny dropped. "I told you—I'm not having a kid. I just need somewhere to stay."

The silence grew awkward.

"I'm sorry. They would have told me something as important as that," Carol said, looking up and holding Lizzie's glare.

"If they left in such a hurry, they wouldn't have had chance to tell you every detail of things they'd arranged, would they?" Lizzie could feel she was gaining momentum. "I came in to collect the keys this morning from Andrew, but as he's not here, you can give them to me."

Carol hesitated.

"Don't you believe me?"

"I'll try and contact them again," Carol replied slowly. "I'll ring you when I've got through."

She turned away, taking that as the end of the conversation and expecting Lizzie to leave, but Lizzie didn't move from the table.

"I'm not messing about, Carol. He told me to pick up the keys. I haven't time for all this coming and going."

"I thought you had a boyfriend in Rigby. Why don't you stay with him until I talk to them? I just want to do everything by the book, I'm sure they'll say yes and then I'll give you the key. You can understand that, can't you? That I want to keep things absolutely squeaky clean?"

"Are they in the office or the library?" Lizzie began walking towards the nearest door.

"Come on, be reasonable! I could lose my job!"

"I need to move my stuff in before it gets dark," Lizzie insisted.

Carol seemed to come to a decision and headed into the shop. "I've got work to do and I'm not getting involved. Don't make this difficult for me. Judith trusts me implicitly, and I have to do what I think is best."

"And what about Andrew's promise to me?"

"I only have your word." Carol's voice was measured and quiet.

"You're calling me a liar?"

"I need to check."

"I need it *now*!"

Carol walked behind the desk.

"Stop being so mean!" Lizzie lost it, sick of obstructions and people and nothing ever going right. "I'm not dossing in that manky chalet park another night, Carol. Any decent person would at least offer me their floor, and there are millions of rooms up there."

"Then ask one of your friends for a floor to sleep on." Carol splayed her hands on the desk. "You are not staying here. No way. No. Never. This is their house."

"The gatehouse, then."

"Come back tomorrow."

***

Carol glared at Lizzie, willing her to stop asking. She'd never liked her, but she could tell she was desperate. She had that crazy look on her face again, but what else could Carol say?

***

Andrew listened to his breathing slowing down. He tapped his palm against the floor; it made no sound. He could hear voices, or maybe they were in his head. He opened his mouth, but no sound came. A warm, thick liquid filled his throat, but he couldn't gag. He couldn't feel any part of his body except a gentle ache in his lungs lulling him to sleep. He no longer tried to lift up his head from the stone floor. Female voices rang out, but they weren't real. They merged with the resonance in his ears and the vibration in his chest. With relief, he realised his torso, legs, arms, fingers and face had lost all sensation. The air changed. A door slammed. He forced out a last word. It sounded to him something like help. The pulsing of his blood grew fainter. He tried to call out again, but liquid filled his nasal cavities and all that came out was a dull gurgle and a dribble that mingled with the thick stickiness he lay in.

***

Car tyres skidding over gravel, Lizzie pulled away from the castle, dreading another night in the car but willing to put up with anything rather than return to the chalet park. And there was the gatehouse, at the end of the drive, tempting and empty. Braking, she peered at the dark windows, turned off the ignition and got out, slamming the car door hard. She covered the ground quickly and grabbed the front door latch, jiggling it in frustration. Locked. Though it was futile, she thumped the wood repeatedly then, as if remembering something, hurried around to the back door, pushing her way past sagging bushes to throw her weight against it, wincing with pain when it refused to give way.

A small top window stood ajar. She looked around for a ladder, a dustbin, something to stand on and reach—even a nearby tree—but nothing came to hand. Kicking her way back around the building, she studied the windows with their ornate grilles covering the glass. She hadn't noticed them before, but they must have been there, so ingratiated into the stone was the metal. With both hands, she grabbed the bars of one and shook relentlessly, but the grid remained rigid. Looking up at the upper windows, she saw that they were all protected by similar grilles.

Briefly, she thought about driving back up to the castle and ransacking the desk in the library, rifling through the till and forcing open the safe to find the keys, but it was most likely useless. Carol would have hidden them by now. She'd had enough. She'd get out now, head inland, reach York, find something, someone to stay with.

Driving north along the cliff road, she tried to stop shaking. She hated this feeling of panic; hated it as much as she hated her anger. She needed space from it, a place to breathe, to feel the universe cool her head, and with that thought, she opened the window and pressed her foot harder on the accelerator.

The cliff stretched barren. Flat outcrops of coarse grass lined the edge on one side of the grey coast road; on the other, rusted railings holding back the undergrowth of the estate boundary strobed. She knew the road well because she drove down it once a week to the village hall where she posed for the local art club. It wouldn't take her long to join the A171, where she'd fly with such speed away from Carol, Andrew and the entire wretched estate.

The heat in her head took a long while to abate this time. The banging in her forehead had reached its peak. She hated Andrew as much as she hated herself for believing in him. She hated Jez for opening the inklings of hope. She put a hand to her cheek. It blazed like a furnace.

She sped past scrub and sea, but she needed the road to go on forever. The wind caught her hair, and she narrowed her eyes against the rush of air. There were no other vehicles in sight. Lifting her foot off the pedal as she neared the left-hand turning that met the high wall of the estate, she felt the car begin to float. She loved that feeling of weightlessness. The car didn't lose momentum as it swung around the corner, only there was something there, in line with the bonnet—another object, bright and floating, the figure of a woman, a familiar skirt blowing in the wind. The car rocked as she slammed her foot on the brake. The crack of a tyre bursting rang out, and a flurry of crows rose squawking into the air from high, dark trees.

Chapter Twenty-Four

SECONDS LATER, THE car faced back towards the way it had come. Hands gripping the steering wheel, Lizzie stared at the inert body lying about twenty metres away. The woman's bright skirt lifted in a gust of wind. Startled crows settled again in the tall trees. Branches creaked. The car engine ticked. Lizzie concentrated on taking deep breaths.

Beyond the woman's body, the sea sparkled. The sky spread clear and blue. Several minutes past. The engine's ticking slowed. The woman's skirt fluttered. Lizzie peeled her hands off the steering wheel. Opened the door. Her hands shook. She waited, but the tremors slipped through her body. She looked at the dry, crumbling ground and placed her feet one at a time on the road. She let the moments pass before prising herself out. Gripping the car door, she raised her head to look at the mound of vivid clothing. She didn't know how long she leaned against the car door before walking tentatively towards the crumpled cerise and blue pile, but it seemed like hours. Staring down at the twisted body, her chest tightened. A breeze ruffled her hair. Gulls wheeled overhead. She could hear the sea hitting rocks. No traffic drove by. Nobody walked along the clifftops. Nobody to ask what to do.

It was the woman from the chalet park. The one who'd worn a kimono and cooked the hottest chilli she'd ever tasted. One leg turned unnaturally. Apart from that and the fact that her eyes stared skywards, and that she was lying in the middle of the road, she could have been taking a nap. Marilyn Hopper. That was her name. Lizzie crouched down and splayed her hands on the ground for balance. She knew she ought to check, but it was obvious Marilyn was dead.

Lizzie looked around. The dense woodland over the wall seemed to watch her. A twig snapped. A rabbit sped over the mound. She puffed out her cheeks. She didn't know how to check if Marilyn was alive. She walked back to the car, sat in the driver's seat, pulled the door closed and switched on the engine. It turned over, and she watched the wind catch the cobalt-blue skirt again. She should have tucked it in to stop it blowing.

Her bag had fallen into the foot well; retrieving it, she rummaged inside. Pressing in Andrew's name, she listened to the dial tone. When it remained unanswered, she leant back her head, fumbling to turn off the engine. Surely, even in Spain, he should answer. Silence. Scrolling down the contacts again, she pressed another name.

It didn't take long for the police car to appear. Phil Chorley walked towards Marilyn's body then bent down stiffly, lifting one wrist and leaning close to her face. Lizzie watched through the windscreen as he circled the corpse. He registered skid marks that she hadn't noticed.

"I think a tyre blew," she said as he opened her door. "I heard it go."

Without saying a word, Phil strolled slowly around the car, looking down at the tyres. When he reached the boot, Lizzie closed her eyes, unable to watch. She listened to his careful tread. She must be dreaming. This couldn't be real. She wondered how any of the last few days could be real. She was in a parallel universe. She'd wake up at any moment.

Phil stood by the open door. He glanced at the dent in the bonnet. "I'll have to breathalyse you," he said.

She followed him back to the police vehicle as he talked rapidly on his transmitter. She kept her eyes fixed on the sea.

He opened the boot of the police car, then stood silently, not looking at her as she breathed into the apparatus. Checking it, he held it up to show her there was no evidence of alcohol in her system. Without speaking, they walked past the body and returned to Lizzie's car.

"What speed were you doing?" he said, peering inside.

"Aren't you going to say anything to calm me down?"

"What do you expect me to say when there's a dead body lying there?"

Tears welled up. "I don't know. Something reassuring?"

He glanced away. "I phoned for the ambulance," he said.

"You should've phoned 999, not me. Shit, Lizzie. I'll have to take a statement."

"I wanted somebody I knew who wouldn't..." She paused. "Somebody who knows me."

"What speed were you going?"

Lizzie shrugged. She pressed her hands together. "I wasn't looking at the dial. The road was empty."

He glanced at Marilyn and shook his head. "How come you didn't see her in time?"

"I turned the corner and she was just standing there."

"For Christ's sake, didn't you try and avoid her?"

"Why d'you think there's skid marks?" Lizzie felt a surge of anger at his tone. "The tyre went. I bet you couldn't have controlled your car."

"This is bollocks, Lizzie. All the tyres are fine."

"Don't mess with me, Phil, I heard it." Her voice came out too loud. "The front one. The passenger side."

"Stop it, Lizzie. You're going to need legal aid."

She looked down at the nearest tyre and kicked it before striding rapidly to the passenger side. Bending, she ran a hand over the tyre. She looked up at Phil. "I *heard* it," she repeated. She slid her hand over the metal until she reached the rear wheel. She barely gave the fourth a glance.

"I did hear it blow," she said. "I don't know why the tyres look okay. Maybe something blew in the engine, but whatever it was, there was no way I could have avoided her."

He looked back at Marilyn, then the junction, then at the sky. Eventually, he looked back at Lizzie.

"Have you got your driving licence?"

She reached inside the car for her bag.

"Where were you going?"

"Does it matter?"

He checked the licence and handed it back. She didn't like the look on his face and wondered briefly what she ever saw in him.

"How long before you called me?"

"Straight away."

"Where were you coming from?"

Her mouth dried up her words. She felt sick. She was going to throw up. She began to sway.

"You'd better sit down," he said.

Lizzie slumped sideways onto the driver's seat and leant her head on her knees. It seemed barely a moment before she heard the ambulance arrive. Two people climbed down. Another police car arrived, and Phil went off to speak to the driver. Lizzie glanced away at the sound of a camera clicking as a red-haired policeman took photographs. Phil busied himself talking to the ambulance crew. Once the body had been photographed, the female medic crouched and rested her ear against Marilyn's chest whilst looking at her watch. She lifted Marilyn's wrist, watching sixty more seconds tick away. Laying the arm back down, she flicked a narrow torch over the unflinching pupils and finally looked up at her colleague then at Phil and the other officer Lizzie thought she recognised.

She said something, and they all looked at her. *What?* They huddled in a deep discussion.

Lizzie looked away. Let them talk about her. She was used to it. She leaned her head back and closed her eyes listening to footsteps approaching.

"D'you want them to look at you?" Phil asked.

She could hardly get the word out. "Who?"

He nodded over his shoulder. The female medic shaded her eyes as she stared at them.

"No." Lizzie shook her head. "I'm fine."

Phil waved his hand, and the medics disappeared inside the ambulance.

"Why couldn't you have missed her?" he said. "You've only made it worse."

She didn't know what to say. She'd turned the wheel and pressed the brakes straight away. She had tried. She hadn't been drinking. She opened her mouth, but her jaw felt too heavy to form words. She sensed his impatience.

"I told you," her voice came out like someone else's. "She was smack bang in the middle of the road. I swerved but…"

He glanced at the high wall of the estate and a green, wooded knoll rising behind. "You were in a bad mood, weren't you?"

Lizzie felt the sway of injustice.

"Will I go to prison?"

"Depends how angry the family are with you."

"She has no family," said Lizzie. "I know who she is."

"You know? Why didn't you say? Who is she?"

"I don't *know her*, know her," Lizzie's voice rose louder. "She lived at the chalet park where I've been staying. I was going to tell you about it. It's horrible, full of weird people. A chalet collapsed into the sea. I was going to…but…well, things happened." She stopped, looked at the ground, at her feet. She turned her head, looking away from him.

"What's her name?"

"Marilyn Hopper."

"Here." He held out a packet of cigarettes, then flicked the lighter. Lizzie shook her head, and he raised his eyebrows. She felt the wave of now familiar tears mounting and kept her eyes on the road in an attempt to stop them. He put the packet back in his pocket.

"Phil? Can I have a word?" the other officer called, lifting his mobile away from his ear.

Phil raised his hand.

"How d'you know she's no family?" he asked.

"I can't remember." Lizzie hugged herself. "Someone said— I think it was a woman called Mavis…or it could have been Jez. No, it was Mavis. I'm sure it was her. She was talking about her family. I don't think any of them have anyone much. She said Marilyn was on her own, but that doesn't mean she has no children, does it? There could be an ex-husband or sisters. Brothers. I don't know. I just got the impression. I'm probably wrong. I don't know why I said anything. I'm usually wrong, aren't I?"

"Okay, okay." Phil walked away, half turned to her, half to the officer Lizzie recognised—*what is his name?*—who beckoned him over, still listening on the phone. "We'll go over this again later."

Lizzie sat on the grass at the junction, looking out to sea as they measured skid marks and took stock of her car. *Simon Bradbury.* She'd remembered. Her senses were coming back. The sun felt warm now. She could smell grass and soil. A car passed quietly along the road before she registered its approach.

Eventually, Simon came and stood behind her. She knew without turning around it wasn't Phil. Phil had scuffed boots, but Simon's were shiny as gloss paint. She wanted quiet, no talking, no movement, only stillness.

Sunlight sparkled on the water, and she could feel her cheeks growing pink. The damp grass beneath her palms was reassuring. *Fade away,* she thought. *Please let me fade away.*

"Miss?" His voice cut in. "D'you need anything?"

Her elbow rested on her raised knee, hand on forehead. Did she need anything?

"I'm fine." She turned, catching his eye.

He remained still. What was he doing? The only sounds were the breeze in the grass and a gentle shush of waves. She had no control over anything. She turned her eyes to the water.

"What d'you think, Phil?" She sensed Simon look over his shoulder and heard footsteps approach.

"Post-mortem." Phil stood on the other side of her, hands in pockets.

"Is it normal to do a post-mortem?" Lizzie kept her eyes on a large boat nearing the horizon.

Phil faltered. "They always need to check the body."

"Are you sure you're all right, Miss?" asked Simon.

Lizzie walked towards her car while the other two continued talking. She knew they had spoken to their boss and that they'd talked about her; that they were deciding what to say to her, how to say it, what words to use to say she was under arrest.

"Sorry, you can't drive." Phil jogged to catch her up. "And I'll need your keys."

She glanced at the other officer, but he was crouching, pretending to examine the tarmac as if he hadn't heard. She looked at Phil. He shook his head.

"Keys," he repeated, holding out one hand. "Got to treat you like I would anyone else."

She hesitated, feeling their hard edges in her palm.

Phil snatched them. "I'll run you back from the station."

"Haven't you already asked me all you need to know?" She was tired. Tired of everything.

"I need to take down your statement."

"Can't you do it here?"

He shook his head. "If you don't want to hang around at the station, I'll drive you back to the park after, but then you'll have to stay put until someone comes to see you again."

"That's it?" she said. She didn't know him, in his uniform, with that voice and that look on his face.

"Then you'll be charged," he said.

"What with?"

"For Christ's sake, Lizzie. I'm not sure. Could be manslaughter." His voice was too loud.

They both waited for the red-haired officer to come over, but he didn't. No-one looked their way.

"I'll need my things from the car," she said.

A tent had been erected where Marilyn had lain. It seemed worse than the exposed body. She hurried past, aware that some of the officers standing around were watching her. Phil opened the boot. She leant against the car door. She tried not to notice how he ran his hands around the sides of the boot, breathing in deeply over and over.

He eventually lifted out her suitcase. "We'll let you know when you can have it back," he said. His eyes flicked from side to side, and she realised he was looking at the bedding. "D'you want this box?"

"What box?"

"These bits of food?"

Before she reached him, the noise of vehicles caught their attention. Half a dozen cars and vans pulled up at the end of the road. Phil looked as nervous as she felt. He straightened his jacket. She pushed back her hair. Plain-clothed personnel and police officers with dogs swarmed like the first attack of an army.

Chapter Twenty-Five

POLICE TAPE FLUTTERED across the stretch of side road as it had at the entrance to the cliff path at the chalet park. Signs announcing an accident and calling for witnesses stood at a distance from the vehicles parked half on the verge of the cliff highway. Inland, another sign and more tape would be closing off the road at the junction with the A171.

The road linking the two filled with activity. In the passenger seat of Phil's car, Lizzie waited for someone to tell her when she could leave.

**

Chief Inspector Harry Sayles studied the tyre marks on the road again before scrutinising the battered Renault. A small, grubby, white tent protected Marilyn's body from view. He walked up to the canvas flap and held it back.

"Well?" he said.

A freckled face looked up. "The bullet definitely did it," the woman said, "but the car hitting her didn't help."

Sayles looked around at his officers. He needed that gun and a suspect as soon as possible. He glanced at the grassy knoll and almost-bare trees towering over the high wall of the estate and then at the long, straight road that led inland away from the sea. The fact that the deceased had been thrown by a car and landed here rather than where she would otherwise have dropped, complicated matters. And this, after the business with the chalet on the beach and the two dead bodies there. Why did it all have to happen at once?

An officer with rolled-up shirt sleeves kept his Alsatian on a tight lead as he followed the verge on the near side of the wall, stopping as the dog sniffed for a moment before moving on. Sayles' deputy, Greg Taylor, said he'd speak to the driver. Sayles left him to it. He wanted that weapon.

He looked down the long, straight road inland again. No houses or side roads there to explore. Open scrub made it impossible for anyone to hide. He looked towards Phil's vehicle and Greg leaning against the passenger door, talking to the woman seated inside. He'd seen her at the station before. She was an odd one. Hearing the sound of raised voices, he looked up sharply to see several officers, two with dogs and three others with beaters, clambering up the small hill inside the estate.

"Careful," he shouted, waving his arms. "You're not on an afternoon picnic."

He rubbed his head, going over what the forensic team had deemed to tell him at that point. The bullet had been fired from a rifle aimed at a distance to the victim's left, entered straight into the heart and been fatal. Who the hell around here killed anything but rabbits? Must have been an accident. The shooter had scarpered, though. Probably some poacher from Beamstown or possibly further inland. Stupid sod, giving him paperwork and a pain in the backside. And the woman. Who the hell was Marilyn Hopper?

The men with their dogs scoured the area meticulously for signs of any disturbance. Several stretched up to examine branches while others prodded dense holly bushes and laurels.

"Make sure you look up as well as down," Sayles ordered. He strode up to the wall before turning abruptly and walking back until his view became obscured by the buttress of stone.

Returning to the junction, he looked up and down the empty road. The wall ran along the boundary of the estate to his right, ending as spiked railings took their place. On the far side ran a wide stretch of long, untamed grass and then the sea, vast and glittering. He turned back and studied the activity around the car and tent. He wondered if it had been a more local poacher who had struck her and, panicking, run off. Poaching was rife and on the increase, and several landowners had been on his back about it. He closed his eyes and listened to a distant bird, a dog barking and the last of the year's leaves rustling loose from the trees.

Bullets like the one lodged in Hopper's body could be found in rabbits and foxes all over Yorkshire. It was from the type of gun fired on farm after farm across the moors. It was imperative they found the weapon, and from the information they had, it was most likely local. He didn't like it. He'd much have preferred it to be some offcumder. He shifted his feet. He'd best make a start, and that meant calling at Moorland Castle.

He was relieved when Greg Taylor strolled over to join him.

"Well?" Sayles asked, realising it was becoming his catch phrase.

Taylor took a swig of bottled water. "She's in shock."

"Did she see anyone else around?"

"Didn't even see the woman she hit until she was flying through the air."

Sayles rubbed his nose. Bradbury had checked her record. Clean licence; a bit of a disturbance at her boyfriend's flat. Nothing proved. He waved Phil Chorley over.

"Have you got a statement?"

"I was going to do it at the station, but we were hanging about, so I've taken it here. If that's all right with you?"

"Take her home," Sayles said. "We'll talk to her again tomorrow."

"Do I stay with her, Sir? She had all her belongings in her car. I'll have to get the bedding out of the boot. Is that okay?"

Sayles studied him for a moment, then shook his head. "She can't go anywhere without her car, and that park, from how you describe it, will keep her isolated. No, you don't need to stay. Just read her the riot act."

Taylor watched Phil head off. This Lizzie Juniper seemed properly shaken. He hated incidents like this; everyone suffered. He'd have to take a look at that chalet park for himself as well. From what Taylor had said, nobody should be there, and now he'd sent this young girl back. *Bloody place.* He mentally retracted all he'd ever said about Hull.

***

Moorland Castle looked abandoned when they pulled up at the front entrance. The door stood wide open, but there were no signs of life. They strolled inside.

"Hello?" Taylor called out.

Noises emanated from the closed glass door to the left, and they headed straight for it. The gift shop was in a state of disarray with books in boxes and shelves half emptied. Two young women stared at them in surprise.

The blonde stood up. "We're closed now until Easter," she said.

Sayles and Taylor both held out their IDs.

"We want to talk to either Mr. or Mrs. Booth," Sayles said.

The girls answered in unison: "They're not here."

"Which one of you is in charge, then?" Sayles asked after their jumbled explanation as to where the owners had gone. Again, their answers were inconclusive. The only clear facts were that they were minions and that Carol Bailey, the manager, had gone on an errand. In her absence, they could speak to Jim Wright, the estate manager. They found him in a building around the back in the courtyard.

Sayles surveyed a line of rifles and guns in a locked case. He didn't know why, but he hadn't expected to find so many and on display. The office was extremely tidy too. He hadn't expected that either. Jim Wright was watching him. He definitely looked as if he didn't like people—a man after Sayles' own heart.

"There's one missing," he said, looking at Jim.

"Mrs. Booth backed the Range Rover into the rack before I'd had chance to load them up for the shoot. The trigger were broke on that one. We were one gun down."

Taylor looked at the rack of guns. "How did that happen?"

"She knocked shoot rack right over. We were lucky it weren't more."

Taylor studied the rifles one by one. "Hasn't the gun been fixed?"

"Mr. Booth said to keep it for spares. We rarely need twelve now."

"Are the shoots not attracting numbers anymore?"

"On the contrary. They're big business. We get pop stars, politicians—even supermarket chiefs these days. They tend to bring their own guns, that's all. Take any of them out." He nodded to Sayles. "They're not loaded."

Taylor immediately took hold of the nearest and felt its weight before smelling the metal.

"Any residue?" Sayles asked.

Taylor grimaced at his carelessness, took out his handkerchief and held the rifle more carefully.

"You won't damage any by handling them." Jim turned away and perched on the edge of the desk." "Takes a badly driven Range Rover to do that. That one hasn't been fired in over a month."

"So where's this spare parts gun kept?" Sayles asked, looking around the pristine office.

Jim unlocked an old fortified cupboard in the corner and gathered various pieces from a shelf. He tipped the sections on the desk, then a box filled with springs and various small parts. Sayles rummaged through, holding pieces together, at a loss how they should fit. "Did you know Marilyn Hopper, Mr. Wright?"

"Yes, I knew her," Jim answered the less than subtle enquiry while he watched Taylor bag up the gun parts. Straight away, Sayles knew what Jim's tone meant; even so, he thought a man like Jim Wright and the woman he'd seen out on the road were incongruous acquaintances. This man seemed dignified, quiet, if with little money; she looked coarse, smelt of alcohol and had a wad of notes in her purse. That pointed to random poacher again. It obviously wasn't an opportunist or a chance holdup that had led to her demise.

Taylor interrupted his thoughts. "Do any of these get used?"

Sayles waited. They had to be seen to follow all leads.

"Just the two at this end," Jim said. "I sometimes need to scare off birds."

"These two?" Taylor indicated.

"I'm very strict over my vegetables," he said, "especially when I'm planting out. Mr. Booth likes to see off any foxes, but we've not been bothered much this year. He's not been out lately, if that's what you're thinking."

They could weigh up this gamekeeper easily. Worked here all his life, lived in a nearby cottage since he was born, generations of his family based in the vicinity. Didn't socialise much; didn't do anything much except look after the estate; above all, loyal to the landed gentry.

"We may want to ask you more questions later," Sayles said. "And I'll need the key to this case. This the only one?"

"Mr. Booth has the other." Jim took the rifle and put it back into the cupboard. Sayles and Taylor watched in silence before catching each other's eye.

"Right. Well, thanks for your time. We can see you're busy with the big event for tomorrow night." Sayles headed for the door. "Shame Mr. Booth won't be there. He always seems to relish presiding over the fire."

Jim secured the gun case and locked it deftly. "I have nothing to do with that. If you're wanting to know anything, ask Madam up at the house."

"Is Mrs. Booth still here?"

"Carol Bailey. She's in charge when they're off gallivanting in Spain." He began putting pieces back into the box on the desk. "Right madam, she is."

"Carol Bailey's the one who lives with Officer Chorley, Sir," Taylor said to Sayles.

Sayles caught Jim Wright's eye. He'd tell Taylor later about keeping private matters private. "You wouldn't happen to know why they went to Spain earlier than normal this year?"

"It'll have been *her* idea," Jim said, crossing to the corner cupboard and checking the door was properly closed.

"Did either of the Booths know Marilyn Hopper?"

"Ask Carol Bailey."

Taylor forced a laugh. "She seems to be the one who knows everything round here."

"It's unusual for them to go before the firework display, isn't it?" Sayles persisted.

"And lots of people going to be around who wouldn't usually be," Taylor added.

Jim shrugged again. He wasn't one for hanging around social events; they could see that.

"We'll ask Carol," Taylor sighed. "And the key?"

Jim placed it firmly on the desk.

"Who's lighting the fire this year?"

Sayles pocketed the key. "We'll ask Carol," he said.

"Marilyn Hopper was an alcoholic, you know." A voice from the doorway made them all jump. "Hello. I'm Carol Bailey." The woman moved swiftly back outside. Jim shook his head and began checking the line of rifles.

Chapter Twenty-Six

THERE DIDN'T APPEAR to be anyone about at the chalet park when Phil carried in Lizzie's suitcase and bedding and instructed her not to leave. It was almost dusk, and he turned on the lights.

She made him a cup of tea before he had chance to stop her. She spooned in the four sugars he always took and placed it on the table.

"What were the dogs for?" she asked, folding her arms.

He blew on the steaming mug. "Procedure."

She laughed. "You don't know anything. You're nothing to do with real crime. You just deal with moving people on when they're minding their own business."

He tipped back the mug, burning the top of his mouth, before placing it on the table. "I'll see you in the morning," he said. "Don't mess up."

Grabbing the mug as soon as the door closed behind him, Lizzie hurled it into the sink. It didn't break but spun noisily, spraying out its milky-brown contents whilst retaining the mound of sweet, greying sludge in the bottom.

She kicked the sink unit, then turned and slammed the sole of her shoe against it. The small box of food on the worktop rattled. Through the open doorway, she could see her case and duvet and pillows hastily dumped on the bed. Panic rose in her stomach as sounds from outside put her on immediate alert. She waited for Phil's car engine to start up.

Then someone shouted; it sounded like Randolph. She closed her eyes, tense. *Let him kick off. Let Phil see what a place he's abandoned me in.* She waited for more raised voices but instead heard the sticky scream of strong tape being stretched out. She peered from behind a curtain and saw Phil pressing down police tape across Marilyn's doorway. Randolph dragged on a cigarette and watched.

"What's that?" Randolph jerked his head at the taped door.

Phil glanced back at Lizzie's chalet, and she moved out of sight.

"Police tape."

"I meant, what's it for?"

"It's to protect Miss Hopper's belongings."

Lizzie smiled. Phil would be cringing under this scrutiny. She wished she could see his face.

"How's she going to get back in?" Randolph demanded loudly.

"She's not coming back right now. She's been in an accident." Phil turned around. He looked embarrassed.

"What sort of accident?"

This was it. She waited for the explosion. Randolph wouldn't take this lightly, and Phil would have to get her out of the place for safety's sake. She shoved the mug back into the box before peering through the window again.

Phil walked slowly down the steps towards his car. Randolph caught up with him and walked alongside. She knew how Phil would be kicking himself for saying anything and wondered what he would say next.

"What sort of accident, I said?" Randolph repeated, directly below the window. Once again, Lizzie drew back.

"Car accident." Phil opened the driver's door. "Now if you'll excuse me."

"What? Is she all right? What happened?"

"I'm afraid I can't give details."

"Is she in the James Cook?"

To her surprise, the man seemed genuinely concerned, and she almost wished Phil would tell him and put him out of his misery.

"I'm sorry," Phil said, "I'll be back tomorrow and I'll be able to tell you more then."

"What's she got to do with it?" Randolph jerked his head in Lizzie's direction.

"Nothing."

"You brought her back."

Lizzie stepped right away from the window. If Randolph saw her watching, he'd be up the steps in a shot, breaking down the door and probably strangling her before Phil could blink. He must have seen Phil bring her down the track in his police car and take her inside, along with the bedding, suitcase and box of food. He'd have noted how long Phil had stayed in there—long enough to have a cuppa—and he'd wonder what had happened to her Renault, then put two and two together and make six hundred thousand.

"Let's not go jumping to any conclusions," Phil said as if reading her mind. He opened the car door and climbed in. "I'll be back tomorrow," he said, shaking his head when Randolph didn't answer and pulling the door closed. Randolph still didn't say a word.

Quietly, Lizzie checked the front door again. It remained locked. She crossed the room and flung herself on top of the bed. Twisting, she tried to pull the duvet over her, but both legs became entwined with pockets of down and it wouldn't yank free. Exasperated, she stood, wafted the tangled quilt so that it spread out. Clambering underneath, she remained still, trying to think what to do. Should she keep quiet and stay—wait for Phil to come back? Should she make a run for it up to the main road and try and flag down a car? Knowing her luck, none would pass all night. She could catch the bus, assuming they passed more than once a day. She gripped the duvet. She was ready to throw things. Kick things. Break everything she could get her hands on. She knew this feeling that was welling up. It happened for the day before her period whenever she had too much to drink or someone said the wrong thing. Some people said she had it too often. If Randolph or anyone was stupid enough to come into her chalet now, she wouldn't be held responsible.

Concentrating on the rise and fall of her breath, she tried to slow everything down—the panic, the fizzing, all the questions bouncing around her head. It was pointless to wish she hadn't been driving too fast; she always drove too fast. In future, she might not be driving at all. In future, she must stay in control. She could do nothing about Marilyn's face and broken body now. The bright-red lips in the pale oval caught mid-speech, a flicker of lilac eyelids, the incongruous gaudiness of clothes and hair, fake and woolly and too long and those horrible dark birds peppering the blue sky. She covered her head at the memory of the raucous crowing and clenched her shoulders against the thudding impact.

Curled foetus-like, she no longer listened to her breath. The noise the crows made as they'd flocked upwards like they knew something dreadful was going to happen filled her head. She'd been sure it had been a burst tyre; she'd heard it as the car swung around the corner, but then the birds rose up and the dark, speckled sky filled her view. Marilyn, caught in the road as the car sped too fast past trees, had been obscured by tiny stones flying up and striking the windscreen with sharp cracks.

Sleep, she willed. *Sleep.*

"I didn't do it on purpose. I didn't mean it. It wasn't me."

But there was no-one to apologise to. She was alone. They could take her away, stand her in the deep-brown wooden box of the accused, question and stare and judge, and no-one would speak up in her defence.

"I didn't kill her!"

Stern faces with despising eyes confirming her guilt would pass sentence.

"I hit her, but I didn't kill her!"

The quiet of the court meant nothing. Guilt seared across the room whatever she said. Whatever she'd done. Ever. In her entire life. Walking with acceptance, without response, heavy-limbed and heavy-eyed, the fight taken out. She didn't care; her body and mind were too tired. *Don't give me a caution or a speeding fine or community service. Put me in a cell, feed me and let me sleep.* Freedom was overrated; she didn't want it anymore. She didn't want to have to think for herself. Incarceration would come as a blessing. And she didn't want any do-good visitors either.

She slept dreamlessly for two hours, and it was pitch-black outside when she woke. Perspiring, she pushed back the duvet and the chill air caught her skin. She looked at the time on her phone then tossed it down, glad of the glow from the other room spilling through the open doorway. It didn't matter that Phil had told her to stay put. It was more important to keep the images of Marilyn at bay. She had somewhere else she needed to be. She'd find a way of getting there. A car was bound to be passing. Loads of people took the back road to Beamstown or Rigby. Loads of people wanted to speed and not get caught.

Besides, she needed the money. Yanking the suitcase on its side, she rifled through clothes, pulled out a dark-blue dressing gown and, shoving it into a plastic bag, looked around for where she'd kicked off her boots.

Chapter Twenty-Seven

S HE HELD THE door open a crack. It was a cold but clear evening, and the moon, just beginning to wane, lit up the field. From somewhere too close, Randolph's and Peter's voices sounded intense, but Jez spoke more calmly.

"Come away." Jez touched Randolph's arm. Swearing, Randolph shrugged off his hand.

She'd become accustomed to difficult customers at The Swan, but she didn't fancy confronting this character right now. She'd never met anyone so cantankerous.

"You bloody well are, Peter," the old man yelled even though Peter walked close enough to hear a whisper.

There he was again, always telling people what to do. She looked at her mobile. She couldn't wait much longer. She peered out again. One of them held a torch. Jez had placed an arm around the old man's shoulders; Peter, the smaller and thinner of the three, walked alongside, nodding his head. Jez stepped back unexpectedly, releasing Randolph. The trio stood for a moment, but she couldn't hear what they said, then Jez looked up and the other two walked away. Convinced he'd seen her, she listened for the sound of footsteps approaching her door, but none came.

To hell with it. She had to set off, otherwise she'd never get there in time. They didn't know she wasn't supposed to leave the park, and what would they do even if they did know? It wasn't their business. Stepping determinedly outside, she noticed clouds had covered the moon. Fumbling, she struggled with the key in the lock.

"You should turn on the light." Jez's voice made her jump.

She turned sharply to see two figures approaching. *Christ.* They were like ninjas appearing from nowhere.

"You don't need to do that here," said John, flashing a large hurricane lamp.

She made a show of putting the key in her bag and marching down the steps.

"What's happened to your car?" Jez asked.

"It's in at the garage."

"Which one?"

"You won't know it."

"There's nowhere close. Must have been a long walk—or did you get a lift?" Jez followed with John close behind.

She glanced at him, then back at John. They were creepy. She increased her pace, relieved that the lights of the chalets lit a path through the field. Randolph might appear at any moment. She couldn't bear his questions, especially as he knew Phil had brought her down. Randolph must have told Jez and John. Suddenly realising how vulnerable she was, she kept her eyes on the uneven ground and broke into a trot.

"Where are you going?"

She tripped but managed to stay on her feet.

"Don't go so fast."

She turned abruptly. "Do either of you have a torch I could borrow?"

"D'you need a lift?" Jez asked.

John caught up with them but didn't offer his lantern.

"Thank you, I'll catch the bus," she said. "D'you think I could borrow that?" She held out her hand to John.

"Ten o'clock in the morning, two in the afternoon," said Jez. "It's just after six in the evening now."

"I'll phone for a taxi."

"It'll be expensive," John chipped in, "and there's no reception for your mobile."

"There is at the top." Lizzie shoved the phone back into her jacket pocket and started walking again. She was almost at the track, but it was impossible to see the rise and fall of the ground, and the dim lights on the sides of the chalets only made the place more unsettling rather than safe.

"John'll lend you his lantern," Jez shouted.

"I don't mind," John raised his voice.

"Give me the keys," Jez said.

"What?" John sounded taken aback.

"Give me the keys. I'll take her."

"But—"

"Come on, quick!" He wriggled his fingers.

Lizzie stopped at the jingle of keys. A car door opened. She looked over her shoulder. By the time she reached the top road, phoned for a taxi and waited for it to arrive, she might as well not have bothered. An engine started up.

She quickened her pace. The car horn beeped. She tried to make up her mind what to do, until she allowed for the fact that there were worse things than being driven by a sad, bitter ex-businessman. She strode over to the car. Stopped. John stood beside the vehicle. That meant Jez sat behind the wheel. If Jez drove her, it was going to be a very different journey to the uncomplicated one she'd thought it was going to be. She had no choice. No bus. No money for a taxi. No passers-by. Resigned, she slumped into the passenger seat. John closed the door and stepped back. Jez looked straight ahead at the grass illuminated by the headlights, waiting. She was determined not to say anything, annoyed he didn't drive off straight away, but just as she was about to speak, he let down the handbrake.

"Seat belt?" he said.

***

John strolled back through the chilly night air along the line of chalets. Reluctantly, he opened his front door and took off his thick coat and gloves. He took his time, trying to ignore the voices emanating from the next room.

"Is that you, John?"

He slapped his hat down on the kitchen unit just inside the door.

"Who else were you expecting?" He turned out the lantern. The murmuring continued, and he knew he couldn't put it off any longer. He took a deep breath and went through to the living room, where the dining table had been pulled out and Joyce, Trevor and Mavis were already seated. John joined them, glaring at his wife as if daring her to say something, and although she looked as if she did want to speak, she didn't.

Trevor broke the silence as he raised his glass. "I think a toast is in order."

They all paused, waiting for someone else to make it, but no-one did, and when the expectant looks at John produced no appropriate response, they raised their glasses, tapped them against each other and made the crystal ring.

"Now you're here, we can begin serving," said Joyce, rising to her feet. "I just hope it's not burnt."

Joyce apologised for not giving them pheasant as she had hoped. She smiled at Trevor in gratitude when he praised the tender rabbit. Mavis insisted over-enthusiastically that she preferred rabbit to any bird and they were grateful that she and John had gone to all this trouble. Trevor again broke the ensuing silence by adding that they should have done this more often, and to that they all agreed, took another drink, another mouthful, another furtive glance at their neighbour, and were glad that they hadn't.

**

Neither Lizzie nor Jez said a word as they drove along the top road. Lizzie found his silence unbearable; adamant she was not going to break it, she stared out of the side window into the darkness of the grounds as they sped past the estate. As a driver, she'd never given much thought to the confined space of a car before, but in the dark with only headlights illuminating their way and no steering wheel to hold or rear-view mirror to check, she became acutely conscious that a passenger had no distractions. The sound of their breathing amplified, and she could almost hear her blood pumping around her body. She steeled herself not to look at him but out of the corner of her eye sensed his leg relax in her direction and his arm sway as his fingers tapped the curve of plastic. The car was an ancient automatic, too smooth and boat-like for her taste. She should have been in her own car, in the driver's seat, changing through gears, looking out for oncoming traffic and travelling alone. *Alone*, she wanted to yell, and not with some weird stranger.

She hated the police; they had gained nothing by confiscating her car, only caused her to take more risks. She closed her eyes, remembering Marilyn's stunned face and the shameful feeling of knowing she'd done something wrong and been found out.

As she reached the point when she thought she'd slam her hands on the dashboard and cause them to crash, Jez turned the car through iron gates and pulled up outside the front entrance of Cobden village hall. Lizzie opened the passenger door.

"I'll park up and wait," Jez said before she'd put a foot on the tarmac.

"I'm going to be at least two hours."

"I'll come in, then."

"No. I'll get a taxi back or a lift from someone." She couldn't let him come in. It would be the worst thing that could happen.

"Okay," he said cheerfully and pulled the door to before she could slam it shut.

She watched in surprise as he drove towards the gates, having expected him to at least insist on waiting and for her to argue that she didn't want him to give her a lift back. She felt angry that he'd taken it so casually, and furious with herself for wanting him to return and insist on giving her a lift. It seemed little consolation that at least this way, she could easily find a reason for never returning to the chalet park. She put out her palm and felt the first spots of rain.

***

John, Joyce, Trevor and Mavis listened to heavy drops fall on the chalet roof. John glanced up. Trevor and Mavis continued to scrape custard and remains of dark blackberries from the sides of their bowls.

"I didn't think it was supposed to rain," said Trevor.

"There's a couple of spoonfuls left." Joyce half rose from her chair as she picked up a serving spoon.

"No, thank you, Joyce, love." Trevor held up his hand. "Don't want to spoil ourselves."

"That was lovely," said Mavis.

John didn't say anything. He poured them all another glass of Trevor's elderberry wine and looked up again at the ceiling.

"I think it's settling in for the night," said Trevor. "That's a pity."

"As if that matters," John snapped.

"We've had some good times here, haven't we?" Mavis shuffled in her chair and glanced at Trevor.

Joyce smoothed the tablecloth and adjusted the napkin she'd laid down by her glass.

"We have." Mavis reached out and patted the other woman's jewelled hand.

"That's right," said Trevor. "Now that's something to be proud of."

"I'll clear the table if you've all finished." Joyce pushed back her chair and was on her feet again, sliding out her hand from beneath Mavis's smaller one.

"Can't we leave it?" said Trevor, his pink face making him look younger than ever.

"Of course, you want to get it all tidy," Mavis blustered and readied to prise herself from her chair, but Trevor touched her arm gently and nodded towards Joyce gathering the dirty dishes.

They watched her falter when she reached the kitchen sink and then stand still, holding onto the edge, her back to the open doorway. Even though there came no sound, they knew she had begun to cry.

Chapter Twenty-Eight

JEZ PUSHED OPEN the door. The room in front of him was full of men and women quietly drawing. A couple closest to the door turned from their easels and glanced at him, then looked back to the beginnings of what looked like an eye, a head or a shoulder on an otherwise blank sheet of paper. Colin Fisher, sleeves rolled to his elbows, a tight, black waistcoat hugging his torso, skirted the room, making his way to the back.

"Are you here for the class?" he asked.

Jez stared at the naked model on the podium.

***

Lizzie struggled to keep her gaze fixed on Mrs. Pearson's pink training shoes and not automatically reach for the dark-blue dressing gown draped on a nearby table. Of course Jez had come back. He must have known they held art classes here. He was an artist himself, for God's sake. She couldn't look at him. Wouldn't look at him.

Jez slung his jacket over the back of a chair. Someone handed him charcoal as he tore pieces of masking tape and fastened a sheet of paper to a board. Desperate to cover up, even though she normally wouldn't flinch at being seen naked, Lizzie racked her brains as to what she could say to have him removed from the class.

Painfully aware of his side view of her and how she hated her profile, she couldn't stop herself blushing. Mr. Johnson, directly in her eye line, winked. Colin called out. She turned to look at him.

"No, don't move," he said. "Just to let you know we have a new member."

"Actually, Colin…"

"You don't know each other, do you?"

"The name's Jez, and we came here together," said Jez.

She turned, head only, to look at him.

"Keep still."

She glared back at the clock. Her entire body felt as if it were bright red.

"Thank you." There was an edge to Colin's voice.

She kept still. She knew what Colin would be thinking and planning, and he would not be able to keep his tongue bridled for long.

The sounds of charcoal brushing over paper, pencils being sharpened, brushes feathering lightly and the scrape of a knife patterning out skin tone, faded beneath Colin's careful tread. *Don't let him*, she told herself. *Don't let him do this to you.* She concentrated hard on the clock on the back wall until the numbers blurred. She would have liked to close her eyes, but having started the session with them open, she couldn't now change position. She had a trick, though, of stopping herself from seeing her surroundings. She knew everyone in the room scrutinised her closely, but she let them grow hazy and until they were indistinct shadows.

Marilyn's crumpled shape appeared. Right there in the middle of the clock. A heap of clothes barely forming a body, hair fluttering in the wind and a billowing skirt. One leg twisted and a shoe cast off. No sound, then a gull, a gust, the sea and that clammy, cold sickness on her skin. *Thud.* Marilyn's body hitting the bonnet of the car. Foot down hard. *Screech. Skid. Stop.* Breathing heavily and keeping her eyes tightly shut, gripping the wheel so hard it made her hands ache. Eyes wide open. The road empty, except for a mound of bright clothing and the billowing skirt.

She jolted, transported back to the room and becoming conscious of hands moving, eyes flickering up and down, hands moving again. *Does it show? Can they tell I've killed somebody?* Faces blurred like a watercolour wash, and she stared at the clock and concentrated so hard in the hope that no-one would guess what she could see.

Colin shifted position. Jez lifted his head. She wouldn't let them in.

Phil had been no help. He had removed himself and thought she would go to prison, or that was how it seemed to Lizzie. She pictured grey, cold concrete and a shelf as a bed with a thin blanket and a small, high window with a bird outside and a bowl of gruel. *Prisons aren't like that*, she told herself. A newspaper said that prisons had gyms and cinemas and people to give you a hug. It sounded better than real life; better than the chalet park. Maybe it would be simpler if she went to prison. She could stay there forever and never have to worry about struggling to survive.

She was shutting down. She'd done this before but usually stopped herself. Now it seemed as though it was the best response. *Shut down, Lizzie. Let your mind and body go numb so that you don't have to think. Get up, eat, walk, sleep when told. You will be clothed and fed and kept warm.* She could either stay naked, posing for the art club forever on this podium, or curl under clean, white sheets and sleep for eternity.

"Carrie?" The unexpected volume of an exterior voice was like a hammer hitting her skull.

Almost everyone in the room looked up.

"Carrie?" Colin made a fake show of rubbing his hands together. "I hope you remembered to put the water on and set out the biscuits."

He'd done that on purpose.

Holding mugs of tea or coffee and part-eaten biscuits, the group strolled around the room studying each other's sketches. None of them admitted they didn't have the skill to capture the intangible expression on Lizzie's face. Instead, they talked about brushstrokes, lines or the colours they would use.

Distanced, Lizzie, now enveloped in her dark-blue dressing gown, walked up and down, shaking out her legs. Dunking a digestive biscuit into her mug of tea, she sucked it slowly. Jez fell into step beside her.

"Why did you come back?" she asked.

"Want another?" He held out a packet of biscuits.

She took three. "I want you to go."

"What d'you get out of doing this?"

"Money."

Mr. Johnson beckoned her to look at his portrait. She turned her back. "Can't you just leave?"

Jez sipped his tea as if this was normal. "I came back because it's raining, and I didn't want you to get wet."

She could see Clara Frasier had heard and regretted starting the conversation, knowing there'd be gossip over their instant coffee and custard creams.

"Well, thank you, but I've got a lift."

"Who with?"

"Colin."

Jez looked at Colin chatting to a woman who looked sixteen.

"I want to paint you properly." Jez bent his head towards her, his hair almost touching hers. "I don't want to paint you like this."

The colour in her cheeks spread down her neck, and she involuntarily turned her head.

"I want to paint what goes on behind those eyes."

Clara Frasier studied the lines she'd made and picked up her pencil. A figure behind yawned, stretching arms high then glancing about as if embarrassed and quickly retracting them.

"There's nothing going on behind my eyes," Lizzie said. "Ask anyone. They'll all tell you—Elizabeth Juniper has no brains."

"Why do you say that?"

She swallowed the last of the soggy biscuit. People put their mugs back on the trolley and returned to their seats. Voices lulled as they separated to their easels.

"Let me paint you?" he pleaded, his voice still hushed. Clara Frasier bent her dyed head forward. "Not here. Relaxed by a window in your chalet with the light of the low November sun catching your hair. I want to capture the way you push out your lips when you half-agree with what someone's said, and the way a thought flashes across your face when you're listening to someone but pretending not to."

No-one, not even the so-called artists in the room, had ever paid her that much attention.

"No."

"We could do it tomorrow."

"I'm busy."

"It won't take long."

"The light wouldn't be right. It's bright in here. This is your only chance, make the most of it."

The sounds of pencils and brushes and charcoal tentatively started up. Colin's cowboy boots echoed.

"You get to keep this sketch if you let me paint you properly," Jez said.

"Is that instead of getting paid? I'd want to be paid."

"A portrait by Jez Maiden could be worth something one day."

Lizzie thought about it, thought whether she needed another painting of herself; thought whether it was a good idea to let him see behind her eyes...thought whether she could stand him not looking at her as closely as he did now. She clutched the mug tightly.

"I'd prefer cash," she said.

"I'll have you know the upper classes always paid the artist to paint them, not the other way round."

"I'm working class. What did they do?"

"They went to bed with the painter."

She burst out laughing.

"Most of the upper classes slept with the artist as well, of course."

"And how much money do these posh women give you?" she asked, staring him directly in the eye.

But before he could more than smile, her name came at her like a pistol shot.

"Lizzie." Colin marched towards them. "Everyone's waiting."

When she didn't move, he lifted the mug and remaining biscuit from her hands and smiled. She knew that smile and what it meant. Without hesitation, she undid the robe, slid it from her shoulders and walked to the podium.

"Lose the chair," Colin said.

Jez placed his mug on the trolley and returned to his seat. People busied themselves. Lizzie stood, waiting. Colin strolled to the back of the hall and stood by the door.

"Sit with your legs to the side and lean on your hand." His voice boomed across their heads.

"Which way?" Facing left or right?"

He raised his eyebrows in mock despair. "What's she like?" he asked the room.

Laughter spluttered back.

"This hand?" She waved the right hand, two fingers forming a V.

"Right buttock down. Right hand flat on the podium," he said.

Lizzie let herself drop. "Bastard," she muttered. What was worse, though, was that Jez saw everything.

"Don't forget to drape yourself," Colin said. "Both feet to the side."

"I was just going to."

Annoyed that Jez would get the impression she was unprofessional, she struck a pose with legs splayed elegantly to the side. Leaning, she dropped back her head.

"This suit you?"

"Finally." Colin over-pronounced the syllables, playing to the crowd.

She stared upwards, fighting back the words she desperately wanted to hurl at him.

"Is it as bad as it looks?" Jez asked in a low voice.

Again, she didn't respond because if she had, the torrent surging through her would escape and never stop.

"Relax, Lizzie." Colin's voice turned sticky as black treacle. "How can anyone draw you properly if you're as tight as a fan belt?"

She heard laughter again. Colin circled the back row, pretending to be interested in one of the younger women's attempts at capturing her jaw line, the curve of her stomach or the angle of her breast. She knew he'd be touching the paper, running his fingers over her curves as if he were touching her body. Jez's quiet whisper jolted her as it rose out of the scratches of charcoal, quiet mumblings of conversation and Colin's measured footsteps making sure no-one forgot his presence.

"Please let me paint you tomorrow. It can't be as bad as this, can it?"

He asked. He said please. It made all the difference, didn't it? The words went through her head. *At least he asked. Only another thirty minutes.* She could wait, put on her clothes, take the money and never return. She could do that, and for tonight, she could bide her time. Colin did it to provoke her, but she wouldn't give him any of the satisfaction he craved. She wanted that money. And what would Jez pay? Easy money. *Think of the money.*

"Not a bad likeness," Colin said, bending over Jez's shoulder and peering from the easel to Lizzie then back again to the sketch. Jez did likewise, his eyes lingering longer before looking away again. Lizzie didn't move, concentrating on deciding who she was going to ask for a lift into Rigby and from there to York and from there to London and from there to South Africa or South America or Australia or wherever as long as it was as far away from Cobden as possible.

"That's good." Colin pointed at a spot on Jez's portrait. "You've particularly caught the weight of her breasts and the beginnings of muscle tone in her upper arms."

Jez didn't utter a word. Maybe she would take a lift with him after all.

"Not bad." Colin threw over his shoulder, glancing at Carrie's attempt. "Better, much better," he said. "Try and keep your wrist loose."

The half hour dragged, but anger kept Lizzie alert.

"He must come again, mustn't he, Liz?" said Colin, nodding at Jez as everyone packed up their paraphernalia.

"What do you think?" Jez untaped the piece of paper from the board and turned it to face her. Reaching slowly, she took it from him, studying the indefinable emotion he had captured on her face. It wasn't anger. It wasn't boredom. Or hysteria. She couldn't even describe what it was, but the picture looked like she felt. Jez put out his hand to take it back, but she pulled it away.

"Thank you. I don't need to do another sitting. This is good enough." She clasped the portrait to her chest and walked quickly towards the door behind the podium.

Colin leant against the doorway while Lizzie, fully dressed now, pushed her dressing gown into its bag.

"Can't you ever let me get changed in peace?" she said.

His eyes flicked up and down. "Are you and him fucking?" Lizzie reached for her coat. "He'll be just like that wanker Andrew Booth and give you the push after a few, you know." He waited, and when she didn't respond, continued, "As long as it's clear you don't come knocking at my door in the middle of the night again."

She carefully slid the drawing into her bag and, holding it close, sidled past him and back into the brightly lit hall.

Chapter Twenty-Nine

S HE STOOD IN the doorway watching red taillights as cars pulled away through the open gates, wondering what would be best. She couldn't make out who was driving which vehicle, but she'd need to risk it and flag one down if she wanted a lift. She'd assumed Jez would have waited, but he wasn't around when she came back into the hall, and by the time she reached the entrance, she saw that not only he but most of the usual members had left.

"Don't let it bother you," she told herself. "Of course he went. You told him you were staying with Colin."

She asked the few women who still lingered, but they said sorry, they lived in nearby villages. She wanted to go in the opposite direction and much further than they were prepared to take her. Suddenly it seemed as if no-one lived in Rigby anymore except Colin. Standing outside, she tried to calculate how long it would take her to walk and if it were possible in the dark without a torch.

A horn sounded, jolting her back to blurred lights and damp drizzle. John Carmichael's old, heavy car pulled up. The passenger door opened. Lizzie bent to see Jez and commanded herself to bite her tongue and accept. A minute later, she sat in the passenger seat and watched rain stream down the windscreen. Misty beams of other cars glowed hazily until Jez flicked the windscreen wipers on double speed and their view cleared.

"Belt up." He waited, peering through the glass. She pulled the seat belt across her chest, reminded of the last time, and the time before that, when she'd been told the same. She was beginning to realise that Jez only explained things when he wanted. He turned the fan on full, and the heat quickly came through; she glanced at him, offering a quick smile in thanks.

As they drove along the dark cliff road, Lizzie racked her brains as to how she could persuade him to turn the car around and take her to Rigby. It was late. Most places would be locked up for the night, and she couldn't afford a big hotel but couldn't think what else she could do when she didn't want to return to the chalet park.

They drove in silence. She didn't know what he was thinking but felt he must be able to hear the muddled thoughts clamouring in her head. Soon they would pass the spot where Marilyn had lain crumpled and broken, but she must keep calm. As long as she was warm and in comfortable surroundings, she'd be all right, but the chalet was old and dilapidated—an ideal environment for negative thoughts to fester and pull her down into that suffocating void she dreaded. Of course, it was illogical because dead people didn't come back, but now that the vision of Marilyn was in her head, she couldn't shake it.

They passed the end of the road at the edge of the estate, and she looked the other way. The railings stretched to their right; tall, dense woods loomed dark and forbidding. By this hour, the house would be locked up and Andrew and Judith would be in bed. Carol was wrong. There was no way they'd be in Spain with the bonfire imminent. Andrew would have said something; he *always* said something. They'd have gone to York for a day or two, maybe London on estate business. It had to be that.

The thought of the chalets made her panic. For a moment she wondered if Jez had taken it for granted that she would stay with him after the attention he'd shown her in the hall. She'd accepted a lift, climbed in willingly and fastened the safety belt. She looked across at him, and he glanced back, his eyes sparkling in the dark.

Please let him be different. Please don't let him be a bastard as well.

"I'm sorry I've got to take you back," he said without turning to look. "You'll be in more trouble than it's worth if Phil doesn't find you there." He stared at the patch of road illuminated in the headlights. "You don't want him being kicked out for not doing his job properly, do you?"

She held the edge of the seat. "How d'you know he's coming?"

"He's an old mate."

"He had no right to say anything." They were all connected. All of them knew everyone else. That's why she wanted to leave. They all knew her history and her every movement. They probably had her next move planned out and were going to text it to her.

He glanced at her again; defiantly, she held his gaze.

"He thought you needed a friend," Jez said.

Looking sideways into the dark, it dawned on her that he had driven her to the art class because Phil Chorley had told him to keep an eye on her. They probably all knew about the accident.

"Just so you know," he said, "Marilyn was a very close friend of Randolph."

It never ended. *There* was the catch. She knew there had to be one, and Jez had delivered it. He didn't really care for her well-being. He wanted to get her to do something and blackmail was how he would try and make her. Well, he was on to a losing battle.

"Thanks for telling me," she said.

"I lived next to Marilyn for five years."

That clinched it. Five years was long enough to more than care about someone. Five years was enough to make you fight.

"It was an accident," she said. "She was standing in the middle of the road. It was too late to swerve."

"You still need to come back to the park."

She kept her voice steady. "Who says I don't want to go back?"

"If I could, I would take you anywhere else."

Yes, she thought, *that's right. You take me somewhere else, take me to Timbuktu, London, the Shetland Islands, heaven. Hell. I don't care.*

She debated whether she should give in, see what they all had to say, see what Phil wanted in the morning and then decide what her options were. Take the anger and grief on the chin. Explain the inexplicable to people who wouldn't listen. She was so sick of it all that to go along with it would almost be a relief. She could stand there and take their abuse. She'd done it on numerous occasions from people she knew. She'd had it from Colin that very night. She could certainly take it from strangers, then leave. Move on.

"Will you pull over for a minute?" she asked.

He turned the wheel, the car slowed, and he turned off the engine.

"Thanks." She undid her seat belt. He undid his and turned towards her. "Do the others know about it?"

"Only Randolph."

She pictured Marilyn's inert body and wondered what she could say.

"Are you afraid?" he asked.

"No," she said a little too loudly.

"They all loved Marilyn."

"I know." She was scared of everything about the park now, but she couldn't admit it. "I don't think it'll be very thoughtful to go back, that's all." She waited, but he didn't say anything else.

"Tell me something?" His words made her look up. "Tell me if you want to be remembered as the one who always makes the wrong choices."

She frowned, not sure what he meant. "I said I'll be there to see Phil, and I will." She tried to make her voice sound firm, but he caught her hand.

"I don't mean that," he said.

"Don't come to the art class next week. It wasn't fair of you to come." She could feel herself unravelling.

"I still want to paint you."

"You've drawn me." Maybe he would pay. *Ask him.*

"Yes, but there's no colour in a drawing. You need shades of warmth in your cheeks."

Why was he so insistent? She didn't know him. He didn't know her.

"Do you want the picture back?" She extricated her fingers and began to pull the sheet of paper out of the bag.

He looked as if she'd slapped him.

"Don't come," she said, tears pricking her eyelashes.

"Please sit for me tomorrow, Lizzie."

There it was again. How dare he use her name against her, so gentle and caressing? She couldn't understand how his saying her name made her insides ache.

"Here. Take the picture." She held it out.

"Okay." To her surprise, he took it back. "I'm sorry. I was being pushy. You've got enough on. 'Course you don't want me painting you as well."

She hadn't planned on kissing him. She touched his face carefully, her fingers tracing the contours of his cheeks, his nose and jaw line. He reached out, making her shiver as he ran his hand down her neck, his thumb stroking the line of her collarbone.

The picture slid off his knee. She felt like a teenager snogging in the dark. He smelt like a mixture of dry woods and grassy dunes, and she wondered briefly what she smelt like to him. But kissing was one thing she could do right, make others do what she wanted for once. She stuck in her tongue, held his head close. Made the noises she knew men wanted to hear. She didn't expect him to kiss back the way he did, matching her tongue with his own. If only the gearstick wasn't in the way. He was good. Way better than Colin. They had to stop at some point, though. She had to come up for air.

"So, you're okay about coming back?" he said.

"I don't have any choice." She wiped her mouth. *Who's fooling who?*

"Wait here for just a bit, would you? Help yourself to the whiskey in the back."

"What?" She gasped as a cold wind blew through the open driver's door. Almost immediately, it slammed closed, and she sat alone in the eerie silence. That wasn't what her kiss had intended. Scrambling decisively out of the car, she looked frantically around.

"Jez?!" she shouted.

The wind howled through the trees on the estate, and waves thundered against rocks far below the cliff. Jez was nowhere in sight.

Chapter Thirty

PETER GLANCED AT his watch again before closing the gap in the curtains. A small pan standing on top of the stove grew too tempting, and he couldn't resist lifting the lid. The still-warm rabbit stew smelt good and gave him pangs of hunger. Swiftly replacing the lid, he walked back to the window and looked to see if Randolph had appeared.

It seemed longer than a couple of hours since they had said goodbye to the others. Joyce had handed him a dish of rabbit stew and closed the door on them. They'd stood for a minute in the cold and dark wishing they were inside, warm and about to sit down and eat, but they would have to wait. It was Mavis and Trevor Cummings who sat at the Carmichaels' mahogany dining table that night. Peter could only imagine what it would be like. A heavy cloth with matching napkins setting off the patterned gold and white china. Candles flickering and glasses sparkling. Mavis uncomfortable in lilac and pink, freshly washed and curled hair and a smudge of eye shadow. Joyce, smart in dark green, in her element, ladling soup into flat bowls and passing them around. John pouring elderberry wine that Trevor had brought. No-one speaking about what was to come later.

Brought to his senses, Peter looped the woollen scarf around his neck, zipped up his grey anorak and pulled on a woollen hat. Ready.

He strolled into the bedroom and lifted a fawn blanket off the parcel. Kneeling down, he gazed at the heavily reinforced box within a box and recognised the sense of excitement that rose in his stomach. It fluttered upwards through his chest, all the way to the crown of his head. He knew this reaction. It was the same sensation he felt when laying fuses and watching the resulting explosions that sent chunks of buildings high into the air amongst the smoke of concrete and smell of crumbled stone.

"We haven't got all night." Randolph's voice cut into his reverie, and he prised himself to his feet.

Less than an hour later, Peter and Randolph reached the bottom of the cliff path, each carrying a heavy backpack. Now that the wind had blown away the rain, a waning yellow moon, peering through strands of cloud, glowed over the beach, illuminating foaming waves as the two men scrambled over the shingle. The cliff cast shadows and Randolph and Peter, dwarfed between the dark sea and towering land, moved haphazardly. Randolph stopped to catch his breath and regain his balance by splaying his legs. Satisfied, he nodded, and Peter continued to lead the way across the debris-strewn beach. Shining their torches, catching the edge of floor, chair or rock, Randolph occasionally stumbled, cursing, steadying himself and readjusting his rucksack while Peter remained quiet, keeping his eyes fixed on the beam ahead.

Randolph knocked into Peter who, with his torch trained on the ground, had come to an abrupt halt. "What's up?"

Peter pointed the beam of light at an opening in the rock face. They exchanged looks. Pushing past, Randolph disappeared from view; a few seconds later, Peter followed. Randolph leant against the roughly hewn wall and for the first time, glad of the cover of dark, allowed himself a moment of calm. Hearing Peter enter, he flashed his torch directly into Peter's face.

"What are you waiting for?"

***

Back in their chalet, Trevor and Mavis sat opposite each other in their winter coats at the Formica-topped kitchen table. Mavis had tied her favourite pink scarf under her chin, and Trevor put on his flat tweed cap. She pointed the tip of a knife into the centre of the Victoria sponge cake she had baked the morning of the picnic. If one dollop could kill a dog, a slice would be enough for each of them. She hadn't meant Campion to die, but the others insisted it was for the best: they couldn't leave him behind. Trevor had carried the stiff animal from the woods where John had found it to Randolph's cabin.

"At least it was quick," he reassured.

Mavis tried not to think about poison being painful.

Levering out a generous slice, she laid it on a white side plate, cut a second slice and placed it on another piece of their wedding china, then put down the knife. Trevor poured tea into green cups and smiled.

With a shaking hand, she wiped away a tear. Automatically, Trevor reached across the table and cupped her cheek in his hand. She leaned into it and held his gaze. He didn't need to say anything. She didn't need to. Picking up the larger slice of cake and gesturing for her to do likewise, Trevor pursed his lips in a kiss. Looking at him through watery eyes, she lifted her piece of light sponge as he opened his mouth wide to take a bite.

"Let's not!" Mavis dropped her slice and reached out to stop him.

He lowered his hand. Leaning forward again, he said in a gentle voice, "It'll be easier this way, I promise."

Her lips trembled. "It doesn't seem fair on Shelley and Gordon, when they didn't have any help."

Patiently replacing his piece of cake and catching her fingers with his own, he squeezed her hand.

"After what they went through, this feels like cheating somehow," she said. "And what would Randolph say? This wasn't part of the plan."

"I don't want you upset."

She attempted a smile. "I'm braver than I look."

"I know how brave you are," said Trevor. "Maybe I'm doing this for me." Mavis's eyes brimmed with liquid. "I wouldn't change anything even if it meant we'd have another thirty years."

"Nor would I." She smiled.

"Well, then."

"At least we're not ill in hospital or in a home," said Mavis. "That would be unbearable, and I couldn't face not being together. You're right. I'm sorry." She toyed with the slice of cake, crumbling its edges and watching them roll.

"I'm not sure I could live on that housing estate," he said. "But I'll do whatever you want." He stroked her hand. "Anything you want. I'll deal with Randolph."

Tears dropped like globules of mercury. "I don't want to be a coward."

"We're not cowards."

They sat in silence for several minutes before Trevor gently released her hand and, standing stiffly, picked up the two plates, tipping the slices into a bin under the sink before returning to the table.

"Let's drink our tea," he said.

***

Jez listened for voices but heard none. If he'd gauged Lizzie right, she'd be curled up on the back seat, downing the flask of whisky with its added sleeping pills. Once she drunk it, there'd be no way she'd be driving back to the chalet park—or anywhere else for that matter. And doused asleep, she wouldn't hear the explosions.

Kneeling on the wet ground beside Mavis and Trevor's chalet, his trousers immediately damp, Jez pushed the prepared dynamite down the piping. Peter and Randolph had done a good job of preparing the remaining chalets. They should have done this for Shelley and Gordon, but Peter had thought they were close enough to the edge not to warrant it. What impressed Jez about

Peter was that he adapted quickly to changing events. He didn't waste fire, nor did he skimp when warranted.

He'd hoped the concentration required to make no sound whilst ensuring the explosives were properly set would prevent him from thinking about Lizzie, but they didn't. He hadn't told Randolph; hadn't told anyone how she threw him off-kilter, but he sensed Randolph's suspicion. He'd hated leaving her on the top road, but he had no choice. He had to know where she was that night. He hoped that she slept, oblivious to everything. He looked at his watch; Randolph and Peter would be waiting. He lit the long fuse and hurried away from Mavis and Trevor's chalet as fast as he could, sprinting to the path that led down to the beach.

Halfway, just as he lit a cigarette, he heard the explosion. It shocked him, even though he'd expected it. At least it would be instant. They would have felt nothing. He pulled on the cigarette and waited for his heart rate to slow. Peter had been right: the detonation this time took only the chalet. The cliff, they'd see to later.

The tide was on its way in, and he negotiated his way down the steep incline with only the moon to light his track. Randolph would be wondering what had kept him, but he wanted to give himself a breather before having to cope with any abruptness from the old man. It was proving more complicated than they'd envisaged with Lizzie in the picture. He thought how she had looked in the car, with hair curling over her cheek and tickling her mouth. And that kiss. He never thought he'd be affected by a kiss. She drew problems to her, but maybe he could help. Maybe she had come to the park for the reason that *they* could help. He really hoped she stayed in the car. He threw away the remainder of his cigarette and trudged resignedly across the pebbles until he reached the cave entrance.

Straight away, the cold and damp penetrated. Noises told him that work was underway, and the moving beams of light helped him locate Randolph and Peter. Lifting his arm, he shielded his eyes, blinded by a direct glare.

"Well?" The instantly recognisable venom of Randolph's voice.

"Ready when you are."

Peter's voice was anxious. "It went off all right?"

"Didn't you hear it?" Jez picked up the hurricane lamp left at the entrance, swinging its glow across the dark sand. It could hardly be called a cave; it was more of a scoop within the cliff but eerie enough to be left unexplored.

Randolph turned his back and shoved Peter from behind. Jez lifted the light. Peter moved carefully, taking a reasonable amount of dynamite from a bag on the ground and pressing it into one of the holes they'd taken turns to drill into the rock earlier in the summer. Peter lifted more from the bag and filled the hole completely before securing a fuse and letting it hang to the ground. Moving around Randolph, who took longer, he began the process again. Jez liked watching Peter work. He admired him because he moved assuredly, without panic or hesitation. Jez had wanted to paint him in action, but Peter had refused.

"Make me like everyone else," he'd said.

Jez had, even though none of them were like anyone else.

"I'll light the fuses," he said.

Randolph trained the bright beam on him again.

"Thanks," said Peter. "That'll be a help." Even in the shadows, he looked tired.

"You two go back up, I'll join you when it's done," Jez said.

Randolph glanced across at Peter, who refused to look away from the rock. Jez knew he'd be thinking about Mavis, wishing it hadn't come to this for her.

"Would you put explosives in the other side as well?" Peter's voice gave nothing away. "We'll finish off quicker if you can do that."

"Sure. Just tell me where they are."

***

Once the two men had left, Jez made his way to the other side of the cave and awkwardly divided the remaining explosives into the drilled holes. Standing back, he turned off his torch and plunged into coal-like darkness, ran his thumb over the switch, daring himself to withstand the increasingly numbing cold for longer. He waited. He might die there if the torch wouldn't switch on again and he couldn't find the exit. Would that be so bad? He'd thought before about wading out to sea and letting his feet lift with the current, allowing himself to float, grow numb, slide away from his body, knowing he didn't mind. Sometimes that seemed like the right thing to do—take the short swim to oblivion. With people relying on him, he couldn't do that yet. Flicking the light back on, he unravelled cable across the sand and out through the cave entrance. A breeze buffeted his face whilst an aroma of seaweed brought him back to the task in hand, and he fumbled in his pocket until he grasped his lighter. They'd soon know if Lizzie had drunk the whisky or not.

***

Alert for the sound of the blast, Peter sipped tea at the kitchen table, secure in the knowledge they were a safe distance from the cliff edge. They had kept their torches trained on lighting their way across the ground to Randolph's chalet so that they wouldn't look at whatever remained of Mavis and Trevor's chalet or if John and Joyce had panicked.

He silently prayed that Jez was able to make it to safety. He didn't want the experience to be as drawn out as it had been for the Westons and had packed more than sufficient dynamite into the holes so that the cliff would collapse swiftly and hide the real source of the chalet's extinction. He slurped his sugary tea again, tensed now for the sound of exploding rock.

***

Randolph stood at the sink and poured himself a glass of water, gulping down the cold liquid as he looked at the brown and mauve clouds circling the moon. He glanced at the clock, filled a second glass, and steeled himself to look at the scene of destruction.

***

Jez headed straight across the beach to the sea rather than risk being caught too near the cliff. He didn't want to be anywhere near when it blew. He pulled out his lighter. A noise from above made him hesitate. He glanced up. Someone shouted from the clifftop. Stepping backwards, he peered at the rock face, higher, making out soil then scrub and grass in the tangerine glow of the moon. He still couldn't see but the shouts came louder and more frantic. Stepping back again, he made out two figures against the sky, waving their arms and shouting.

He couldn't make out the words that came in a torrent of panic.

He cupped his hands to his mouth. "What?" he shouted so loud his lungs hurt.

And then, he heard.

"You blew up the wrong one."

Chapter Thirty-One

A FAINT NOISE BOOMED somewhere in Lizzie's head, but she remained inert, cocooned in warm blankets. Doped by whisky, body relaxed and brain fluffy as wool, she didn't register any importance in the sound. It triggered something, though, and in minutes, maybe an hour, there seemed no way of knowing, she opened her eyes. Unsure if she were dreaming, she looked lazily out of the window. Her neck hurt. She felt sick—hungry sick and groggy as if she'd been drinking all day. A half-empty whisky bottle lay on the seat. She never drank whisky. She hated whisky. She closed her eyes again, but the grip of pain in her head made sleep impossible now.

Slowly pushing back the blankets, she opened the door and clambered out. The night breeze hit; disorientated, she turned around. A large moon cast an eerie, orange glow, and the ever-present crash of waves and whisper of ghostlike branches were the only sounds. Shivering, she walked back to the car. She should have known she couldn't rely on Jez. He was a stranger. A strange lad. No wonder he lived in a strange place. She drove off slowly, concentrating, clenching the wheel, eyes fixed on the road, driving so slowly she could have been walking. It seemed as if she'd been driving for an interminable time when she saw the familiar lay-by loom just ahead. She pulled up, opened the door and retched. Eventually, cold and sweating, she stood up, welcoming the breeze that hit her face.

The soft light made the chalet park beautiful. Clouds hung purple and brown. The sea tickled the shingle. It looked so peaceful. It looked like an idyllic place to live. The cliff edge darkened.

The chalets glowed. She looked along the line of buildings. The field seemed different. She stepped closer to the edge of grass, noticing a gap in the line of dwellings. The line ended too short. There was one missing. She stepped forward again, confused, and then she realised. The last chalet had disappeared. Her head was fuzzy and tongue dry and rancid, but she wasn't dreaming. She looked back at the car. She could drive down and see what had happened. She listened to the wind. Maybe she was dreaming.

***

Randolph and Peter met Jez at the top of the cliff path. Panting heavily, Jez bent over to catch his breath.

"Are you an idiot?" said Randolph. "What the hell were you doing?"

"I don't know! I was at Mavis and Trevor's. I was sure. I don't know, Randolph. Peter, I don't know what happened."

"You'd better think up something fast before Trevor gets here," Randolph said. "We've not seen them yet."

Jez looked up, struggling to focus on Randolph's rounded features. Peter remained silent, face pale and drawn. At least the Carmichaels hadn't time to have second thoughts. At least they were already swimming in oblivion. *Keep thinking that,* he told himself, *and not about Trevor and Mavis wondering when it's going to happen.*

"I think we should go and see if they're all right," Peter suggested quietly.

"Useless fuck," spat Randolph.

"It would have been quicker and easier blowing the two chalets together." Peter's voice sounded flat. "I did suggest that."

"Each has their own time slot," Randolph interrupted. "We agreed."

"We didn't take people's reactions into consideration," said Peter. "I take responsibility for that. I wasn't thinking about civvies."

"Reactions?" scoffed Randolph. "Just because we haven't all been in the army doesn't mean we lack discipline."

"I meant Mavis and Joyce," Peter shot back uncharacteristically. "Trevor will be out of his mind."

"What about the Alum mines?" Jez looked at Randolph, then Peter, his head scrambling for a solution as he pictured Trevor and Mavis, trusting and scared.

"What the hell are you on about?"

"We can say it was a gas pocket." Jez picked up momentum. "It blew before we were ready. I'll go tell them right now. Otherwise, it won't make sense." Words tumbled out of his mouth; he was grateful he could focus on doing something rather than standing helpless.

"Won't make sense? 'Course it doesn't make sense! What the hell are you on about?" Randolph was apoplectic.

"It might help explain why the wrong chalet blew," said Jez. "Don't you remember? We looked at plans of the mines at the library. There will be gas down there. We won't be able to explain to Trevor how it ignited, but in his state, he probably wouldn't think to question that."

Jez looked from one to the other. Randolph struggled for words. Peter looked at the sky.

"We should give Jez's suggestion a shot," he said.

"Yes!" Jez slapped his arm.

"It's the only way to justify the mistake. We don't want to admit...not when Mavis will be terrified, and Trevor will want to take her out of here straight away."

"Thanks, Peter," Jez cut in. "I'm sorry, honest, Randolph. I don't know how it happened. Maybe in the dark...maybe I rushed and panicked. I'm just...I don't know. I'm sorry, but can't we think about Mavis and Trevor now?" He couldn't admit that he had pictured Lizzie and him side by side in her car, windows open, breeze blowing through, sun shining, driving, driving, heading far away. He could never admit that he'd seen a flicker of hope.

"Fuck, Jez, I didn't expect this from you."

Jez shook his head, splaying his hands.

"John was a white-collar worker," Peter broke their silence.

"What's that got to do with it?" snapped Randolph.

"He wasn't a soldier," Peter glanced at Randolph. "This isn't how a man like him should die. It would have been better to have shot him. It's my fault. I should have planned better. I'm out of practice. I'm—"

"Don't be stupid! We're making a statement, not carrying out assassinations. Like we said, the cliff goes, we go. That's the whole point, and we've got to get on with it. When we're done, you go back onto the beach and blow that last fuse, do you hear?"

"John wanted to wear a suit," Peter persisted. "He had it hanging in the wardrobe with a shirt and tie."

Randolph coughed, scuffing the grass with his boots.

"I'll tell Trevor it was gas in the mines," confirmed Jez, aware of Peter's movements but keeping them in his peripheral vision. "He'll understand. He knows about geology."

"You blow up the Carmichaels' chalet when Trevor and Mavis are sitting there with cups of tea and you want to rationally explain it? Bloody hell, Jez. Bloody hell," muttered Randolph.

***

Jez came to a standstill as they reached Mavis and Trevor's chalet and likewise, Peter and Randolph slowed, all three wondering why they hadn't appeared.

"What d'you think they're doing?" Peter looked nervous.

"What the hell would you be doing?" said Randolph. "For Christ's sake, they'd better not see any of this."

"What are we going to say, then?"

"Gas," said Peter.

"He won't sodding care," Randolph spat. "They'll have packed their bags and be phoning the police."

Trevor opened the door.

"Is Mavis all right?" Peter blurted out.

"Of course she's not, you idiot," snapped Randolph, stepping in front of him. "Fuck, Trevor, who knows what this place is gonna do?"

"We think there was a gas explosion in the mines under the park. It went off and...what can we say, Trevor?" Jez moved into the spill of the chalet's light. "Are you okay?"

"Mavis is hysterical." Trevor came down the steps. "We were ready."

"Why don't you go back in and stay with her?" Randolph grasped the balustrade, blocking Trevor in.

"What a mess." Trevor turned to look towards the site of the explosion. "We thought we'd been struck, it was so loud. And then—Oh my God, Randolph, this was the mines?"

"Bloody mines. We hadn't counted on them."

"John and Joyce wouldn't have known anything," Jez added.

"But that's worse. John and dear Joyce." Trevor strained to look at the gash of cliff.

"We need to think straight." Randolph frowned at Jez. "Peter'll check on the mine. He's got equipment—sensory stuff, a device..." He trailed off, but Trevor didn't notice, merely staring in apparent shock.

"Yes, yes," Trevor reiterated. They watched him, shoulders hunched, walk back up the steps. "If it's gas in the mines—" he turned, worried "—that could blow again. Don't we need to get out straight away?"

Jez glanced quickly at Randolph. They hadn't thought of that.

"I'm going to get Mavis and me ready," Trevor nodded. "Where's John's car?"

"I left it on the top road," Jez said, ignoring Randolph's questioning glance.

"If we say, what," continued Trevor, "ten minutes? Meet at the car? Will you bring it down?" He looked at Jez.

"Where will we go?" asked Peter.

"It's too late to go anywhere," Randolph said.

"There's houses for us at Beamstown."

"You're right, Trevor," interrupted Jez. "The cliff could go again. Just grab what you need. I'll fetch the car. Let's say an hour—is that enough time for everyone?"

Randolph looked furious but didn't say anything. Trevor looked ashen. He nodded and opened the door. They waited until it closed.

Peter glanced at their faces incredulously. "We're all leaving?"

"'Course we're not," Randolph snapped.

Hearing voices, they listened, reluctant to move.

"D-don't leave me," Mavis stuttered as if she were cold. "D-don't leave me again."

They knew the scene: Trevor would be trying to stay strong, wondering how he could go into the other room and pack their clothes, collect photographs and knickknacks; it was unrealistic to think they could be ready in an hour.

The three men looked at each other in realisation. Sixty minutes wasn't long at all.

***

Lizzie made up her mind quickly. She slipped into the driver's seat and carefully turned the car around. But it wasn't as easy as she'd thought. Automatics were strange beasts. But the gates beckoned; the driveway, too easily familiar. Pulling up outside the main doors of the house and turning off the engine, exhausted, she began to sob. She thought she'd be efficient, but it was as though she'd been accumulating grief since childhood, and now the tears were finally flowing, nothing would prevent them. Clutching the wheel, she left them to stream uninterrupted down her cheeks. Nothing made sense anymore. If Jez were dead, she'd finally give up. If she were sent to prison, she'd have to. She was too tired of the effort it took to get through a day. The thought of finding somewhere else to live seemed insurmountable. Jez had presented a glimmer of hope, and if he'd been killed, then life was too cruel, offering up then snatching away. She should go inside and raise the alarm; she should have phoned the police direct, dialled Phil's number as she usually did, driven down to the park and found out what had happened. She'd abandoned them.

Wiping her cheeks with shaking fingers, she peered through the windscreen. The front of the house, in darkness once again now that the security light had extinguished, towered ominously. The gravel, illuminated by headlights, looked unyielding. She turned them off and rested her head on the steering wheel. Her eyes, sore from crying, begged to close, and her head throbbed unbearably. Phoning the police would not be welcomed by Randolph and the others, she knew that. She'd be in serious trouble with everyone, but she needed to know for sure that they were safe.

She shouldn't have left, she berated herself again. She shouldn't have gone to the picnic, met Jez, stayed near Andrew, driven after all that whisky, any of it. There was no logic to anything anymore. Maybe there never had been. She reached for the ignition key and jumped at a tap on the window. Jim's anxious face stared in at her.

***

Randolph and Jez exchanged glances; they knew what the other was thinking. Neither moved and then Peter turned around, glancing at Marilyn's chalet, then Trevor's closed door.

"We can't," he said, turning around again. "Maybe to a stranger, but not Trevor, not when he's unsuspecting. He said himself that's the worst thing."

"We'll have to get a move on." Jez took off the backpack and handed it to Randolph.

"Thank Christ that girl isn't here." Randolph grasped the bag, gauging its weight.

"I think we should respect their wishes," Peter said.

"Thought you were an army man." Randolph stepped towards him. "What's best for the team?"

Peter didn't answer, so Randolph moved the beam of his torch and Peter slowly bent to the ground. Jez glanced up at the hill. Thank God she hadn't turned up.

"Open the bag, man," Randolph urged.

"We'll have to keep quiet." Jez kept his voice steady, giving back his attention. "We don't want Mavis and Trevor—"

"What about the fuse on the beach? It's exposed," said Peter.

"Bugger that for now, we have to be quick."

Peter held out his hands. "Pass some to me."

Glancing up, Jez saw headlights moving erratically and heard voices whooping along the top road. He hoped the young drunks hadn't hit John's car. It worried him now, leaving her up there in the dark. He looked at Randolph and Trevor, but they took no notice, preoccupied with pressing dynamite into the ground, so Jez quickly took fuses out of the bag. This was worse than lighting the fuse. Worse than laying them earlier or in the cave. His hands trembled, and he dropped one, then froze as a sliver of light illuminated his hands. Trevor's shoes thudded down the chalet steps.

"Come inside," he said. "Mavis and I want to talk to you."

Chapter Thirty-Two

L IZZIE OPENED HER eyes to the faded morning light of Moorland Castle library. Still groggy, she must have fallen asleep as soon as Jim left. His kindness had surprised her, the way he'd brought a quilt down from upstairs and insisted he'd find out whatever had happened at the park. She smiled; he hadn't wanted her to go upstairs and use one of the bedrooms; he always did things properly. Pulling the thick cover up to her chin, she watched a figure come into the room and open the curtains. He must have stayed awake all night. She sat up, eager to hear what he'd found out. As she did so, sunlight flooded across the carpet, and squinting, she covered her eyes, her forehead heavy as a lump of iron. *Never again.*

"Jim?"

Only it wasn't Jim standing at the long windows.

"I told you not to leave the chalet park. What am I going to say to my boss?" Phil Chorley strode impatiently across the carpet.

So Jim *had* called the police; that's what he meant by finding things out. She was on her own again, left to talk her way out of another corner she'd recklessly backed herself into.

"Carol phoned me," Phil said, "but she said she didn't let you in, so what's going on?"

She closed her eyes to think. It didn't sound as if Phil had spoken to Jim after all, and she might get him in trouble if she said how he'd taken care of her. She kept her eyes closed. If she couldn't see him, the minutes would pass and she needn't say anything. It seemed better to say nothing. She couldn't tell him about Jez and sitting in the car and what it felt like kissing him and how he'd abandoned her and how she'd retaliated by abandoning him because she was angry and too scared to go down and see if he lay at the bottom of the cliff covered in stones and wood. She hated how irrational it all sounded. Phil would say that was nothing new.

"I'll fetch some tea." Carol's voice infiltrated her throbbing head. She opened her eyes. Carol stood there, as neat and immaculate as ever, staring at Phil, who nodded meaningfully back. Carol left again, leaving the door open wide, heels clattering across the hall. If her skull hadn't felt so heavy and eyes so painfully dry, Lizzie would have screamed.

"I've got some news for you." he eventually said. With a sigh, he dropped his hat on a low table and slumped onto the sofa opposite. Exhausted, Lizzie listened. This was it. This time, he would take her down to the station, and from there, the long, drawn-out process to slam her behind bars would begin. Again, for the umpteenth time, she thought prison would be the best option, but most importantly this time, she wouldn't have to go back to the chalet park.

"You didn't kill Marilyn Hopper," he said.

The clock ticked louder. All the sounds of the old house could suddenly be heard. Cracking of antique furniture, the dull swish of heavy curtains as a gust snuck through the single-paned windows, a kettle boiling, a teaspoon stirring liquid. They looked at each other.

"I didn't kill Marilyn Hopper?"

"No." He brushed his sleeve.

"But I hit her with my car."

"The post-mortem revealed that a bullet went straight through her heart. She died before—"

"A bullet? Are you kidding me?" *Let it stop. Just let me die too.*

He glanced at the door. "We're looking for a rifle. I thought—"

"You think I shot her then ran her down?"

"Don't be flippant—"

"She was standing in the middle of the road," Lizzie interrupted, unable to stomach any details. "She was looking straight at me."

"The coroner said she died before impact. When you hit her, she fell with the force of the car, but she would have fallen even if you hadn't arrived. Technically, you're not responsible—"

"Stop it!" Lizzie shouted. "That's impossible. Don't joke about it." She knew she'd hit Marilyn full on. "Just arrest me now or whatever it is you've come here for."

"It's so you know your position." He leant forwards, about to touch her hand, then sat back again.

She remained silent.

"She was shot near the wall of the estate," Phil began again. "She must have wandered into the road." He ruffled up his hair, then smoothed it down.

Lizzie was glad he wasn't looking at her. She didn't want him to read her mind. Who would shoot Marilyn? It was rubbish. Nonsense. No-one shot women like Marilyn. Jez said they all loved her. No. It had been the car. She remembered the sound of the woman's body hitting the car bonnet.

"I'm sorry, but you'll still be charged for dangerous driving." His voice was so low she almost couldn't hear him. She could see the look on Marilyn's face and the bright skirt lifting up in the breeze.

She interlocked her fingers and held them tight. "What does this mean?"

He strolled to the window. "Look, I'm not an expert, but you might just get a caution. You weren't over the limit, and it is a blind corner."

There it was. The get-out clause. She was so tired of get-out clauses that flung her back to real life.

"We're concentrating on looking for someone else now," he said, turning around.

If this were true, he wouldn't have come up to the house alone. Phil didn't have sufficient authority; he was the acne-faced boy she'd sat behind in maths. A smartly dressed chief inspector would be telling her this if it were true.

"Why didn't you say anything before? How come the ambulance people didn't say? If it's true, why didn't you tell me straight away? I've been going through hell. I could have left. I didn't need to stay around. I didn't need to..." She stopped. She couldn't say what she had done or what she'd seen.

"I'm sorry. I couldn't tell you, and you're not completely free to go." Phil looked worried. "Where's the tea?" He strode out into the hall, and she could hear him pacing about. "Carol?" There was an edge to his voice.

She looked at the grate with its remnants of a fire and ash spilt on the hearth. *It should be cleaned up.* She could do that. She could clean the entire house if they wanted. She'd do it for a bed and a few meals a day, but people weren't kind. They didn't help those they saw every day—much better to help some stranger they'd hired through some sodding agency.

His footsteps grew louder. Pushing away the cover, she stood, taking a step towards the door then indecisively back again.

"Will you tell me what's going to happen?" she asked when he reappeared.

"I can't say." He held the door open, embarrassed.

She tried to arrest the fatigue that seeped through her veins and muscles and bones and the pain in her head. If she could sleep for a few hours, she'd be able to make sense of what he'd said. She'd be able to walk out of here, go back to the park and face whatever she found.

"You should never have phoned me direct." He picked up his hat, toying with the brim. "It's put me in a difficult position."

"I knew I'd been driving too fast, and I panicked."

"Okay." His voice turned cold. "We can't talk about this right now. It's—ah, Carol, brilliant." He held the door wide as Carol entered.

"You can't talk about what?" Carol looked pointedly at him as she held out the tray. "I thought that's why you were going to see her at the chalet park."

"Well, that's where she's supposed to be," he said hesitantly.

"I don't know why I bothered phoning you. Here, take it. I do have better things to do, you know." She put the tray down hard on the coffee table, making the cups slosh their contents.

"Do you know everything?" Lizzie looked at Carol.

"No," Phil cut in before Carol could answer. "This isn't the place, and it's not fair on you, Carol. I'll take Lizzie…Miss er… I'll take you back to the park to go through procedures when you've finished that." He nodded to the tray. "And you're to stay put this time."

"We can't go back there," Lizzie said. "Take me to the station."

"You were told not to leave."

"It's collapsing into the sea! I think your boss will understand me not wanting to stay there."

He couldn't know. Jim couldn't have told him. Maybe no-one had heard the explosion; maybe it had only been in her head.

"Apparently—" he began.

"Can't I sign whatever it is here? You don't mind, do you, Carol?" *Anything, anything.*

Phil looked at Carol again, waiting for her answer.

"I don't think that's appropriate," she said.

"Fine. The station, then."

"Whose is that car outside?" Carol asked, lifting a mug to her lips, her voice casually antagonistic.

Phil looked accusingly at Lizzie, who glanced at Carol then away again.

"I borrowed it. It belongs to someone at the chalet park."

"Who? Do they know you've taken it?"

"It's fine. I just need to return it."

Phil looked incredulous. "You're not allowed to drive. You were speeding. You're not allowed to drive while we're investigating. This is a serious offence."

"You get a fine for speeding, not a prison sentence. Just cos you're wearing a uniform, you think you can tell people what to do. I can still drive."

She blushed, angry with Carol and the way Phil had turned on her, angry with herself that she'd drunk half a bottle of whisky and couldn't think clearly enough to reason her way out of this nonsense.

"What do you recommend, then?" Her voice sounded far away, even to her.

The room began to shrink. She put out her hands, feeling for the sofa behind.

And then they began talking. They said her name. He gave directions for her to do something. She jolted back to consciousness.

"Please, Carol," he said. "I need you to follow in your car."

"I don't see why you have to return it. Get whoever it belongs to, to come up here."

"Where are the keys?" He turned to Lizzie, and she saw his face, over-large, puzzled, too close, and Carol behind, staring.

Chapter Thirty-Three

S HE WAITED, COLD hands clasped on her lap, as Phil climbed behind the wheel of John's BMW. Carol followed in her shiny white Nissan. They passed Andrew's old dog, stretched on the grass at the front of the gatehouse, and she thought how stupid the dog at the chalet park had been; how stupid all dogs were to love their owners so much. She turned her head to gaze out of the window, eyes still sore and head aching. She yearned for a soft bed and to be left alone for a long, uninterrupted sleep. As if noticing, Phil blasted out the heater, and she closed her eyes.

Think. Kick yourself into gear and think.

He drove at a steady pace, checking in his mirror that Carol continued behind. Lizzie sucked in her bottom lip, looking out of the side window again, trying to find a reason why they shouldn't go to the chalet park, at the same time annoyed that he kept well below the speed limit as if making a point.

"I still think the station would be best," she said. He didn't answer.

It would be horrible if Carol and he came down and found out who remained and who didn't. They'd put their stamp on the atmosphere, and it wasn't their right. Mavis would be distraught, Trevor upset, Joyce tight-lipped. *Please let Jez be all right, though. Whatever happened, let him be safe.* Bringing Phil and Carol to the park would be another betrayal, but she couldn't think how to stop them, and with every second, they drew closer. Soon, Phil would see the cliff and the hole where a chalet should be, and then there'd be bedlam. There'd be police and medics and all sorts of people scraping and digging and measuring and ordering Mavis around, touching her precious ornaments and cups and saucers and packing them off, and she'd be crying as they were sent their separate ways. Above all, the thought of not seeing Jez again hit her like a kick in the stomach, but she could think of no way to stop them driving down. Left alone, they'd move out more easily; they'd take the offered flats. *But don't push them. Don't belittle them and shove and bully.*

They were on the last stretch. The sea seemed to taunt; fields opened out. She sensed the chalet park below even though they couldn't see it. She glanced at Phil. He looked in his rear-view mirror at Carol again.

And then, directly ahead, she saw the bus. The Rigby to Beamstown shuttle stood at the stop on the far side of the entrance to the track. Seeing it too, Phil slowed.

"You don't need to bother coming down," she said. "John's been keeping his car up here, you know, for safety's sake. I'll take the keys down to him."

Phil glanced at her as if she was an idiot and checked behind again. Lizzie looked over her shoulder. Carol would see the collapsed chalet as well if they got any closer. She looked at the bus. With surprise, she saw Jez shaking Peter Hawksworth's hand.

"It'll save you getting caught up with that lot." Lizzie shuffled in her seat, itching to find out why Jez had left her and that bottle on the back seat.

"What? Don't be stupid. I'm taking you down," Phil said, turning the wheel.

"He can drive it." She pointed to Jez. "I think Mr. Carmichael will create less of a fuss that way."

She could tell Phil was thinking about it.

"If he sees you driving his car, he could seriously lose the plot," she added, knowing this would clinch it. Phil hated confrontation. God only knew how he'd become a policeman.

The bus indicated to pull out, and they watched Peter walk down the aisle, looking at his feet. Lizzie waited, hoping she didn't seem too anxious. Peter swung into a seat on the side nearest the sea, a long, tube-like shape sticking above his head. And then Jez waved, and Peter nodded briefly before Jez turned and strolled towards them.

"Better have a word?" she said as Phil turned off the ignition and she pushed back her seat belt and opened the door.

"Wait," Phil ordered.

But she was already out, running towards Jez.

"He mustn't see what's happened," she said. "Say you'll drive John's car down."

A flicker of bemusement coloured Jez's face. Walking on, he met Phil, shook his hand and gently manoeuvred him around, making sure his back faced the sea.

"Don't think John will be too happy seeing you driving his precious BMW." Jez was the picture of calm. "Good one bringing it back, though. And Carol." He glanced across and waved cheerily. "Well thought ahead, getting her to follow."

"Hi, Jez." Phil bristled. "This one here is giving me trouble."

They both looked at Lizzie. She held back a retort and grinned instead, spreading her hands in agreement, playing the game she knew so well.

"Come on, get in," Jez said. She hurried back to the car. "That's all right, isn't it, Phil? Bet you've more important things to be getting on with."

Phil looked as if he would contest the offer, but after a moment's hesitation, he gestured for Jez to take the car.

"Thanks, Phil." Lizzie waved to Carol, unable to hide her relief.

Jez didn't immediately sit in but put an arm around Phil's shoulders and led him towards the white car, talking animatedly. Lizzie couldn't hear but watched Jez manipulate Phil into the passenger seat, pat the roof and gesture a farewell. To Lizzie's surprise, Carol put her foot down straight away and, making a large loop, headed back the way they had come.

"Why did you leave me last night?" Lizzie shouted as Jez sat behind the wheel. "And what was with the whisky?"

Without answering, he turned on the ignition so that Lizzie had to quickly slide into her seat, but he didn't move off.

"It's okay," he said. "Got to wait a second."

Pressing down the window, the fresh breeze blew on her face, and she breathed in deeply, wondering what she was doing now that she was alone with the residents in this remote spot. When they still didn't set off, she turned to look at him. He concentrated on the dashboard.

"Are you going to tell me?"

And then they set off, as if he too wanted to play games. She looked ahead, steeling herself for the people. As they neared the bottom of the track, the lack of activity made her uneasy. Now she was back, she remembered that first night too vividly. The sounds and the couple in the chalet. She couldn't look. Something bad had happened. She sensed it. Knew it.

"Where is everyone?"

Jez swung the car onto the flat. Peter's chalet looked closed up, and she realised he'd gone for good. She was glad he'd been sensible. He seemed a quiet, nervous man who should be taken care of, and although relieved they'd be out of danger, the thought that the place could be empty made her sad. She craned to hear Mavis and Trevor calling out to each other but could only hear the sea, birds crying overhead and wind stirring the grass. Even Randolph shouting would be preferable to this eerie atmosphere. Surely John would have waited to see what had happened to his car. Had they all really gone? Steering past Marilyn's colourful shack, she kept her eyes fixed on Mavis and Trevor's front door, nervous now and wondering if Jez had waited specifically for her return.

And then with a gasp, she saw the vast open space where the Carmichaels' chalet should have been. There was too much sky and sea. Uneasy, she glanced around: the other chalets were all closed up, and it was only then that she noticed there was no debris from the disappeared chalet—no broken piece of chair or torn shirt or battered tin of beans. No signs that it had ever been there. It was as if it had imploded, leaving only scorched earth.

Panic pounded in her chest as Jez curved the car around the rear of her chalet and parked up between it and Randolph's. The old man came to meet them. He looked as if he hadn't slept or changed his clothes in weeks. His matted, grey hair stuck out, and thick stubble created a splattering of coal dust across his jowls. She could run if need be, but Jez touched her hand gently as he turned off the ignition.

"Tell me what's happened," she said. "I need to know."

"It's all right. Randolph won't hurt you."

She still didn't open the car door. She didn't understand. She'd never understand. She wanted to stay cocooned, safe. They could make a getaway—did she dare to suggest it? Randolph stood with folded arms, watching them.

"Come on." Jez opened his door. "I'll see you safely inside so you can get some sleep, then I'll pop by later and see what's best to do."

"You've got to be joking. I can't sleep. How can anyone sleep? What's happened? Where's that chalet gone?"

"I'm sorry I left you in the car. I was coming back. I was."

She looked at Randolph. He didn't move. She wasn't getting out of the car. Whatever Jez said.

"I fell asleep, you know. When you left me. After I'd drunk that whisky you left. I fell asleep, but I did hear the noise of the cliff collapsing."

"It's okay," he said. "It's not dangerous. These chalets are far from the edge."

"I don't trust it." She watched Randolph walk towards the car. "I don't trust him."

Chapter Thirty-Four

JIM WRIGHT USED a sharp knife to cut back the long, whippy shoots on the roses. He sliced them about halfway down, angling the blade away from the centre of the plant. He worked steadily, moving slowly from bush to bush, bending now and again on one knee and cutting a sucker off at soil level. He could see the bonfire from where he worked; it was the best to date, and he wasn't going to let any young hooligans spoil it. He'd caught them mucking about earlier in the week and now, before retiring to bed, made it a ritual to check no-one came around getting up to mischief.

It had been a surprise to see an old boat of a car parked on the drive. All set to turn the courting couple away, he'd been lost for words when he heard sobbing and even more taken aback when he recognised the person inside. He felt sorry for Lizzie Juniper. Aware of Andrew's ways, he had never said anything, but it made him feel like the father he'd always wished he could be, carrying her into the house and settling her in the library. She belonged there more than Andrew's jumped-up wife, and it gave him some satisfaction. Seeing the copper's car on the drive in the morning angered him, but he should have guessed. It was typical of women like Carol to snitch on those most in need of help.

He made a mental note of the dead stems and woody plants that would need heavy pruning when spring came. Nearby, Gloucester sprawled on the path in a patch of sun.

"Only you and me to see out the year, boy," he said.

He could see Inspector Sayles and his deputy, Taylor, talking with Carol Bailey on the drive. As soon as they left, she would be over, telling him what to do; that was unless they came over and talked to him again.

The memory from earlier that summer still made him smart. He had been carrying a bunch of roses up to the house, late blooms that Mrs. Booth had picked out that morning. Walking around to the front in the opposite direction to the crowds of visitors, he'd had to cradle the bouquet to protect it from being knocked. He jutted out his bare elbows and felt satisfied by the looks of surprise, sometimes shock, invariably anger, when his arm made contact with a tourist. And then unexpectedly, out of their ordinariness, she had emerged through the crowd, at odds with the rest in a long, flowery dress, thick cardigan and long scarf wafting tantalisingly sheer.

It happened as though in a dream. She turned her head and smiled at him, and he moved towards her, lifting the bouquet of the sweetest scented roses and placing them in her arms. She took the gift as if it was the most natural gesture in the world.

"Thank you," she said in that all-encompassing way she had.

"Thought you might be able to use them," he mumbled, ashamed at his gruffness and forgetting that the roses had been destined for the main house. She hadn't seemed to notice the uncomfortable shifting of his eyes as she burrowed her face into the petals. She inhaled deeply, and he couldn't help but watch, intrigued by the brightness of her thick, red hair that was close enough to touch. She might not notice if he put out his hand and stroked the gleaming tresses that shone in the sunlight. She lifted her face, eyes watery with pleasure, postbox-bright lips parted.

"You're very thoughtful, Bill," she said before drifting away on a cloud of synthetic fragrance.

He stood, letting tourists jostle against him, immune to their puzzled and disgruntled looks. Slowly, he turned and retraced his steps, his pace increasing to match his pounding heart, rounding the rear of the house and striding into the kitchen gardens away from the hordes. As he reached the neatly planted rows, his stride faltered. A cold shadow eclipsed the sunshine, and he tried to figure out why he'd let himself sabotage the glorious event of conversing with his childhood crush, Marilyn Hopper.

Words tumbled around and around in his head. Clouds gathered above him. Her dress had been dirty around the hem. She wore old, scuffed shoes. Too much make-up aged her. She'd dyed her hair over a cracked bathroom sink. Eyes gleamed of cider not softness. And then he heard her voice again and with the voice, came her words.

"You're very thoughtful, Bill."

The rainbow that had arched over their heads, her melodic voice, the radiance in her eyes that gazed into his, all splintered into thousands of shards. He became once again the grey-haired bachelor who wore old, baggy and grubby clothes, his whole being weathered by a life spent in the sun, wind and rain. Like a punch in the stomach, he had been reminded that even a woman like Marilyn Hopper would never deign to treat him as a contender for her notice, let alone her heart. That glorious sun-filled moment fractured, and he, the romantic male lead, was thrust back into what he really was: the old, insignificant, hired hand.

In that one-syllable word, that hard guttural stop of a name that wasn't his, he had been slapped down into remembering where he belonged. It didn't matter to her whether he were Fred or John or Will or Ted. He was anybody, nobody, nameless to the people who were somebody; the people holding the power. And with that thought, he reiterated the name she had called him. Over the following days and weeks, it grew into a mantra.

"Jim," he spat it out. "Jim, not Bill. My name's Jim, not bloody Bill."

It amazed him how he could form his mouth into such a sneer of hatred. The sound changed too, becoming a globule of spit in a stagnant pond. There was no word he hated more. It hurt not only him but all his ancestors because it rendered the one thing that mattered to them worthless.

His father had drummed into him the importance of a man's name. His grandfather had been given the job of gardener here on the strength of it, as had his father, and then he had taken up the mantle.

He was Jim. Jim Wright. His father and grandfather had been Jim Wright. Everyone knew that. She knew that. He hadn't travelled all over the world, but the people around Rigby and Beamstown thought him a good, reliable man. His name had meaning.

And she had carelessly called him Bill. He looked down at his hardened, scarred hands. They shook.

Months later, on that November late morning, he walked around the edges of the estate, checking for any breaches in the fence or wall. With the majority of leaves gone, it was easier to see if any stones had fallen, sections collapsed or damage been done. With the gun resting over his shoulder as was his habit, he trudged through the undergrowth, making note of where he would need to return. The ground smelt damp, leaves already mulching underfoot. Crows gathered in the high branches standing chill-black against the azure sky. A couple of small mounds of fresh earth erupted on the grass. He hated moles; he'd been known to shoot the odd one. Every year, they spoilt some green area of the park. He pointed the barrel at the telling signs of upturned soil. At that moment, he saw a flash of colour through the trees; a deep royal blue, a pink jacket and the bright red of her hair. She would have been recognisable even standing across the way at Rigby Abbey. Through the sight of his gun, he followed the colour of her as she shimmered in and out of sight.

The swish of blue cotton and the sun on her gleaming hair made her appear young again. She closed her eyes for a moment, the flash of purple shimmering on her lids, her mouth bleeding lipstick. The breeze sent a whistling through surrounding tall trees, and her shadow flickered over the grass. He no longer saw her damaged prettiness but only the arrogant tilt of her chin as she leant back her head and let the fading scarlet locks shake out behind. The sun fell full on her face, bleaching it chalk white. Her heels clicked harsh over the tarmac, and then suddenly she twirled around, skirt splaying like a rose head. Trees moaned. Her shoes, childlike, tapped. A car engine sounded in the distance. A crow called out. And then she started laughing. He flinched. She laughed uncontrollably; standing in the middle of the road cackling as she no doubt had when showing her friends the handpicked roses he had bestowed on her.

He felt the smoothness of the barrel with his hand. She swirled again like the little girl in the school playground, swishing the folds of skirt, shaking her long, loose hair, determined to enjoy the moment at any cost. Mesmerised, he gazed at the colour and joy. The sound of the car neared to his right. He turned to look, then back again to Marilyn. She waved.

"Hello, Bill!"

Bill. She'd already dismissed him by turning away, turning her back as she had when she'd called him Bill that first time. He raised the gun. A car blurred in his peripheral vision. It travelled too fast. An old Renault swung around the corner of the estate. The car slid out of control. He closed one eye, squinted and fired. Crows rose out of the trees in a cacophony of noise.

The car scraped heavy, spewing up stones, then it hit her, and she rose, limp as a scarecrow in the air, a moment of slow motion before she fell to the ground. The car spun noisily on itself to face the way it had come. Tyres left their mark on the tarmac. Her skirt lifted and fell in the breeze. She didn't get up.

Trees wavered, scattering a few remaining leaves. Then came silence as the crows settled again in the treetops.

Chapter Thirty-Five

LIZZIE LUGGED HER suitcase down the steps. Randolph carried a plastic bag as he reappeared from Peter's chalet. She hesitated. The suitcase weighed heavy. She'd be crippled dragging it up the track to the top road. She glanced back at Randolph, doubting he would even acknowledge her. This was stupid. He'd be glad she was leaving so they could get on with whatever they wanted to do.

He trudged towards Jez's chalet, seemingly in no hurry, his face turned to the ground, as unreadable as usual. Soon, he was inside, kicking the door closed behind him. There was no-one else about. She dragged the case onto the grass.

Randolph came back out of the chalet, followed a minute or two later by Jez. The sight of his tall figure clenched the permanent knot in her stomach.

"Can I just check something?" Jez shouted after Randolph.

"Where is she?" Randolph's voice caught on the air.

"Leave her alone. She's getting by best she can."

Randolph glanced up at the track and said something she couldn't catch before Jez disappeared inside again and Randolph trudged back to Peter's chalet. She wondered what he was doing there when Peter had left, but only fleetingly; she had enough worries of her own.

Edging around the upper side of the chalet, she saw John Carmichael's car. She'd forgotten about that. She could borrow it as she'd done before, but this time leave it on the top road while she caught the bus. She glanced at her phone. Ten past one.

And then she heard the soft sound of voices emanating from Mavis and Trevor's chalet. John and Joyce would be inside with Trevor and Mavis. She couldn't take his car. They'd be preparing to leave right now. She could ask him to drive her up the track to the bus stop, though. She bent down to look through the car window. The keys hung from the ignition. She tried the door handle. It opened. Without hesitating, she yanked open the back door and pushed the case with all her strength along the seat. She glanced over her shoulder: Randolph and Jez were busy, sorting out what they wanted to take, no doubt.

***

Randolph strolled across the grass again, two plastic bags in his hands. He went back inside Jez's chalet. Straight away, she walked across the grass, resolute that she would do things right for once and ask for a lift. Three steps and she'd be inside. She glanced to her left. She liked the Cummings better than anyone else. They'd be the kind of grandparents she'd have loved to have had. She looked again. The broken ground stretched inland, clearly visible on the other side of the building. It could go at any moment. She had to make sure they were leaving right now. All of them.

Leaping up the steps, she tapped on the door. Hopefully, they would see sense and come with her straight away if she chivvied them along. No-one could stop them if they were adamant about leaving. *Safety in numbers. Remember that.*

The Carmichaels would be with them, John probably still stunned, Joyce maybe hysterical. Mavis and Trevor would be trying to be discreet, methodically going through all the drawers and cupboards, she in the bathroom gathering toiletries, he in the bedroom lifting down boxes. John and Joyce would be in the living room waiting with no possessions of their own but determined not to seek help. Would they be in a fit state to unquestioningly do as she asked and do it immediately? She knocked again and opened the door.

"Hello?" she whispered, closing the door quickly as she stepped into the kitchen. "Trevor? Mavis?"

No-one in sight, but she could hear them talking.

"Joyce? Hello? Mr. Carmichael?"

She walked further into the empty room. The table still showed the remnants of a snack with two cups of cold tea, a jug with milk beginning to form a thick surface and a teapot. Pale cake crumbs. Perhaps John and Joyce had gone down onto the beach trying to salvage some of their clothes and treasured belongings or to merely see for themselves, in daylight, that this had really happened. Mavis would be upset, and it struck Lizzie that they might want to be left alone. Through the window, she saw Randolph reappear. She glanced back at the front door with its curtain pulled neatly across the glass. Of course, John and Joyce may have been taken to hospital to be treated for shock. She listened.

Mumbling came from one of the other rooms, but the doors remained closed. Voices outside came through as well.

"You'll be all right?" Jez's voice.

"Bit late to be asking me that."

She placed her hand on the handle of the door nearest, then hesitated, wondering what she would say. She pushed it open. Two toothbrushes stood erect in a jar on the sink. A new bar of soap lay in a dish, and clean towels, neatly folded, hung from a rail. She listened again. The voices came from the room next door. She tiptoed across the thin pink carpet and tapped gently.

"Hello? It's Lizzie."

No answer. She knocked a little louder.

"Mavis? Trevor? Are you okay?"

Grasping the handle, she glanced out of the window. All that was visible was the sea. She opened the door.

Mavis and Trevor lay fully clothed side by side on the bed. Lizzie looked down at them, taking in their smart clothes and polished shoes. Mavis held a beige handbag over her stomach; Trevor clutched a Bible to his chest. She'd put on pale lipstick. He'd combed his hair. Lizzie became aware of her breathing. They couldn't have been more different from the old couple clinging to each other in that first chalet on that rainy night. The cheerful voices in the room seemed inappropriate. She walked to the bedside table and sharply turned off the radio.

A minute later, she faced the front door.

"Breathe," she told herself, teeth clenched to keep them from chattering. "Just keep breathing."

Sunlight shining through the square glass pane in the door illuminated all the tiny yellow daisies on the curtain covering the little window. She imagined Randolph's face pressed up against the other side, ready to snarl his hatred, or Jez, turned into someone she didn't know, primed to knock her to the ground. She waited, but no shadowy profile appeared, and still she didn't move as she struggled to contain the pinpricks in her eyes. With great effort, she grasped the handle and pulled.

At that same moment, Randolph came out of Peter's chalet again, carrying two more plastic bags. He stopped. Lizzie froze halfway down the front steps. They stared at each other for a moment.

"Oy!" he shouted.

Jumping down the remaining steps, she heard him call after her again, but with hairs rising on the back of her neck, she didn't wait. Instead, feet pounding on grass, head bursting, she heaved for breath as she reached the car and yanked open the driver's door.

"Jez?" Randolph's voice came urgent.

Shaking, she scrambled inside, grasped the ignition key and turned. She took off the handbrake and looked up. Jez stood directly in front of the car. Randolph waited only slightly behind, puffing and wheezing. Into drive. Foot down. Jez didn't move. Randolph stepped towards her. Tightening her grip on the wheel, moving forward, she stared at Jez, willing him to shift. He didn't react. Randolph looked confused. She pressed her foot a little harder and turned the wheel to skirt the chalet, but they were too close. Randolph stepped backwards. Frowning, Jez jumped sideways, one hand slightly raised as if he wanted to speak but didn't know what to say. She picked up speed.

"Get out of that car!" Randolph pushed past Jez and slammed his hand on the roof.

Shaken, Lizzie automatically jammed her foot down. The tyres spun on the soft earth. Randolph reached for the door. Jez remained still. Randolph, running now, banged the boot with his fist. The sound reverberated, and she couldn't help but check in her rear-view mirror. As she pulled away, the tyres gripped. Concentrating on the ground directly in front, she pressed her foot fully to the floor. Out of the corner of her eye, she caught the flash of the bus on the top road. She accelerated. The car bumped over potholes, straining up the steep track. She came down a gear.

The bus stood at the top of the track. *Quick*, she begged. *Please, please wait for me.*

She stopped, jumped out. Leaving the keys jangling in the ignition, she yanked her suitcase from the back seat and left the door open.

"Wait!" she yelled, the case banging against her side as she gesticulated. "Hey!" She couldn't believe it. The bus began to pull away. "Stop! Stop!"

Chapter Thirty-Six

STARING OUT THROUGH the freshly cleaned window at the flashing sea, Peter sat on the same bus as had left the same spot at ten o'clock that morning. He sat with his hands clasped over the cardboard tube on his knee, determined not to let anyone see how tired he felt. It didn't seem right that passengers climbing on and off the bus were ignorant of what had happened to the chalet park, but he watched placidly as they greeted the driver, chatting animatedly before settling into a seat next to someone they knew. *Soon you'll all know*, he thought. *Everyone will know about Moorland Chalet Park.*

One woman nodded politely as she took the seat in front; a small child stared unsmiling. No-one sat beside Peter, and he steadfastly kept his gaze on the pale cardboard cylinder and brown sleeves of the anorak Randolph had given him.

He hadn't seen Mavis and Trevor again last night. He'd left, not wanting to disturb them, but he regretted it now. Mavis would think he didn't care, and he admonished himself for not having written a note and pushed it through their door. Randolph hadn't said much. Peter didn't suppose it mattered now. He looked out of the window again, his breath steaming an oval patch on the glass, and wondered if they would see the spectacle from Beamstown.

***

Lizzie dropped her suitcase in frustration. She turned around and looked down at the park, then at John's old car, then the park again. The distant figures of Randolph and Jez stood by the cliff, but no-one else came into view. They obviously didn't care about the car anymore. Odd after making such a fuss. And it would be the fastest way out of there, away from them, safe and far away from all trouble—if that were ever possible. She could take it.

She should take it.

Grasping the handle, she began walking in the direction of Rigby, dragging the case roughly behind. "You're out of that hole," she muttered to herself. "That's all that matters. If you take it, they're still with you. Forget it. Forget Jez and the lot of them. Don't think about it. Let them get on with it. Get back to normal. Get your life back. That's what you need to do."

But it wasn't long before she began to struggle with the awkward suitcase. She couldn't keep up the level of anger it took to walk at the pace she'd set. The suitcase hurt her arm. Slowing, she looked behind her for a car coming that might give her a lift. She stopped, dropped the case on its side and sat on it to wait.

Moorland stretched clearly visible under the still, crisp sky. The sea, choppy and grey, basked in the afternoon sun. Minutes passed. Half an hour. Not a car in sight. She stood and pulled up the case. Plovers called out. A breeze built speed across the coarse scrub and browning heather. Orange and pink tinged the horizon. She walked on, weighing up if she should stop at Moorland Castle after all, persuade Carol to help her in some way. Her right arm began to tire, and she swapped hands, relieved to reach the woods and outer wall of the estate. The sun flickered its orange beams through the trees, losing its warmth as the contrast between light and dark grew more pronounced. Descending rapidly now, the sun spread its aftermath through bare branches. Shadows crept out of the fading day. The suitcase, increasingly awkward, slowed her down. She switched it back to her right hand, glancing nervously at the darkening parkland as she neared the front gates.

***

Even before John's ancient BMW sped up the track with Lizzie Juniper in it, Randolph turned his back and strolled slowly to the grassy cliff edge to face the grey water.

"Let her go." He struck a match and lit a cigarette. Jez flexed his arms above his head, and Randolph glanced at him, flicking his wrist to extinguish the flame.

"She'll be upset about Mavis and Trevor," Jez said, dropping his arms. "Never mind John and Joyce's chalet."

Randolph sucked viciously, then handed the cigarette to Jez, and they stood side by side, passing it between them as they watched waves clutching at the beach.

Randolph couldn't remember a time when he hadn't been able to look at the North Sea. He gazed to his left at the four remaining chalets where once there had been twenty or so, then to his right where caravans had spread out on the far side of the track. He remembered the constant activity and the noise of people's voices. They had erected picket fences and planted gardens lined with white-painted stones, positioned brightly coloured gnomes and concrete statues of everything from Greek gods to hedgehogs. He recalled the smell of fresh emulsion and gloss, of bronzed faces in evening sunshine, the grind of lawn mowers, sizzle of frying bacon and the long-gone sound of children playing. In his mind, Randolph could still see footballs rolling across the field and summer-dressed figures turning cartwheels, could still smell the freshly mown grass.

"Are you sure you want to do it?" Jez asked. "I don't mind taking over if you don't feel up to it."

A gull cried loudly overhead, and they both looked up.

Randolph threw the butt over the cliff. "No. I'll do it."

"Well, let me set the last two." Jez turned around. "Then it's all yours."

Randolph nodded. He wasn't going to let anyone, not even Jez, see how difficult this was for him.

He cleared his throat. "We haven't given up, have we?"

"'Course not," Jez said, stressing the words. "No-one can take your England away. It's in here." He stepped forward and lightly tapped Randolph's chest.

"You go on." His voice was gruff. An old man's voice. "I'll be with you in a minute."

Jez hesitated, then walked off towards Peter's chalet. It was too late to change tack now. Too late to run away and think of alternatives. Randolph didn't move. On the beach below, wet sand gleamed, and seaweed stretched like green bubble wrap across the pebbles. The remains of chalets littered incongruously over rocks and sand. He frowned. The wind had turned chilly and it would soon be dusk.

It was as though he were eight years old again, knowing he should go home for tea but reluctant to leave the shore with its rock pools of treasure.

He licked his lower lip, tasting the air as he always did at the water's edge; hair ruffled, face buffeted, chin raised. He didn't want to go, but time was running out. He wasn't a grand man, needing to live in a place like Moorland Castle; nor did he feel he belonged in a housing estate surrounded by people with whom he had nothing in common. The chalet park was his home. The sea. The air. The cliff. He didn't belong anywhere but at the sea's edge.

It went through his mind that he should utter a farewell, thanks, some words at least. None of the prayers he knew seemed fitting, yet he couldn't go without some mark of occasion. He wasn't an eloquent man and he struggled. The prayer of St. Ignatius Loyola seemed the most suitable, but it reminded him of school, and he'd hated school. The force of grey water rippled, and the light faded in the ever-changing sky. Grass brushed his legs. He moved his feet, testing the slightly wet ground, and sighed. And then it came to him unbeckoned as he looked down at the earth, and he began reciting the lines he'd learnt by rote as a child, as he'd learnt all these things.

At first, William Blake's words about the hills and valleys and industrial towns of England tumbled haltingly from his mouth, but then, more and more forcefully, they came as both a surprise and a comfort. He didn't believe in God. He didn't believe that Jesus had ever stepped foot in England, but he believed in the past, unsung heroes and the beauty of the Yorkshire countryside that existed in spite of industry and greedy men. He opened his mouth wider and sang. He wasn't going to apologise for the pleasant pastures and green mountains, and when he finally shouted out the word "Jerusalem!" he felt the stark chasm of his chest rupture and tears pour down his lined cheeks, and he began to shake with emotion.

***

Silently, from behind, Jez touched his shoulder. Taken off guard, Randolph yelled out.

"Randolph," Jez said quietly. "Come on, mate. Let's go."

Randolph waved Jez away whilst obstinately staring out to sea. For a moment, Jez studied the older man's shoulders. "Let me do it."

Randolph shrugged him away. "Go on, get on with you."

Jez hesitated, then, hands shoved into pockets, he reluctantly strolled towards the cliff path that led down to the beach.

***

Randolph coughed raggedly and wiped his face with a crumpled handkerchief before turning his back on the sea and trudging resolutely towards Lizzie's chalet, clutching the box of matches.

Several hundred yards away, the branch caught, and with it, Randolph lit a fuse stretching onto the grass. Shambling sideways, he lit a second fuse that snaked towards his own chalet and began to feel the excitement of action. As he jogged across to the Cummings', his legs began to shake. It would soon be dark. Now Marilyn's then Jez's.

Finally, he lit the fuse that led to Peter's doorway. It sparked and sizzled, spreading towards the building. An explosion almost knocked him off his feet. The first chalet had detonated, quickly followed by the second, and he fell to the ground, nerves frayed at the volume and force of the blast. Debris fell, bouncing and splitting, and he instinctively covered his head.

He gave a quick glance at the fuses. Each one sparked towards their destination. He stumbled towards the cliff, glad Jez had insisted on such long fuses to snake and twist over the grass before doing what they were primed to do. The week had been so much harder to endure than he'd imagined. He hadn't taken into consideration how Mavis and Joyce would react, and the effort of containing his own emotion after the initial outbursts had taken its toll. He couldn't bear to look at Mavis last night. What was worse, he'd let Marilyn down. He couldn't stomach that she wasn't with them at the end. It had been her nightmare that she'd be left behind, and now she had been, her body splayed on a cold slab for anyone to gawp at. Sorry wasn't good enough.

He no longer flinched as the other chalets exploded, littering the grass with broken Derby and blackened plastic flowers. He no longer cared if he were struck. Let the knives and forks and kettles and bars of soap fall. It didn't matter. Nothing mattered now the noise ripped into the sky and made the earth groan. Let everyone see the scarred land and the broken buildings. Let everyone wonder why they had done this. He rubbed his chin. Jez would wonder why he was taking so long. They had a final fuse to light. He should go, but he no longer had the will. Jez could do it. Jez knew what needed to be done. This was his land. Randolph Brook's Jerusalem.

***

Leaving Randolph to gather his composure, Jez dodged around the flapping police tape and trotted down the path, glancing behind every now and then and listening for Randolph's heavy tread. He was a strange old beggar. It had surprised Jez to hear him singing that song; he always acquainted it with jam and his mum disappearing on Monday nights to the village hall. Lizzie would probably have laughed. She was odd too. He wished he'd explained to her what they were doing. Now he'd never see her again, and even if he did, she'd keep her distance as if they'd never met. He ducked his head and felt a thump of excitement as an explosion cracked the air.

***

Lizzie dropped her suitcase on the drive. Spinning, confused, almost stumbling, she screamed at the boom of a second explosion. Tensed for another, she waited, then, fumbling around for her case, jumped again and again as a third, fourth then fifth roared in succession. She held her breath, squealing at a sixth blast.

The noises came from the direction of the coast. It seemed like fireworks, a whole lot going off. It sounded the same as when the mine had blown near Whitecross. Trapped gas, they'd said. She wondered then about the old ruins near Rook Bay. There were old mines all along the coast.

Night had almost fallen. Animals called out from the woods. She shivered, waited, tensed, but no more reverberations rang out. Hands shaking, she took out her phone and stared at the screen, unsure what to do.

"Forget it," she told herself. "No-one will thank you."

***

When Jez reached the beach, he looked at the cliff for signs of cracks and movement. The gentle rush of waves sounded so normal. The night was anything but normal. He looked up at the path, but Randolph hadn't appeared. They still had the cliff to blow from the beach, but he was nowhere in sight. And then Jez spotted him, right on the top, near the edge. *What the hell is he doing? Of course. I should've guessed.* Randolph singing 'Jerusalem' had been a sign. His figure seemed so small up on the clifftop. Smoke billowed dark into the trails of the day. Sparks spiralled overhead. The figure remained still. Waiting. The sea hushed again. Jez raised his arm. The sea gently murmured. Without a sound, Randolph fell.

Chapter Thirty-Seven

S TUMBLING ACROSS PEBBLES, chest pounding, he cursed, trousers soaked as he splashed through rocky pools. In his haste, he slipped on wet clothing and seaweed-covered boulders. Eyes fixed on the spot where Randolph had fallen, he staggered towards the cliff base. Slowing, he approached the distorted mound. The light hadn't completely faded, and he could still see enough to find Randolph. Panting heavily and legs trembling, he looked down at the surprisingly small body. Blood flecked the surrounding stones. Wind lifted a few strands of grey hair, the rest red and rigid, too clogged to move. He'd never noticed Randolph's bald patch before, but the stubby fingers of one hand dabbling in a pool of green water were as familiar as his own. He looked back up at the cliff.

A canopy of white stars sprinkled through the inky grey, crackling and snapping. He shivered. Night had fallen.

**

Grabbing her case, Lizzie struggled up the uneven drive. She told herself not to think about it. Not to question. She'd left the chalet park. It was none of her business. She yanked the case, thankful the noise of its wheels drowned out any calls in the undergrowth. Eyes fixed on the track ahead so as not to see how darkness crept in on her, she lifted the case in both hands, ignoring the ache in her arms and soreness of her palms. It was with relief she crossed the top car park and front sweep of drive and looked up at the majestic battlements of the house.

Night enveloped completely now, and the ground-floor rooms sent their electric glow spilling onto the gravel.

Pausing by the library window when the security light triggered, she caught sight of Carol dancing to loud music. The front door stood open, and she automatically headed for it, struggling awkwardly inside and praying the outside light would extinguish before Carol noticed. An old pop song blared through the closed library door. Carol couldn't have heard a thing of what was going on outside. With the suitcase banging against her shins, Lizzie crossed the entrance hall and headed straight for the stairs, desperate to find a bedroom and collapse for the night. She shifted awkwardly up the steps, suitcase tapping her shins and pausing as the penultimate tread creaked. The high cheery vocals cut out.

"Phil?" Carol yelled.

Lizzie heaved the case up the last step and hobbled along the threadbare carpet.

Downstairs, the library door opened, followed by a long pause as the house remained quiet.

"Phil? Is that you? I'm not in the mood for messing about."

Outside, the wind gusted, and branches of nearby trees groaned. Rapidly crossing to the front door, Carol pushed it closed and shot across the bolt. The telephone rang.

Lizzie glanced down the panelled landing, which petered into darkness, and listened to Carol's clipped tones emanating through the open library doorway.

All she needed was time to make a plan. A night's rest and she would be ready for a fresh start, maybe catch a bus to York and find a job there. Opportunities in the run-up to Christmas would be plentiful; then there were sales throughout January, and then who knew what could take off? She'd make a plan, anything but think about the noises she'd heard ringing out from the coast.

She listened. The phone call must have finished, and she strained, trying to discern what Carol did next. Footsteps resounded across the hall. Almost immediately, they stopped. There was the sound of the bolt on the front door being pulled back, a draught then the door slamming and once again, quiet.

Feeling her way along the panelling until she found an opening, Lizzie edged inside. With the glare from the outside security light illuminating her way, she crossed the floor without any hazard. About to draw one of the heavy curtains across the mullion window, she noticed sparks like fireflies dancing into the dark sky. She pressed her face against the glass. The bonfire blazed brightly. A day early.

Carol prowled around the parameter, stepping nearer to the burning wood then back again, flinching at the fire's scorching heat. Automatically, Lizzie leant on the sill, yanking the catch; when the window wouldn't open, she tapped her knuckles on the glass. Carol didn't hear her. Instead, her shadowy figure strode out of sight in the direction of the rose garden and greenhouses.

Lizzie waited, fascinated by the intensity of flames and sound of wood spitting and cracking. The stuffed figure of Guy Fawkes sagged as the chair it sat on shifted. Enthralled, Lizzie watched as it subsided further, one leg disappearing in a bright eruption of sparks. Straining to look, she followed the flakes of ash and fire as they disappeared into the inky sky.

Minutes later, Carol reappeared, holding the nozzle of a hose tightly in both hands and dragging rubber tubing behind her across the grass. As she neared the fire, she twisted the valve to spray water over the flames. It sent out a fountain of drops that arched through the air but just as suddenly withdrew to a stream, then a dribble and then nothing. Carol shook the nozzle furiously. Flinging the hose down, she strode back and pressed her foot on the rubber. The hose bulged before thundering spray at the windows. Letting the hose twist and snake, Carol took out her mobile and after a moment began talking loudly.

Guy Fawkes scattered ash through the collapsing pyramid, and the base of the fire shimmered flakes of grey and black wood. Reflections flashed across windowpanes, but Carol took no notice as she stalked past on her way to the front of the house.

Lizzie turned and stepped straight into a tall figure holding a finger to his lips.

Chapter Thirty-Eight

CURTAINS FIRMLY DRAWN, Jez turned on a lamp to reveal a large bedroom that looked warmer than it felt. Fawn sheeting covered furniture, creating vast amorphous shapes that whispered of neglect. He dragged a dustsheet off a table and put down a vodka bottle before lifting two mugs out of a bag. Wanting to see him properly, Lizzie turned on a lamp near the door; stunned, she watched him as he unscrewed the bottle lid with a click of its breaking seal.

"What are you doing?" she demanded, angry that he offered no explanation.

Without a word, he began to pour.

"You said the chalets were safe. You said the cliff was sound. There's no storm. Tell me what happened to Joyce's chalet. Do you know…do you know about Trevor and Mavis?"

He filled the second mug.

She caught herself before she spoke again. *Breathe, just breathe.* So this was it. They couldn't bear the thought of the flats at Beamstown. They couldn't bear to leave that wretched chalet park.

"Where is Joyce?" she said. "And her husband? John?"

"Here. Take this." He held out a mug.

"Is Randolph with you?"

"No."

"I've got to go down and help Carol." She suddenly didn't want to talk about Trevor and Mavis or John and Joyce. "You can sit here and drink your vodka if you want."

"It's too late to put out the fire." He held out a mug. "Please, have a drink with me."

She felt she hadn't slept for a week. The thought of having a drink and the ensuing oblivion was appealing. And he was asking, sounding as if he needed her help to get through this, get over it, not to be alone.

"It's not fair Carol's left to deal with the fire," she said.

He smiled. "Always putting others before yourself."

No-one had ever said that of her before, and she wondered if he saw a different person to everyone else—one even she didn't recognise.

"I wouldn't like to have to deal with this place on my own, would you?"

"She won't be on her own. Phil will be here soon." He took a long drink.

Phil wouldn't be pleased to see her, and she definitely didn't want to see him. That's who Carol had phoned, and he always came running. The haven of the room and escape of vodka seemed increasingly her only option, and wasn't that what Jez wanted? She walked across the floor, snatched up the mug and took a gulp, gasping as it stripped down her throat.

"I take it you found John's car at the top of the track?"

"What?" Jez put down the bottle, looking surprised. "But how did you get here?"

"You didn't find the car? Then how did you get here?"

She took another drink and waited, but he didn't say anything.

"I heard loud bangs." She noticed her voice rang too harsh, too out of control. She could tell by his face that he was thinking something over. "It sounded as if the whole cliff had blown up." She didn't care. She wanted to grab hold of him and make sure he was listening. "How did you know I'd be here?" Fingering the mug's handle, she averted her eyes. "I thought I'd leave the car for you and Randolph. A final gesture of goodwill. How stupid am I?"

"You walked all this way?" He sounded astonished.

"I saw Mavis and Trevor lying on their bed. They looked so peaceful. It was sad. I thought you'd need the car for them."

He took another long drink.

She felt embarrassed and reluctant to look at him, wanting to explain but knowing she'd never make herself understood. She should have taken the car and driven away—and kept on driving.

He laughed suddenly, shaking his head, glancing around the room.

"What?" she demanded.

"You must have walked fast."

She didn't want to talk about what she'd done or hadn't done.

"How did you know I'd be here?"

"Great minds think alike."

She crossed to the windows and ran one hand down the folds of tapestry in an effort to hide her emotions. "Do you think they'll see the light from outside?"

He pulled the cover off an armchair and sat down, reaching for the bottle and holding it up again in her direction.

"Tell me what's happened. I need to know what made Trevor and Mavis do it. I liked them. They were kind."

They had made the effort to dress in their best clothes. Trevor's suit and shirt and tie were old, and Mavis's tweed coat was slightly frayed at the lapel. Their faces were pale and waxen and would never smile or laugh at each other again. The brooch on Mavis's collar with its missing diamond chips looked as if it had been well-loved. The photographs of two little girls smiling and freckled in shorts and T-shirts and the dirty cups and plates of cake crumbs on the table when Mavis seemed so house-proud affected Lizzie more than the terror of seeing the Westons' chalet collapsing in the storm. They had loved each other, and she would never be loved or love someone like that. She didn't know which made her want to cry the most.

"You haven't said where Randolph is. I don't want him smashing his way in here, shouting and smacking people," she said.

"Why d'you think I brought the vodka?" He looked tired; as tired as she felt.

She remembered the look on Mavis's face as she'd talked about long summer days with her daughters on the beach, them playing on grass in the evening sun while she washed up tea things by the open window, of reading Georgette Heyer romances and listening to the radio.

"Is Randolph dead too?" she asked. "Is that why you want to get hammered?"

He took another drink. "Moving house is too big a deal for some people."

She looked down at the liquid, so like water, in her cup. "After death, the hardest thing to deal with is divorce."

He still didn't look at her.

"Then changing jobs."

"I thought it was moving house." He looked at her then, fixing her with his green-brown eyes.

"I couldn't kill myself, no matter how hard things got."

He raised his glass. "To Trevor, Mavis, John, Joyce, Marilyn and Randolph."

So they were all dead. Every single one of them. She believed him. She studied his waxed jacket, dark jeans and brown boots encrusted with white salt stains. His long fingers encircled the cup resting on his knee. He seemed different to the man who had tried to save the old couple from falling to their deaths five long days ago. She stepped forward and clinked his cup.

"I saw Peter on the Beamstown bus," she said, surprising herself with the force of her voice. "I'm glad he got away."

"And you and I are safe here." The way he said it didn't sound safe. "Does Carol know you're here?"

She hesitated. She wanted to sound like a definite decision had been made.

"I'm waiting," she eventually said.

"Sit down and wait properly then."

She dropped into a chair without removing the dustsheet. "Did you talk to her when you came in?"

"I wanted to see if you were here first."

The words rang in her head. She knew there was a reason why she'd ended up in the chalet park, but she couldn't quite work out why yet. She'd felt it immediately he opened the door and she'd smelt the woody scent of apples. And it was hard. Too hard.

"I'm glad I've found you," he said. "This was my first port of call. I was going to try your scraggy boyfriend next." He paused, waiting for her response, then leaned forward, arms resting on thighs, mug dangling empty from one hand.

"Ex," she said. "He's an ex."

She tried to work out what else to say. If she told him she was glad he'd come, he might lean back and let her words hang, and she'd be left exposed and looking stupid. He might say he was glad he'd found her because he'd only come to find the car. If she didn't say a word, he couldn't throw it back.

"So you're going to stay here?" he eventually asked.

"I've nowhere else to go."

"I know." He didn't sound sarcastic or proud to know what having nowhere to go meant.

She kept her eyes on the liquid glinting in her cup. "What about you?"

"I've nowhere to go either. We're like two dinghies drifting at sea."

"Well," she tried to smile, "better than being tied up in a marina on a short rope."

That's what she always told everyone even though it's what she secretly wanted. Drifting wasn't fun. Drifting meant being battered. It didn't make life simpler and more fun, not in the way knowing where you'd come from and were going back to did. In reality, it made it more complicated because drifting meant not trusting, and not trusting meant you pushed other boats away, and that meant being a dinghy all on your own and never finding a jetty to tie yourself up against.

"How did you get here?" she suddenly wondered. "You were quick. It took me ages to walk."

He put down his mug on the table. "I know a short cut," he said. "If you hadn't been in such a hurry, I could have shown you."

She couldn't tell whether he was joking or not.

He leant forward again, almost touching her knees with his hand. "It's okay. Randolph scares me most of the time as well. I'm just sorry you were so frightened of us you had to bolt."

"I wasn't...I'm not."

"We can go back and get the car if you want. I can drop you wherever you want in Rigby." He walked to the window and peered around the curtains.

Disappointment flowed through her. Of course he didn't want to be her friend. He was merely being kind. She realised it was madness to think that life could change; she wouldn't see Jez again after tonight. He'd come to the castle to make sure that happened.

She put down her mug next to his. "I'm going to stay here tonight. I'll catch the bus to Rigby in the morning. Thanks for the offer, but I'll be fine."

"Has anyone told you you're like a breath of fresh air?" he asked.

She looked away. "Of course they have. All the time."

"You don't realise it, do you?"

"Have you eaten anything? I'm starving. There's probably something left in the kitchen." She was already moving towards the door.

"Why are you so frightened of everyone?"

Her head was beginning to fizzle again. Why didn't he go and leave her be? She'd spent years trying to infiltrate groups, be part of a crowd, mingle with people, but had always been pushed away. Now she wanted to be left alone, he wouldn't leave.

"Of course I'm not," she said. "I'm dumped among strangers in a lonely old place that's falling into the sea and you all act really odd and don't care people are dead and Randolph's hitting everyone and shouting and running around all secretive with stuff and Mavis and Trevor are lying in their best clothes and then all those explosions and bangs and you don't tell me anything…" She paused, overwhelmed. "Of course I'm not frightened."

"How were we supposed to talk to you?" he said. "We tried to make you welcome, but you kept running away."

"That's not fair!" She couldn't believe it. "I had to be places. I had work and things to do, and why should I be friendly, anyway? We were told to leave. The housing people said we should leave. I wasn't running away. That's unfair."

"Life's not fair. Surely someone must've told you *that*?"

She didn't answer. Everyone told her that.

"What do you want me to say?" he said. "That Trevor and Mavis have been planning to commit suicide since spring?"

"Don't joke about things like that. They could've been happy somewhere else."

"In a rabbit hutch in Beamstown?"

"Alive."

"Feeling they were dead."

"Same sky, same sea, same bloody accents."

"They'd been planning it since spring. We all had."

She wouldn't be angry. She wouldn't cry. They were nothing to do with her.

"I thought you were dead," she said.

Silently, tired of pretence, she stepped forward and rested her head against his chest, and he leant his cheek on her hair. She heard his cup on the table. His coat felt hard and cold touching her skin, like it had on that first rainy night. They didn't say a word.

Eventually, she stepped back. "Wait here," she told him. "I'll go down and get some food. We'll have a picnic and finish the vodka."

She left him standing in the room whilst she trod carefully along the dark corridor past portraits of Andrew's unyielding ancestors, towards the main stairs and the light emanating from below.

Chapter Thirty-Nine

SITTING IN BEAMSTOWN'S bus station, Peter rested the cardboard tube on the metal seat at his side, checked that Randolph's letter remained in his top pocket and then carefully unfolded a small greaseproof packet on his lap. As he chewed a well-peppered egg sandwich, he looked around at the graffiti-scrawled walls and seats declaring that Josie loved Kyle and Danielle loved Nicky.

Outside, a taxi driver glanced at him briefly then away again. Two men stood talking. A group of giggling youngsters in dark clothes looking like shadows ran past.

A shout in the distance. "Oy, you buggers!"

Another group, older this time, spun him around as they hurtled past, leaving him disorientated. As kids, he and his friends had kept quiet on Mischief Night. There had been no gunpowder that night, only mischief, but this lot had lost the whole idea of what 4th November meant. Traditions were lost. The world had changed and not for the better. He glanced over his shoulder and kept close to the wall so that he wasn't caught off guard again.

Even so, coming around the corner of the Broomfield Shopping Centre, he collided with yet another cluster of youths. The two tallest, a girl with black hair and a lad wearing a bright-blue cap, struggled to carry a large 'house for sale' sign between them. He smiled to himself in memory of the similar tricks he and his friends had played. This was more like it. Straightening his shoulders, he thought how he too was part of this anarchic night when, without warning, numbing pain seared across the back of his shoulders. Crumpling to his knees, he broke the fall with outstretched hands. The cardboard cylinder rolled into the gutter. Reaching out, he yelped as a white trainer stamped on his fingers. He heard laughter, shouts, no longer friendly.

"Hit him again."

"Kick him."

"Old bastard."

"Fucking creep."

"Teach him to laugh at us."

"In his balls."

"Head."

"Let me in."

He curled into his shell. The cardboard tube struck his shoulder, and he cradled his head, trying to dissolve into the pavement but only managing to leave his spine exposed. Somehow, their feet forced their way under and up into the softness of his stomach, and he retched. As his body began to unfurl and his head explode in red orbiting particles, new shouts erupted. There came the bullet-like sound of imploding glass and then a grating, throbbing siren. And then they were running, large feet and small, stampeding as a pack of excited children at a birthday party.

The car alarm penetrated the muted noise in his head, and a huge black van of a car lit up like a spaceship. The cracked 'For Sale' sign now protruded out of the vehicle's broken sunroof, and then, out of nowhere, lights panned across the wall and a police car pulled up. He clenched his stiff fingers. His hands shook. Footsteps on the road. Distorted voices. With trembling fingers, Peter felt for the cardboard container in the spill of the flashing vehicle.

"Did you see any of them?"

"I were driving. You're on lookout."

"Will you do the biz on this one? It's going to be a long night."

"They're only kids."

"Yeah, yeah, and it's only tradition."

"Mischief Night were always my favourite night of the year."

Peter listened. It had been his too. Returning home, bright-eyed from the cold and excitement, distractedly eating digestives and drinking cocoa, parents indulgent, listening, shaking heads, tutting, pleased. What would they think, seeing him on the ground, that small wiry boy now an old man ready to die?

"The owner of this monster will cause shit, rich bastard," the older, cynical voice reminded him.

"Should turn itself off in a minute," a younger voice said.

It dawned on Peter that they hadn't stopped to save him from being beaten to death but rather to catch whoever had broken a window in the towering four-by-four blaring too loud and flashing so brightly. He felt swamped with both despair and relief that they still hadn't seen him. He reached out his arm, stretching tentative fingertips, and rolled the tube towards him. The officers lingered in the road on the other side of the line of parked cars. Any minute now, they would skirt the bonnet and step onto the pavement and see him.

He tried to move, but pain stabbed through his limbs, through every organ, every bone and muscle in his body. Outstretched on the wet concrete, one bruised cheek cold against the kerb, he closed his eyes. If he couldn't see them, then maybe they wouldn't see him. If he remained still and flat, maybe they'd walk over him as if he were a pile of leaves. He could do this. He could become invisible; he'd felt invisible for a long time now; a few more minutes would be no problem. Through the rushing torrent in his ears, he heard boots move. He let his body relax. *This is the end; please let them find me. Let an ambulance arrive and white-clad forms place me on a stretcher and carry me swiftly to a place where neon lights blanch my skin and shining implements repair my organs, but please God, let my body survive until a priest arrives.*

Randolph, Jez, Mavis and Trevor filtered into his mind. If he died on the pavement or in hospital, they would all be forgotten and he would be in hell. He felt Marilyn hold his hand in support. A wave of nausea swept through him again, and he stretched out his fingers. One trembling arm followed, then the other. Mavis anxiously dabbed his forehead; Trevor silently willed him on. Randolph stood disapproving, arms folded, issuing expletives.

As he had many times, with bombs screeching overhead, he separated his mind from his body.

"Move the parts," he ordered. "Come on, move."

One limb at a time, quietly in the dark, keeping close to the ground and in the shadow of parked cars.

Distant noises dulled to the sound of footsteps. Consciousness ebbed. They stopped by the front bonnet, tapping buttons on their machine.

"Andrew Booth?" a surprised voice. "Isn't he from Moorland Castle up by Rook Bay?"

Peter heard the machine again. Three cars drove past sounding their horns. Andrew Booth had come into Beamstown as well. Right now, he couldn't figure out why. It didn't matter; that was for Randolph and Jez to worry about. He closed his eyes and let his mind fall blank before heaving up his body and dragging himself along the damp ground like an earthworm.

Finally, achingly, he reached the rear of the next vehicle, another homogenised car, as smooth and shiny as the next. Slowly and painstakingly, he crawled, the cardboard tube crunching under his weight until he reached the boot of another. Dragging himself to his knees, he winced, struggling for breath. His legs took his weight, arms balanced him, neck supporting his aching head. One officer climbed back into the police vehicle while the other stood in the middle of the road. Gradually, he rose to his feet, pressing against the back of a car and resting his forehead against the rear window. He didn't fall back down. Breathing heavily, he pulled the knitted hat Randolph had given him from his anorak pocket. The officer in the road walked back to the vehicle without noticing him slumped in the dark amid the cacophony of sound. Voices grew distant. Doors slammed, and the vehicle pulled away, leaving him alone.

He leant against the car for some time, wondering if it had crossed Randolph's mind what dangers Plot Night could hold and that all over town youngsters would not be sticking chewing gum to door knockers, taping up letterboxes, piling leaves in front of doorways, but instead throwing stones and beating up strangers. And worse, much, much worse. It was a long time since either of them had been out on 4th November.

As he crossed town, he heard countless car alarms, shouts and running feet, and cringed at every sound. These weren't covert terrorists as he and his pals had been; they were more like marauding gangs. He concentrated on putting one foot forward, then another, and again and again, over and over, making progress, nearing his goal, blocking out all shouts and alarms and activity. He kept walking, reciting over and over to himself.

"Keep going, keep going, keep going."

All these years, Randolph had kept going, fighting their corner, lobbying the council for sea defences, grants, services that would make their lives tolerable. Randolph's belligerent letters had secured for them mains water and gas delivered in huge canisters. The Royal Mail had agreed to deliver letters to their doors and not leave them in a box at the top of the hill. Randolph's dogged determination had made it possible to live as human beings in a crumbling chalet park. If Randolph could keep going against the odds, so could Peter Hawksworth.

He turned the corner, down the long strait, step by step until he looked up at the Royal Hotel. Across the way towered the foreboding redbrick town hall. He stumbled off the kerb. A car horn blared, and he stopped, blinded by headlights before staggering across the road, all the while checking for oncoming traffic. At last, he was there...almost there. A woman let the door swing back, too much in a rush to hold it open. He caught it. Stepped inside. Walking purposefully up to the front desk, he took out Randolph's letter from his breast pocket. A young woman buttoning her coat barely glanced at him.

He kept his head down. "Is this the basket for the interior post?"

"As if you didn't know," she said, bending to pick up her handbag.

Hesitantly, he placed the letter carefully on top of a pile in a wire tray and turned away at the instant she looked up.

"Oh, I thought you were...my God, what's happened to your face?"

Involuntarily, he put a hand to his cheek and felt the rough graze that seared across his skin.

"I fell." He pulled down the side of his hat. "I'm a clumsy sod."

She began opening a drawer. "I think we've got a first-aid kit somewhere."

"It's all right," he said. "I'll give it a wash."

He walked as steadily as he could towards the stairs. If he could just get down to the room below...

"Excuse me?" Her voice echoed across the vast chamber.

He froze. He should have asked permission. She was the type who liked to be asked. He raised a hand, nodding his head, praying she would understand.

He half turned, gesturing vaguely to his face. "You don't mind if I get the dirt out?"

Silence. He'd have to turn around completely to see her response. He steadied himself with the stair rail.

"I've found some plasters," she said.

He squeezed the rail. The steps curved around. If he let go, he'd fall.

"It's just a graze," he said. "Best let it breathe."

"The gents' are down the corridor." She moved out of view. He could tell she had lost interest.

***

The night security guard appeared from a small room on the right of the hall and strolled up to the desk.

"There's an old man going in the toilets," she said. "He shouldn't be long." He nodded, not wanting to drop into conversation. "Have you seen what it's like outside?" Tying a scarf around her neck, she headed for the front door. "Is it raining?"

"Like a smog with all them fireworks," he said. "Keep an eye open for those nippers out there."

She laughed. "Night, then."

He followed her to the door and watched her trot across the road. Reaching in a pocket, he pulled out a packet of cigarettes and lit up. Shouts and cries smattered the air. Two young lads walked across the pedestrian area, pulling plants out of the long, low troughs.

"I'm watching you!" he shouted as they continued to tear out small evergreen shrubs.

Chapter Forty

SHIVERS OF YELLOW, green and pink stars and crackling silvery cascades peppered the sky above the towering roof of Moorland Castle. They flared then faded as vast waterfalls of fluorescent sparks twinkled down from booming explosions. Lizzie sniffed as she rounded the house and caught the forceful heat of the flaming pyre. The smell of gunpowder belched in the air as increasing numbers of fireworks detonated. The noise, sight and blazing warmth coming out of the dark hit her full on. Jim stood too close to the fire; shocked, she roughly pulled him by the sleeve of his jacket. He stumbled back, staring at her as though she were a stranger.

"Jim?" she said. "Jim, it's me, Lizzie. What's happened? Have you seen Carol?"

He came to then, nodding recognition before looking back at the bonfire.

"Have those kids done this?" she asked. He didn't answer. "There's going to be a lot of upset punters tomorrow night." Another rocket screeched above their heads, and she jumped.

Seemingly oblivious to the heat, Jim neared the blaze again. "Without Mister Andrew here, it don't really matter," he said.

"'Course it does." Lizzie glanced at the upstairs window, wondering if Jez was watching. "Carol's worked hard for this. And you—you've worked hard too." When he didn't respond, she touched his arm again. "Thank you for looking after me the other day."

He turned his watery eyes on her.

"I lit it," he said.

Before she could think what to answer, Carol marched towards them with a face pinched as a nettle sting.

Lizzie stepped automatically in front of Jim. "It was an accident."

"I've called the fire service," Carol snapped. "And the police."

Lizzie glanced at Jim, but he remained staring at the flames.

"Don't you think they'll have enough to do tonight?" Lizzie faced Carol again. "We were just talking—it's probably those kids that are always mucking around, and they'll be well out of here by now—"

"Don't you dare go anywhere," Carol interrupted, her face ugly with anger as Jim turned to go. "Don't either of you move." She strode back to the front drive, phone in hand.

"She's no right to talk to me like that." Jim's voice was barely audible.

Retreating from the searing heat, Lizzie remained silent.

"You're a jumped-up shop girl," he shouted after Carol.

Lizzie held his arm. "Why the hell did you do this, Jim?"

"No class," he said. "Talking to me like that. Mister Andrew knows there has to be respect. He was brought up to it, but that wife of his, she hasn't a clue. And Carol—" he said the name with venom "—she's of the same mould. Can't be doing with women like that."

"Jim? Are you listening? You've just thrown away thousands of pounds of their income. She's not exactly going to be understanding." Even as she spoke, she knew it was too late.

Jim had always seemed dour but harmless, and she realised how little she knew him. She didn't know anyone well when she thought about it. Not Colin, Phil, Andrew or anyone she'd ever come across, and none of them really knew her; not what she was thinking and feeling deep down. She wondered if it was merely her desire to be understood that made her think Jez could read her mind. And even that illusion had been shattered; she hadn't a clue what drove him. She took out her mobile, more for comfort than to make a call, and rubbed her thumb over the keypad.

The firelight flickered over them both, casting shadows. Jim seemed preoccupied, nudging ash and wood off the path with his boot, and she studied him warily from the cover of her fringe—his tall, wiry frame, comfortable, sagging wax jacket and, to her unease, glinting in the orange glow, the long barrel of a gun at his side. For a second, in the wavering shadows, like sunlight dappling through rustling trees, she recognised the coat and boots and gun, not because she'd seen him walking with it about the gardens or across the yard or tending the flower borders as he always did, but somewhere else. Slowly, she stepped back further, remembering the figure she had thought merely another slender sapling overlooking the wall at the edge of the estate. Jim's arm lifted.

She stared through the cracked windscreen...

She dropped the phone. Before she knew it, he reached out. Panicking, she bobbed down to retrieve it first, and they looked into each other's eyes. That was it. She ran across the grass, tripping over the path in her haste.

Once more, the security light triggered, flooding the front of the house with its bright glare. She searched frantically, but no-one was about. Assuming Carol had gone inside, Lizzie ran straight through the front door. Plunged into darkness, she noisily bumped into the centre table. The vase of Michaelmas daisies tipped, hitting the wood with a crack, and water spread across the table and dripped onto the rug.

"Shit."

Hurrying up the stairs and reaching the bedroom, she pushed open the door and stumbled inside. The lamps had been turned off, and she reached for the switch, desperate now to see.

"Jez?" she whispered.

His voice came from the window. "Thought you were going for food?"

"What's happened to the lights?"

"Leave them."

His voice sounded different, and she wished she'd gone to the kitchen after all and not tried to play peacemaker.

"I can't find her. She's not inside," she said. "It's Jim. He lit the bonfire and he's gone crazy letting off fireworks, and I think he killed Marilyn. Jez, I'm positive it was him."

"Jim wouldn't kill anyone." Maybe a stray dog that's worrying sheep, but that's as much as it gets. He definitely wouldn't sabotage anything that could affect the castle."

Thrown into doubt, she tried to remember if it had been a dark sapling rather than a figure she'd seen on the rise. Everyone said Jim was a good guy. It was normal for him to carry a gun. Loads of people did around here.

She reached out, trembling, for the lamp. "Can't we put on a light?"

"Wait one minute. Let me look outside."

"Carol said she's called the police."

He turned to look back through the curtains. In the silence, they heard the penultimate tread of the staircase creak and approaching footsteps, a few moments of stillness, then the snap of a rifle being locked. Lizzie tensed, wondering how long it would take before the door flew open and Jim towered in the doorway, aiming his gun, completely insane.

"He's gone in one of the other rooms." Jez touched her arm, making her jump. "If he thinks the police are on their way, I guess he's keeping a low profile." He hesitated. "Like we should."

She frowned. Were they hiding from the police? She often wanted to hide from everyone. Whatever happened now, it would be better than carrying on the way she had. Something had to change. She couldn't hide forever.

"Let's both go back down," she said. "I'll tell them I saw a gang of kids mucking about. So what if Carol asks what we're doing here? I don't think that'll be a priority right now."

"That should keep them busy." His voice came out bright. "You go down, and I'll warn Jim, and Lizzie? Best not mention either that Jim and I are here."

"Don't go near him," she said. "He may suddenly take a crack at you."

"All the more reason I find him. He won't turn on me, but he could on someone he doesn't know, especially if they take it into their heads to be a bit rough."

Of course they had to protect those who couldn't protect themselves.

"Okay," she whispered. "Let's go, then." She turned to the door, fumbling for the handle.

"Lizzie, wait a minute." His voice sounded different again. "I'll meet you." He reached out and cupped his hand over hers. "Far side of the car park?"

His fingers touched her hand, his mouth so close to hers she felt it move. In the back of her mind, she knew Jim had shot Marilyn and she would never know why. She couldn't save him, just as she hadn't been able to save Mavis and Trevor or the others, but they could try. Everyone had to try.

She pressed down the door handle.

"Let's not get arrested ourselves." He smiled, that rare lightning flash of humour, and with that look, she saw the glimmer of an alternative. The old house with its dark panelling and back stairs had secret means to make people disappear.

She grabbed his arm.

"How did you get here so fast? Show me. You know a quick way out of here, don't you?" Her heart thumped with possibility.

His smile dropped as if he would protest, then tentatively, without a word, he stepped onto the corridor. She hesitated, wondering why he wasn't more enthusiastic, but then followed him, hand firm against the panelling, eyes fixed on the beam of his torch. He headed in the opposite direction to the staircase and front entrance, to the left, further into the passages of the house. Quietly, she walked behind him, past heavily framed portraits of unsmiling men and women. Two suits of armour gleamed then receded. Chairs glowed with beeswax then dulled. Thoughts of where they could be headed beckoned, but when Jez abruptly stopped and pushed one of the wooden panels, she could only stare in surprise. Standing to one side, he gestured for her to step into the darkness.

Chapter Forty-One

STRAIGHT AWAY, COLD air enveloped them. Jez pulled the door closed and shifted the beam of his torch slowly over a wall, revealing a tunnel's tar-like entrance.

"Okay?" he asked.

She shivered. "I don't understand."

"It leads to the beach."

She sensed his hesitation that there was something else he wanted to say.

"What is it?" she asked.

Jez's eyes lit up as torchlight caught his face, and she knew she'd been right: he formulated another plan.

"There's no point in us both going back," he said.

"What d'you mean, go back?" She panicked. "What are you talking about? If you really wanted to get Jim, we should have gone together, but it's too late now."

"Jim's not a murderer," Jez reiterated. "We can't leave him to the mercy of that lot. You know that."

"All right. Let's see if he'll come with us." She didn't want to—it was anything but what she wanted—but she fought her natural reaction to run and readied herself.

"I'll be five minutes and we'll catch you up."

He moved; the panel door opened.

She reached for his arm. "What? No. I won't be able to see."

"Here." He pressed the torch into her hands. "I've got another. The quicker I find him, the sooner we'll all be out of this place."

Before she could say anything else, he pulled another torch out of his jacket pocket and was gone.

Flashing the beam over uneven stone, studying the pocked and shadowy rock, she dallied over whether she should set off and hope they'd catch up. She peered into the tunnel. The drop in temperature made her gasp. Bracing herself, she took a couple of paces before turning back again. Jim had a gun; if Jez took him by surprise or Jim didn't like what Jez said, or just completely by accident, he might use it. Jim knew her best. Jim had carried her into the warmth of the house from the car. He didn't judge her; she didn't judge him.

Out in the corridor, voices reached her immediately. She raised her torch in the direction of the sound, but there was no-one to be seen. Following the threadbare runner, she moved the beam over glinting suits of armour, chairs and paintings, looking for doors. Wood panelling gleamed, and the faces of Andrew's ancestors appeared and disappeared as she hurried past. Then she caught sight of the dark crack of the priest hide door standing ajar. Male voices emanated from within, and a circle of light flashed intermittently. She felt the wall for a light switch, but the bulb didn't come on. Fumbling her way with one hand, she trained the torch on each narrow stair as she crept tentatively upwards. Rounding the top step into the room, the sight of two men met her.

"Jim? Are you coming?"

Neither answered, and Jez lowered his torch so that it shone its circle on the ground at his feet.

"Are you coming with us, Jim?" She was determined to remain in control. She shone her torch directly into his craggy face.

"I said we'd catch you up." Jez's voice was quiet, his face shadowy in the edges of light.

"Then let's go." She turned.

"I told you, I'd do it." Jim's voice was almost inaudible.

"Do what?" Lizzie flashed the torch at their faces again. "Why are you hanging about up here? We've got to go."

She waited. Neither of them spoke. Jim cleared his throat and then silence again. She half wished she'd gone down the tunnel and forgotten about them. This time last week, she'd been staying in the spare room at the fish and chip shop. Two days ago, she'd been looking around council flats. This time tomorrow, she could be in one. She remembered her suitcase, in the bedroom where she'd left it. It seemed unbelievable she'd forgotten about it after dragging it all the way up here. They'd definitely have to leave by the front entrance now; she'd never be able to carry it down the tunnel unless she came back later, sometime, maybe tomorrow. Maybe.

"What were you arguing about?" she asked.

No answer.

"Let me light it." Jim's measured tone, as if he were stating the most logical act in the world, made the air tingle with the brutality of the simple statement.

"Light what?" she demanded, lifting the torch again. Police officers could run up the stairs at any moment, and then they'd all be hauled down to the station and made to answer questions as to why they were there. She'd never thought Jez could be lost for words. Quiet, yes, but never unsure. He merely stared back at Jim.

"Let him light what?" she repeated.

"It doesn't matter." Jez turned his face out of the glare. "You're right, let's go."

She wanted to hit one, if not both of them.

"Thank you, you know I'll do it right," Jim said.

She knew he meant something to do with the house; something to do with the dark oak panelling, the family portraits and ancient furniture, velvet sofas and the dog's basket by the Aga.

He looked at her directly with no obvious emotion.

Then he said, "I'm going to blow up Moorland Castle."

She glanced at Jez, then back at Jim. He meant it. He meant the front door that she wanted to leave by, the tall chimneys, the bedroom with her suitcase and the bottle of vodka, the china cupids in the library and spilt purple flowers on the polished table in the hall; the entire building that had been a family home for centuries. The only thing she wasn't sure of was whether he wanted to blow them up as well. She remembered Marilyn's twisted limbs on the tarmac and skirt billowing in the wind. She knew she was right; it had been Jim's figure on the wooded hillock.

"Jim, whatever it is, let it go," she said. "Doing this is huge. There'll be no going back. It's the castle, for God's sake. You love Moorland Castle. You love Andrew. You can't do that to him."

"Get out."

"No." She'd make him listen. "Carol might be downstairs. There might be others who could be hurt." Astonished she was arguing so logically, she drew out time, as much time as she could to get him to change his mind. "Jim, you love this place, don't…"

His eyes sagged, tired, skin drained; he'd had enough.

"You're young," he said.

She tried to see if the gun hung there, held tight against his leg, but his hands moved freely, and there was no sign of it in the circle of light.

"You can't blow up Moorland Castle when there are still people here," she reasoned.

"There'll only be me." He turned back to Jez.

She stared at his profile. Jez was right: he didn't appear capable of shooting anyone.

Jez looked at Lizzie. "We've got time to get out."

"You can't agree with this." She took a step forward. "This is nuts."

"I killed someone." Jim's voice sounded choked. "There's nothing for me now."

Silence again. Jim shifted his feet. Jez didn't say anything.

"Let's go." She shone the torch directly into Jim's face. "Come on, Jim. Let's leave this place for Andrew and Judith to come home to."

He squinted, putting up a hand to shield his eyes from the glare.

She tried to keep her voice steady. "You don't have to do this."

"My job is to protect Mister Andrew," he mumbled. "Jez, give me your torch." He held out his hand.

"Andrew can protect himself." Lizzie flashed the beam again. "That's one thing he's brilliant at. Come on, let's go!"

The more questions she asked the less she felt she understood. She wanted to see what Jez thought, but she didn't want to let Jim out of her sight. Still, he didn't say a word. Confused, her palms grew sweaty and her cheeks burned.

Jim held his hand out more forcefully. "I'm not going to change my mind."

"What do you mean? What are you talking about?" Her heart beat painfully. "This is crazy."

No-one said anything again. Lizzie swallowed, aware that the atmosphere between them was growing increasingly fractious.

Jim's quiet voice broke the silence. "The dynamite's ready to set off."

Lizzie glanced behind them, her scalp pricking like sunburnt skin.

Jim moved first, grabbing the torch from Jez. Without thinking, Lizzie grasped his sleeve in an attempt to hold him back, but he thrust her off easily, and she staggered, grappling to maintain her hold as their shadows towered over the ceiling.

"Lizzie!" Jez's voice came out of the darkness. "Jim, leave her alone."

She couldn't see him but heard Jim clamber over the wall. Painfully scraping her hands on stone, she followed.

"Lizzie."

"You've lit the bonfire and let off all the fireworks. You've ruined Carol's night—can't that be enough for you?" She panted, flashing the torch. "Just because you've killed one person doesn't mean you have to kill more people." She reached out trying to catch hold of him again.

"Jim, wait!" Jez's voice resounded in the small space.

"I won't let you destroy the house," she shouted, angry now. "This is Andrew's family home. It would kill him. You love this place too. What would you do without it? What if you killed someone else? Jez? Say something!" She flashed the beam on his face.

He looked dejected. "It's time we weren't here," he said.

"No!" She swivelled around, fixing the torchlight on the gap into the second chamber. "It's in here, isn't it?" She dropped on her knees, pushing his legs aside and bending so that her head touched the stone floor. She pointed the torch into the secret hide.

Jez scrambled over the wall, but she'd already caught the overwhelming aroma emanating from the enclosed space. Covering her mouth and nose, she fell back, banging her torch on the hard floor. Holding her breath, she shone the light back through the gap. A body, sprawled dark and inert, filled the floor of the tiny room. Recognising the tweed jacket, she gasped and tightened her grip on the torch, slowly moving the beam down the patched sleeve and thick corduroy trousers to brown brogues. Jez knelt beside her.

"Did you do this?" She looked up at Jim, shining the beam directly into his face.

Confusion filled his eyes.

"I moved him in here," he said. "But I couldn't..." His voice caught, and he looked away.

She felt ashamed for asking. He had nothing but the estate, overseeing grouse hunts, raising chicks, maintaining the grounds and the ritual of morning talks with Andrew. Without Andrew, he had nothing. She wanted to rest her head on the cold stone and feel its solid weight against her skin.

She lowered the beam. "D'you know what happened?"

"He wouldn't want to be found like this."

"Then let's move him. We can lift him out between us. Please, Jim. He should be in the family grave. We can do this."

"He's the last of the line." Jim's hands shook, and the beam bobbed over their figures. "Who'll inherit the place? Her?"

"It doesn't matter, we need...who do we need to call?" She looked at Jez.

"Nobody's moving him." Jim's voice was firm now. "This is his home. No-one else is having it."

"Come on, Jim, this isn't up to us. Judith will want—"

"It's not up to her. He wouldn't want the place selling off."

The lifeless body didn't seem like Andrew. She shivered, unable to imagine his arms strong around her now. It was Jez by her side with his long, sinewy wrists and stretched fingers that were real. She didn't love Andrew; she'd never loved him, or anyone; she only felt need. And now she felt pity. Andrew should be alive, his face reddened by the heat of the bonfire, eyes sparkling at the crowds who came to watch fireworks exploding above the tall chimneys of the house—his home. As a child, she'd gaped at them in awe, seen the tousle-haired son of the owner throwing sticks, striding about and shouting with the authority of someone who knew their place in the world. She'd never dreamt he would share his thoughts with her; never imagined in all her fantasies that he would find something in her that he wanted.

She leant back, the musty, yet sharp stench unbearable. Unable to hold her breath any longer, she pressed her hand down on Jez's shoulder for leverage and rose unsteadily to her feet.

"If Judith wants to sell the place then that's up to her," she directed wearily at Jim's silent figure. "Houses get sold all the time. His family got the place from someone else, you know. They're not the original owners."

"You need to go now. I've got to get on," said Jim.

"What if someone else gets hurt?" She grabbed his hand, hoping the touch of another human being would be enough to pull him back.

"If you go now, no-one will."

His skin felt dry and hard. Lines ran deep across the palm etched with dirt that wouldn't wash out.

"Don't make Andrew into some sort of saint," she said. "You don't owe him anything."

"Shows you didn't know him. He kept up the old ways and looked after everyone that worked for him."

"Okay, he made sacrifices." She felt heartened. "So think about it. He'd want the house to go to someone else so we all keep our jobs." She paused. "Keep its history. If you destroy the place, it goes against what he worked for."

His shoulders drooped under the wax jacket. His skin, leathered by the elements, showed the paleness of exhaustion. He'd had enough. She knew that feeling, recognising the dread of having to start all over again.

"You know that won't happen." Nudging past, he snatched the torch from Jez and bent down. He flashed the beam back at her. "Let me show you something."

"I've seen," she said, stepping back. "I don't want to look again."

She knew she'd be sick if she smelt the contaminated air and instinctively held her breath.

"Here." Jez held out a handkerchief. "Have a look at what Jim wants to show you."

She looked at the handkerchief, clean and white, gleaming in the dull light, then at Jez. He too was tired, but his eyes encouraged her to do as Jim said. She grabbed the handkerchief and, holding it over her nose, bent to look back inside the hole.

Jim shone the torch over the walls, skimming the top of Andrew's body. She couldn't make out what he illuminated at first and was about to sit back as he caught her arm. Reluctantly, she looked again. Focusing on the uneven surface of the stone walls, she saw that holes had been drilled all around the perimeter and cords snaked down to the floor gathering in a central pile of what looked like unwrapped fireworks.

"It's all set," said Jez, his voice chilly in the dark.

Horrified, she sat up.

Jim's eyes glared pink. Rummaging in a pocket, he drew out a box of matches, glanced into the hole, then back at them.

"Now take your torch and bugger off."

Chapter Forty-Two

PETER HAD NO intention of cleaning his cuts and grazes in the gents' toilets. Instead, making his way down the curving stairwell, he sensed the familiar tenderness of bruising developing over his abdomen and arms.

He reached the last step and headed for a large, wooden door on the right. Once inside, he closed his eyes and, with shoulders slumped against the wood, rested the cardboard tube on the ground. It felt as though pressure built inside his head. His body ached all over. He forced himself to look around. All was as Randolph told him it would be. He let the tube slip from his hand, and it bounced as it hit the flags. He jumped at the noise. His nerves coiled tight. Not good news for an ex-soldier.

He waited to see if anyone upstairs had heard. No-one came, and he exhaled deeply; he couldn't afford to make any more mistakes. He shuffled over to a pile of disused and broken furniture in the corner, looked behind at several boxes stacked neatly. Next to them, propped against the wall, were wooden picture frames, as arranged. He carefully lifted one then another and carried them, two at a time, until eight lay on the floor. Wincing, he lowered himself onto the flags. Closing his eyes again, he reminded himself that every day, soldiers endured horrific injuries without complaint.

He took the lid off the cylindrical container and unrolled eleven canvases. Gordon and Shelley, John and Joyce and all the other members of the community, himself included, soon stared up at him. Emptying a box of tacks on the stone flags and pulling a small hammer from an inside pocket, he began stretching canvases over the frames. He worked steadily, taking his time as Jez had taught him, until finally, he looked down at the young woman who'd come to the park barely a week ago. He'd hardly paid attention to her during those first few days. He could recall only two occasions: when she first arrived in her beaten-up car and on that sunny afternoon when they'd sat around eating Marilyn's chilli. Jez had captured her indecisive gaze well. That's what had struck him about her. He'd been amazed when Jez pressed the rough sheet of paper into his hand.

"Hot off the press," he'd said.

He looked down. Randolph glared up at him.

"All right, all right," he said aloud, tapping in tacks as he pulled the canvas taut. "Keep your hair on."

He tried not to look at the paintings too much after that. He didn't want to catch Marilyn's red-lipped pout or Mavis's grey-eyed warmth, but he couldn't help himself. He needed to see their faces again. Randolph defiant. Gordon stoic, and Shelley, the cancer shadowed under her eyes. John and Joyce, stiff and uncomfortable. His own, medals shining. Jez's self-portrait was remarkably lifelike. Trevor, well…Trevor. He smiled. Mavis's soft gaze comforted him. Her skin glowed of late-summer sun, reminding him why he was doing what he did. Saved especially until last, he propped Mavis and Trevor up in front of his own portrait and formally said the goodbye he'd neglected to make earlier. He glanced at his watch: he was on schedule.

Jez had been right. By being methodical, it hadn't proved too difficult, and he felt calmer now they sat taut over their frames. He stretched a sheet out on the floor, placed the canvases on top of each other in the centre, gathered in the corners, tied a knot and carefully tested their weight, straining as his arms trembled at the awkwardness of its shape.

***

Susan Harper lay awake, balancing uncomfortably on the edge of the divan while Jack, her two-year-old son, lay spreadeagled in sleep at her side. She didn't know why, but the memory of seeing Randolph Brook lurching up the town hall steps unsettled her. With a headache threatening, she couldn't face talking to anyone else that evening, particularly that persistently belligerent old man. He collared her at that time of day on a weekly basis, and she told herself that missing one ranting session wouldn't do him or her any harm. Something was different, though. She rarely left on time, but last night, she'd wanted to pick up Jack promptly so he wouldn't see any of the kids up to tricks and ask questions she didn't have the energy to answer. It had been a long day finalising suitable properties for the chalet residents and removal vans for all their belongings, but she'd managed it.

She sighed. Tomorrow wasn't going to be easy with emotions at play. Moving the remaining residents out before the bulldozers arrived would be traumatic for everyone involved. Plus, she'd had to add the younger woman to the list. She wished the old couples had gone to live with relatives, but realistically that had never been an option. Hopefully, they'd be organised and grateful to leave after the weekend's tragedy. Carl had kept in touch with Randolph to check they were organising themselves, but she couldn't know for sure how it would pan out until the actual time of eviction. She closed her eyes, willing herself back to sleep, but the memory of Randolph in his familiar brown anorak rankled. She sat when an image pierced her memory. There had been something different about his gait and manner; she was certain of that now.

Downstairs in the kitchen, as the kettle boiled, she pressed the town hall's number on her phone.

"Did Randolph Brook leave anything besides the usual brown envelope?" she asked George, who was notably frustrated by the interruption and grumbled that she'd taken him away from a freshly made cup of tea.

"Like what?" he asked.

"A long packet. You know, one of them cardboard tube things you put posters in." She tried not to sound impatient.

"I'll have a look," he said, and he took his time, as it was a couple of minutes before he came back on the phone.

"Just the same old," he said.

"No, there should be a long cylinder," Susan explained. "It might not have my name on it."

George sighed heavily, and she heard things being moved around the desk. "Nope," he said.

"Check on the shelves behind you and on the floor. It's quite big. It should be obvious."

"Can't see owt," he said. "Lisa probably put it somewhere safe to give you in the morning."

"Was she still there when he came in?"

"Yeah, he spoke to her, but it wasn't—"

"Did she say anything to you about it?"

"She asked if it were raining."

Susan sighed. She wouldn't be able to sleep now. "Okay, thanks. Never mind."

"You want me to go and look, don't you?" His tone was resigned.

"Would you mind?" She couldn't pinpoint why, but she knew this was important. "I'll phone you back in ten minutes."

After putting down the receiver, she sat on a chair, wide awake. When she phoned again, he still hadn't found it. She couldn't sleep now, but it would be futile to phone back a third time and ask him to open the letter that always said the same thing.

***

It was almost midnight. Peter waited at the base of the stairwell until the sound of footsteps faded away. As Randolph had said, George began his rounds like clockwork, first checking the front door bolts, then setting off up the stairs to the first floor. Peter heaved the bundle of canvases and ascended the small flight of stairs, one careful step at a time until, breathing heavily, he rested the frames on the floor of the entrance hall. He listened again. Silence. He glanced at his watch. He had thirty minutes before the security guard came back downstairs. Hurrying as quickly as he could manage, the wooden frames knocking against his shins, he glanced up the main stairwell and listened again.

Randolph had drilled into him which door to head for even though he already knew. The main hall was a grand room. He'd been to a ceremony honouring soldiers from the Falklands War there years ago. He would never forget the gleaming wood of the parquet floor, the vast alabaster ceiling, magnificent chandeliers and dark oil paintings of town dignitaries. He limped across the floor and pressed down the iron handle.

***

Across town, Susan remained seated at the kitchen table, coffee mug in hand, wondering if she was overreacting, even though something Mavis Cummings had said kept coming back. She'd asked about family. Susan had told her she had a little boy. Mavis said she shouldn't work because the years when they are young go too fast and you never get them back. All stuff she'd been told before. It had annoyed her. But then there was something different. Mavis had taken her hand and whispered, "Don't stay late on Plot Night. Get yourself home. Do something nice with your little boy."

Susan picked up the phone and dialled 999.

***

Peter knew exactly where to position them. Logically, he set about the task, propping up each painting under that of a local dignitary. He wished he could physically replace them, but the old paintings in their heavy frames could not be easily or quickly moved, so for a while, his friends would have to rest on the floor. It seemed ludicrous, now that he surveyed the ordinary faces against those stern and imposing men, that they would ever hang in such lofty surroundings, but Randolph had been convincing. Peter glanced at his watch again. He'd taken too long. He took one last look at Mavis, feeling a hollow pit in his stomach that it had come to this. It wasn't his way, but Randolph had assured them all that this was how they'd make their mark. He looked at his own portrait and wished he had been a stronger man.

A crack against one of the windows snapped him back to reality. A light flared outside, sizzling and spitting bright sparks. Laughter. *The little bastards.* He let out a long sigh and bundled up the sheet. At least he'd be able to rest for two hours before the security guard's second round of inspection—when he'd be able to bring up the boxes.

Footsteps from upstairs rang out as Peter carefully closed the grand chamber door. He pushed the handle down as if to escape back inside, then turned to face the vast, open space. The sound of boots approached from the floor above. He took several steps forward. The stuttering cough of the security guard echoed. Peter reached the top of the curving stairwell and caught his breath. Footsteps resounded from the main staircase. Holding onto the balustrade, legs almost collapsing under him, Peter hobbled down the steps. He stopped. Loud banging resonated from the front door. The security guard's heavy footsteps hesitated, then set off again, more deliberate with each step. Bolts rammed back.

One foot resting on the bottom step, trying to calm his breathing, Peter listened to the distant booms and shouts.

"Is there anything up?" The security guard sounded worried.

"Can we come in?"

A pause, several pairs of feet, then scuffling; kids voices, some swearing and other unidentifiable noises. The door closed and then there was quiet until someone moved.

"Sit that rabble over there." The commanding voice again. Kids protesting, shuffling feet, an order, a threat, scuffling, giggles.

"Sit down and don't move." Another voice.

"I'm Police Officer Bradley. This is Police Officer Bentley and Officer Boscombe. And you are…?"

"George Copperthwaite. Security."

"So, George." It must have been Bradley still speaking. "We spoke to a Susan Harper, chief housing officer here. She seemed very concerned there was an intruder in the town hall. Do you know Miss Harper?"

A grunt.

"Do you know who she could be talking about? She mentioned a name. Mike—what was it?"

Peter strained again. Mumbling voices.

"Someone called Randolph Brook. She said you knew him?" Simon Bradbury's voice rang clear.

"Oh, him."

"Have you seen him tonight?"

Peter peered up the stairs, desperate to hear the answer.

"Not tonight, but there was another feller."

"Gaz, shut those kids up? Another man?"

"Well, I heard that lot outside. Told them off for pulling up plants, you know. Can't have them wrecking council property. Are you keeping them in here long? I mean, are you taking them off, you know, like…" His voice petered out. No-one seemed to speak for a while, and then George again, louder, decisively, almost gleeful: "A chap came in to use the gents'. Lisa went—"

"Lisa?"

"Lass on reception. She let this old chap in. He was a bit scuffed up, liked he'd fallen or something, so went to tidy himself in the toilets. She went off home, and I stood at the door watching she were safe like, with these young hooligans about, tossing stuff around."

"Did he come past you when he left?"

"What? Er, no, I don't recall that he did."

"So you didn't see him come out of this front door?" Footsteps resonated over the open space.

Peter retreated a couple of paces down the corridor.

"I've got other duties, you know?" A scuffle of feet, youthful objections, a low tone of authority. "I'd have kept an eye on him if she said he was dodgy."

"Where are the toilets?"

He coughed. "Down there."

"Is there another exit?"

Peter tiptoed towards the room he'd vacated earlier.

"Straight down?"

"By the steps. On the left."

"Where do the steps go?"

Peter opened the door to the downstairs room.

"Mike. Come with me."

"Are you gonna tell me what he's done?" the security guard asked, then called out, "Oy, you little buggers, leave those envelopes alone."

Peter didn't wait to hear what the other officer did. He crept inside and carefully closed the door.

It went quiet. He sighed with relief. A rattle of keys made him hold his breath. Footsteps. They were coming down the stairs. He hurried over to the pile of broken furniture. There was nowhere to hide. Maybe another room would be better. He started towards the door when the handle turned. Stepping back again, he caught a chair leg with his foot and stumbled.

"Hello." He recognised the voice of the red-haired Simon Bradbury. "What d'you think you're doing in here?"

Unable to catch his balance, Peter stumbled backwards over chairs and stools, groaning as his back dug into the hard edge of a table leg.

Rushing forward, Mike grabbed his arm to stop him falling.

"Get off me!" Peter flailed, twisting as he rolled onto the floor. The cold, hard concrete came as a shock. Footsteps ceased. He turned his head; a pair of boots shone by his side. Simon looked down at him.

"Get caught up in something, did you? That looks sore."

Silently, Peter struggled to his feet, brushing down his trousers and straightening his cuffs.

"Have you been drinking?"

Peter stared in disdain.

"What are you doing here?" Simon asked. "This is no place to set up home, you know. Come on, mate, you don't have to be this desperate. You'll be properly housed. You can't squat here."

Mike pulled open one of the boxes from behind the furniture pile.

"Bloody hell."

Simon glanced over his shoulder. "What is it? The old man's belongings? Kitchen sink and stove?"

Mike lifted a cardboard box. "See for yourself."

Peter remembered everything that he and Randolph had spoken about over the past year. He remembered as if it had been yesterday how he had felt returning from the Falklands and hearing those familiar Rigby accents cocoon him in wool, and how he was swept over with gratitude to be back home. Randolph had trusted him, and he had only completed half the job.

Without warning, he pushed Simon in the stomach. Taken unawares, Simon reeled back into Mike who, stumbling backwards, dropped the box. Simon, tripping, tried to catch his balance and grasped Mike's arms. Peter dragged the box from the floor, almost falling over in his haste.

"Stop!" Simon shouted as he crashed into the pile of furniture, groaning as he half pulled, half pushed Mike away while Peter staggered breathlessly into the corridor.

Chapter Forty-Three

THE BEAMS OF their torches flickered over the roughly hewn rock roof and rock walls. A moment later, Jez disappeared into the tunnel. Tripping over the uneven floor in her haste, Lizzie followed. She tried not to panic when she couldn't see him and was almost overwhelmed with relief when his heels appeared in her circle of light before they disappeared again. Heart thumping, trying not to think about the rock piled above her head and encroaching to her sides, she concentrated on keeping his disappearing and reappearing legs in view.

It could have been minutes or an hour that they'd been shambling over the stony ground, when a shudder reverberated through the rock.

Instinctively, Lizzie covered her head. Spirals of dust fell from the walls. No downfall came. Lizzie pressed one hand over her mouth to stop from screaming.

"Keep calm," Jez said.

"I don't want to die."

Their breath clouded in the cold. Sweat ran down Lizzie's neck. She shivered. Jez shifted his feet and flicked the torch ahead again.

Face moist, Lizzie wiped her cheeks before following once more. They moved rapidly now, and Lizzie kept up. She wanted out as fast as possible. This had been a stupid decision. She couldn't believe he'd come up this way. It couldn't be far; it couldn't. Her legs were buckling. She couldn't breathe. *Don't panic.* Stumbling and tripping over the uneven ground, eyes on the rocky floor, hands sore from catching against rough walls, back, neck and legs aching from bending and stooping, shoulders hunched, elbows held in, she followed.

***

Dawn already stretched over the ruins of Moorland Castle as it cast its irreparably changed imprint on the charcoal sky. The side wings remained intact, but the middle section that had housed the central chimneys, main bedrooms, library, entrance hall and priest hide lay in rubble. The parkland behind could now clearly be seen; tall exposed trees towered beyond broken greenhouses and high brick walls. Dark, crushed undergrowth curled close to the building, bordering the sodden grass, trampled by boots and water hoses. Shards of glass glinted over lawns; stones littered flower beds; walls dripped with spray. Delicate flakes of ash from the bonfire floated in the air, sprinkling the grass like grey confetti, and Carol, looking drawn and exhausted, walked aimlessly, mobile phone dormant in her hand.

She turned to Phil. "I don't know what to do. What am I going to tell Mr. and Mrs. Booth?"

Phil stared at a long curtain flapping through the gaping hole of a window. "The police will see to all that."

"They'll blame me. They left me in charge." Carol's voice came thin and high.

"It's not your fault—" He stopped mid-sentence as they watched stretchers being carried past.

"Oh my God, two. Two, Phil! There are two bodies."

Phil put a hand on her shoulder. "Breathe."

She pushed him aside. "Who are they? Let me see."

One of the medics shook his head.

"It's all right," Phil said, catching her arm. "Let them get on with their job. We'll know the full score soon enough."

She walked aimlessly, staring at her mobile phone as if she hadn't heard. "Who should I ring now?"

"You've moved them pretty fast," Phil said to the medic.

"We were given the go-ahead," the short-haired brunette snapped. "It doesn't have to be dragged out."

"Can you tell me who they are?"

"Not a chance," said the female medic, determinedly blocking him from nearing the stretcher.

The man shrugged. "The remains can be identified easier in the labs."

"Where'd you find them?"

The paramedic glanced at Phil as if he were stupid, then nodded his head towards the gaping expanse of rubble.

"Someone said the priest hide. They're still looking."

"Shit. Are there any more bodies?" Phil glanced up as Carol meandered back towards them.

"What were people doing in the priest hole?" she demanded. "Nobody should've been in there."

"Time, Carol. It takes time." Phil took her arm, leading her away. "Come on, let's go sit in your car."

"It could be a tourist, one of them kids…anyone." Carol's eyes widened.

"You don't get tourists in the middle of the night," said Phil. "And kids wouldn't know how to find the place."

"I bet they would. Jim's always chucking them out of places they shouldn't be."

Footsteps crunched over gravel, voices shouted, and generators rumbled.

"Stop worrying." Phil put his arm around her again. "We'll find out who it was."

"I can't believe how lucky we were." Carol shivered as the doors of the ambulance banged shut. "I could still've been in the shop sorting things…upstairs…anywhere." She paused, waiting for him to voice the same.

"Yes, but we were at the gatehouse. Someone wanted us out of the house. I actually have to say thanks to Jim for lighting the bonfire."

"Jim?" She put her hand to her mouth. "Oh my God, where is he?" She groaned. "Oh, no. Lizzie."

"Don't jump to conclusions," Phil said. "We don't know anything yet."

Phil watched the ambulance drive off rather than let her see the expression on his face. They stood isolated, squinting at the floodlights illuminating the building like a film set as fire crew began to rewind cables and hoses, police officers brought dogs down from vans and the solitary figure of the man in charge slurped from a tin cup.

Seeing Gloucester lying flat to the ground a short distance away, Phil tapped his leg, glad of the distraction.

"Poor mutt," he said. "Who's going to look after you now?"

Carol glanced at Phil as he stroked the Labrador.

"You don't need to stay with me," she said. "I'm okay. I know you're itching to do your detective stuff. If anyone needs me, tell them where I am."

He glanced at her, his face now open and alert.

"Are you sure? I'm not on duty, I don't have to."

She bent to ruffle Gloucester's fur. Phil watched for a few seconds before striding across the gravel, eyes alert for officers he knew.

***

Standing by the main desk in Beamstown Town Hall, a hastily dressed Susan Harper frowned at a group of youngsters shuffling about on one of the long benches.

"Don't even think about those boxes," warned an officer, folding his arms.

Their voices babbled in protest, drowning out the crackling voice on his walkie-talkie.

"Who are they?" Susan nodded to the group.

"Criminals for making me miss my night out." Lisa thumped her handbag down on the desk. "But don't worry. Someone's on the way to throw them into their cage."

A tall, brown-haired lad with a bright-blue cap, jabbing the air at one of the officers, caught their attention.

"We never saw a fucking four-by-four," he yelled.

"Choice," said Lisa. "See what I mean? Criminals."

The officer pushed him roughly back down. "Watch your language."

"Hey, you can't prove anything, I've got my rights. Wait till my mum—"

"Sit there and shut up."

Susan turned back to the desk as Lisa handed her a brown envelope.

"An old man dropped it off last night."

"Our resident Mr. Charming." Susan nodded. "Never disappoints."

"No. I told that police bloke it wasn't him." Lisa unwound a scarf from around her neck. "Taylor—something like that. I told him I'd have been here all night if it was that freak. It was another old bloke. He came in just after you left. Didn't you see him? His face was all bleeding, and he was acting really weird. One of them nutters. They're all the same."

Susan turned the envelope over in her hand. "Did he say who he was?"

Lisa shrugged, taking off her coat as Susan studied Randolph's distinctive scrawl, wondering why he hadn't delivered it himself.

A police cordon had been set up across the stairwell to the basement, and senior members of the council spoke in low tones about the paintings in the grand hall and the contents of the boxes stacked by the front desk. One man stood deep in conversation with a couple of plain-clothed police officers.

Lisa caught Susan's eye. "Are you going to bother opening that?"

Susan ran a maroon-painted nail under the flap and pulled out a single sheet of blue paper. As she read, her face flushed hot then cold. Lisa had gone. She glanced across the hall. Thomas Grant, the council leader, dominated a small group by his superior height and weight.

"Where's them social workers?" Thomas Grant yelled.

"It's a busy night."

"I want more officers down here," someone said.

Susan held out the letter. "Mr. Grant? You need to read this."

When Grant finished reading, he handed the blue sheet of paper to a woman standing close by. She read it and passed it on until Deputy Police Inspector Greg Taylor quickly perused the handwritten message. He gestured to two police officers standing by the main doors.

"Get a couple of men over to Moorland Chalet Park," he ordered.

Susan's jaw ached. She needed to stop grinding her teeth. She could lose her job over this chalet park.

Grant turned to a woman in a striped suit. "People are going to want to know what's been going on."

The woman waved a folder. "I'm on it."

"We need all the facts—what we've been doing about this place and these people. Have they asked for help? What the Environment Agency has done. What we've done. Should they be there in the first place?" He rattled through points. "We'll need a cast iron statement."

"I'm on my way over to the park as well," Susan said, determined she wouldn't be sidelined.

"Everyone's dead." Peter's voice interrupted from across the hall.

The teenagers fell quiet.

Peter sat on the end of the wooden bench, staring at his hands. "It's Plot Night, what do you expect? Something has to be blown up."

Chapter Forty-Four

GRANT AND TAYLOR strode quickly across the floor. Taylor pushed the youngsters out of the way to sit next to Peter. They shoved each other, and the ones at the far end of the bench were forced to stand. Taylor waited for Peter to speak again. Peter continued to study his grazed and dirty fingers. Susan remained at a short distance.

"Are you saying everyone's actually gone ahead with this lunacy?" Taylor hesitated over the words, his mind trying to connect Marilyn Hopper's death with the ones at the chalet park. He knew all this would be in the headlines. His boss would be livid. A place like Moorland Castle didn't blow up and residents die in their homes without people wanting to know why. There had still been no contact with the owners of the castle. Forensics was examining the two bodies found in the ruins; they had corpses stacking up as if they were in Manchester or London.

He looked down at Peter, frowning at the bruises over the old man's cheekbone and a smarting graze above one eye. He glanced towards the front doors. "Where's that ambulance?" he shouted.

Peter looked sideways. "You'll remember them all, won't you?"

"Why couldn't you have spoken to Miss Harper's team before doing something as ludicrous as this? You're all lunatics."

Susan stepped forward. "We have spoken, and I was always at the end of a phone. I've arranged everything—transport, removals, housing…"

Peter ignored Susan and stared at Grant. "Randolph said you'd only be interested when bodies were involved."

"What's that supposed to mean?" Grant snapped.

"What do you know about the castle?" Taylor persisted gently, giving a warning glance to Grant, who turned away in exasperation.

Peter looked patiently at him.

"I supplied the explosives," he said.

Taylor held up his hand in warning to the others again. "And the chalet park?"

"We'd nothing left to lose." He turned his hands over again.

"Are you saying this is some sort of suicide pact?" Taylor sensed Grant move and the kids edge forward. He gestured for an officer to herd the kids back.

"Where's Randolph Brook?" Susan sat on Peter's other side. Everyone was taking him for an idiot, but she knew different. Taylor glared, obviously annoyed at being interrupted, but she leant closer. "Why did you deliver his letter? Where is Mr. Brook?"

"You know Randolph," Peter said, sitting up straight. "We thought the grand hall for the portraits. Replace those old capitalist buggers."

Grant looked furiously around.

Peter's grey eyes shone. "Who do you think people would rather see up on them walls? Folk who are ignored and treated like dirt and who have nowhere to go or folk that do whatever it takes to destroy them?"

"The ambulance is outside," someone called.

Taylor stood, putting out his hand. "Mr. Hawksworth?"

Grant blustered. "Give me a good reason why I should give the go-ahead to putting up pictures of a bunch of people nobody has heard of."

Taylor leaned in to help Peter stand. "Mr. Hawksworth? Can you walk?"

"We may not seem important to you," Peter said. "You might think we don't matter because we're not the type to make a fuss, but it's funny because people like us outnumber the likes of you." He paused again, waited, but no-one spoke, so he continued.

"If you got out there and knocked on doors, you'd meet men like Randolph Brook and women like Mavis Cummings."

"Now hang on a minute—"

"You send our youngsters—yeah, like you lot." He nodded towards the kids. "Yes, you. Watch out, or they'll pack you off to places devastated by war to help poor sods get their lives back on track, but they turn a blind eye if the likes of you need a little help here. It's not only the sea that's taking away our lives, it's people like you and you." He prodded his bloodstained finger in the air, first at Grant then Susan.

"Mr. Hawksworth, we don't send—" Susan began, but Peter cut her short.

"If you put our portraits up in that other room and let off them fireworks tomorrow in the main square, people will say, 'Do you remember that day? Let's go see those paintings hanging in our town hall that look like someone I might know.'"

"They won't give a toss."

Taylor held up his hand to silence the man to his left.

"If our likenesses are hung on those walls, if nothing else, we'll remind you lot not to forget people who feel invisible and unheard, and if you let off these fireworks that I guarantee are better than any you've ever seen or ever will see, you'll be giving everyone a sense that they aren't on their own. Every individual in Beamstown, up coast, all way to Rigby, will be part of that crowd. They'll be a group and not stranded on their own in bloody high-rise." Peter's face already drooped with fatigue. "We need that," he muttered. "Human beings need that."

Susan looked down the list of ten signatures scrawled on the sheet of paper in her hand, old couples and lonely old men and those who didn't belong anywhere, and she felt overcome with exhaustion.

"Geroff me!" A voice shattered the quiet.

They all looked up. An officer grappled the tall boy with the blue hat away from the boxes. Struggling and kicking hard, the boy broke free, crashing into the pile and the top one, already opened, fell sideways, startling them all as it thudded to the floor. Brightly coloured shapes spilled across the tiles. The other kids, jeering and whooping, leapt to their feet, chasing the escaped fireworks, gathering up all they could hold and ramming them into pockets.

"Put those back!" yelled Taylor.

Officers began yanking flailing and cursing kids away from the fireworks, pushing them roughly and grabbing coat sleeves and collars as they wriggled past.

"Get them into the main hall until social services arrive," Taylor ordered above the shouts.

No-one noticed Peter rise to his feet.

"The three of you stay with them." Taylor gestured to another officer entering through the front doors.

A black-haired girl struggled, screaming against her captor as he propelled her after two others into the main hall. With a trembling hand, Peter tapped the group's ringleader on the shoulder. Noticing, Susan glanced around with concern. The uniforms were otherwise engaged, and Grant held Taylor's attention. The tall boy turned, his face open with surprise, and before anyone could stop him, Peter clasped his shoulders, pushing his face up close.

"Mr. Hawksworth?" Susan tapped his arm, but he shrugged her away.

"Do you remember me?" Peter spoke quietly to the blue-capped boy. "Do you remember kicking and punching me to the ground and hitting me with a big for-sale board?" The boy desperately glanced at the others, but Peter stepped even closer. "Hey. I'm asking you a question." His voice cut across the now hushed hall. The lad nodded, backing away, but Peter pressed forward again as Grant raised one hand for attention and Taylor reached for Peter's arm.

"Mr. Hawkworth...Peter, I think—"

"I remember every second of how you and your friends hit me over the head and kicked me in the stomach." Peter nudged Taylor away. "I remember creasing up in pain on the dirty wet pavement with my bleeding hands in the gutter as you and your mob smashed the roof of that big black Range Rover, and how the alarm nearly burst my eardrums and its flashing lights scared you all away. And you ran. You ran away like the little cowards you are."

Still holding onto the lad, he looked pointedly at Taylor. "That vehicle belongs to Andrew Booth up at Moorland Castle. Did you know that? I bet you did, you jealous little tyke. What did you do to him, eh? Come on, you brave little tosser, tell us what you did."

Other kids reappeared from the main hall, shouting encouragement to their leader as two officers tried to restrain them. Others watched aghast. A woman in a long woollen coat, a large bag over her shoulder, stopped inside the doorway, a look of incredulity on her face.

"They're all yours," Peter said before an officer took his arm. The woman watched with bemusement.

"You know nothing about me, you crazy git," shouted the brown-haired ringleader. "You know nothing!"

He strained against Taylor's tight hold, and the newcomer walked quickly towards them, issuing protests.

Peter turned, his eyes dark and tired, his pale face drawn.

"I hope you remember everything you did." He pointed again at the lad. "Because by God, I do and kicking old gits like me will get you nowhere. Kick up a fuss, kick up a storm, but don't bloody well kick old sods that you'll probably turn into fifty years from now."

Chapter Forty-Five

LIZZIE EMERGED FROM the dank cave to the sound of waves foaming on the shingle. The noise filled her ears as the sea-drenched wind bit her face and hands. She grimaced, catching her breath and closing her eyes to withstand the brightness of the sky. Steadying her feet, trembling, she adjusted to the exposed beach after the dark, confined space of the tunnel. They'd not been crushed to death. They'd not run out of air, but this was too much. In an attempt to keep the feeling of dizziness at bay, she bent over, hands grasping knees, and fixed her gaze on a myriad of smooth, pale stones and broken, jagged shells. Minutes passed before, wondering what had happened to Jez, she looked up.

Slipping over rocks, arms outstretched to maintain balance, he came towards her. Embarrassed that she felt so shaken, she tried to gauge on what stretch of beach they had emerged and saw the cliff towering above them, grey-black, gashed and ragged.

"I can't believe we've made it." She tried to sound light-hearted as he approached. "Are you all right?"

"Yup." He nodded. "Just wanted to check something."

She wanted to ask what he imagined the castle looked like after the blast and how he felt about it, but it seemed pointless. No answer would explain how on earth this could be the logical culmination of the past week.

"I wish I understood why you've all done this," she said.

He glanced up at the broken land. "D'you want to get out of here?"

"Of course I do. Did you think I'd be stopping?"

"You look frozen."

"You don't look so great yourself!"

"A hot meal will sort me out. Roast beef and Yorkshire pudding. What about you?"

She glanced at him again. He looked as if he would fall over.

"Let's just stand here for a minute and catch our breath," she said.

***

The small group of teenagers were driven away in the gunpowder-fumed morning air, parents clamouring with social workers, and police officers stepping back with relief. At the hospital Accident and Emergency, a doctor dabbed Peter's wounds with antiseptic and told the officer with him that he'd have to wait for an X-ray.

At the town hall, as telephones began to ring and meeting rooms filled with voices, hands clasped behind his back, Thomas Grant moved down the line of canvases propped up against one wall of the grand hall. Susan Harper, following, scrutinised the faces staring back at her. It was as if they could have spoken at any moment, telling her things she didn't want to hear. How these people could have stayed in the clifftop park amazed her. She leaned closer. The handwritten names at the bottom left-hand corner of each canvas suggested nothing extraordinary. How could she be blamed for not taking care of people who had got themselves into such difficulties?

She studied Jez Maiden's unruffled gaze and wondered why a talented artist like him hadn't left the place. If she'd explained more clearly, maybe they would have understood what was on offer and this would never have happened. She frowned at Peter Hawksworth's surprisingly intelligent features. These people weren't lunatics; they'd thought it through carefully.

Grant waited for her in front of Randolph. Now the old git was gone, she realised she would miss his obnoxious weekly tirades.

He'd been one of a kind, never to be replaced. Even though they needed proof, she knew Peter didn't lie. These people, barring Peter Hawksworth, were all dead, and these paintings were all that remained. Glancing at the last likeness, a sketch of the youngish, chestnut-haired woman who had arrived at the park the previous week, Susan frowned. The woman's eyes, flecked with distrust, glared into the distance, her face, caught at an angle, showed cheeks rounded and speckled like a farm egg. Susan stood back, unable to comprehend how this young woman could have given up so completely and so quickly.

"These are the people you were rehousing?" Grant broke into her thoughts. She swallowed, nodding.

"Yes." She cleared her throat. "I found alternative properties for all of them."

"Then what's this about?"

She could hardly bear to say the words. "They didn't want to leave their homes."

"What do you mean?" He leant forward to peer more closely at Randolph. "Those chalets were a death trap."

She could imagine people whispering in the corridors and see her name the subject of emails. The smell of furniture polish overpowered the room.

"They're very good, aren't they?" she said, clenching her hands and willing him to agree.

"Not bad," he eventually commented, walking along the line again. "Who did them?"

"Jez Maiden. He lives…lived at the chalet park. That's him." She pointed.

"Is he famous? Should I have heard of him?"

She looked away from his intense gaze. "Maybe now that he's…" She stopped. Braced herself. "Dead."

Grant made a small noise in the back of his throat.

"D'you think the general public would like to see pictures of ordinary people in the town hall?" she said.

"Where were this motley crew from, did you say?" He seemed not to notice, bending closer to look at Marilyn.

"Moorland Chalet Park." She hated him. His back, shoulders, hair curling over collar, shower of dandruff, black, shiny, tightly laced shoes. His voice.

"Near Moorland Castle?" He looked thoughtful. "I take it that land used to be part of the estate?"

"They sold it off years ago," she said. "That bit of coast is our responsibility."

He made that noise again.

"How come I don't know about it?"

"It's down a rough track, so you can't see it from the main road. You have to know it's there. It's so remote in fact, no-one heard the explosions that went off there last night."

He pulled out a large, creased handkerchief and blew his nose. "I suppose you should call in, get yourself down there."

"One of my team will be there now. And bulldozers are going down tomorrow." She kept her voice matter of fact. "It's just above Scarbeck, south of Rook Bay. The erosion is bad there, but it used to be a beautiful spot, years ago."

"There are other beautiful places," he said. "We can't protect the entire coast. That's what these people don't realise. They think the coffers are inexhaustible."

"Yes, but we are liable."

She looked at his wide shoulders and big face as he folded the letter decisively and handed it back to her. She gripped the list tightly as the echo of his strident steps crossed the gleaming honey-brown parquet.

***

Lizzie lifted strands of grey hair from Randolph's pale cheek and gently felt the icy skin with her fingertips. A blackening tar-like mixture congealed across his forehead, and a stain haloed the sand around his skull. She knew faces like this. Ingrained downward-looking lines on battered men's and women's faces she saw every day in Rigby. This angry old man was no different to any of them. His rigid fingers dug into the dark, splattered pebbles as if trying to scoop a fistful, his other hand emerging grey blue and yellowing mauve from the sodden cuffs of his jumper, fingers dabbling amongst the swaying fronds of green. Resting on her haunches, she looked at Jez's back. She wondered what he was thinking. Gulls wheeled and cried over their heads. She glanced up in disgust.

"We've got to move him," she said. "Jez? We can't leave him here."

Randolph looked too vulnerable to hate now. His frayed shirt collar framed the lilac skin of his neck. His thick wool jumper looked even more ancient amongst the whitened shingle. Grey trousers clinging wetly to twisted legs made them look thinner than they probably were, and one shoelace escaped untied, snaking in the water like a small adder.

"He stays here," Jez said.

"We can't leave him." Lizzie glanced up at the gulls again. "We'll have to tell somebody to come and get him."

It had been hard enough leaving Andrew in the cold priest hide; she couldn't abandon a vulnerable old man to the elements as well. It felt like the sea rose up inside her, sweeping away her equilibrium.

"Of all the things we thought we couldn't do, this is the easiest," he said, holding out his hand.

Lizzie rose to her feet, pushing away his arm, tears running down her cheeks as if the sea escaped. "I'm not leaving him."

"It's only a body, Lizzie. Randolph is part of the land now, or the beach. Crushed bones in the shingle, whatever way you want to look at it."

His voice said it all. He couldn't have cared more for a loved brother. Her tears subsided, drying salt in patches on her skin. She pressed his arms away, turning to the cliff, her back to the water.

"You go on," she insisted. "I'll catch up in a minute."

He walked away, hunching his shoulders. Lizzie glanced back down at Randolph; for the first time since she had met him, he was quiet and still.

It did look as if he belonged there; it would be a crime to carry him away from the shells and rock pools.

"Wait," she called.

Jez stopped, half turned and waited until Lizzie, scrambling over the uneven pebbles, caught him up. Leaving a trail of footprints, they walked across another outcrop of wet sand.

"People will think we're dead as well, won't they?" she said.

His hands touched her shoulders as he turned her to face him. Seeing how he struggled to maintain composure, she slipped her arms around him, glad for the warmth of another human being.

She didn't know how long they stood wrapped closely together, but it didn't seem important that they hurry. It was as if only they and the sea existed, its gentle rush a permanent reminder that it would never leave. She glanced over his shoulder. The cliff towered over them, as painful as burnt, smarting flesh, the only movement the gentle wind ruffling the scrubland grass. And then without warning, the cliff began to move. Rivulets of soil crumbled gently, cascading like dusty waterfalls.

She watched as a gust caught the surface and dislodged another delicate downpour. "It's going to go completely, isn't it?"

They picked their way past a long row of groynes leaning useless and forgotten in the shallows.

Here, they stepped over more and more debris. A sand-stained curtain fluttering in the breeze caught Lizzie's eye. The intact floor spread at an angle several metres away. Releasing Jez's hand, she stepped onto it. It shifted as the sand beneath compressed. With her weight on it, the wood steadied, and she strode swiftly across the expanse, ignoring the creaking readjustments. She turned slowly around. Amongst the broken furniture, clods of turf and mounds of rubble, she began to pick out scattered possessions.

It was the small items that caught her eye: a bright-red toothbrush; a jar of face cream; a supermarket brand of digestive biscuits. She turned again and gazed through a splintered wall into the bathroom with its upturned toilet and cracked turquoise sink. A short distance away, on green rocks, a huge white gull perched on the edge of a bath.

After a while, she walked back across the shifting wood and stepped down onto solid ground, gasping at the sight that greeted her. A man's watery eyes stared up into hers. Crouching, she pushed up a sleeve and reached into the mossy pool to drag the edge of a painted canvas from under the chalet floor. It caught, but she tugged and wriggled until with a jolt it came free. Sitting beside the man, a tanned, sunken-eyed woman stared out from the portrait. Lizzie let the water drip onto the pebbles. Jez walked towards her and she looked down again at their resolute faces.

"I had to do another one of Gordon and Shelley," he said.

"How'd you mean?"

He took the painting and lowered it back into the water. Their shimmering expressions winked back at her.

"Portraits keep you alive," he said.

The cliff whispered more downfalls of soil, and they both looked up.

"We could take John's car, if it's still where I left it," she said. She stood slowly, realising the time for explanations had passed.

Jez glanced back the way they had come, to Randolph's inert figure. She followed his gaze.

"Let me lay one last fuse," he said.

"No." She touched his arm. "Let the cliff do its job in its own time."

Already she could see them driving up to Scotland with the Bowles' abandoned caravan in tow. They'd meander along small, barely negotiable roads towards a different coast, one which wasn't eroding, and find another resting place—a place to have the baby. An heir to Moorland Castle had come too late, but it didn't matter. Everybody here believed she and Jez were dead, just like the other chalet park residents.

She took his hand, leading him towards the cliff path. "Do you think people will remember folk once lived here?"

A few more stones tumbled onto the beach. A plover rose in flight, called out and disappeared from view as it headed inland.

Acknowledgements

I originally self-published *Erosion* in 2012. Writer and bookshop owner Bob Stone of Write Blend, Liverpool, read it seven years later and told me to send it to Debbie McGowan of Beaten Track Publishing. He thought she would like it. Plus, he rated her as a brilliant editor and publisher. I agreed: *Erosion* did need the eyes of a brilliant editor and an award-winning publisher to give it a second chance of being seen! Thanks so much, Bob!

Luckily, Debbie did like it and my thanks to her for her prompt response and above all, excellent editing. Her skill and knowledge of the written word is astounding. Thanks too to the eagle eyes of the two other proofreaders, Estelle Maher and Jor Barrie. I am honoured to be part of the Beaten Track team.

A reader often picks up an unknown book by an unknown author because they are drawn to it by the cover. With this in mind, many thanks to the artistic talents of Miranda Estevez-Baker. Not only that, when I asked her for another firework here and a bit more red there, she never lost her patience with me.

Of course, without the Yorkshire coast, this story would not exist. Nor would it exist without my memories of the Yorkshire folk I have known and still do know. I am continually grateful for both the beauty of this county and the resilience of its people. My stories could not have been written without them.

And lastly, to all those who have supported me in my writing endeavours, a heartfelt thank-you.

About the Author

Yorkshire born Ruth Estevez is a YA and Adult fiction writer.

Ruth takes inspiration from place, particularly from her native Yorkshire. Themes that link her books are identity, being the outsider and what people will do when literally living on the edge. These themes, present in Erosion, are also present in her previous novel, a tale of a real-life female smuggler Jiddy Vardy, and its sequel, Jiddy Vardy – High Tide, coming April 2021.

With a background in theatre and television, from acting and stage management to writing, Ruth has travelled to remote Yorkshire schools, top security prisons, Shakespeare's Globe to Emmerdale. Writing credentials include scriptwriting on TV's Bob the Builder and creating her own little books, inspired by those of the Bronte children at Haworth Parsonage.

When not writing or organising young persons' reading and writing competitions with the historic and beautiful Portico Library in Manchester, Ruth can be found travelling to Drum and Dance Festivals in her flower-stickered camper van, Doris.

You can contact Ruth on...

Instagram @ruthestevezwriter

Twitter @RuthEstevez2

Facebook @RuthEstevezM

Website: www.artgoesglobal.wordpress.com

By the Author

Meeting Coty

Jiddy Vardy

Coming 2021

Jiddy Vardy – High Tide

The Monster Belt

Beaten Track Publishing

For more titles from Beaten Track Publishing,
please visit our website:

https://www.beatentrackpublishing.com

Thanks for reading!